Campbell Armstrong was born in Glasgow in 1944. He was awarded his BA degree from the University of Sussex. Three years after his first novel was published in 1968, he moved to the United States, where he taught creative writing. He lived there for twenty years with his wife and children, and produced twenty novels before moving to Ireland in 1991. Following the international success of *Jig* (1987), many of his books, including *Brainfire*, *Asterisk* and *Death's Head*, are once again available in the United Kingdom.

D1390074

By the same author

Jig
Mambo
Mazurka
Brainfire
Agent of Darkness
Asterisk

CAMPBELL ARMSTRONG

Death's Head

Grafton

An Imprint of HarperCollins*Publishers*

Grafton
An Imprint of HarperCollins*Publishers*
77–85 Fulham Palace Road,
Hammersmith, London W6 8JB

Published by Grafton 1993
9 8 7 6 5 4 3 2 1

First published in Great Britain by
Collins 1972

First published as *Death's Head*
by Campbell Black

ISBN 0 586 21745 2

Set in Times

Printed in Great Britain by
HarperCollinsManufacturing Ltd

For Olivia Sayers

'I prayed with them. I pressed myself into a corner and cried out to my God and theirs. How glad I should have been to go into the gas chambers with them! Then an SS officer in uniform would have been found in the gas chambers.'

– SS-Obersturmführer Kurt Gerstein

'I swear to thee Adolf Hitler
As Führer and Chancellor of the German Reich
Loyalty and Bravery.
I vow to thee and to the superiors
whom thou shalt appoint
Obedience unto death
So help me God.'

– SS Oath*

PART ONE

Berlin, September 1945

1

It sometimes surprised him that he was still alive; that his body, like some flawed machine, continued to function of its own accord. It had nothing to do with the lack of food and the sickness he frequently felt; it was the simple fact that beneath the surface of his brain and body there was no real reason for his life to go on. The idea of death and dying fluttered every so often on the darker edges of his mind, as if it were some kind of wounded butterfly seeking its last glimpse of light. And yet death terrified him because it brought still one more unanswerable question: what is it like *not* to exist?

He lay for a time with his eyes open, staring at the broken shaft of sunlight that came through the hole in the masonry. Outside was a large expanse of rubble, a desert where there had once been a city. He could hear various sounds – someone moving across the stones, a foreign voice screaming an order, the rattle of a passing truck. Not far away the Untergrundbahn used to run through the Alexander-Platz and he recalled the crowded red and yellow cars without affection. Everything then had been efficient, murderously so, the people moving with the sort of insane regularity you associate with clockwork.

He did not move for some minutes. There was nothing to move for. There were no special events that differentiated one day from the next. His environment, the architecture of his life, had become the stark remains of the bombast of the Third Reich. Fallen concrete eagles could be seen amongst the ruins, looking like birds that have always been too heavy to fly. Stone swastikas that rang when you struck them with slabs of brick, as if they retained fading echoes of the million voices that had once

9

sustained them and given them meaning. It was as if some giant hand had crushed everything and the thousand-year concept of the Reich had ended – not in a chamber in the Wilhelmstrasse – but in a few granules of dark dust and the pathetic sight of colourful flowers growing out of slag heaps.

Rising, very slowly, he went towards the hole in the masonry and blinked in the bright morning light. Yesterday he had placed a piece of bread in the pocket of his coat and he felt for it now. A blackish kind of bread that tasted vile if it had any taste at all. But that was something else; he doubted now whether he could tell the difference between any of the scraps of food he put in his mouth.

He went outside after he had chewed the bread and stood for a time. The sunlight was hard against his face. On good days he found that he lived only for the present time. All his thoughts and instincts were devoted to the single achievement of dragging himself through yet another day. On bad days his mind kept returning to the past, as if by searching there he could find a single seed of justification for what he had done. But his thoughts of the past had a peculiar texture: they weren't like memories of events he had lived through himself. They were distant from him, and they were cold, like the memories of a stranger he could never hope to know.

Moving carefully across the rubble he stared at the faces of the few people who had ventured out. There had once been another Berlin. A summer day would have drawn them out in their thousands to the cafés and beer restaurants on the Unter den Linden, to the *Königin Victoria* and the *Kranzler*, to the *Admiral* in the Friedrichstrasse. A touch of sunlight and the young men with their girls would have been outside on the terraces, laughing, talking, thinking of love.

A couple of Russian soldiers in their absurd and grubby uniforms were talking on the corner of the street. He walked past them as quickly as he could. They could stop

10

you and ask to see your papers and yet beneath their seriousness was the constant feeling that they wanted to turn you into an object of fun. They stopped talking as he went past and he waited to hear them call to him; but they didn't, and when he glanced back once he saw that they were hunched together lighting cigarettes. The simple act of passing them seemed to have drained him of energy. He leaned against a wall and caught his breath and observed with some alarm that his pulse was hammering away under his flesh. Uniforms; nothing but uniforms. Now and in the past, his whole life seemed to have been dominated by uniforms. Something extraordinary happened to a man when he climbed inside one: he ceased to exist, he became nothing more than the sum of his various insignia. The brown-shirts of the SA, the black of the SS, the steel-blue of the Wehrmacht, the cold white of –

Something caught his eye above and he turned his face upwards. A flock of birds, nothing more, frightened by the sudden backfire of a truck. Feeling cold all at once, he walked on: even if there was nowhere to go, the mere act of walking generated some kind of heat.

They sat in a prefabricated hut made from rusted slabs of thin metal. They went there day after day with their belongings in cheap suitcases usually kept shut with pieces of string. Some brought children along and the children waited in artificial silence like creatures that have had every spark of life obliterated in them. Sometimes he imagined that they looked older than their parents, that they were the ones who had recently fought a war and returned, with incurable wounds, from some forlorn front. Their dumbness and silence was a mask of sheer incomprehension.

He entered the ante-room and sat on a bench near the door. The place depressed him. It had the same effect upon him as a doctor's waiting-room except that here nobody was looking for a clean bill of health. If you wanted to speak you spoke in whispers. But there was nothing to say. Apart from himself there was an old couple holding hands tightly as if any break in their contact would be an irrevocable loss, a young woman with an emaciated baby, a man in a patched overcoat not unlike his own. The Wilhelmstrasse wasn't far from here. The centre of the world until a short time ago: now, the men who had manned it with all the dedication of soldiers protecting something pure and holy, were either dead or about to die. It caused him an intense pleasure to think of this. The mad Goebbels, whose shrill voice he had heard on a hundred radio broadcasts. Heini, unprotected by his monolithic SS, crushing the poison capsule between his teeth – a banal death and yet somehow a predictable one. And poor Adolf – it was said that his corpse had been burned and taken away by the Russians.

A door that led to an inner room was suddenly opened and a young man in uniform stood there with a sheaf of papers in his hand. His expression was that of someone who has stretched his patience to its limits and has realized he is fatigued beyond belief. The old couple rose slowly and still holding hands disappeared through the door which was closed immediately.

The man in the patched overcoat whispered something and Grunwald leaned forward to hear what was being said. The man turned his hands over and looked at them. His hands were filthy and the cuffs of his coat ragged.

'I didn't hear you,' Grunwald said apologetically.

The man smiled. 'It hardly seems worthwhile,' he said.

'What doesn't?'

'Waiting here. What are we waiting for?'

Grunwald sat back against the wall and was silent. There wasn't an answer to that question. People waited for different reasons.

The man took a rag from his coat and spat into it. In spite of his appearance, there was still a sort of faded dignity in his movements. It was a peculiar German trait, Grunwald sometimes thought, that they could look like demobilized officers of the Wehrmacht even in rags. Or possibly this young man had fought valiantly for the city of Berlin, surrendering his uniform for a cast-off coat in some dark cellar only when he learned that the Führer had taken his life. Even then some part of him would go on struggling; even in defeat he would still respond to the rallying-cries of his imaginations. And where did it all lead to? Grunwald stared at the young man and then at the woman with the baby; he loathed these people and yet his hatred was involuntarily touched with a sense of pity. He despised them as he despised all Germany and he found some consolation in the thought that the Reich, like some proud animal finally hunted down and slain, was crawling now with the parasites of occupation.

He got up from the bench and looked through the window. Outside were the same old shells of buildings where the bombs had fallen and the fires had spread. It was amazing how quickly you could become accustomed to the architecture of destruction. You realized that it had all looked very different once, but somehow the new environment was the only possible one. As he turned round to look at the young man again, the woman's baby uttered a tired cry. She cradled its head with her hands and held it tightly against her breasts. Grunwald was reminded of the baby he had come across only a few days ago. Nobody had taken the trouble to bury it; it had simply been placed, naked, amidst a pile of broken stones. Its hands were clenched, the lips a dark colour of blue. Sickened, he had stepped back from the sight, thankful at least that the eyes had been closed.

The door opened and the old couple came out. The woman was sobbing, the man was trying desperately to console her. Grunwald returned to the bench and sat down, staring at the floor. The young man continued to

13

spit from time to time into his rag. The woman, carrying her baby, went towards the door where the young officer was waiting. And then there was a long silence.

The officer could hardly have been more than twenty-five. His thick hair had been closely and crudely cropped by some insensitive army barber and there was a pale blue tint to the area at the back of his solid neck. The tiny room in which he sat was barely furnished; a desk, two hard chairs, a filing cabinet. The desk and the floor were littered with bundles of papers, some tied with string or ribbon. A decrepit paraffin heater burned in one corner, hissing noisily sometimes, filling the room with a smell that choked and sickened Grunwald.

The officer looked at Grunwald and then at his identity papers. His manner was that of a man who would have liked to be brisk and efficient, but who was overwhelmed with the volume of papers and the length of his working day.

'Grunwald. Leonhard Israel Grunwald.' He said the name as if it were something solid he could taste but with the uncertainty of someone trying an exotic food for the first time. His German was precise and correct even if his accent was poor. He rose and went to the filing cabinet and began to look through it.

'I have no record,' he said at last and slammed the drawer shut. 'It doesn't surprise me. I hardly have records for anybody. When anything comes in it gets filed.' He looked at Grunwald hopelessly. 'But of course very little comes in.'

Grunwald wished he could open the window. The smell of paraffin was overwhelming now. He undid the top button of his shirt and watched the officer return to his chair. He picked up a pen and searched for a piece of paper.

'I will take the necessary particulars.'

'What particulars?' Grunwald asked.

'Information that I require.' The officer yawned and covered his mouth with a hand; the hand, Grunwald noticed, was smeared with stains of dark blue ink.

'I forget things sometimes,' Grunwald said and wondered what special talent this young man brought to his job. Was it simply the case that he had been chosen because he could speak German? He was young, conceivably ambitious – so why should he be content in the sort of post that at best could only be described as a stagnant backwater? Picking his way amongst the scattered relics of humanity that the Reich left behind was hardly a task of any great importance: what did people matter when politicians were squabbling over territorial gains and slicing Europe as though it were a stale birthday cake? Somewhere great decisions were being made, but it wasn't here in this shabby prefabricated hut.

The officer looked at his pen with the disgusted expression of a man who joined the army because he wanted to carry a gun. 'Place and date of birth,' he said.

'Munich,' Grunwald said. 'April, 1908.'

The officer put his pen down. 'Who are you looking for?'

Grunwald said, 'In 1939 I had a wife and a son. My wife was thirty years of age. The boy was five. We lived in an apartment in Wendl-Dietrichstrasse in the Neuhausen district of Munich. All things considered, it was not altogether an unpleasant apartment.' Grunwald stopped, conscious of the monotonous way he had been speaking; and yet why should he speak otherwise? He was reciting only dead facts, he was speaking of the fleshless skeleton that had once been his life. It did not call for a tone of animation.

The officer stopped writing and put his pen into the ink-bottle. For no apparent reason he said, 'I fought all the way from the Polish front, driving the Germans back. I don't know what I expected them to be like. Perhaps I imagined they were supermen. But they had nothing to offer until we reached Berlin and then they fought like insane men. Young boys, old men, anybody who could carry a weapon – they came out against us. And I asked myself, What are they protecting? Don't they know the war is already over? What do you imagine they were fighting for?'

The officer smiled: 'I asked myself, Where was all the great efficiency I'd heard so much about? What kind of people send out schoolboys with machine-guns and old men with grenades?' He rose from his desk and went to the window and, as if conscious for the first time of the heavy smell of paraffin, pushed the window open. 'The great efficiency was a myth. The infallibility was a lie. I know what you are going to tell me, Herr Grunwald.' He paused a second. 'You had a wife and a child. And one day, they are no longer there. They vanish. You ask questions but there are no answers.'

Grunwald looked at the officer. 'I arrived home. The apartment was empty. Someone had come in a truck and they had been taken away. I never saw either of them again.'

The officer shook his head. 'That was their real ability, you see. That was the real gift. They could take a single human being, or a million human beings, and they could deny that they had ever existed. And they did it very well. They did it with great skill.'

Grunwald was sweating: why had he come here? What was the point of it all? The young officer knew only a part of the truth.

'You never saw either of them again,' the officer said, and began to write. 'Give me their names.'

'Martha Sara Grunwald, unmarried name Brock. And Hugo Israel Grunwald. Aged five.'

The officer shrugged. 'You know that there isn't any hope. The chances of their being alive are practically zero.'

Grunwald moved his head. They were dead, he knew

they were dead. Nothing would alter that conviction. Why had he come here? Simply to have confirmed what he already knew to be true? He rose from his chair.

The officer said, 'One thing puzzles me. How did *you* survive?'

Grunwald watched the young man's eyes. They were pale and blue: he might have been German, one of Himmler's ideal men. He waited for Grunwald's answer, tapping his pen on the desk.

'I survived in the easiest possible way,' Grunwald said, and moved towards the door. He opened the door and peered into the ante-room. There were more people than before, some Germans, some Jews, all of them seeking a shred of comfort through the humanitarian auspices of the occupying army. Why did the conquerors bother? Grunwald wondered. Was it to compensate in some way for the thousands of German women they were said to have raped? It was an easy solution: stick some young officer in a tiny room and let these poor defeated bastards think that something was being done for them. It was easy and it was cheap.

The officer said, 'Come back in about ten days.'

Grunwald, nodding his head, moved through the ante-room and into the street. A squad of Russian soldiers was parading lethargically up and down, working through pointless military manoeuvres – up with their rifles, down with their rifles, twenty paces forward, about turn, twenty paces back. Grunwald knew that he wouldn't go back to see the young officer. How did *you* survive? The question, the expression in the young man's eyes – these things pained him. These were the things that would deter him in the future. How did *you* survive?

Crossing the street, he turned his collar up against a thin rain that had suddenly begun to fall.

2

Munich: which was where the barbarism had begun. When Grunwald thought of Munich he remembered less the empty apartment and the holiday snapshots in their thin frames than the sight of broken windows and desecration – the great worm that slithered over the city dressed in brown, a marching worm that carried its swastika like a prize insect it was about to devour. He remembered the boycott and the emergence of the SS. The martyrs of the Feldherrnhalle. The crowds in the Königsplaz. The Braun Haus in the Briennerstrasse. It seemed to him, recalling the city now, that wherever he looked people had altered: their faces had changed and they had become hard and hardness was a new sort of ideal. But it entailed suffering. Those who had been woken in the night and disappeared in the direction of the Dachauerstrasse in dark cars were the natural victims of the new social order. For Grunwald, until early 1940, it had meant not only fear but a profound emptiness in his life, a feeling that no matter what happened after the end of the barbarism nothing could ever be the same. And how could it? How was it possible to go back and erase the shapes and shadows of the past? But Grunwald did not think of Munich often. If he was to survive in Berlin, the past was nothing more than an irrelevant encumbrance. The burning synagogues, the yellow stars, the identity papers with the statutory J, the transports and the empty echoes of machine-guns – these were disorientated images in no way connected with each other.

He walked towards the Wilhelmstrasse. Goebbels's Ministry for National Enlightenment and Propaganda: where were they now, all those Germans who had been enlightened? You did not simply switch off a light that had burned with such intense power for so many years simply because the Minister himself was no longer in residence.

The Wilhelmstrasse. It was here that they had thrived, crazy conductors leading a mad orchestra into a complex and incomprehensible piece of music. It was here that they had planned the new Europe.

Now, where they had once ruled, another army existed. Grunwald watched a crowd of Russians, their rifles strapped to their shoulders, looking for all the world like a band of sightseers. They called out to each other, laughed, made jokes: they were like men sniggering at a funeral.

He moved forward and drank some water at a hydrant, washing it around in his mouth before spitting it out. Above him was a huge portrait of Stalin nailed to what had once been the entrance to a building; the building itself was mostly destroyed but the face, hard as granite, seemed to work upwards and away with an expression of contemptuous distaste for so much destruction. The Russians were moving off down the Wilhelmstrasse in the direction of the Unter den Linden where, at the Brandenburg Gate, hung even more portraits of Stalin. It seemed to Grunwald that there was little difference between these blurred photographs and the crucifixes hung in Bavarian Catholic homes: how did you choose between the intentions of those who had taken the trouble to nail such things to walls? Talismanic devices, whether political or religious: there was nothing to choose. Turning away, he went back in the direction of the Alexander-Platz.

Martha had said to him one morning in August 1939, 'I don't think I can go on.'

He had been dreading these words. They meant that she had reached the end of something and that he would have to make a decision. It was still possible to leave. A

19

vast sum of money could buy a passage to America but America seemed so distant and the decision such a momentous one. And there was something else besides: blindly, without real reason, he had refused to accept as a permanent state of affairs the anti-Jewish measures taken by the National Socialist government. Somehow he had always imagined that these were temporary stipulations, created for simple propagandist purposes. It was nothing more than that. In a few more months everything would be normal again.

Martha had argued against this blindness. He was a coward, he was blinkered. If he thought things were ever going to improve, then he was stupid. Every day she had watched the Jews being stripped of yet another segment of their dignity; even now it was impossible for her to speak to her German friends without putting them in some kind of danger. Fraternization had been forbidden. They were living in a prison. Had he ever *heard* of Dachau?

Grunwald recognized an element of truth in her arguments and yet still managed to convince himself that they were not in immediate danger. He did not think of himself as a Jew in any case. First and foremost he was a German.

Martha had spoken of the Night of the Broken Glass. What had happened then? Grunwald agreed that it had been a terrible thing – but was it really anything more than the actions of a few extremists?

And Martha had said, 'I don't think I can go on.'

Those were the last words she had spoken to him. He left the house and went to his office in the Kaufinger-strasse, thinking how difficult life and work had been in the last few years. It was only just possible to survive but the commercial restrictions against the Jews made anything other than the barest living difficult. Martha was probably right: life had become a burden, a constant struggle against a system that had denied them almost every human right. Why not leave? Why not?

When he returned home that evening both his wife and son had gone. He never saw either of them again.

The man in the cellar, who had been eating something, hastily covered the food with his coat when Grunwald entered. A little surprised, Grunwald said nothing: he hadn't seen the man before but in these days strangers came and went, saying neither where they had come from nor where they were going. Grunwald stood against the wall. The man, shading his eyes as if afflicted by the brightness of an electric light, shrugged apologetically and then removed the food from beneath his coat and started to eat again. When he had finished, he wiped his lips with the back of his sleeve. He was, Grunwald supposed, in his middle forties. It was impossible to be sure. Everyone seemed ravaged by war and appearances were no longer a safe indication of age. The man got to his feet.

'I came in out of the rain,' he said and shuffled around the cellar. Stopping by the gap in the masonry, he looked out across the expanse of rubble. And then he shook his head in disbeleif. 'Are you a Berliner?'

Grunwald said, 'I come from Munich.'

'I hear things are bad there now. Even worse than here.' The man was still shaking his head as if to say that nothing could be worse than Berlin. He turned to look at Grunwald.

'You're a Jew.'

Grunwald did not reply. The statement still had another shade of meaning; more than a fact, it was an accusation. The man stumped around the room, avoiding slabs of fallen brickwork.

'You're a Jew. I used to be able to smell a Jew from forty yards.'

'A keen sense of smell,' Grunwald said. 'It must have been useful.'

The man laughed: a brief, emaciated sound. 'Don't get me wrong. I didn't have anything to do with any of those

21

camps. That was bloody stupidity.' And he laughed again, so that Grunwald did not know whether to take him seriously.

Grunwald sat down. The man came close to him and it was only then Grunwald realized he had been drinking heavily; his breath was stale and alcoholic.

'What's your name?'

'Grunwald.'

'Mine's Schoen.' He sat beside Grunwald and crossed his legs. His face, Grunwald noticed, was scarred in two or three places and the little finger of his right hand was missing. 'Have you got a woman?'

Grunwald shook his head. 'I don't.'

Schoen took a small knife from his coat and began to pick at his fingernails. He removed the dirt from beneath the nails as though it were important to keep up some standard of hygiene. 'I had a woman until last week. Know what she did? She chucked me out because she took up with an Ivan. He brings her presents. I suspect he's got a bigger prick than me. That's what I suspect.'

Grunwald felt suddenly hungry. 'I'm sorry to hear that.'

'She wasn't a bad sort. I met her at one of those bloody rallies at Bad Harzburg or some such place in 1937. Or was it '36? Then I bumped into her again just after the Russians got here. Nostalgia, that's all. Sheer nostalgia.'

Schoen slumped down with his head against the wall. He talked for some moments and then, almost imperceptibly, he was asleep. It was a solid, drunken sleep and when Grunwald was sure that he wouldn't waken, he slipped his hand into the pocket of Schoen's coat. There were two squares of dark chocolate wrapped in a scrap of newspaper. He ate them hurriedly and then went outside, feeling like a robber.

'I can't go on. I don't think I can go on.'

Only the night before last Herr Schumann had been taken away by the Gestapo. Nobody knew where. What harm had Herr Schumann done? By any standards of orthodoxy, he wasn't really a Jew. A man of mild manners, reserved, civilized – what had Herr Schumann done? What was happening in Germany?

'I don't think I can go on.'

Only last week, when Herr Kramer protested to his landlord about the inordinate rise in his rent, he was visited by someone from Gestapo HQ who accused him of treachery through his unwillingness to contribute to the Reich economy. Herr Kramer was made to walk up and down the Maximilians-Platz wearing a placard round his neck. *I am a Jewish swine.*

And so the apartment was empty one day. The photographs in their tin frames beaming at him from the shelf. Everything neat and tidy. And empty. His life could never be so empty again. In a panic, his mind turning over and over, questions and fears racing through him, he had asked the neighbours. Only Frau Lindmann had seen anything. The truck, as if it were some ambulance of terror, had finally called. Yes, Frau Grunwald and the child had been taken into the truck. Yes, the people who had taken them were from the Gestapo.

At Gestapo HQ, Grunwald had been kept waiting for more than three hours. His fear, like the sequence of dread in some hostile nightmare, had increased with every minute; not simply for Martha and the boy, but also for himself. Would he ever walk out of this place again? SS-Obersturmführer Mayer, a little man in a uniform that was too large for him, had eventually invited Grunwald into his office. Trembling, shaking with a rage he knew was ineffectual, Grunwald asked to see his wife and son. Mayer smoked a pipe which he lit with deliberate slowness, spoiling match after match. He blew a cloud of smoke upwards at the ceiling and when he spoke he gave the impression of someone deeply concerned – he was a cultured, civilized human being: as were all members of the Gestapo. Reports of atrocities were exaggerated.

Germans did not behave like that. Being a member of the Gestapo was a great responsibility. The security of the Reich depended on the Gestapo. And Obersturmführer Mayer, like all his colleagues, did not wish Herr Grunwald to think that the Gestapo had been instrumental in the disappearance of his family. Why would it do such a thing anyway? Admittedly, measures against the Jews were strenuous; but these were difficult times. Just the same, Frau Grunwald and the child had not been taken by the Gestapo. For what purpose would they have been taken anyway? It amounted to the old story, in Obersturmführer Mayer's opinion: Frau Grunwald had a lover, and, in the natural course of these things, had left her husband. That was all. He hoped he had set Herr Grunwald's mind at ease. He was the unlucky victim of an unfaithful woman. Nothing more.

Grunwald waited, as if he were waiting for the truth to be revealed all of a sudden. But Mayer's mask remained unaltered. It did not even change, when the distinct sound of a human scream, muffled from several rooms away, penetrated the air. Mayer rose. He was extremely sorry.

Outside, in the burning sunshine of the street, Grunwald was confused. He felt suddenly all hope had been drained away from him. He walked up the Neuhauser-strasse, the sun hammering down at him. He did not want to go back to the empty apartment. He was afraid now for his own life. And he realized that if Mayer, or someone like him, chose to append his signature to an arrest order made out in the name of Leonhard Grunwald, he was utterly powerless to act.

He had to wait almost a year for his own arrest.

Cautiously he returned to the cellar where Schoen was still asleep. His head to one side, his hands clasped together over his groin, he was snoring. His mouth hung open. Except for the noise he might have been a corpse. Grunwald moved towards him. It was ridiculous that war had brought him to this – and yet there had been much worse. He searched quickly through Schoen's pockets. He found some money in a small leather purse and he took the purse as well. Then he left the cellar, wondering why he cared so much, in such an instinctive way, for his own survival.

3

The American soldier, who had come out of a cellar bar, said that his name was Jacob: Grunwald could call him Jake, if he liked. His uniform was crumpled and he had been drinking heavily for the last twenty-four hours, or so he claimed, sleeping only in snatches, drinking himself sober and then back through various stages to drunkenness again. He put his arm around Grunwald's shoulder and spoke in poor but comprehensible German. He was sorry for the German nation: a proud people, who had contributed much to civilization and Christ, look at them now. He was sad that they had swallowed old Adolf's medicine, a blood tonic that had turned into an unpalatable poison. That was the trouble with politicians and dictators – they spoke a load of bullshit and the great mass, like cattle lining up at the trough, had devoured it wholesale. Still, he was having some fun. You could get a fräulein for the price of a few cigarettes or a bar of soap. And he'd been doing just that, screwing his way across the whole damn city. He gave Grunwald a cigarette and offered him a drink from the flask of whisky he carried. Grunwald accepted both. They were in the Kurfürstendamm and Grunwald, after so much walking, was tired.

'I oughn't to be talking to you,' the American said. 'They don't like it. They don't like to see us talking to the – what is it called? – the remaining population. Fraternization is out. Right out.'

Grunwald, handing back the flask, said, 'I'm a Jew.'

Jake held out his hand. 'Shake. My great-grandmother on my father's side was a Jew. I guess that gives me a fair percentage of the old blood.' The American took the flask and, without wiping it, held it to his lips. He was about thirty and his hair was cut close to his head and Grunwald thought that if you changed his uniform for the one of the young Russian officer there would be very little difference.

'Where are you from?' Grunwald asked.

'Boston,' Jake said.

'I almost went to America once,' Grunwald said, pronouncing the name as if it were some fabled land across impossible seas.

'You've had a hard time, I suppose,' the American said. He returned the flask to Grunwald.

Grunwald shrugged and drained the flask. 'I'm sorry. It's finished.'

'Plenty more of that. I've got my hands on a whole supply of the stuff.' The American was silent for a time. It was hard not to form the impression that he was some kind of tourist, travelling at his government's expense; and Grunwald felt, rightly or wrongly, that he himself was simply an item of local colour.

The American said, 'I've got to go to Nuremberg next month. The trials. I'm on duty at the trials.'

'Why bother to try them?' Grunwald asked.

'Search me. There's got to be some sort of face put on the whole show.' He slapped Grunwald on the shoulder. 'Look, let's get some more whisky. It isn't far from here. I've got the address written down somewhere.' He searched in his tunic and produced a small notebook. Between its pages there was a scrap of folded paper. 'Augsburgerstrasse. That isn't far from here. Maybe you better lead the way. I can't get the hang of the directions around here.'

They walked towards the Augsburgerstrasse and the American hung on to Grunwald like someone whose fear of losing his way is almost desperate. As they went down the Augsburgerstrasse, the American started to laugh.

'I like you!' he said suddenly. 'I like you. You're the first local I've come across who isn't out to screw me.'

Grunwald smiled. The soldier's large arm was like a dead weight on his shoulder.

They climbed a flight of stairs and Grunwald noticed the various pieces of furniture littered around the place. Mattresses, old sofas, chairs. The smell of excrement was strong. The American said that it was like a shithouse and there was a touch of shame in his voice, as if it were his personal responsibility to keep the place clean. At the top of the stairs they went into a corridor that led off from a strong wooden door. The corridor ended at another door. The American took the key from his trousers. Beyond was a large room sparsely furnished. The light was poor because curtains had been drawn across the windows. When his eyes had become accustomed to the dimness, Grunwald saw that there was a young girl asleep on a bed in the corner. The American touched her lightly on the shoulder and she woke. She seemed alarmed to see Grunwald in the room.

'Who is he?'

The soldier silenced her by placing his fingers gently on her lips. 'A friend of mine. It's all right. We've come for a drink.'

The girl sat up, smoothing her hair from her face. Grunwald saw that she was very young, probably little more than sixteen or seventeen. Her body was thin and the bed upon which she had been lying was dirty. She stared at Grunwald and then, touching the soldier's face, placed her lips against the side of his neck.

'You know where the stuff is,' she said.

The American went to the other side of the room. He removed a threadbare rug and then a couple of loose floorboards. He put his hand into the space below and took out an unopened bottle of scotch. Breaking the seal, he said, 'Plunder. From an officers' mess by kind courtesy of the Wehrmacht.'

The girl found some cups in a cabinet and gave one

without a handle to Grunwald. He drank slowly. Alcohol, which he had never consumed regularly in the past, seemed to befuddle his thoughts. The girl, the American, the room – they were receding from him at an alarming rate as if he were witnessing them down the wrong end of a telescope. The girl sat on the soldier's lap. Her name was Ursula and she never left this room because in May she had murdered a Russian soldier who had raped her. The American explained all this in a dry, factual way and the girl listened to him without expression. The Russian soldier, Anatole, had been dragged up to the attic and shoved in a cupboard. The cupboard had been locked and the key lost. The body was still there.

'Germans and Russians,' Grunwald said. 'There's not much difference.'

Ursula looked at him angrily. She might have been pretty once, Grunwald thought. Her thinness had robbed her of her looks even if there was still a suggestion of beauty.

'There's a great difference,' she said. 'How can you say something like that?'

Grunwald sipped the whisky. He felt that he was floating out on a dark ocean; a seabird that has lost the power of its wings.

'It's easy to say,' Grunwald answered.

'Adolf had the right idea,' the girl said, and laughed.

'He had hundreds of ideas,' Grunwald said. 'He was an ideas factory. He never stopped having them. I'd say that his last idea was the best he ever had.'

'Which was that?'

'To commit suicide.'

The girl stared hard at Grunwald. He could not understand her open hostility. The American was laughing at their argument, like someone enjoying a hugely private joke. He passed the bottle towards Grunwald, who reached for it.

The girl said, 'Why should he come here? What did you bring him for?'

'I told you. He's a friend. I invited him for a drink.'

'You never think of asking me first,' she said.

'Why don't you shut up?'

Grunwald poured himself a fresh drink. Ursula rose from the American's lap and, moving across the room, sat on the edge of the bed. Watching her, Grunwald wondered about her past: he saw her as a schoolgirl with plaited fair hair and rewritten history textbooks, new biological studies compiled by the brilliant scientists of the Reich, Wagner played at regular interludes, compulsory study of how Bolshevism and World Jewry had combined to bring Germany to its knees like some out-of-condition boxer. The whole thing was odious to him – the great Teutonic myth, the grandeur, the Bund Deutscher Mädchen. It was the rhetoric of insanity. And this girl, this child, had been caught up in it like a scrap of paper in a hurricane.

The American sat on the floor and lit a cigarette.

'You should smile more. You look fucking ugly when you don't smile.'

The girl bared her teeth. 'I don't care.'

'You'd soon care if I stopped coming, wouldn't you? You'd soon begin to care then.' The soldier reached for the whisky and filled his cup. 'Jesus, I wish we had some ice. There isn't a drop of ice in this whole lousy country.'

Listening apathetically to their conversation, Grunwald closed his eyes. He thought of the dead Russian in the attic: fighting all the way across Poland to be murdered by a German girl – it seemed meaningless. How had she murdered him? When he was asleep had she taken his gun and shot him? He tried to imagine this young girl with her finger on a trigger and the mouldering body in the cupboard upstairs. Death scared him: he had seen so much of it, and yet it terrified him.

When he opened his eyes, and realized with surprise that he must have fallen asleep, he saw that the soldier and the girl were lying on the bed. The American stared at him.

'You talk in your sleep. Did you know that?'

Grunwald was embarrassed. 'What did I say?'

'Nothing I could understand. A lot of gibberish. It sounded like you were in pain.'

The girl said, 'You were probably having a nightmare.'

'I can't remember,' Grunwald said, 'I can't remember a nightmare. I don't even remember falling asleep.'

The American passed him the whisky. Grunwald poured some into his cup and drank; he felt drunk now.

'And you snore,' the girl said. 'Your mouth hangs open and you snore.' She got up from the bed, climbing over the soldier, and lit a candle that sat in a dish near the window. The single point of moving light created shadows in the room. The faces of the soldier and the girl were alternatively yellow and white as the flame moved.

The girl said, 'What did you do in the war?'

'Nothing,' Grunwald said.

'You must have done something. Everybody did something.'

'Stop talking about the fucking war,' the American said. 'I've had it up to here with the war. It's all I ever hear. Did you have a good war? Did you have a bad war? What did you do in the fucking war? It's all I ever hear.'

Grunwald watched the girl come closer to him. She stood in front of him: her expression was suddenly strange – like that of someone about to offer a piece of poisoned fruit.

'Come on. You must have done something. Why don't you tell us about it? What are you afraid of?'

Grunwald said, 'I'm not afraid of anything.'

The girl laughed. Grunwald had a sudden impulse to reach out towards her and touch her. She seemed all at once so insubstantial that she might have been only another shadow in the room. He dropped his hands to his side. It had been a long time since he had touched a woman. Turning away from him, the girl went back to the bed and sat beside the American. But she continued to look curiously at Grunwald.

'It doesn't matter a damn what people did in the war,' the American said. 'All that's finished. If you survived, you're pretty lucky. And the dead don't have any complaints. It doesn't matter a shit.'

The girl turned away from him and looked at Grunwald. 'I wish I could get one of the windows open. This place stinks.'

Grunwald stared at her. Her mouth hung open. She seemed acutely vulnerable all at once, as if the change in her expression made her look like a child again. But no; she wasn't a child. She was a woman, she had been raped by the Russian, she was visited regularly by the American – and how many others? Grunwald thought of the things one had to do to survive. Rising from the chair he went to the window and drew the curtain back a couple of inches. In the street below several people were moving back and forward with a kind of aimless furtiveness: they were like creatures carrying unimportant secrets to destinations they knew they would never reach. The girl approached him. He was conscious of her breath against his face.

'Everything was happier before the war. Didn't you think everything was much nicer then?'

He could not tell if she was deliberately trying to provoke him. He said nothing. She touched him on the elbow and continued, almost in a whisper, to speak.

'I was only a child then, of course. But I felt a certain kind of atmosphere in Germany. What's the word? Jubilance. Everybody was jubilant. Nothing could happen to the Reich. Didn't you feel like that?'

What was she trying to do? Did she genuinely imagine that he hadn't suffered even during those halcyon days before the destruction of Europe? He turned to look at

32

her. She was smiling slightly. Before he could interpret her expression she moved away.

The American, who hadn't been listening to her, said, 'Know what my trouble is? Know what it is? I'm fucking homesick. I want to go home.'

'Why don't you have another drink? It's the only damn thing that keeps you happy.' The girl gave him the bottle. He ignored it and caught her by the waist. She pulled herself free, laughing softly. The soldier rose from the bed. He spilled the bottle. Reeling, he lost balance and struck himself hard against the wall. He moved towards her again. A chair toppled over and, catching his legs against it, he fell to the floor. He sat there for a time, dazed, more drunk than he had realized.

Grunwald picked up the empty bottle and looked at the puddle of liquid on the floorboards.

'I'm fucking homesick,' the American said. He got to his feet with surprising agility and snatched the empty bottle from Grunwald's hand. And then, as if berserk, as if something in his mind had suddenly broken, he lunged after the girl. Still laughing, she moved quickly away from him. She stood by the window, her hands on her hips, and when the soldier threw the bottle at her head she ducked. Grunwald expected to hear the noise of broken glass but the bottle, trapped in the curtain, dropped intact to the floor.

'You're drunk out of your mind,' the girl said.

The American stared hollowly at her for a second and then looked at Grunwald. 'Sometimes I'd like to kill the bitch. I'd like to throttle her.'

Grunwald asked, 'Why?'

The American shrugged. 'No reason. No real reason. She just makes me feel violent sometimes. That's all.'

The soldier returned to the bed where he lay down. Within minutes he was snoring. The girl went towards him and, as if the earlier scene had never happened, began to stroke his hair. Grunwald looked from the window into the street. Everything, even now, fell into patterns of random violence. It made no sense. But then nothing did. The great war should have seen an end to violence.

He watched the figures that moved in the street below. A couple of military policemen had stopped a soldier and were asking to see his papers. Everyone, in uniform or out, had to have papers. Without them, you might just as well be dead.

He was walking up the Neuhauserstrasse again with the sun killing him. Martha and the boy. Martha and the boy. A couple of SS men were walking in his direction. Involuntarily he moved into the doorway of a shop and pretended to be looking at something in the window. He emerged again only after they had gone past.

Later in the evening, when Herr Kramer called, Grunwald had at last accepted a simple fact: in the Third Reich certain people were no longer human beings. They had no rights. Their fates depended on nothing more substantial than the casual whims of an insane regime.

Herr Kramer took off his spectacles and polished them as was his habit on the cuff of his shirt. He said, 'Maybe you would like a glass of wine. A cognac.'

Grunwald moved his hands in a tired fashion. 'I don't feel like anything, thank you.'

Restlessly he rose and walked up and down the room.

Herr Kramer said, 'I feel a great sense of doom, Leonhard. And I am afraid for all of us.'

Grunwald began to search for his cigarettes. Anything, anything at all, that would prevent him from having to listen to Kramer. But Kramer continued, his voice rising and dropping with predictable regularity.

'We could argue that these times will pass. But what sort of argument would that be? It's like saying that some day in the distant future the sun will no longer rise. No, Leonhard. I think we are doomed. Everything we have seen happening, and everything that I fear is going to happen, only adds weight to what I already feel.' He began to tap his fingers on the arms of the leather chair. He was silent a moment. 'We are already dead.'

Grunwald looked at him. The late evening sun touched the bare flesh of his scalp, suddenly and comically seeming to transform him into a visionary. Herr Kramer had nothing more to say. Soon he would return to his apartment and sit there pontificating to himself, meditating the wild injustice of everything even when his door was being hammered down.

Grunwald said, 'Why did they take Martha and the boy?'

Herr Kramer shrugged: 'I am not a psychiatrist, Leonhard. You have my deepest and sincerest sympathies and my heartfelt hope that they will be returned to you. But you cannot expect me, a simple schoolmaster – forcibly retired – to understand the labyrinthine workings of the National Socialist mind.'

Later, when Herr Kramer had gone out into the night, Grunwald opened a bottle of cognac and drank himself into a hollow state of oblivion. He crawled into his empty bed and slept immediately, dreamlessly.

It was almost dark. Grunwald woke with a headache. The room was silent except for the sound of someone breathing. The candle, now almost burnt down, gave out a spluttering flame. He looked around. The girl, Ursula, was sitting upright on the bed, staring at him. The American had gone.

'Jake had to leave. He was due back at his base hours ago.' She lit a cigarette from the candle. 'He insisted that you stay here until morning. If you want to stay, that is, I don't care either way. If Jake hadn't specially asked, I would have thrown you out.'

Grunwald shivered and drew his coat around him. He could barely see the girl now because the light from the candle was dying rapidly. The room appeared to shrink. He felt too tired to leave and begin the search for somewhere to sleep.

'I'll stay,' he said.

'That's up to you. You'll have to sleep between the chairs. Or on the floor.' She started to take off her clothes. She crossed her arms over her breasts, a gesture of curious modesty, and pulled the blanket towards her body. Grunwald watched her for a time, aware of the way her eyes seemed to burn against him.

She was silent for a minute. And then she asked, 'Do you want to sleep with me?'

Grunwald shook his head.

'You want to sleep with me, don't you? You want to get in beside me. Don't you?' She crushed her cigarette out on the floor. 'When did you last have a woman?'

Grunwald said nothing.

'The way you looked at me before. I could tell what was in your mind. I knew what you were thinking.'

Grunwald said, 'You're wrong. You're quite wrong.' He lay on the floor, his coat drawn tightly around him.

'You don't even understand your own motives, do you? You want to fuck me.'

He turned on his side. The sudden pain in his head was like a burning needle.

She said, 'I only want you to know that I couldn't stand you near me. I couldn't bear to let you touch me. I'd die before I'd let you come within an inch of me.'

Grunwald sat up. 'Why? I don't understand why.'

She was silent for a long time. The candle was finally dead. The darkness around him was hostile and indifferent. They had done their job well, the propagandists and the teachers of the Third Reich. They had proclaimed a new biological order in which certain species were unfit to survive; they had created a new order of vermin. It didn't sadden him now to realize this, or to remember. It angered him.

The girl, as if quoting from the scriptures, said, 'The Jew is not a human being. He is a symbol of putrefaction.'

Grunwald closed his eyes. The girl's last statement, like a relentless echo, rebounded again and again through his brain.

4

He was alone in the room. Even though the curtains still covered the windows he was aware of a fine light filtering through. It was early morning. From the street below came a variety of sounds: someone was revving up an engine and a radio was playing a song in a foreign language he couldn't recognize. When he sat up he saw that the girl's bed was empty. Rising, he moved towards the bed as if he wanted to be certain that she wasn't there. The blanket was twisted untidily. On the floor lay an empty pack of American cigarettes. A tattered pair of stockings hung from the mantelpiece: they were damp, dripping slightly, and had been placed there to dry. He touched them. And then he withdrew his hand. He went to the window and pulled a curtain back. Outside, the morning was bleak and grey and touched by the approach of winter.

The light that fell into the room revealed things he had not noticed before. There was a framed photograph on the wall: the girl Ursula, aged perhaps about eight, smiling into the camera. Her fair hair was coiled on the top of her head. A front tooth was missing. A child of the Reich, he thought: what had they done to her? Beneath the snapshot, pinned to the wall with a rusty tack, hung one of those lapel badges people used to wear, depicting a swastika on a strip of black cloth. Grunwald put out his hand to it and ran his finger down the length of the cloth like a blind man feeling for an unfamiliar object. And then he ripped it from the tack and crumpled it between his fingers. It dropped from his hand to the floor and lay there, unrecognizable and black, a dead insect.

In a cupboard he found some biscuits which he ate

slowly. They were dry and stale and tasteless. When he had finished them he wondered about the girl. Where was she? If she never left the apartment, as the American had said, why had she suddenly chosen to leave it now? He took one of her cigarettes and lit it, coughing badly: it was a habit he had given up years ago. It must have been in 1940 when he had last smoked a cigarette. After 1940 there hadn't been much opportunity to continue the habit and little emotional energy to suffer the symptoms of withdrawal. Now, smoking for the first time in so many years, he wondered where the girl had got to.

He was taken, as were so many others, in the summer of 1940. It seemed an absurd exercise, a day's outing at the expense of Reichsführer Himmler, a trip to a holiday camp in some remote part of the countryside. But there was a distinct absence of gaiety about those who were pushed into the trains and the trucks; and as those SS men who were supervising the whole operation began to detect this attitude of insolent ingratitude amongst the travellers, so their acts of brutality seemed to increase. A young man of about eighteen had his face split open with the butt of a revolver. A girl of fourteen, in an old school uniform was dragged into a siding and silenced behind a row of rotten, derelict railway trucks. And so these savageries had continued as the train moved towards Mauthausen; and Grunwald could only think how extraordinary it was that he had never visited Austria before and how stupid that his first visit should be under such restrictive circumstances.

Someone said to Grunwald, 'They tell us nothing. They haven't said where they're taking us.'

'A pleasant Austrian resort, I believe,' Grunwald said – wondering why he felt such an intense sense of freedom. Packed amongst a hundred other prisoners, how was it possible to feel like this? He could only suppose that it was because the thing he had long expected was at last actually happening. Until then, he had been imprisoned by his own dread, by his own fear of the unknown. Now, at least, he knew where he was being taken.

Finishing the cigarette, Grunwald decided that it was time to leave. It hardly mattered if he saw the girl again or not. It was pointless to wait in her apartment; what was he waiting for anyway? He had a last look round and then went to the door. Outside, he stopped on the landing. The building was silent. Above him there was a great gash in the roof where the masonry had collapsed. He made his way between the ruined items of furniture that cluttered the stairs and he began to walk down. Somewhere, perhaps in the street, a radio was playing American dance-band music. On the landing below he found the girl.

She was sitting with her back to the wall. Her hands were crossed in her lap. Her legs were apart. One broken shoe lay some inches away from her. The ring on her left hand looked painfully tight because the bone of the ring-finger was the colour of chalk. Her hair had fallen across her eyes and her mouth was open, giving her once again the appearance of a vulnerable child. Her blouse was open, and her breasts visible. They were thin and white and the nipples hardly apparent.

She seemed to be asleep. Or, like a child in a child's game, pretending sleep. Only the opening of the flesh around her neck and throat indicated otherwise. Grunwald wanted to shake her, bring her out of her sleep. But that was quite impossible. Someone had taken an instrument – a knife, razor, anything sharp – and had slit her across the throat. The blood had drained away, running over her neck and shoulders into a pool on the floor beside her. He stepped away. Who had done it? The American? Had he come back and killed her?

Mesmerized, Grunwald stared at the girl. It was difficult to avoid the feeling that really she wasn't dead, that she

40

was merely pretending: synthetic blood, a fixed posture, breath held back into the lungs – a grotesque joke. He was trembling. The sight of death did this to him. He touched the girl's arm. Strangely her flesh was still warm but the heat was rapidly leaving her body. Moving back, he leaned against the wall. He hadn't liked the girl. But seeing her now brought back some of the fears he had been suppressing himself, some of the sounds and sights and smells that had been haunting his mind restlessly. He went slowly towards the stairs. Nobody would care that she had been killed. There would no investigation and no arrest. Another prostitute slashed – so what? An official shrug. A blind drawn on a dirty window. A file closed.

A man and a woman were climbing the stairs towards him. A sense of panic assailed him. The man, hanging grimly to the woman's arm, raised his head and saw Grunwald. The woman, sensing something, stopped. Climbing the last steps slowly, the man reached the landing. Grunwald felt he should apologize – for being there, for the girl's body, for the fact of his existence. The man caught his breath and told the woman to fetch a doctor. She didn't hestitate. Grunwald heard her footsteps ringing down the stairs as she turned and ran.

'It's too late for a doctor,' Grunwald said.

The man, as if a practical solution to the problem were exclusively his, leaned over the dead girl. He was breathing heavily. 'You're right. It's too late for anything but an undertaker.' He straightened up and looked at Grunwald.

'Do you know the girl?'

'Only vaguely.

The man took off his cap, a belated mark of respect. 'Did you find her like this?'

'She was lying there. Just as you see her now.'

The man spat. 'A pretty thorough job all the same. See the clean line across the throat. Whoever did that to her knew exactly where to make his cut. Very tidy.'

'I hadn't thought about it like that,' Grunwald said.

The man replaced his cap. His face was grubby and bearded and yet, incongrously, the clothes he wore were clean and neat. He said, 'We've got to get a doctor anyway. For the death certificate.'

Grunwald turned his face away from the girl. The man lit a cigarette. 'It's nasty,' he said. 'Neat and nasty.'

'Yes,' Grunwald said. He wondered if he might leave now – there was nothing for him to do here. He remained where he was, experiencing the odd sensation that he had been completely stripped of any purpose or function. He looked at the man who was smoking silently. Somehow the smell of the place seemed more intense than before and he was aware of the large numbers of flies that floated through the air, as if they had come from nowhere in the hope of picking at the girl's remains. He looked down the stairs to the landing below. A thin light filtered through some broken glass.

'Any idea who might have done it?'

Grunwald shook his head. He could have mentioned the American, but what would have been the point? If he remained silent it was a relatively simple affair: a young prositute murdered by an unknown person. If he opened his mouth and mentioned the soldier, it threw open all kinds of complicated possibilities.

'She's only a kid,' the man said. 'We'd better wait here until Elsie comes back, with the doctor.' He sat down on the cold stone and crossed his legs. Grunwald remained standing, his eyes fixed to the point of light coming up from below. He listened to the sound of the man smoking, the faint whisper as the cigarette came apart from his lips and the swift intake of air when he drew the smoke into his throat.

'You live around here?' he asked.

Grunwald said, 'Not exactly.'

The man seemed satisfied with this answer. 'Elsie will bring a doctor. There's one that lives a couple of streets away. If he's at home. They're kept pretty busy these days, I imagine.'

'I expect you're right,' Grunwald leaned against the wall. The scent of tobacco, the smell of excrement, the noise of the flies, and the unbearable presence of the dead girl – these things combined to sicken him. He felt dizzy and for no apparent reason afraid. He wished that Elsie would come quickly with the doctor so that he could get away from the place as soon as possible.

The man sighed and threw down his cigarette. He looked at his wristwatch. 'What's keeping Elsie, for Christ's sake?'

'Perhaps the doctor is busy.'

The man nodded and clenched and unclenched his fists in a show of impatience. He sat back against the wall and took his tobacco tin from his jacket.

After the April boycott in 1933 Martha asked him to think seriously about leaving Germany. It was the first time she had made such a request and Grunwald was surprised. It was true that the position of the Jews was worsening but this was a fact that Grunwald unhestitatingly attributed to the poor economic situation. As soon as this improved it would follow that the position of the Jews would improve as well – but Martha, who had been shocked by the boycott, disagreed. After all, what had the *Völkischer Beobachter* said a few days later. *Saturday's boycott is to be regarded merely as a dress rehearsal for a series of measures that will be carried out unless world opinion, which is against us at the moment, definitely changes.* A dress rehearsal: what would the real thing be like? The SA would exchange their propagandist leaflets and warnings to the Jews for rifles, and their random acts of violence for the swifter discipline of the machine-gun.

Wouldn't Grunwald leave? Why wouldn't he? What did he owe to Germany? Didn't he see that he was like a cripple who after all other treatment has failed persists in being ministered to by a crank? Didn't he see how dumb his faith was? Did he imagine that because he himself hadn't been beaten or terrorized in a public street he was safe? Did he believe that nothing could ever touch him? That even obscure laws created in Nuremberg were irrelevant to his life?

Martha's questions remained unanswered and eventually for a time she stopped asking them, as if she were prepared to play along with Grunwald's game. When she heard that something had happened to Frau Becker or to Herr Zuckerman or that Rabbi Gerstein had been abused in the street, she mentioned these facts like someone discussing surprising changes in the weather: a freak snowstorm in the middle of July, a heatwave on New Year's Day. Her outbursts were infrequent but when they happened she poured them out hurriedly as if she were reciting some catalogue of misery, repeating every act of vandalism and violence so that she might make Grunwald see the strength of her case. And when Grunwald eventually realized, it was much too late.

He loved her. In many ways he admired her. She was more intelligent than he was, and more perceptive. When the boy was born he hoped that he would inherit her traits rather than his own. She had a certain courage that he could never hope to emulate and he realized, many years later, that even if she had died in the most painful and degrading of circumstances, she would have died with her courage intact. The thoughts consoled him in a small way.

He never stopped to wonder how the boy had died.

The man had lit a fresh cigarette. When he heard the sound on the stair below he stood up and turned to Grunwald.

'That might be Elsie now,' he said.

Grunwald did not know how long he had been standing in the same waiting position. His limbs were numb and

44

frozen. He watched the stairs and saw the woman come into view. She had a headscarf knotted tightly around her hair and it was glistening with fine drops of rain.

'I've got the doctor,' she said.

'It took you long enough,' the man said.

Elsie whipped off her scarf and shook it. 'I couldn't find him at first.' She had reached the landing and saw the dead girl for the first time. 'Oh, Jesus. Who did that to her?'

The man shrugged. 'Do you know her?'

Elsie said, 'I've seen her a few times. She didn't say much. She kept to herself.'

There was another noise on the stairs below. A slow, heavy footstep; the sound of a man who realizes it is too late to rush. For some reason Grunwald shivered.

He watched the man's shadow rise against the wall and then the man himself came into view.

'Here he is,' Elsie said.

The doctor was wearing a broad-rimmed hat and a threadbare black overcoat. In his right hand he carried a leather bag. He walked with an odd swaying motion, as if his movement originated in his shoulders rather than in his legs.

Grunwald stepped back against the wall. The sudden fear that he felt was like a flash of light. The doctor climbed the last few stairs and reached the landing.

'This is the girl, Doctor,' Elsie said, as though such an explanation were needed.

Without speaking the doctor put down his bag and then leaned over the girl's body.

Terrified, Grunwald watched. The doctor's hands probed the wound in the girl's neck. He had seen those hands before. He stepped back as far as he could, afraid again.

The doctor stood up and looked at Elsie. 'A death certificate. That's all I can give you. Someone will have to be notified. Someone will have to come and take the corpse away.'

Grunwald heard the strange clipped voice that had a faint hypnotic quality about it. He had heard it before. It came to him again, a fading echo.

The doctor picked up his bag. He wiped his hands on a rag and then pulled on a pair of gloves. He looked at Elsie and then at Elsie's man. And finally, inevitably, he noticed Grunwald. The expression on his face did not alter. He said, 'She's been murdered. There's no doubt about that.'

Grunwald felt faint. Before he knew what he was doing he said, 'Doctor Schwarzenbach.'

The doctor looked puzzled. 'Schwarzenbach? You must be mistaken. My name is Lutzke. Doctor Lutzke.' He shrugged his shoulders and turned to the woman. 'If you'll return to my surgery I'll give you the certificate. And then we can notify the authorities.'

Grunwald stood upright, forcing his body away from the wall. He felt intensely weak: something had entered him, something had struck all the strength from his body. He watched the doctor turn to go down the stairs.

'Doctor?'

The doctor stopped. 'Yes?'

Whatever he had intended to say would not be forced from his mouth. 'Nothing. It's nothing.'

The doctor gazed at him for a second and then, to the woman, said, 'If you'll come with me.'

Elsie followed him down the stairs

Schwarzenbach. Gerhardt Schwarzenbach.

Grunwald stood for a time on the street. The man had said that he would stay long enough to make a statement to the authorities. Grunwald had replied that he would return. Rain, driven by sharp wind, numbed his face. He started to walk.

Schwarzenbach was in Berlin. Calling himself Lutzke.

And still practising medicine. Dr Schwarzenbach.

On the corner of the street Grunwald wondered which way to turn. He had a sudden desire to urinate and went behind some rubble. He thought of the dead girl and how ironic it was that Schwarzenbach had been the one to sign the certificate of death. He thought of Schwarzenbach's hands touching the flap of damp skin round the girl's throat. Schwarzenbach had perfect hands and had always been proud of them. He polished and protected them as if they were sensitive instruments that had to be kept beautiful because they were on permanent display. He wore gloves in cold weather so that the icy air could not get at his skin and in summer he covered his fingers with a protective liniment. He thought more of his hands than of anything else and he guarded them as someone might guard a priceless relic.

Gerhardt Schwarzenbach was here in Berlin. Grunwald realized for the first time what this might mean.

He walked until he reached the junction of Kurfürsten and Potsdamerstrasse and then he hesitated. The rain was falling heavily now and he had to find shelter quickly.

5

The tables in the darkened room were crowded and waitresses had to push energetically through if they wanted to serve drinks. Over everything hung a blanket of tobacco smoke so thick it seemed deliberately to have been woven in the air. Away in a corner, partly hidden by a curtain, a man played a piano and sometimes a sad-faced girl would get up and attempt to sing over the noise. Most of the customers were American soldiers but here and there Germans sat drinking in tight little groups, men who were making a decent living on the black market and who could afford to spend time discussing world affairs and how, since the fall and surrender of the Reich, Germany had become a better place to live in. Grunwald took some coins from his coat and asked for a beer and the barman, staring at him as if a memory of a time when Grunwald would not have been served had crossed his mind, drew the beer slowly from the tap.

Grunwald looked for a chair but none was vacant. Eventually he decided to stand near the pianist and listened to the girl as she made yet another attempt to sing her song to an unwilling and uninterested audience. He was aware of a curious mood about the place; it was somehow transitory and people were drinking as if they suspected that next day the supply of alcohol would cease to exist, as if some sort of decree would prohibit them from ever drinking again. The girl opened her mouth and shouted the first line of her song and as she sang her body swayed back and forth to the rhythm of the piano. The pianist, a thin man in shirtsleeves, touched the keys with an expression of contempt. Grunwald, suddenly cold, put his free hand into the pocket of his coat. It was impossible,

48

even in the midst of so much noise and human company, not to remember Schwarzenbach leaning over the body of the girl and the sight of his fingers on the slashed throat.

He felt a sensation of fear. It was connected with Schwarzenbach; it had something to do with seeing the doctor again and something to do with the way he had so casually brushed aside Grunwald's utterance of his name, and his insistence that he was called Lutzke. And yet it was more than merely seeing Schwarzenbach again. Other phantoms seemed to come alive and the questions that had frequently gone through Grunwald's mind appeared to answer itself. Where were they now? The Obersturmführers, like Mayer, the doctors, like Schwarzenbach, the other thousands of men who had manned the machine and made it run with barbarous efficiency? The answer was that they still existed – under other names, living in other districts, doing other jobs. Their uniforms safely tucked away at the bottom of trunks, their party cards dutifully burned, they perhaps raised hens and collected eggs and men like Mayer, retired forcibly in their prime, presumably tended flowers in rural Bavarian gardens and persisted in denying that they had ever done anything else. And Schwarzenbach? What did he feel now when he came across a typhoid case or cured a child's measles? Or found it difficult to get the right sort of medicine when he needed it? Or brought a new baby into the universe?

For a moment Grunwald was conscious of his own physical self: the shabby overcoat, the unshaven face, the thinness that seemed to emphasize his appearance of Jewishness. And seeing himself in this way brought back yet another image – of a thousand men walking through mud towards an unknown destination, like soldiers searching for a battlefield upon which no war could conceivably be fought, a thousand men ploughing through acres of mud in falling, cutting rain, some sinking in marshes, some stumbling, all moving as fast as they could, hurrying, the ice of the rain slashing through their garments, aware of the cry of the dogs that came up through the darkness out of the electric lamps and the noise of men in greatcoats who carried rifles and sometimes fired random bullets into the crowd.

Grunwald listened to the girl singing: a soldier came back from the war, from a faraway front, and couldn't find his girl because she had died in an air-raid. A thousand men had gone across the mud and some had fallen and you could sometimes hear the clutching noise the mud made as it sucked against their flesh. And the dogs. The rattle of chains. The sullen cries of the dogs and the shouts of the guards and the way the lamps penetrated the darkness, gathering into their bands of light the frozen breath of a thousand men.

Gerhardt Schwarzenbach had practised medicine in a surgery near to the Prinzenstrasse. The house was nineteenth century and Schwarzenbach's name, together with that of his partner Dr Muller, was embossed on a brass plate nailed to the front door. The doctors occupied rooms on the ground floor, Schwarzenbach's being to the rear of the house with windows that looked into a small, walled garden. The Munich practice was profitable and popular chiefly because Schwarzenbach was efficient: his patients often thought that he regarded the human body as a mechanic might a machine, that he conceived of human existence as nothing more than a mass of physical impulses and reactions. But he was efficient, and this fact cancelled the impression of aloofness that he presented.

Grunwald had visited him on several occasions and Martha, early in her pregnancy, had consulted him once. Martha had gone to another doctor shortly after, arguing that she didn't like Schwarzenbach because he seemed uncaring. But Grunwald, who considered this a perfect example of irrational feminine intuition, continued to consult Schwarzenbach until the autumn of 1935. At that time he had been suffering from severe headaches.

Early in October 1935 he paid his last call. Schwarzenbach kept him waiting in the reception room until all the other patients had gone – even though some of them had actually arrived *after* Grunwald – and when Grunwald entered the surgery Schwarzenbach announced that he could no longer regard Grunwald as a patient. It appeared, Schwarzenbach said, that in view of the Nuremberg Laws, Grunwald would be well advised to seek a doctor of his own race. Besides, as a member of the National Socialist Party – in which organization he was held in some esteem – it could hardly help his career if it were discovered that he had Jewish patients. There was the additional fact, of course, that the practice had become too large and unless the number of patients were kept to a reasonable limit, everyone would suffer. Schwarzenbach had spoken these words without once looking at Grunwald, his eyes fixed to the window and the dishevelled garden at the rear as if he were discussing the failure of his flower-beds. Grunwald looked round the office: it had not occurred to him before, in spite of his suspicions, that Schwarzenbach was a Nazi. The gleaming instruments, the white coat hanging starkly on the back of the door, the tidy desk, the neat bundles of papers – what had political affiliations to do with the practice of medicine?

Grunwald asked, 'If you saw a Jew dying, and no Jewish doctor happened to be available, would you treat the man?'

Schwarzenbach said nothing for a long time but stared at Grunwald as though the question were too naïve to deserve an answer. He then moved to the window and pressed his forehead against the glass. 'Adolf Hitler has clearly stipulated the way in which the Jews of Germany are to be regarded.'

'What about you?' Grunwald asked.

'Me? What do you expect me to say?'

'I don't know. What do you want to say?'

'I don't have to answer your questions, Herr Grunwald.'

'It's up to you, naturally. But what are you? A doctor?'

Schwarzenbach looked angry. 'A good doctor, Herr Grunwald, as most of my patients would testify – including yourself, I imagine.'

'Until now, yes,' Grunwald said.

'And because I refuse to treat you, I'm no longer a good doctor?'

Grunwald said nothing. He watched Schwarzenbach walk up and down the room. He was a man in his middle-thirties, already almost bald; a few strands of soft dark hair covered his skull. He was a neat man and Grunwald could imagine him meticulously hanging his clothes each night before he slept in his well-made bed. He wasn't married although some of the patients in the waiting-room sometimes whispered of a vague love-affair that had gone wrong; and that he carried the scars of the shattered romance like some veteran returning from the front with his medals of martyrdom. It was Schwarzenbach's walk that fascinated Grunwald: it was like that of a sailor who has spent his life struggling against head-on gales in rolling ships.

Schwarzenbach said, 'I don't want to see you here again. I don't want to treat you again. The laws of the Reich – the laws of the Führer – are inviolable.'

For one moment Grunwald thought that he was joking and that the solemnity was a charade, something that could not be taken seriously. It was like the feeling he had when he watched the Liebstandarte march past and heard the noise of drums.

'Do I have to say anything more?'

Grunwald got to his feet, still waiting for some explanation that would clarify everything. But there wasn't an explanation; there was none to be given. Schwarzenbach remained grim and silent and did not even turn to look as Grunwald left the room.

Several years passed before he saw Schwarzenbach again. During that time he heard two things, both – as he then thought, unlikely rumours. The first was that Schwarzenbach had been invited to advise on the so-called Reich euthanasia programme. The second that he had been seen in the Marienplatz, in the autumn of 1938, wearing a resplendent new black uniform.

And now Schwarzenbach was in Berlin, calling himself Lutzke. Grunwald closed his eyes: all at once he was tired, he experienced a fatigue that seemed to sink through his bones as if they were blotting-paper and the noises around him – piano, the song, the empty rattle of human voices – came from a long way off. He looked up at the ceiling where a single lamp, shrouded in smoke, burned bleakly. He got up from the table and went outside and wondered if he should go back to the house in the Augsburgerstrasse. The dead girl – there would perhaps be questions to answer. But the idea was point-less. It wasn't death he wanted to see: he wanted clean air, fresh air, an atmosphere that hadn't been polluted by the scents and stenches of destruction.

He crossed the street. A wintry wind flapped through his thin overcoat. He saw in a sudden flash of cold insight the dilemma of his life. He had a duty to speak out, and to tell what he knew.

Schwarzenbach. No mistake. The face, the voice, the hands, the manner of walking.

Suddenly he was afraid again. The wind seemed to crucify him with driven shafts of ice. *Dr Schwarzenbach – will you save my life? I am afraid of dying. I want to live.*

Was that the way it had been? Had it happened like that? In Chelmo concentration camp, in the bleak back-waters of occupied Poland, had he really genuflected in front of the good doctor like some half-mad slave pleading to be spared? Spared from what? From precisely what? He thought of the barbed-wire strung across the dead

53

landscape like an artificial horizon imposed upon nature by a crowd of lunatics and the memory seemed to drag out of him some deep longing to be free, to forget.

Schwarzenbach. He had a duty to reveal what he knew. He is in Berlin and the war is over and he is one of the men you are looking for on the count of crimes against humanity in occupied Poland. What are you going to do?

An American sergeant went past him, bent forward against the lash of the wind. Grunwald, hurrying, caught up with the soldier and fell into step only a few paces behind him. It would take only a few seconds, it would take no more than that to expose Dr Lutzke. He held his breath.

The soldier swung round and stared hard at him.

'Beat it, Fritz.'

Grunwald brought his hands out of his overcoat.

'Look, fuck off. No cigarettes. No chocolate. Unnerstand? Now fuck off.'

The soldier walked briskly away and Grunwald, motionless, watched him go. A sense of imposed silence fell across him. He felt despair, loneliness.

It was impossible to speak out against Schwarzenbach. He saw that now. He saw the frailty of the past and realized that, if he were to tell the truth, the whole skeletal edifice would come toppling down. And it would fall not only on Schwarzenbach but on himself because the guilt was something they shared between them.

PART TWO

Berlin, September/ October 1945

6

Waking suddenly in the dark as if an external noise had disturbed him, he reached out for his wristwatch on the bedside table. He went to the window and held the watch at such an angle that it caught the thin light from a lamp outside. Three-twenty. What had awakened him? What had happened to disturb him? He found his carpet slippers and went through to the room that served as a kitchen – although of course it was only a kitchen in the loosest possible meaning of the word. The plumbing was crude and makeshift and the wall-basin was badly cracked. When he filled it to the top water seeped through. Christ, why did nothing function properly any more? Wherever he looked he saw the patches people had used to cover things that had been casualties of the war. It was a pretence. You had only to remove the patches to see. He went through the kitchen on to the small room beyond that he used as a surgery. He turned on the light and looked around; and then he realized something else as well. He was afraid. Fear, like something hanging lightly from the ceiling of a darkened room, like a dry cobweb, had touched him. Returning to the kitchen he poured himself a small glass of cognac and sat for a time at the table, listening to the continual drip from the faucet. When he looked from the window he saw how black the sky had become. The absence of light was suddenly appalling. His hands were shaking. It embarrassed him to see just how badly they trembled; and yet it would have been worse if there had been anyone else present to notice it as well. He sipped the cognac very slowly and enjoyed the taste. It pleased him to think that in an age of tastelessness there was still something he could enjoy.

When he went back into the bedroom he knew that he wouldn't be able to sleep. Not now. Sleep had been driven from him. He turned on the reading lamp and looked distastefully at the way in which the bedsheets had become so crumpled. Was he really such a restless sleeper? Then he went to the mirror and began to sweep what remained of his hair across the baldness of his forehead. A vain thing, really, but he felt the need to keep up appearances. He put on his trousers, shoes and a shirt; and then he pulled on his overcoat and went outside to the landing. The stairs were dark and utterly silent. And yet – strange what darkness did – he imagined that someone was waiting below. Looking down, he almost expected to see the flare of a match or the arc of a torch. But there was nothing. Nerves; he was simply nervous. As he started to descend he listened to the slight echoes of his own footsteps. When he stopped just once the echo continued briefly, but in a hollow way, like someone catching his breath.

Outside, the night air was freezing cold. His breath hung in the darkness. The streets were silent. The houses that remained standing were like mausoleums; and between them those that had been gutted reminded him, absurdly he thought, of rotting limbs. Their shells were of various shapes and sizes and they seemed to threaten him. It was hard to imagine this place as it once might have been. Instead, he could see only the blind windows and the broken arches, the courtyards filled with rubble and dust and splinters of masonry and charred beams. Berlin: a tinderbox. The Reichskänzlei, the Reichs-Arbeits-Ministerium, the Reichs Justiz Ministerium. These seemed to him, as he thought of them now, like flowers that had been severed and had died. The Unter den Linden, the Friedrichstrasse, the Brandenburger Tor, the Pariser-Platz, the Tiergarten beyond: now all monstrously and hideously devoured.

He continued to walk. An anaemic moon broke

through the clouds. It looked like a curved chip of ice, pale and insubstantial. As it broke it made even more hideous the ragged buildings around him, covering them with a white light that looked like frost. And then when the moon sank the darkness dropped again. By the time he had reached the woman's house he was shivering. He let himself in with the key she had given him and stood for a time in the unlit entrance hall and wondered if he should wake her. What difference would it make if he did? He could turn now and leave but the thought of the long walk back didn't appeal to him. Moving forward, feeling his way against the wall, he stumbled over something metallic. There was a loud echoing noise and although he waited for some response – a door to be opened, an angry voice – he heard nothing. When he reached the door of the woman's room he pushed it open. There was a smell of candlegrease and tobacco smoke and something else altogether – the scent of the woman.

He found her lying across an old sofa. Her breath was stale from cheap alcohol. With some disgust he shook her and she woke; he whispered his name and felt her body go limp under his hands.

'For Christ's sake, what time is it?'

He found a candle and lit it. Even in the pale, flattering light she looked ugly.

'What time is it?' she again asked.

'I don't know.'

She sat up, rubbing her hands through her hair. 'You choose the strangest times, don't you?'

He stared at the candle flame. Why had he bothered to come? To rid himself of the fear? No: he would not admit that he was afraid. When he turned to look at the woman she was lighting a cigarette. She was fat and hideous. He had decided this before. When he lay with her flesh pressed flat against his he was reminded of old butcher-meat; he was reminded of the fact that decay touched not only buildings and cities but flesh as well. When he lay sweating against her and listened to the moist sound that their bodies made together, it disgusted him. He had decided all this before – so why had he come? What hatred had brought him all this way across the darkened city? And yet it wasn't hatred: when he thought about it, he realized that he felt nothing. Hatred was something strong. It was an emotion you reserved for your enemies. The woman meant nothing to him.

He put his hands on her shoulders and pushed back the thin blouse that she wore. Her skin felt rough. She suffered from some minor ailment that sometimes affected her skin, causing rough, red patches. A lack of vitamins; a lack of hot water and soap. Too much alcohol.

'You don't give a damn how I feel,' she said. 'I'm bloody tired. I'm really bloody tired.'

'Shut up.' He took the blouse from her body and stared at her naked breasts. Their hugeness appalled him. The nipples were cracked and dry. She lay back on the sofa and dropped her cigarette to the bare floorboards where it smouldered and died.

'Undress me,' he said. 'Hurry. Undress me.'

She removed his overcoat and unbuttoned his shirt. He felt her fingers upon the buttons of his trousers. Her face was utterly blank. The candle burned in her fair hair. She brought her face forward and placed her lips against his belly. He felt her moist tongue against his flesh and her fingers undoing his trousers. What had brought him here? Fear? But he had never been afraid before. It was a feeling he had never experienced. In that sense he could safely say of himself that he was not and never had been a coward. He had never failed to face up to the facts of life, to the facts of his own existence.

He watched the candlelight in the woman's hair and he placed his hands upon her neck. Involuntarily she stiffened; her body became tense. She moved her head back and forward in slight, imperceptible movements and he thought of the girl, the dead girl, the dead girl in the

Augsburgerstrasse he had seen the day before. She had been slashed across the neck, an expert cut, a clean slash through the jugular vein. She had looked like a broken toy, a figurine in whose existence he found it impossible to believe; and he was indifferent to her death. He had been quite indifferent. He imagined that there were those who would have said that he was callous – and yet if he were callous then he was proud of the fact. Callousness didn't have to be a pejorative description: to be callous you had to be hard. And where was the virtue in being soft? He thought of the girl as he tightened his hold on the woman's neck, as he held hard to the back of her head and tensed his body in preparation. A dead girl.

But it wasn't only the dead girl. There was that fucking little Jew. That fucking little Jew who had stepped forward and called out a name. Schwarzenbach? Who was Schwarzenbach? The man was dead – if he had ever lived at all. There was only Lutzke. Dr Gerhardt Lutzke. The Jew was mistaken, his memories were false, completely false, and because of that he had made a mistake. Was that why he was afraid? Because the Jew had mentioned the name? No: he had to remind himself that he wasn't afraid at all. Nobody could ever say with any certainty that he was Schwarzenbach, and nobody could ever prove it. He had papers to prove that he was Gerhardt Lutzke. And that was what he would have to remember now.

The woman was lighting another cigarette. But first she wiped her mouth against her sleeve. He adjusted his clothes and waited for her to say something, hoping that she had nothing to say and that she would remain silent. She was an object. He had used her as anybody would use an object.

'Satisfied?'

He didn't answer. He was fascinated by the flame from the candle and how it moved back and forth even though there was hardly any draught.

'Well – you bloody well ought to be,' she said. 'Waking

me up at this time of day.' She touched the back of his head and with mock tenderness said, 'Poor thing. You must have been desperate. Were you desperate?'

He pushed her hand away. 'I gave you something. I want it back.'

'What did you give me?'

'You know. I want it back.'

She began to cough. The cough disgusted him more than anything else; more than her breasts, more than her body. It was the kind of cough that came deep from her lungs. 'Are you talking about that photograph?'

'That's right. I want it back.'

'I thought you wanted me to have it as a keepsake.'

He clenched his hands in anger. 'Look. Just give it back. Forget you ever saw it.'

The woman shrugged. 'If that's what you want.' She dragged a wooden box from behind a curtain, opened it, and began to rummage through it. She took out a photograph and looked at it.

'Why do you want it back? Are you afraid of something?'

He took the photograph from her. He put it into the pocket of his overcoat. As he did so he knew that sooner or later he would have to destroy it.

'Are you afraid it might fall into the wrong hands?' she asked.

'Forget you ever saw it, will you?' He felt the photograph inside his pocket and wondered why he really wanted it back. The notion that he was afraid returned to him again and he tried to push it from his mind. He wanted the photograph back simply because it was his personal property. There was no other reason. How could there be? In a moment of stupid weakness, when he had been boasting to the woman, he had given her the picture. It was of himself in SS uniform taken in 1939 against the background of the Schöner Brunnen in the Adolf-Hitler-Platz in Nuremberg. He hadn't worn the uniform often and this, so far as he could recall, was the only photograph that showed him wearing it. He hadn't needed to wear it except during great occasions and even now he couldn't recollect why he had put it on in Nuremberg in 1939. But why did he feel that he would have to destroy it? It was a harmless snapshot. It didn't incriminate him. So why had he asked for it back?

'Just forget I ever let you see it,' he said.

The woman said, 'All right. I've forgotten. But tell me one thing – why do you want it back?'

'Mind your own bloody business.'

He began to button his overcoat. Outside, it was beginning to get light. He looked at the woman and for some reason felt a touch of pity for her. He allowed the feeling to pass. He was becoming soft, that was the trouble. He was losing his edge. Once, he had been as hard as a razor, a fact he remembered with a mixture of shame and pleasure.

'Are you going?' she asked.

He left some money on the table and went out without saying another word to her. In the street it was bitterly cold: an empty wind drifted up through the barren buildings. He thought of the Jew but that hardly mattered now. Berlin was a large, broken city. He was hardly likely to see the Jew again.

Until midday he saw a whole sequence of people in his surgery and he listened to their complaints. There were cases of dysentery, malnutrition, bronchitis, venereal disease, gangrene – the last being the complaint of an old soldier who had sustained a serious wound during the defence of Berlin. He treated his patients as well as he could, but it was hard without the proper supplies of medicine. Ultimately he didn't care; he regarded death as a fact of nature and any attempt he made professionally to prevent it from occurring was bound to be feeble. The best he could do was simply to alter the calendar of dying;

to push the date back as far as he possibly could. Besides, he sometimes wondered if any of his patients were worth the trouble of saving. They came to him – thin people with faces he failed to recognize and names he barely remembered – and he asked himself how many of them had been responsible for Germany's defeat. Even the old Berlin soldier, whom he regarded with a grudging respect, must carry some of the blame for failing to protect the last stronghold of the Reich. And when he realized how little he genuinely cared for his patients, he knew it was because the things he had believed in, the themes and concepts in dreams that had sustained him, lay somewhere about him in ruins.

This sense of wreckage had changed him. Even his appearance, over which he had once spent so much time, had become shabby now. When he looked at his face in the reflection of a mirror he was invariably touched by a moment of pain. And when he examined his reflection closely he experienced the odd sensation that somehow he no longer existed. His name, for example – what was his name? The letters that came to him were addressed to Gerhardt Lutzke, Doctor of Medicine. And his patients called him Doctor Lutzke, and when they did, sometimes when they did, he had difficulty in remembering that they were addressing him.

At first, at the very beginning, he used to imagine foolishly that they were talking to someone else, another person who had silently entered the room behind his back. Although this feeling passed, it seemed to him that he had assumed more than a new name, he had taken on a new life – easily, calmly, as one puts on a new overcoat. He was a different person. The mirror reflected a different face. And all that remained of the past – apart from his memories – was the photograph. When he had looked at it earlier it even seemed that the person who had been snapped against the Schöner Brunnen was a child, a boy dressing up for the day in the ancient militaristic cast-offs

of his father. It was nonsense of course. The ideas that
went through his mind and sometimes seemed to burn
there were often nonsense. He hadn't lost either his
identity or his beliefs. It was called a period of transition.
The old world – *his* world – had ceased to exist, but he
felt, along with so many others, that it was merely a
temporary cessation. A day was coming; a better day was
coming, and when it came everyone would see that
nothing had really changed.

When he had finished his surgery period he went into
the kitchen and scrubbed his hands under water that he
had previously boiled. There were tiny sores along the
backs of his fingers. He couldn't remember where they
had come from. At one time they would have worried
him greatly, more so than they did now. He spread some
ointment over them: in a day or two they would heal. He
poured a small glass of cognac, noticing that the bottle
was almost empty. He realized he would have to negotiate
with a black marketeer for a new bottle and he hated the
thought. It seemed to him criminal that Germans had
been reduced to such activities – some, he had heard,
were even making a fortune in scarce commodities. But
this was perhaps symptomatic of a new period of cynicism.
There had been cynical periods before, certainly, but
Germany had always risen to transcend them. Some
people he had spoken to recently were even starting to
talk of a rebirth and there were rumours, probably
entirely untrue, that a former Wehrmacht General –
whom the rumours failed to name – was secretly reform-
ing an army in Southern Bavaria. He liked to hear such
rumours, becuase they demonstrated that some people
still cared, but he could not bring himself to believe in
them.

When he heard a sound coming from his surgery, he
thought for a moment that perhaps it was yet another
patient visiting him after hours. He went towards the door
and hesitated. Whoever was in the surgery was walking

very slowly up and down the room. He put his hand against the door and pushed it open. The man in the surgery was wearing the uniform of a captain in the United States Army. He was standing by the window, looking out into the street. In one hand he held a briefcase; and for a moment Schwarzenbach imagined that the captain had come in connection with the dead girl in the Augsburgerstrasse, yet that, he realized immediately afterwards, was most unlikely. What connection could there be between a US captain and a dead German girl? He felt uneasy and he thought of the photograph in the pocket of his overcoat: he should have destroyed it, he knew he should have taken it and burned it. But why was he reacting like this? He was behaving like a guilty man who has something dark to hide.

'Dr Lutzke?' The American was a man of about forty. He had an easy manner, a natural charm, that Schwarzenbach immediately suspected.

'Yes,' Schwarzenbach said. 'Can I help you?'

The American said, 'May I sit down?' He moved towards a chair and laid the briefcase on his knees. 'Do you mind if I smoke?'

'Please do,' Schwarzenbach said. He stood behind his desk and absently touched the paperknife that lay across the blotter. 'I'm not sure how I can help you. If you've come for my professional assistance – '

'Nothing like that, Dr Lutzke,' the American said. 'I ought to introduce myself. Captain Eberhard.'

'Captain Eberhard,' Schwarzenbach said. He sat down and stared at the American. A man of forty, but still apparently youthful; a facile charm that came from confidence, and a confidence that came from a good education and upbringing. Schwarzenbach could imagine him being adept at athletic pursuits – tennis, basketball, swimming. And he probably danced well, talked well, and in his own territory was known as a good mixer. These thoughts went quickly through Schwarzenbach's mind. He had known Americans like Eberhard before. Once, as a medical student, he had gone to the United States. A dismal place, he thought: but that had been in 1924 and perhaps it had changed since then. His only memory now was of warm nights filled with banal talk and young girls whose mothers had educated them to think in terms of making a good marriage. There had been stiff, polite young men from private schools who made conversation as if they were playing a game of poker.

'What can I do for you, Captain?' Schwarzenbach asked.

'I'm not sure yet,' the American said. He was smiling. He had been wearing the smile for some minutes now as though it were fixed to his face permanently; an affliction of some kind, Schwarzenbach thought. And yet he still felt uneasy. He thought of the photograph again and wondered if he was worrying needlessly. A photograph proved nothing. You could not say that a photograph was evidence of anything.

'There must be some reason for your visit,' Schwarzenbach said.

'Yes. There is.' Eberhard seemed in no hurry to express his purpose. He continued to smoke his cigarette and, to Schwarzenbach's vague annoyance, flick his ash on the floor. The conquerors could do as they pleased, he supposed, even in the most inconsequential of ways.

'Perhaps you would be kind enough to tell me,' Schwarzenbach said.

'Of course. You must be a fairly busy man. There's a lot of sickness around these days.' Eberhard smiled but still did not seem in a rush to explain. He finished his cigarette and crushed it in the ashtray on the desk. 'I like your country, I must say. I only wish I'd seen it before the war.'

'It was different then, of course.' Again the sense of unease touched Schwarzenbach. If only the man would come to the point; instead, he seemed content to wander in pointless circles around whatever it was he really wanted to say.

'I can easily imagine that, Dr Lutzke.'

Was Schwarzenbach mistaken? Or had Eberhard said the word 'Lutzke' with an undertone of mockery? Of disbelief and doubt? He played with the paperknife. Otherwise he knew that his hands would begin to tremble. He felt suddenly sick: it was as if a deepening shadow had fallen across his mind, obscuring everything around him.

'How can I help you, Captain?'

'Oh – did I say you could help me?' Eberhard was grinning stupidly.

'I can't remember. But I imagine that you're here because you think I can help you in some way.'

'How do you imagine you could help me?'

Schwarzenbach felt a growing sense of despair. It was impossible not to think that the man was trying in some devious way to trap him. But why? What did he suspect? Did he suspect anything?

'Until you tell me why you're here, I don't know how I can help you,' he said.

Eberhard made as if to open his briefcase and then apparently changed his mind. He drummed his fingers upon the metal clasp. 'You don't enjoy having us in your country, do you?' he asked.

Schwarzenbach shrugged. 'We lost the war. You won. The spoils of victory.'

'But you don't like it, do you?'

'It hardly matters what I like, does it? My opinion is totally irrelevant.'

Eberhard opened the briefcase this time, glanced inside, and then closed it again. 'Would you say you were a patriotic German, Dr Lutzke?'

Schwarzenbach stared at him. What was the point of the game with the briefcase? What did it contain? Incriminating documents? A weapon? A warrant for his arrest? He tried to relax, to restrain his imagination.

'I love my country,' he said.

'Good. I like to hear that. Why shouldn't you love your country? Some people think patriotism's a little old-fashioned, you know. But you have every right to love it. I love the United States of America. So I guess we're both patriots, eh?'

'I imagine so,' Schwarzenbach said. He was aware of a slight finger of sweat touching his spine, running down to the base of his back. What did the man want? What was he here for?

'Then maybe you don't agree with the thing that's going to happen at Nuremberg,' Eberhard said. 'We've got Goering, Hess, Keitel, Rosenberg, Streicher, von Schirach, Kaltenbrunner.' Eberhard paused and Schwarzenbach noticed that he was counting on his fingers as he rattled off the names. 'And there's Neurath, Funk, Schacht, von Papen, Seyss-Inquart, Jodl, Raeder, Doenitz, Hans Frank, Speer, Frick, and Fritzsche. Have I missed anyone out? That's quite a line-up. All the top brass except for a few. Do you agree with that? Do you agree they should be tried?'

Schwarzenbach looked down at his desk. For a moment he said nothing. His mind had become a petrifying blank. And then; 'They're your prisoners. You can do what you like with them.'

Eberhard was drumming on his briefcase again. 'I don't know what to make of that answer, Dr Lutzke.'

'Did you come here just to ask me that?'

Eberhard shook his head. 'I'm from Military Intelligence. I should have mentioned that fact. I'm sorry I didn't.'

'What difference does it make?'

'Perhaps quite a lot.' Eberhard put the briefcase on the floor where it fell over face down. 'I want to see your identity papers, Dr Lutzke.'

Schwarzenbach tightened his grip on the paperknife. 'I have no objection to your seeing them. Can I ask why?'

Eberhard searched for his cigarettes. When he found them he lit one and tossed the match to the floor. 'A routine check. That's all.'

Schwarzenbach took the papers from his jacket and passed them to the American. Eberhard didn't study them. He flicked through them quickly as if they weren't of any real interest to him. And then he handed them back.

'Nuremberg is only the start, Dr Lutzke,' he said. 'We have a list of names that is a mile long.'

'Why should that be of interest to me?' Schwarzenbach asked.

Eberhard didn't answer. He got to his feet and picked up the briefcase. Smiling, he turned to Schwarzenbach. 'I'm sorry to have taken up so much of your time, Dr Lutzke.'

Schwarzenbach walked with him to the door. As he was leaving, he turned to Schwarzenbach and asked, 'Do you intend to stay in Berlin long?'

Schwarzenbach said, 'I'm needed here.'

'Yes,' Eberhard said. 'Yes, you are.'

And then the captain was gone.

He took the photograph and tore it into tiny pieces which he flushed down the wc. He tried not to think of Eberhard's visit. But it puzzled him. Why had he been part of a routine check? And what exactly *was* a routine check anyway? And why, when he had produced his identity papers, had Eberhard shown so little interest in them? And for what reason had he wanted to know whether Schwarzenbach intended to remain in Berlin? It puzzled and worried him; it was the feeling that he was being pursued by a shadow, something without physical substance. He tried to put these thoughts out of his mind. He was worrying too much. Eberhard's visit had been nothing more than a routine check. That was all. He supposed that Eberhard would be calling on a great many people,

70

looking at thousands of identity papers. And he, Dr Lutzke, was just one of that number.

And then he remembered the Jew. He remembered Grunwald in the house on the Augsburgerstrasse and the coincidence sickened him, the coincidence of the meeting upset him. Had he managed to convince the Jew that he was Lutzke – and not Schwarzenbach? Or had Grunwald remained certain? If so, had he been talking to the authorities? Would that explain Eberhard's visit? Would that make clear one of the reasons why Eberhard had mentioned Nuremberg and the war trials? Was it to frighten him? Make him feel that he, Eberhard, knew Lutzke's real identity, and that it was merely a matter of time before the net closed around him?

These questions circled Schwarzenbach's consciousness; and at the back of his mind was the odd feeling that he *really* was afraid, that some new emotion had penetrated him. The Jew – who would have guessed that the Jew could have survived? And that he would turn up in Berlin? That was the frightening thing: it was the feeling that the Jew's existence plunged him back into the past, to the recent as well as the distant past, into the trap of his own memories. Coincidence – it seemed such a frail thread, a thin chance, a random occurrence completely indifferent to the affairs and destinies of men.

He felt better after the bits and pieces of the photograph had vanished – and yet, throughout the day, there returned to him curious sensations of uneasiness and anxiety.

7

The house that Schwarzenbach visited every Thursday evening was situated in a street near the Kaiser-Allee. Helmut Broszat lived in a tiny apartment on the top floor. Broszat, a man in his early fifties, assembled together secretively a regular gathering of former SS men. When Schwarzenbach arrived that evening and was shown into the front room there were already several men present; apart from Broszat, he recognized Seeler, an ex-Hauptsturmführer in the Wirtschafts und Verwaltungshauptamt, whose responsibility had been for the deportation of Jews from occupied Hungary: Katzmann, who had organized the last stages of the defence of Berlin and who, according to his own testimony, had been close to the Führer himself at the end; Urbach, who had worked in the Central Security Department of the Reich. They were drinking wine and talking aimlessly. As he entered Schwarzenbach wondered why he continued to come. He supposed it was for a sense of camaraderie because these were men who had lived through the same experiences as himself, belonged to the same organization, and who now – like himself – had reasons of their own for wishing, at least publicly, to disown their pasts. And yet, like himself, whenever they talked it was invariably about the past: the future was too difficult either to comprehend or to anticipate. Some of them were expecting to leave Germany as soon as it could be arranged; others preferred to stay, living assumed lives, hoping that the memories of the conquerors were short and their own disguises infallible. Urbach, for instance, was working as a translator for a firm of lawyers that had dealings with the Americans, and Katzmann had found employment with the city council –

a menial position admittedly, but a safe one for that reason. Broszat and Seeler on the other hand were preparing to leave Germany as soon as the chance arose and Broszat, a perpetual optimist, was always talking of his negotiations with this or that ex-Nazi who could promise him a safe passage out of Europe.

Schwarzenbach helped himself to a glass of wine. The apartment was comfortably furnished and intact – a rare thing these days – and it was Schwarzenbach's suspicion that Broszat paid for it out of old SS funds he had somehow managed to expropriate. As he sat drinking his wine, Schwarzenbach listened to the conversation. It followed a regular pattern: Urbach would state the case for remaining in Germany, arguing that the conquerors could not remain forever and envisaging a revival of the SS in a somewhat modified form – and for that reason he was prepared to stay; Broszat would accuse him of a lack of realism – the old days were dead and gone after all and no matter what happened to Germany in the future, the past that they had worked for could never be revived. The Russians and the Americans wanted revenge and when they were satisfied they would go home, leaving Germany depleted and disarmed. This was very clear. The only safe course of action was to leave.

After he had listened in silence for a time, Schwarzenbach went into the kitchen. The talk bored him and he felt somehow that it was dangerous just to be in the apartment. He imagined what might happen if Eberhard had assigned someone to follow him around and report on his movements. He knew it was unlikely but just the same he felt uneasy about the possibility. He washed his hands and examined the slight sores on the backs of his fingers.

Broszat stood in the doorway. 'Hiding yourself away, Gerhardt?'

Schwarzenbach looked at him. He had first met Broszat at a party rally in 1939 at Freudenstadt in the Black

Forest. And again in Berlin in the summer of 1940. They had kept in touch throughout the war and had met again in May when the war ended. These weekly gatherings were Broszat's own idea. Looking at him, Schwarzenbach wondered if Broszat's name was on Eberhard's list – if such a list existed.

'The atmosphere was too smoky,' Schwarzenbach said.

Broszat leaned against the wall. Once, a few weeks ago, he had shown Schwarzenbach an old wooden chest that contained his SS uniform. Thinking of this now, Schwarzenbach felt slightly ashamed that he had destroyed something so trivial as his photograph.

'I had a visitor today, Helmut,' Schwarzenbach said. 'A certain Captain Eberhard of American Military Intelligence.'

Broszat said, 'That sounds serious.'

'I don't know what to make of it.'

'You shouldn't have come here tonight. Suppose they've put someone on to you – '

'It's too late to worry about that now.'

Broszat asked, 'What did he want?'

'I have no idea.' Schwarzenbach finished his wine. He could hear the conversation that drifted through from the other room. Katzmann's excitable voice rose and fell, his words broken now and then by a statement from either Urbach or Seeler. They were talking on a subject they discussed frequently: the reasons for Germany's defeat. He half-listened to them, lazily, waiting for Broszat to speak.

'How much does he know?' Broszat asked.

'About me?'

Broszat looked into the glass he was holding. 'Did you form a clear impression of him? Do you have any idea whether he suspects you?'

Schwarzenbach shrugged. 'He was a devious man. He enjoyed playing silly little games.'

'And so you don't really know anything?'

'He said that it was a routine check on identity papers.'

'What's a routine check?' Broszat waited for an answer, but Schwarzenbach said nothing. 'It's ridiculous. Ever since they dreamed up the idea of war trials they have become like bloody limpets. They never let go of an idea as soon as it enters their heads – an American trait. Protectors of the Western world. That's how they see themselves, Gerhardt. As bloody boy scouts!'

Schwarzenbach listened, but found no consolation in Broszat's words. He became silent, thinking of the Jew in the Augsburgerstrasse, more than a little amazed that the man hadn't perished in the war. It was possible, just possible, that the Jew had believed him. But it was hardly likely. He remembered the shock that seemed to penetrate and freeze his brain when he heard the Jew call out the name. Had he shown surprise? Had his facial expression betrayed him?

Broszat said, 'They've got a Nuremberg mentality now. They see war criminals lurking on every bomb site. Criminals – Jesus! It's ridiculous.'

Suddenly Schwarzenbach felt angry. Broszat was correct. They were being made to feel like criminals, hunted men, they were being forced to walk in shadows with false identities and forged papers – and for what reason? Because they had believed in a certain set of ideals? Because they had worked and surrendered their lives to these ideals? Where was the crime in that?

Broszat said, 'It only emphasizes what I'm always saying. If we can get out of Germany, right out of Europe, we should do so. We can't be safe here. The world has changed, Gerhardt. The Americans and the Russians have introduced a new set of rules and the old laws don't apply any longer. They don't kill Jews – they stick them in hospitals or send them back home in Red Cross trucks. This isn't our world. Everything is different.'

Schwarzenbach wondered what it would be like to leave Germany, and resented the thought. A furtive journey

across Europe, an uncomfortable trip to a place like
Egypt or South America, exiled forever – and he resented
the idea. It was a journey that many men had made,
driven by fear, terrified of vengeance, but it was not for
him.

He asked, 'When are you leaving?'

Broszat said, 'As soon as I can. The sooner the better.
It takes a little time to arrange. But I am working at it.'

'It isn't right,' Schwarzenbach said. 'My place is here.
This is still Germany. It might have changed, but it's still
Germany.'

Broszat said, 'I sympathize with you, Gerhardt. But
sometimes I feel the hangman's rope round my neck. And
I can't stand having nightmares.'

They went into the other room. Katzmann, half drunk,
was sprawled across the carpet. Urbach was offering
round a pack of American cigarettes. Schwarzenbach sat
beside Seeler and listened to the dying conversation.
Sometimes he found it hard to believe that everything had
come to this: a weekly gathering, futile talk, a swastika
flag that Broszat took from beneath his mattress and
tacked to the wall for each meeting, sentimental recollections of the past. And it ended always in the same way,
with either Katzmann or Broszat proposing the toast – the
Oath of Honour – which Schwarzenbach now found
meaningless and pathetic. But, like the others, part of
him still responded to the words, the same part that
refused to accept as entirely true the report of the Führer's
death. Seeler argued that Hitler was in hiding. The suicide
was Soviet propaganda. If the Führer were really dead,
why hadn't a recognizable body been exhibited? In any
case, was it credible that a man like Hitler would have
committed suicide? Urbach supported Seeler's argument
and Katzmann, who claimed to have spent a great deal of
time in the Chancellery towards the end of the war, firmly
believed that the Führer, together with his new wife, had
fled south. If there had been a suicide, then surely he

would have heard of it? Therefore it was either Soviet nonsense – or better still a story spread around by the Führer himself, to deceive his enemies into believing that he was dead. There was an air of naïvety about these arguments that Schwarzenbach recognized but at the same time they were expressions of a genuine longing. It was impossible to believe that the man was dead, that the hard, exciting voice he had listened to countless times at rallies or over radio broadcasts had finally been silenced.

He drank more wine and became dizzy. Mostly the conversation was about the period before the war, a time of promise and achievement, of nights spent dreaming and planning the shape of the world to come; of their days as SS cadets and their pride in being fully accepted after the probationary period; and Seeler, who had been an SS man before any of them, could even recall the action against the Brownshirts and how he personally had gunned down half a dozen of the bastards.

Katzmann proposed the toast at midnight. They stood in front of the swastika flag and raised their glasses. They said the words in unison: *I swear to thee, Adolf Hitler* . . .

Later, when the meeting had broken up, Schwarzenbach and Broszat went to a cellar bar near the Prager-Platz. Broszat, a little drunk, wanted a woman and Schwarzenbach, who was tired, felt that he needed a glass of schnapps before bed. The bar was almost empty. It was off-limits to the military and only a few Germans were present, drinking quietly together in a corner. If anything reflected the way Germany had changed, Schwarzenbach thought, it was the mood he continually encountered in bars. The songs, which had never been sad before, were now tastelessly filled with a quiet suffering. The drinkers consumed quietly and spoke in whispers, like conspirators who no longer have anything left to conspire over.

Broszat bought beer for himself and schnapps for Schwarzenbach. They drank together in silence.

Schwarzenbach felt uneasy again; it was like a fever that constantly kept returning to him, a nagging irritation that entered his mind when he least expected it. The weekly gatherings invariably depressed him in any case; the futility of harking back to past history was all too apparent to him and although there were some of the old responses, he recognized the uselessness of his feelings. Broszat was right: the only thing to do now was to run. But running implied guilt and he could not accept that he was guilty of anything. He was a scientist. He had always been a scientist. And the source of all scientific advance lay in the value of experimentation. That was what had been expected of him and that was precisely what he had supplied – his scientific services, for the sake of the Reich. Human life, by that criterion, was worthless. If you thought of history as one monstrous river that never ceased to run, then human existence was as fragile and insignificant as a particle of water. But he did not need to justify himself in this or any other way. He had never performed a single criminal act. He wasn't a criminal.

Broszat said, 'It's so fucking quiet in here. It's like a tomb.'

'What do you expect?'

Broszat shrugged. He drank his beer and looked round. Everywhere people were whispering: they had become a nation of whisperers. It was as if they were afraid to raise their voices for fear of offending the dead. Was that what losing a war meant? The voices that had been raised in the Luitpold Arena in Nuremberg not so very long ago had become suddenly dumb.

Broszat said, 'I want a woman. That's the way to forget the whole bloody thing.'

'Is there any way of forgetting?' Schwarzenbach asked.

Broszat went to talk to a girl who was standing at the other side of the bar. She was thin and looked tired; Broszat put his arm around her shoulders and after a moment Schwarzenbach saw them leave the bar together. He felt suddenly depressed. The country was bankrupt; everything had been squandered. Even a man like Broszat found it necessary to squander himself. He thought about the woman he had visited the previous evening and felt the cold metal of the key in the pocket of his overcoat. Life had become a sequence of useless gestures, a series of hushed voices in darkened rooms: somewhere along the way mistakes had been made and they were now living through the results of these errors. People whispered: what were they whispering about? What had become of everything? The pointless post-mortems of the past, the fruitless analyses of errors, the cold realization that the world had turned upside-down and that new emotions – fear, anxiety, hopelessness – had entered his life: it was the feeling that wherever he turned, wherever he looked, he was destined to be reminded of everything that had taken place so long ago in the past.

He ordered another schnapps and drank it slowly. His mind became blank.

He was awakened early, shortly after seven, by the sound of someone moving around in his surgery. He rose quickly from his bed, put his coat on over his pyjamas, and went through the kitchen to the room beyond.

Eberhard was standing by the window. He looked alert and cheerful and smiled when he saw Schwarzenbach enter. He was carrying his briefcase in his left hand and Schwarzenbach saw that it was chained to his wrist by a length of linked metal.

'I apologize for disturbing you so early,' Eberhard said. 'The door was unlocked.'

Schwarzenbach went to his desk and sat down. He had a slight headache, a result of the mixture of wine and schnapps.

'I normally rise at this time,' he said.

'I don't,' Eberhard said. 'But today I felt like a change.'

Schwarzenbach said, 'A change sometimes does one good.'

'Exactly. Exactly. You know what I think? I think you and me are going to get along well.' Eberhard's smile, fixed and hard, was suddenly threatening. For the first time Schwarzenbach realized that the man's expression was totally devoid of humour.

'It's damned cold in here,' Eberhard said. He rubbed his hands together and the chain rattled.

'What can I do for you?' Schwarzenbach asked.

'Well, Dr Lutzke, it's a funny thing.' Eberhard paused, and looked as if he were about to tell an obscene joke. 'In my job, I sometimes come across anomalies. Little things here and there that don't quite make sense. Do you know what I mean?'

'Not really.'

'Look. Suppose you had a patient and he had all the symptoms of – say, lung cancer. And yet you couldn't find any trace of cancer in his lungs. Now that would be funny, wouldn't it? That wouldn't add up, would it?' Eberhard looked pleased with the analogy.

'I would then deduce that I had made a mistake in my original diagnosis,' Schwarzenbach said.

'Well, in my profession it isn't as simple as that. I keep records, you see. And these records aren't always complete. Now that worries me. I've got a tidy mind. Like yourself, I imagine.' Eberhard lit a cigarette. Puzzled, Schwarzenbach waited: what was going to come next? He felt tense now.

Eberhard said, 'I'm coming to the point. I don't want to alarm you, but I've got a file on you.'

'On me?'

'A routine matter, Dr Lutzke. But I've got a file on you.'

Eberhard paused. Schwarzenbach felt that now, more than ever before, he had to remain calm. He had to keep his expression blank. He had to reveal nothing and yet look as if there were nothing to conceal in any case. He crossed his hands one over the other. He was going to remain calm.

'Now my file on you doesn't make sense,' Eberhard said. 'There's one or two gaps in it. And this worries me. Basically, I'm really a clerk. I've got a clerical mentality. I like my records to be complete. And your file isn't.'

'In what way is it incomplete?'

'Well, it doesn't seem to tell us anything about your war record. Do you know what I mean?' Eberhard's smile was suddenly infuriating.

'My war record?' Schwarzenbach looked surprised. 'Is it beyond the resources of the United States Army to discover what I did during the war?'

Eberhard laughed. 'No, not really. But that would take time. It's a whole lot quicker if you give me the information straight.'

'Why should my war record interest you?'

'Well, we're interested in medical personnel.'

Schwarzenbach shrugged. 'My war record is quite uninspiring, Captain. I carried on in general practice.'

'That's what we thought.' Eberhard took a notebook from his pocket and flipped it open. 'Now where would that have been?'

'Between 1938 and 1942 in Munich. And from 1942 until the present time in Berlin.'

'That's fine,' Eberhard said. 'That's all we wanted to know.'

Schwarzenbach stared at the American. It was extraordinary that he had not noticed the captain's moustache before; a faint line of sandy hair about the upper lip – grown, no doubt, to detract from his boyish face, to give him authority.

'Don't you want any more details?'

'No, that won't be necessary, Dr Lutzke. We don't need too many details.' Eberhard stood up. He closed his notebook and returned it to his pocket. For some reason his hand appeared to be shaking. But why? Cold? Nervousness? Schwarzenbach could not imagine that the captain suffered from nerves.

'Again, I'm sorry to have bothered you.'

Schwarzenbach rose from the desk. 'It isn't any trouble.'

Eberhard went to the door where he paused. When he turned round he was no longer smiling. 'We're just beginning to find out what went on in some of those concentration camps. A grisly business.'

Schwarzenbach looked at the American a moment. Why had he mentioned the concentration camps? Why? It was strange – strange simply to append it to the conversation like that. Again Schwarzenbach had the feeling that this man was hunting him – yet it was impossible to tell from his expression exactly how much he knew. And if he really knew anything, if he possessed information and was not merely suspicious, then who had told him? Schwarzenbach pushed his hands into his overcoat. His skin seeped moisture even though he felt intensely cold. He could not take his eyes from Eberhard's face. Exactly how *much* did the bastard know?

Eberhard smiled again. And then, when he had gone, and the sound of his car had faded down the street, Schwarzenbach went into the kitchen and sat at the table, his hands pressed flat to the surface. What would happen when Eberhard decided to investigate his past? When he started to check the dates of Lutzke's war record? How much could he uncover there? Schwarzenbach returned to his bedroom; a heavy sense of fatigue had fallen across him, and he could not think straight. Certainly his identity papers were good, insofar as they were real and not forgeries. And his story would stand a certain amount of exploration. Before the end, before the final collapse, it had been possible to fabricate reality – it had been possible to discover, in the last chaos of bureaucracy,

82

little clerical men with rubber stamps and anxious expressions who were prepared to issue the necessary papers to those who needed them and could also pay the required amounts of money. And so Schwarzenbach had purchased an identity at considerable cost; and he had purchased a past as well – Dr Gerhardt Lutzke, born 1900 in Munich, student in Berlin University, general practice first in Munich and later in Berlin. It was unfortunate that in the anarchic situation thrown up by war and the desperate bomb attacks made by the Royal Air Force certain things had either been lost or destroyed: not simply national monuments and buildings of historic interest, but records, files, dossiers, the whole intricate machinery of bureaucracy had been partially smashed. Who could tell what truths lay beneath uncleared acres of rubble, or had been dissolved in the aftermath of incendiary bombs? Even those of Gerhardt Lutzke, possibly those of Gerhardt Lutzke, had vanished forever. So who was there left to tell the truth? And what records remained to disprove anything Schwarzenbach chose to say? No; he wasn't worried about the credibility of his story because it would require enormous patience on the part of Eberhard to refute a word of it. The thing that caused him anxiety was that Eberhard – for some obscure reason – felt it necessary to ask the questions that he did. And to drop certain hints into his speeches – war criminals, Nuremberg, the camps. But why? Why?

Schwarzenbach sat stiffly on the edge of his mattress. He experienced a curious sensation of numbness, as if a part of his brain was suddenly afflicted with a paralysis. He lay back across the bed. He felt strangely naked: it was as if an operation were being performed upon him and his flesh, layer by layer, were being pushed painfully back from the bone.

8

The woman was dying. She was suffering from an incurable cancer. Even with the best medical supplies and the most delicate instruments Schwarzenbach could never have saved her. The cancer had afflicted her liver and in all probability had spread to other parts of her body as well. It was hardly worth finding out. The fact of her death stared him in the face; the sad eyes that caught his own, as if she were under the impression that he was a priest, a worker of miracles, who could snatch her back from death. He washed his hands, dried them on a towel, and for a moment enjoyed the sensation of helplessness that he experienced. Would he tell her that she was dying?

'It's painful when I pass water,' she said. Her head was wrapped in a grubby scarf. The part of her skull that was visible was covered with thin hair; but tufts of hair had fallen out and areas of naked white scalp could be seen.

'You already said that,' Schwarzenbach answered. 'There's nothing I can give you.'

'Nothing to ease the pain?'

'Nothing.' Schwarzenbach went to his desk. He picked up his pen and drew a series of interlocking circles on his scrap-pad. Ripping the sheet from the pad, he threw it into the waste-basket. 'I'm sorry, there's nothing I can do to help.'

'What does that mean?' Her thin hands were working together. If he were to explore her, to analyse her complaints, what number of diseases might he find? He wondered about that academically and realized that treating the sick had begun to bore him. It lacked excitement and challenge; it was a deathly game, played out in the dark tedium of what was left of Germany. There wasn't a point to it.

'What does it mean?' she asked. 'Can't you tell me what it means?'

'Do you have relatives?'

She looked at him in horror. 'A son. Yes. I'm a widow. I only have the boy.'

'How old is he?'

'Thirteen.'

'Can he look after you?'

She shook her head. 'Look after me? What do you mean?'

He felt suddenly callous and powerful. He had only to tell her the truth. After all, wasn't that what she wanted to hear? Those grim, imploring eyes – weren't they asking for truth?

'There's nothing I can do,' he said. 'It's a matter of time.'

'A matter of time? How?'

'You are going to die.' He experienced a brief sense of triumph.

Strangely, she remained unemotional. He had only told her what she had feared all along. She was going to die. And when he realized this, he wondered why he had cared to be truthful. The woman closed her eyes for a moment.

'I'm not afraid. I'm not scared,' she said. 'It's just that the thought makes me sad, that's all. I find death a sad thought.'

Schwarzenbach looked at her. Her ugliness, the wastage induced by the sickness, repelled him. He turned his eyes away. He had always preferred beauty and order.

'It makes me quite sad,' she said. 'But I had to know.'

She sighed, as if at the thought of her own life ebbing away like some precious liquid spilled. Her stupidity amazed him: what was sad about death? He had to get her out of the surgery quickly now. He stood up.

'There's nothing more I can say.'

'Of course, I understand.' She tied the ends of her headscarf together and, rising slowly, shuffled towards the door. Half-smiling, she went out. He watched as the door swung shut behind her and then he went into the kitchen to finish what little remained in the bottle of cognac. So she would go away, like an insect crawling beneath a stone, and she would die: it puzzled him always that people could not accept death unemotionally, regard it for what it was – an historical fact. They tied it up in mumbo-jumbo and religion, and they tried to defeat it with medicines and drugs, but it remained a constant thing. You could not cheat it. You could not do anything but ultimately accept it. It irritated him now to think of the incredible fuss that was being raised about the millions of deaths that had taken place all over Europe – as if it were possible to differentiate between those who had fallen in battle and the rest who had perished under other circumstances. In reality there was no difference. An enemy was an enemy. There wasn't one sort of enemy that you gunned down between some muddy trenches or blew to shattered pieces with bombs, and another that you gassed in a concentration camp and burned in an incinerator. All were casualties of war, no matter how they had died.

But now he could hear the voices that were being raised all across Europe and they were clamouring after their revenge. It wasn't enough for them that Germany had fallen, and her land savaged, they had also to root out those responsible for the acts now described as war crimes. And it was the logic of this that he couldn't accept. Was a general of the Wehrmacht, who had lined up his troops against the advancing Russians and in so doing had probably caused thousands of deaths, any less responsible than the SS man who had ushered thousands into gas chambers? Was the arms manufacturer to go unpunished, while those who had made Zyklon B were to be incarcerated?

Schwarzenbach found this astonishing: he had been taught, and he had learned, that the enemies of Germany were to be destroyed, that the means of destruction were irrelevant. And the enemies were plainly visible to all concerned. Bolshevism, international Jewry, and the monolithic structures of capitalism raised by international Jewry. He had accepted this. The Reich, before 1933, had been a sick man, suffering an illness that could be cured only by the removal of the poison. And so, in 1934, along with millions of others, he had joined the National Socialist Party. He hadn't agreed with everything immediately, of course. Some measures taken by the new regime seemed extreme and offended a large number of intellectuals and he had found himself, in those early months, looking disapprovingly at some of the acts taken by the Government.

But slowly, inexorably, impressed by the weight of propaganda and the new mood in Germany, he realized that he had to look at National Socialism from the standpoint of history: the Reich, after all, was designed to last for a thousand years. What were a few harsh acts against the judgement of history? What did it matter that blood was spilled when something unique was happening?

Besides, the voices of the intellectuals were fading to whispers, and many of the former opponents of the regime began to appear at Party rallies. They had realized that democracy was a false concept that held out impossible promises; only National Socialism was real. He discovered in himself a new sense of purpose that sometimes rose to a frenzy. You had only to attend a Party rally to realize that here was something real and lasting. You had only to stand with a hundred thousand others to recognize that what you were saluting and shouting about had nothing to do with the little man with the moustache

– it was a belief in blood and in the purity and supremity of the German people. The rest of Europe might perish, but Germany would not sink under the pressures of communism or Jewry. It would destroy those evils. And he found himself actively supporting their destruction. He could remember the torrent of enthusiasm that had swept the country like rain after several seasons of drought, he could remember the way in which it suddenly meant something – an intuitive pride, a nationalistic ambition, feelings he surrendered to with all the bliss of a man who discovers love after years of indifference and hopelessness, feelings that were – for the first time in his life – intangible, almost irrational, and that at the same time flooded him, breaking down the dams of futility and absurdity, lending to everything a blinding sense of purpose. He could recall the masterly arguments of the Führer and the frenzied speeches of Goebbels and the way the mass rallies – burning like a monstrous ocean of light – stirred and moved him as he had never been touched before. He was caught up by, and ensnared in, the fervour of the new mood, the approaching brilliance of the new Germany that had risen like some hungry animal fed for the first time. Transported, discovering within himself hidden depths of what he took to be passion – and it *was* passion of a kind – in 1937 he put his professional services at the disposal of the SS during one of their frantic and energetic recruiting campaigns. It was a pinnacle: it was a mark of his belief and faith. He understood for the first time a new kind of pride: the stiff black uniform, still smelling of newness, the runic SS on the lapel, the sense of belonging to something more important and in its way more tangible than even the frenetic gatherings at Nuremberg. It was as if his natural intelligence were totally subjugated to an utterly different concept of himself, to a shining ideal of what man might become. He became deaf to the fading arguments of resistance and blind to the various aspects of inhumanity required by the new order: Jews streaming to travel agencies, people rounded up in the streets and shunted off like bundles of waste-matter, the sight of a bonfire of books and synagogues flaring – these were merely the passing symptoms of cleanliness. A house was being put in order. What were these minor acts against the prospect of the ultimate victory? There was the uniform; there were the badges. People looked at you when you walked in the street in your uniform. A sense of power was released, and, once released, you could never be the same man again. You learned to live in a new way. The professional skills you had acquired were no longer your own, but had been placed at the service of the Reich. Everywhere there was the hoarse sound of acclaim, a sound that carried upwards, always upwards, amongst the flags and banners that announced the death of yesterday's Germany.

In 1939, Helmut Broszat had said to him, 'There will be a war before the year is out.'

They were drinking together in a beerhall in the Neuhauserstrasse in Munich. Schwarzenbach had desperately tried to remain sober, but in trying to keep up with Broszat, who drank quickly and hungrily, he realized that he was in the first stages of drunkenness. The hall was filled with men in SS uniforms. There was a great deal of noise, coming as if from a distance.

'I want a war,' Broszat said. 'Regardless of the enemy, I don't doubt that we are stronger.'

'I agree,' Schwarzenbach said. And he did agree. The idea of guns lined up against guns and planes bombing cities seemed for some reason suddenly pleasing. A conceptual destruction, drunkenly created; he hadn't envisaged the reality.

'I want to fight,' Broszat said. 'I haven't fought for a long time.'

Schwarzenbach felt slightly sad that in the event of war

his own services would not be required on the battlefield. For a second he experienced a sensation of great warmth towards Broszat and the urge, the terrible urge, to confide in the man. 'Did I ever tell you what I've been doing lately?'

Broszat shook his head. 'It's a mystery to me. I haven't a clue what you get up to, Gerhardt.'

'It's meant to be a secret.'

'You couldn't keep a secret from me, Hauptsturm-führer.' Broszat was mocking him slightly, using the rank lightly because Schwarzenbach had a place in the hierarchy only on the basis of his profession.

'I've been helping to devise something.' Schwarzenbach wondered for a moment if he should continue. He drank more beer and then leaned closer to Broszat. 'I've been devising something.'

'Devising what?'

'It's hard to say.'

'Don't tell me then.' Broszat, uninterested, turned away.

'I've been killing people.'

'Killing people? What people?'

Schwarzenbach felt guilty; he knew he shouldn't have begun to mention this to Broszat. But he continued, as though it were impossible to stop himself. 'Criminals. Old people. A few Jews.'

'There's no harm in that, is there?' Broszat, cold sober, asked the question harshly.

'It's like this.' Schwarzenbach began to trace a diagram in the pool of beer on the surface of the table. 'They want to devise a programme – euthanasia. Do you know what I mean?'

'I've heard of it.'

Schwarzenbach realized with a sense of horror that his vision had become blurred and his speech thick. He stabbed Broszat with his finger. 'Easy ways of killing. They tell me to choose someone, you see. So I choose.

90

Usually somebody old. Or a political. Even a Jew now and then. And I try different ways to see which is the quickest. Am I making myself clear?'

Broszat laughed. 'There's nothing quicker than a bullet in the skull.'

'No, that's messy. That makes too much mess.'

'But it's quick.'

'I'm not going to dispute that, Helmut.' Schwarzenbach tried to light a cigarette and wondered why he had begun to smoke so much recently. He dropped the cigarette into the pool of beer and when he picked it up again the paper had become unstuck, releasing the tobacco. He sat back in his chair. Somewhere beyond him, the room was spinning round and round.

Broszat said, 'A gun in the skull. A bullet through the brain. That's the best way.'

'You might be right,' Schwarzenbach said, realizing that Broszat had lost interest in the subject.

'More interesting is the fact that I fancy a woman. Right now.'

'Your appetites are appalling, Helmut. You're like an animal.'

Broszat struck the table with his fist and stood up. 'Are you coming with me? Or are you too pissed?'

They went to a house in the Kaufingerstrasse where, in an upstairs room, Schwarzenbach was given a seventeen-year-old girl called Madeleine. Plump and fair-haired, wearing only the black underwear of the brothel, she was sitting crosslegged on the bed. Behind her, as if in imitation of an oriental whorehouse, strings of coloured beads hung across a recess in the wall. Above the fireplace was a swastika shaped out of cheap clay. Schwarzenbach absorbed his surroundings without being entirely conscious of them; he staggered towards the bed and fell face down. His brain, seemingly severed from his skull, was elsewhere – floating somewhere, cut adrift. The girl put a record on the phonograph; a love song about an SS man who has had to leave his girl behind him. The female voice was harshly sentimental and the background music thin and dull. He raised himself to a sitting position and tried to fix his eyes on the girl who was dancing slowly – submerged in her own thoughts – around the room. It was difficult. His vision was warped. Sometimes he saw her as two separate shapes, sometimes as one figure from whom another ghostly shadow seems about to emerge. He felt sick.

When the music stopped, the girl approached the bed and undid the buttons of his tunic. He allowed her to undress him and watched as she folded the uniform neatly, lovingly, over a chair. She placed his boots beneath the bed. He lay back, his head propped against a pillow, and noticed a crucifix on the far wall, hanging directly opposite the clay swastika. The figure of Christ seemed absurd and banal. The tortured expression reminded him of a clown he had once seen in a circus, the seat of his coloured trousers belching black fumes of smoke.

'Let me make love to you,' she said. 'What's the matter with you?'

'I'm sick. I'm drunk.' Schwarzenbach covered his face with his hands. The electric light was suddenly blinding.

'I love your uniform. I love it.' She was standing by the chair running her fingers over the cloth. 'Black – it's a beautiful colour. When I saw you come in, I felt – well, weak. It's the uniform. It makes me feel weak.'

'Leave it alone,' he said. He was wondering why some means of execution were more efficient than others. It seemed a simple algebraic problem: find the value of x, and you have the solution. But his brain would not carry the matter a step further. What was he doing, lying there in a whore's bedroom? There was work to be done. There were problems to be solved. From somewhere, a distance away, he heard Broszat's loud laughter and the sound of something falling down the stairs outside the room.

'Don't I please you?' she asked. 'Don't you like me?'

'I've nothing against you,' he answered. Drunkenness was an ocean: the drunk man was like a tiny slab of timber carried far out to sea. He felt abandoned suddenly, forlorn, as if he had been swept up on a deserted beach.

'I'm only here to please you,' she said. 'I'm only here to please the men of the SS.'

What was she doing now? She was pulling on his boots and marching up and down the room. She was wearing his cap on her head and had one arm upraised in a salute.

'Do you like me like this?' she asked.

He opened his mouth to speak but his tongue was dry and swollen. He felt strangely weightless and wished, with a sickening stab of guilt, that he hadn't drunk so much. It was all right for someone like Broszat who had the constitution of an ox. He watched her approach the bed. She placed her hand between his legs.

'Are you impotent?'

'Leave me alone,' he said.

'Nothing's happening. Why isn't anything happening? Is there something wrong with you?'

'For Christ's sake, leave me alone.'

'Do you want to sleep?'

He didn't answer. What was the quickest way of killing efficiently? The question made him conscious of the irony in his position. All his life he had been working on the problem of saving lives, devising ways and means of keeping the human machine functioning. Now he was concerned with death; with short-circuiting the mechanism in the easiest way. He was aware of a strange roaring sound in his ears; it was like a million voices pitched on the one monotonous note. And there was an image: the old woman, with a name like Tritzschke, into whose naked arm he had pushed the hypodermic needle and who had died, in less than forty-five seconds, twisted in pain. She had been a subversive type, an anti-social element, and consequently her life had been unimportant. The only

93

significant thing was the time element: forty-five seconds.

He felt the girl climb into the bed beside him. When he opened his eyes the room was in darkness and he felt dehydrated and unwell. She laid her hands on his body and he turned over, away from her. She sighed impatiently.

'You make me sad,' she said. 'Don't you like women?'

He didn't answer; he was too drunk to care what the answer might be. In the morning he woke to find himself alone.

He left his surgery in the early afternoon. Walking around Berlin was like travelling through the wreckage of his own past. He had been a National Socialist and a Hauptsturm-führer in the SS. He saw no shame in that. Rather he looked back upon it as something he had had a duty to do; and if he were given the choice again, he would have made the same decisions. He realized with some bitterness that it was impossible to convey to people like Eberhard what the country had been in the years of National Socialism. You couldn't explain to Eberhard that there was no such thing as guilt. Nuremberg was a farce, a pantomime staged for the benefit of Europe's conscience. A morality play based upon a soft and decadent liberalism that had become blind to the real dangers that existed in the world.

He found his way to the cellar bar near the Prager-Platz where he had been with Broszat the previous evening. Katzmann was drinking alone, hunched as he always seemed to be, as if in the fear that someone might recognize his face if he held himself upright. As soon as he saw him, Schwarzenbach knew that something was wrong.

Katzmann said, 'Urbach was taken this morning.'

'Taken?'

'They picked him up at his work. Took him away for interrogation.'

94

Schwarzenbach felt the familiar alarm. 'Who took him?'

'US Military Intelligence.' Katzmann shrugged; 'It's becoming more and more difficult.'

'Will he talk? Will he mention names?'

Katzmann was silent for a moment. 'What do you think?'

'How should I know what to think?'

'Perhaps it's a false alarm. A routine check. Perhaps it's nothing to worry about.' Katzmann smiled; 'In any case, he knows what to do if they put too much pressure on him.'

Schwarzenbach thought of the cyanide, the capsule of poison that Urbach was said to carry. Why should Urbach have to die? Why should any of them have to die? The men in the dock in Nuremberg – why did they have to die?

'It's outrageous,' he said, and the word fell from him feebly.

'It's the new way of things,' Katzmann said – always the realist.

Outside, they walked from the Prager-Platz in the direction of the Kurfürstendamm, and as they walked Schwarzenbach wondered what *he* would do if, like Urbach, he were to be taken for interrogation. How would he react if it came to a straight choice between cyanide and trial? The possibility frightened him. He didn't want to die; not that the prospect of death held any terrors for him but it seemed senseless to be provoked into an unnecessary death by men whom he still considered as his enemies.

He left Katzmann on the Kurfürstendamm and walked for some way on his own. The danger was obvious now: the men at Nuremberg were distant figures, men he had always seen from afar – but Urbach was different, someone he knew, someone who had come to the weekly gatherings. What were they going to do with Urbach? And how much could Urbach tell them? Suddenly he felt as if the threads of his life were being gathered together by unknown hands and as he walked he was conscious of the growing obsession that someone was following him. It was absurd: whenever he looked round he saw no one.

9

The Jew. It was extraordinary that he should awake thinking of the Jew again. Opening his eyes he stared up at the ceiling and considered the coincidence of their meeting, the denial of his identity, the shock of recognition. And Grunwald – what had that little bastard felt? He remembered Grunwald as a patient once, a hypochondriac, suffering sometimes from nervous headaches, bronchial trouble, and adenoids. A grasping little Jew – an importer of some description, he recalled, dealing in cheap costume jewellery, little pieces of coloured glass, items that found their way into brothels and decorated the wrists and fingers of whores – a grasping little man who could talk of nothing else but his illnesses and his business problems. That was in 1934: the following year Schwarzenbach had the pleasure of refusing to treat him any longer. Jews should have Jewish doctors. The National Socialist Government had passed laws – didn't Grunwald realize that? Didn't he understand that now, factually and legally, he was a third-class citizen? But Grunwald's dull eyes had remained dumb and uncomprehending: was he so stupid that he didn't realize what had been happening since 1933? Nobody could now listen without laughing to his claims that he was a German first and a Jew next. If a man were Jewish, he could not be German: the implication was logical and irrefutable.

And Grunwald was now in Berlin. What did that mean? Now that Grunwald was regarded internationally as one of Europe's martyrs, what did it mean? Schwarzenbach felt suddenly angry. He rose from his bed and went through to the kitchen. It was just after eight. He opened the bottle of cognac he had bought the previous evening from a black marketeer. The prices they asked these days were extortionate. He sat at the table and sipped it slowly, turning the glass round and round in his fingers.

He went into the empty surgery. The air was frozen and he shivered. He looked at the instruments and bottles behind the glass front of the padlocked cabinet and he remembered how in Munich he had prided himself on possessing the most modern equipment available. Now everything was crude and primitive: the stethoscope, for instance, was an old one – it had been the property of the Reich, and he had hurriedly packed it amongst his belongings before the long journey back from Poland.

He finished his drink and sat for some time behind his desk, gazing at the smudged impressions left by his fingers on the surface of his glass.

In the summer of 1941 he had been summoned personally by no less an individual than Gruppenführer Rudolf Brandt to attend an interview in connection with his future posting. Brandt had congratulated him on his dedicated work during the Reich euthanasia programme, for his contributions to what Brandt called 'death experiments'. Schwarzenbach, strangely nervous, waited. The meeting with Brandt both elated and puzzled him and yet the Gruppenführer, who clearly had something on his mind that he wanted to express, seemed somehow unable to find the correct words. For some time he discussed the nature of medicine and the importance of scientific advance: progress depended upon discovery, he said, and one could hardly hope to discover if one were not to experiment. All human endeavour in the scientific field was like a huge black map: little by little, as new advances were made, the map began to have tiny white areas. And yet these areas were infinitesimally small, pathetically minute. Black was ignorance, white knowledge. The history of progress depended upon the white areas dominating the black. And then the Gruppenführer, his imagery apparently exhausted, mentioned that he had in mind a very special posting for Schwarzenbach. It was assumed in some quarters that certain parts of the human body were more sensitive than others – common knowledge, really. The erotogenic zones, for example, were extremely sensitive. They were more sensitive than, say, the feet; and yet the base of the feet were in turn more sensitive to touch than the base of the throat. Again common knowledge: but the Gruppenführer was coming to the point: pain – which areas of the body were most sensitive to pain and how could reactions to pain be quantitively measured? Research in the area of pain response was lamentable. People understood very little in that field of study. And wasn't pain part and parcel of human existence, after all? Why, therefore, wasn't more research being conducted into it?

Schwarzenbach was fascinated. When the Gruppen-führer then announced that he was being posted to Chelmno, in Poland, where it was expected of him that he would make use of the facilities there to conduct research into the field of enquiry that had just been mentioned, he expressed his pleasure. The facilities were primitive, the Gruppenführer said apologetically, but much human progress in science had been born in the least likely circumstances. Chelmno, however, could provide one amenity, indeed was especially rich in that amenity – human beings.

In October 1941 Schwarzenbach travelled in the relative comfort of a passenger train to Chelmno, north-west of the Polish town of Lodz. His instructions weren't entirely clear but he took that to mean he had been given a free hand; he could conduct his enquiries as he wished. Pain was a subject that had never interested him very much; the fact that he had been trained to cure it did not mean that he actually understood it. He knew only that it was very easy to induce, if not exactly to measure.

* * *

A car had drawn up outside. He went to the window and drew the blind back a couple of inches. When he saw Eberhard emerge from the vehicle, his first impression was that Urbach had talked – and yet that was ridiculous. Urbach wasn't the kind of man who would reveal anything of importance to the Americans. He knew how to handle interrogation. Schwarzenbach went to the front door and waited until he heard Eberhard's hand upon the bell.

For the first time, Eberhard was not on his own. Behind him stood another man, small and muscular, someone who gave the impression of considerable physical strength.

Schwarzenbach said, 'I heard the car.'

Eberhard smiled. He stepped inside, removing his cap. The other man followed. They went together into the surgery.

Eberhard said, 'Dr Lutzke – may I introduce Major Spiers.'

Schwarzenbach extended his hand but the Major had turned away and was walking round the room like someone taking an inventory.

'You seem to enjoy calling here,' Schwarzenbach said. 'How can I help you this time?'

Eberhard sat down. Schwarzenbach noticed that today he wasn't carrying his briefcase. He was turning his cap round and round on his knees nervously.

'Well, this isn't a professional call from my point of view,' Eberhard said. Schwarzenbach watched the Major, who was still stalking the room, covering the same area again and again in a circular fashion.

'That's a relief,' Schwarzenbach said. But he remained distrustful: why were there two of them suddenly? And what was the Major hoping to find?

'Major Spiers asked to be introduced to you, Dr Lutzke.'

Spiers spoke for the first time. 'That's right. I wanted to meet you.'

'May I know the reason why?'

'It's very simple,' Eberhard said. 'He wants your professional advice.'

'I'm flattered, of course. But don't you have perfectly competent physicians of your own? I'd also imagine that they were better equipped as well.' Schwarzenbach picked up his empty glass. There was a sense of dry tension in the air, and he found it impossible to keep his hands still.

'Well, the Major has this thing, Doctor. He thinks that European physicians are generally better trained to heal. We disagree on this point, because I can't see the difference between an American medico and a German one, but he insists.' Eberhard seemed to want to apologize for his superior officer.

Spiers said, 'That's right. You guys have been at it much longer.' He was standing by the window, perfectly still now.

'And what's the trouble?' Schwarzenbach was unconvinced. It was a charade, but he could play it as well as they could.

'It's my back.' The Major was undoing his coat.

'Let me take a look at it.'

Spiers removed his shirt. Stripped to the waist, he did not seem to feel the cold. Schwarzenbach touched his flesh.

'Where does it hurt?'

'At the base of the spine,' Spiers said.

The man's body was in almost perfect condition. He was about fifty and looked thirty. 'You keep yourself in good shape,' Schwarzenbach said.

'I don't eat meat, Doctor,' the Major said. 'I live on health foods. Honey, fruit, cereals. That's how I do it.'

'Have you been doing any exercise lately?'

'I play some tennis.'

'You've probably strained a muscle,' Schwarzenbach pressed his fingers against the Major's spine and Spiers became rigid.

'That's what I thought,' Spiers said. 'That's what I guessed had happened.'

'Your own army doctors could treat this far better than I. It's a question of having the right medical supplies, and they would be better stocked than I could hope to be.' Schwarzenbach turned to see that Eberhard was examining something on his desk. He tried to control the sudden sensation of uneasiness that he felt. It was all a pretext of some kind; there was probably nothing wrong with the Major's back.

Spiers put on his shirt. 'Thanks for the advice. I don't trust some of those guys we've got. They're all young, fresh out of medical school. I wanted somebody experienced.'

'A strained muscle, nothing more than that.'

'That's great, that's all I wanted to know.' Spiers was doing up the buttons of his shirt.

Schwarzenbach moved towards his desk and saw what it was that Eberhard was looking at. Absentmindedly he had been scribbling on a scrap-pad: alarmed, he realized that he had covered the top sheet with the runic insignia of the SS.

'That's interesting, Doctor,' Eberhard said. He passed the pad to Spiers. 'Isn't that interesting, Major?'

'That's really interesting,' Spiers said, and stared at the pad. 'It's amazing what people doodle.'

'Amazing,' Eberhard said. 'Why would you scribble something like that, Dr Lutzke?'

Schwarzenbach hesitated. A sequence of possibilities flashed through his mind. The Jew, Grunwald, had talked. Or Urbach had opened his mouth. Or perhaps they knew something anyway, something they had discovered by themselves, and he wondered where he had failed to cover his tracks. And then he realized that he was being foolish: they knew nothing, they had only their suspicions to go on, because if they were certain of their ground they

102

would have arrested him long ago. They were trying to harass him: it was an obvious strategy.

'Let me see.' Schwarzenbach took the pad from the Major. 'I must have been thinking about the past.'

'Whose past?' Eberhard asked.

'Germany's.' Schwarzenbach laughed. 'We Germans had to live with these initials for many years. We were terrorized by them.'

Eberhard shrugged and looked at the Major. Spiers breathed heavily, inhaling through his nose, exhaling through his mouth, like someone exercising his lungs.

'Yes – we lived in terror of the SS.'

'Do you think of the past often?' the Major asked.

'Much of the time.'

'Why?'

'Like everyone else I wonder what went wrong.'

Eberhard smiled, that inane smile, that idiot expression. 'Were you ever a Party member?'

'No.' Schwarzenbach put the scrap-pad on his desk. 'I didn't agree with the Party on many issues.'

'For instance?' Eberhard frowned like a student trying to understand his lecturer's argument.

'Need I go into it all?'

'Not if you don't want to.'

'I disagreed with the Party's policy on the Jews. I also felt that it was wrong, muddleheaded, to start a war. I didn't believe in *Lebensraum*.' Schwarzenbach bit the lies off easily, smiling as he spoke.

'Come on, Doctor,' Eberhard said. 'Didn't you get a surge of national pride when Adolf walked into Austria?'

'None.'

'And then Poland?'

'That was a mistake.'

There was a moment's pause. The Major was circling the room again, his hands clenched behind his back. He asked suddenly, 'Have you ever been in Poland, Doctor?'

'Never.'

'Not even as a tourist – I mean, when it became a part of the Reich?'

'I didn't especially want to go, Major.'

Spiers thrust his hands into the pockets of his overcoat. 'I can understand that, Doctor. I can easily see it wouldn't have been much fun.'

Schwarzenbach picked up the pad again. 'We lived with these initials for many years. They are almost a part of every German's nightmare. How could it have happened?'

'Search me,' Eberhard said. 'But happen it did.'

Spiers looked at his wristwatch. 'Thanks for looking at my back, Dr Lutzke. I feel relieved to know that it's nothing more than a strained muscle. I guess one tends to imagine the very worst.'

When Eberhard and his Major had gone, Schwarzenbach drank some more cognac. It disgusted him to see that he was trembling again. But why? They didn't scare him. They could ask questions endlessly. They could probe as much as they liked. They would discover nothing. Ultimately all they could ever hope for was that someone would come forward with positive identification. And that thought brought him back again to Grunwald. Only Grunwald could tell the truth: Grunwald's was the only finger that could be pointed at him. And how could Grunwald speak, without revealing his own complicity?

But he was still uneasy. The thought of Grunwald lay across his mind like a terrible shadow. It only needed a stirring of conscience on the Jew's part – it needed only that, and the entire past would be laid bare like some hastily buried skeleton. Facts and facts: they stretched backwards, always backwards, groping towards a point in time when the first crime had been committed. But it was impossible to remember everyone and everything now. His memories were thick with the recollected faces of the anonymous, nameless people, the sounds of crucifixion, the agonies, his memories ran one into another as blurred as an overexposed photograph. The past was buried and, being buried, was a meaningless thing that could never be reconstructed in its entirety.

In Chelmno he had been given a miserable wooden hut that had been designed as three rooms. One contained a primitive latrine that smelled in warm weather. The others were larger: one he used as his living quarters, the second as his surgery. It became clear to him very quickly that nobody was particularly interested in the work he was doing, nor in the results. At first he made copious notes, filling more than a dozen foolscap folders with the results of his research. The camp commandant, Hans Bothmann, was interested only insofar as the work being done would impress his rival Höss at Auschwitz, but after a few initial enquiries he was rarely seen by Schwarzenbach.

After several months Schwarzenbach realized that there was little point in retaining the records he had kept so diligently and eventually he made notes only in the most casual fashion. Besides, he doubted that the research had any genuine objective value. For one thing, the subjects of his experiments were never in the best of health. Consequently their resistance to pain was lowered and their reactions exaggerated: how therefore was it possible to establish any general facts of universal value? Secondly, the conditions were primitive. He was expected to work in unhygienic surroundings with instruments that were out of date. He devised somewhat naïve means of quantitively measuring pain in terms of heart and pulse reaction but even these left a great deal to be desired. Slowly he realized that he was inflicting pain simply for the sake of inflicting it: the screams that he listened to and the expressions of terror he saw were without scientific value, but he continued to function – partly in the hope that something useful would come out of it all, partly in the belief that he was contributing to the destruction of the

105

enemies of the Reich. But killing wasn't his job primarily: the fact that most people died on his crude operating table was irrelevant. He was a scientist. He wasn't one of those brutes – like the guards – who seemed to derive an animal satisfaction from killing cold-bloodedly.

Step by step he slipped into a deep depression. The work was unsatisfactory. Poland was a dreadful place. The camp itself was bleak. He rarely left the confines of his hut which, in cold weather, was impossible to keep warm. His demands for better equipment were ignored and a personal letter he wrote to Gruppenführer Brandt went unanswered. Everything had been sacrificed to the war effort and science had been relegated. The SS guards were unlike any he had ever come across in Germany: most of them, he suspected, were criminals or lunatics, chosen only for their murderous inclinations. Sometimes in the evenings one of the brothel girls would visit him, but these encounters were hardly ever successful. Bored, he found that the only outlet was in devising new ways of inflicting pain and this occupied most of his leisure time. He ordered books from Germany that never arrived, and newspapers were always out of date. His wireless set needed a valve that he had requisitioned but it was never delivered. The only thing to look forward to was the daily work session: the fact that he had become an official torturer barely crossed his mind. The people who were brought to him knew what to expect when the door of the wooden hut had closed behind them, and since their screams could be heard all around, he imagined that his surgery had become the most feared place in the camp.

The days dragged one into the other. Few people visited him – apart from the girls, who looked on him with awe, and one or other of the commandant's minions, who would ask if he had any requests, knowing that they would never be met. But he continued to work: it was expected of him.

In 1942 he was given six weeks' leave and he returned

to Germany where he felt curiously out of place, like someone plunged out of darkness into a room of blinding electric light. There was a mood of optimism that somehow he found difficult to share; while people could talk about their work in munitions factories, and women might worry about their husbands on distant battlefields, and radio broadcasts were filled with propagandist speeches and martial music, he knew that there was a darker side to the mood. It existed in rural Poland, in backwater places carved out of a sullen landscape, it thrived on death and disease, and it had inspired a murderous new vocabulary. There were no brass bands and no stirring speeches: there was silence.

Early in 1943 he returned to Poland, travelling in hideous conditions on a train that was shunted into sidings with tedious regularity, and he sat – frozen in the icy air of his compartment – staring at the bleak countryside that went past in a sequence of half-caught images: German soldiers heaving against trucks that had frozen solid in the snow, a pack of alsatian dogs howling at the barricaded door of a tin hut, field guns covered with white tarpaulins, sad dark people moving along the side of the tracks as if in the hope that they might eventually lead somewhere.

He found himself wishing that the war was over and that he could go home. What did Poland mean to him? Where was the point in his work? Those stupid frightened faces in the camp and the camp itself, which reminded him of a vast archaic slaughterhouse where people came to receive death like children taking gifts at a Christmas party, meekly, coyly – what did all that mean to him?

A request to Bothmann, asking that his application for a transfer be directed to the proper authority, was received without sympathy. Bothmann was concerned only with the fact that his attempt to dynamite some mass graves into oblivion had resulted in the surrounding countryside being showered with sizeable pieces of human bone. And so Schwarzenbach laboured on. He had his radio repaired and listened to announcements of German victories interspersed with speeches and military music, which helped for a time. But boredom was always beneath the surface of his life; even the girls who visited him – Polish Jewesses who couldn't speak a word of German, and who seemed continually to be changing – were invariably uninteresting. His days became a mixture of the bloody and the tedious: he had become a surgeon of death. And in miserable stinking Poland it was difficult to remember the reason for one's life, or to recall the feelings and beliefs that had brought him there in the first place. He discovered one other disturbing thing: he had become anxious to kill the people who were brought to him, to kill them as quickly as possible, as if the whole point of the exercise were finally and irrevocably lost.

It was in the spring of 1943, at a time when he was experiencing an especially severe depression, that Leonhard Grunwald was brought into the hut.

PART THREE

Berlin, October 1945

10

The weather had become intolerably cold. For some days he had been sleeping in the cellar of a house near Charlottenburg Station. At nights his dreams had been haunted by extraordinary images, most of them for some reason connected with the dead girl in the Augsburger-strasse, and he would wake shivering in the cold, drawing his coat around him – yet sweating, always sweating in the same fevered way. He had not eaten properly for several days. Scraps that he picked up here and there, slops left behind by the military – but strangely he was never very hungry. The idea of standing in one of the food queues was appalling to him. Whenever he thought about the past all he seemed capable of remembering was the journey back from Poland. But why should that be singled out? Of all the things he could have remembered, why that? And he realized, in some strange way, that the sight of Schwarzenbach had released the memories most closely associated with the man: strange birds, dark birds, seemed to shift across his mind like creatures thrown into panic by the sound of a gun.

Sometimes he felt that he was dying and the thought brought a certain comfort. He was afraid to close his eyes at night and he would lie awake listening to the rats that moved through the broken stones. He was a coward: he wanted to close his eyes but there was the penetrating fear that he might never open them again. Death remained an impossible comfort to attain. And so there was nothing for him to do but drag himself through the days that fell across one another in artificial divisions of light and dark. He could die and it would barely matter. It was an indictment of the age – death didn't matter.

But if he was afraid of death there was still the other fear – the possibility of seeing Schwarzenbach again. Lying awake in the cellar near Charlottenburg Station, he imagined what he might feel if Schwarzenbach came through the open doorway and turned a torch on his face; and his limbs seemed to freeze, he seemed suddenly to cease to exist, his heartbeat stopped, his mind emptied of images like scraps of rubbish rushing down a sewer, and he wanted to scream – but speech had died in his throat. Sometimes he tried to convince himself that the man he had seen wasn't Schwarzenbach at all. And sometimes this almost worked. But never entirely.

In 1943, the men who administered the Reich policy towards the Jews shipped several thousand inmates from the Mauthausen camp into Poland. Grunwald was amongst them. They travelled in cattle trucks through the night. Nobody spoke because there was nothing to say. They listened to the racketing of the train and they knew intuitively, as animals on the way to an abattoir are said to know, that they were going to their destruction. Grunwald had worked for more than two years on the quarries in the Mauthausen camp. It seemed to him that survival depended very largely on remaining discreet, anonymous and silent, and so he had spoken to nobody. Human relationships were impossible and inconceivable. People died in the quarries, either pointlessly shot by one of the guards or as the result of deprivation. People were tortured for no apparent reason and Grunwald quickly realized that in the order of things the concept of rational behaviour had been demolished. He became like a snail, able to draw silence around him in the barracks at night, and he discovered in himself hidden depths of strength. It was strength without purpose other than that of surviving. He laboured on the quarries, digging, endlessly digging, a task that seemed just as futile as everything else.

Then Poland. On the train it occurred to him that his

time was running out. He had been found out, his disguise had been penetrated. They were taken from the train to Lodz ghetto and left there for some days. The ghetto was a miserable, defeated place filled with people who seemed surprised that they were still alive. German Jews, Poles, Polish Jews – they were herded into the ghetto which was the last point of rest before the inevitability of death. For almost a week Grunwald lived there. In some ways it was worse than Mauthausen, in other ways better. For example, there was an illusion of freedom in the sense that there were houses instead of barracks. If you didn't look at the barbed wire, and forgot the fact of your hunger, it was possible to create an illusion. Grunwald the tourist, visiting Poland for the first time. But the illusion didn't last. Every day people were taken from the ghetto in trucks and he knew that sooner or later he would be forced to enter one of those trucks himself. It was this realization that shocked him. Where did the trucks go? What happened when they arrived?

He thought of the possibility of dying and sometimes he wondered if Martha was still alive – or had she already passed through a place like Lodz on the way to her own destruction? After a week he was taken from the ghetto and pushed into a truck. He was beaten on the head and shoulders with the butt of a rifle and only half-conscious for most of the journey. Chelmno: it seemed a strange name for the final location of his life and the finality of this, the sudden realization that he was being taken somewhere to be killed, shocked him. But how could he stay alive now? What act was there left to perform as they were driven, more than a thousand of them, through the lines of SS guards into the camp?

He was numb, awkward, barely able to lift his legs. He was stricken by fear and the knowledge that nothing in the world could save him from dying. Around him men and women, as well as a few children, were stumbling through the rain, and sometimes one or other of the SS

113

men would smile, or make a joke, as if it were funny, too hilarious to contemplate, these sodden, miserable creatures fumbling through the rain, a strange joke, and sometimes they lashed out with their rifles against bodies as if this too were a part of the joke. From the corner of his eye Grunwald saw that someone was taking photographs with a small box camera and he tried to imagine exactly what sort of album would contain these snapshots, what sort of eyes would turn the pages and remember – years later – the souvenirs of the war in Poland. And then it was all funny suddenly, it all seemed part of a huge cosmic pantomime, and they were entertainers groping through the rain in front of a small but highly appreciative audience. Dogs yelped. Rain soaked through everything, sleeting, blinding rain. Grunwald lost his balance and fell forward in the mud. Someone kicked him in the side of his body and he rose to his feet. He laughed. He could see the funny side of it now. As he laughed he was taken out of the line and pushed against the barbed wire fence. The Sturmmann's overcoat was stiff, clinging like cement to his body, and his face was covered with rain. In his gloved hands he held a whip that he continually turned around between his fingers.

'What are you laughing at?'

Grunwald was aching from the wounds of the barbed wire.

'What are you laughing at?' The Sturmmann raised the whip. At the very tip of his long nose there hung a globule of rain.

Grunwald covered his mouth with his hand. The insanity of the proceedings was overwhelming. And on such a dull, Polish day. The sky was heavy and piled with black cloud and the rain was never going to stop. It was the setting for madness; it was a mad, crazy landscape.

'You must find something bloody funny.' The Sturmmann held the whip up and his hand was shaking.

The Unterscharführer came up out of the crowd. 'For

Christ's sake, what's going on here?'

Grunwald then felt strangely solemn; the mood, the mood of madness, seemed to have left him. He was alone with the landscape again, watching the crowd stumble past, like people on their way to a spectacle that is never going to take place.

'This man was laughing,' the Sturmmann said.

'For Christ's sake, let him laugh,' the Unterscharführer said. 'If he thinks there's something funny, that's his business.'

Grunwald said nothing. He was alone, isolated within the structure of his own fear.

The Unterscharführer said, 'Get him back into the line.'

The Sturmmann pushed Grunwald forward. As he did so, the Unterscharführer called out, 'No! Wait! If he thinks there's something to laugh about, I know just the place for him.'

Grunwald was dragged back out of the line again. He was marched between the Sturmmann and the Unterscharführer to another part of the camp. He was pushed into a small, tiled room and told to wait, as if there were any likelihood of being able to leave: and he waited until the Sturmmann came back alone to take him elsewhere.

Sometimes Grunwald felt an intense but impossible desire to visit the house where the girl had been murdered; and he felt this desire in spite of the fact that he knew Schwarzenbach lived somewhere in that vicinity. The idea frightened him and fascinated him at the same time. When he thought of his own life, and then of Schwarzenbach, he realized that it almost seemed as if they were nailed together by coincidence. Coincidence was meaningless, he knew. Life was a series of accidents. If you were to draw a graph of a man's life, the high points would be those where accidents had taken place – chance encounters, unexpected meetings, impulsive decisions with consequences that altered everything. If he had not remained with the corpse of the girl, he might never have seen Schwarzenbach again. The memory of the man might have faded in time like a disease that can only be cured with patience and forgetfulness. If he had not met the American in the first place, his life would never have collided with that of the girl. It seemed senseless to make any attempt to impose a manageable pattern on these events, to create out of them some kind of design. The world was chaotic.

Sometimes he still thought of going to the Americans and telling them about Schwarzenbach. But what could he say? The kind of statements he might make, and the truths he could reveal, would only destroy him in the end. And the thought of faceless authority ploughing over his own past, churning up old stones, inducing yesterday's wounds, was painful. He was a Jew in the wreckage of Berlin: he had survived the death camps. These were the only two facts he felt he wanted to reveal. Everything else was irrelevant. The decisions he felt he should make about the future, his own future, were either postponed or abandoned indefinitely.

And so he wandered the city, sifting the past like a scavenger. But in his wanderings he found that unconsciously he walked on the shaded sides of streets and preferred to move only when it was dark. He was like a night animal, compelled by an instinctive fear. He resented fear, which he thought he should have left behind him in the past. But he did not know how to exorcize it.

11

On the second Thursday of October Schwarzenbach went to Broszat's apartment. Sometimes different faces appeared – old acquaintances, former colleagues, old friends of Katzmann or of Broszat himself. Invariably these were men passing through Berlin on the way south, where escape routes were said to be easier. It had taken some of them months to reach Germany from places like Poland and Hungary. They brought vague rumours with them: that the Russians were slaughtering any former SS men they found in the Soviet-occupied territories, murdering without trial and with few questions asked; that high-ranking men like Sturmbannführer Anton Brunner and Obersturmbannführer Gustav Friedl were prisoners of the Russians and awaiting execution. They spoke with despair, men who had seen their lives change inexorably and who had become – in the vast desert that was Europe – victims themselves.

On that second Thursday in October there were two newcomers: Rudolf Winkel, who had returned from Rumania, ill and desperately tired: and Reinhardt Ecksdorff, who had commanded an Einsatzgruppe in Poland towards the end of 1944. Ecksdorff spoke of the terrible vengeance the Russians were exacting upon anyone who had assisted the German war effort in any way. He had seen Poles gunned in the streets because they had collaborated; he had witnessed unarmed German soldiers brutally massacred; he had seen the execution of a group of SS men; and he had survived himself only after several months of hiding and running.

Schwarzenbach listened to all this with a profound sense of pity. These were men who had arrived at the very limits of their despair and who fed now – like blind, hungry animals – on a diet of rumours, half-truths and an inherent belief in their chances of escaping arrest. But he was tired listening to them. Their voices were monotonous, their words filled with false optimism. Winkel was ill and miserable, barely able to speak. He had contracted venereal disease from a whole sequence of Rumanian peasant women. And Ecksdorff, who had arrived in Berlin only that day, was planning already to go to Geneva where he had heard of a group of SS men who had organized a highly specialized travel-agency. Both men wore shabby overcoats; if anything remained of their pride and dignity, it was manifest only in something they occasionally said, or the way they infrequently referred to the past – the better past before the war.

When he had finished listening to them, Schwarzenbach went into Broszat's kitchen and walked around restlessly. Outside darkness had fallen. It seemed to him that it contained innumerable shadows, threatening shapes that were simply waiting the chance to destroy him.

Broszat followed him into the kitchen. He took a fresh bottle of wine from the cabinet and searched around for the corkscrew.

'Is there any news of Urbach?' Schwarzenbach asked.

Broszat shook his head. 'They took him to their intelligence headquarters and nothing's been heard of him since.' Broszat paused by the window, the wine in his hand. 'It's fucking absurd. I don't like it. What the hell are they doing to him?'

Schwarzenbach finished his drink and sat at the kitchen table. He couldn't remember when the atmosphere in Broszat's apartment had last been so tense; and yet the tension seemed to have a hollow centre to it – the uncertainty, the ignorance, the plain fact that none of them knew what was going on.

Broszat said, 'He might talk.'

'It's possible.'

'On the other hand,' Broszat said, and his voice trailed off into a whisper. 'I don't think we should have any more of these meetings. It's too dangerous.'

'As you wish.' Schwarzenbach felt a sense of relief. The Thursday gatherings had become an unnerving burden.

'I don't like it. I don't like the feeling of having a bloody noose around my neck.'

'Have they been to see you?'

'Not yet.' Broszat finally uncorked the bottle and put it down on the table. 'But they've spoken to you. And they've taken Urbach. Who's going to be next?'

Ecksdorff came into the kitchen looking for more wine. He put his empty glass on the table. He was a tall man with an expression that reminded Schwarzenbach of the sort of look associated with visionaries – the eyes seemed to look beyond the debris towards something else, a new world. But the expression irritated him; it was exclusive of everyone, save Ecksdorff himself.

'In spite of our current difficulties, gentlemen, it's not altogether unpleasant to be in Germany again,' he said. He filled his glass and drank from it quickly and, clicking his heels in a slightly ludicrous, self-mocking way, gave the Hitler salute. 'May God rest Adolf's soul.'

Broszat said, 'It isn't safe for you to be here –'

'Nonsense, Helmut,' Ecksdorff said, and sat up on the edge of the table. 'What is safety? I used to say to my subordinates that the cardinal rule of action in the Einsatzgruppe was to disregard safety. Practise what you preach. Another principle of mine.'

Schwarzenbach disliked the man, an instinctive reaction without apparent rational basis. 'Helmut means that Berlin isn't a safe place to be these days. Take a walk along the Unter den Linden and you'll find out for yourself.'

'I'm quite prepared to forgo the nostalgic pleasure of walking along that particular thoroughfare – for the time being.' Ecksdorff waved his glass at Schwarzenbach and frowned. 'We haven't been properly introduced, have we?'

'Not properly,' Schwarzenbach said. 'Lutzke – Gerhardt Lutzke.'

Ecksdorff said: 'Your complexion reminds me of the sort I used to see in Poland – grey and washed-out. Were you in Poland?'

'For a time.'

'On SS business?'

'Yes, of course.'

Ecksdorff smiled, and something in the smile reminded Schwarzenbach of Captain Eberhard. 'Of course, otherwise you wouldn't be here, would you? But I imagine your reluctance to speak about yourself implies that you had some connection with one of old Heini's death factories. Right?'

Schwarzenbach reached for the wine. The man made him uneasy and he felt a sudden shift of anger.

Ecksdorff said, 'But why the reluctance? Why are you so coy? If you had a hand in one of those notorious palaces, don't be ashamed. Do you want me to tell you some of the enjoyable monstrosities that I perpetrated? Do you want to hear?'

Schwarzenbach had a sudden image: Chelmno, the wooden hut, the soiled rags of human beings that were brought to him and placed on the wooden table, the frenzy with which he worked to destroy them. Was he ashamed? No; there was no shame, no sense of guilt in the memory. The responsibility for those deaths lay less with him than with Gruppenführer Brandt – but even that was a nebulous thing. Who could say where the responsibility lay ultimately? Besides, the question didn't interest him.

Ecksdorff was still staring at him; the eyes, brilliant and grey, penetrated him, and he felt as if Ecksdorff's stare were a fine instrument designed to probe the fragile tissues of evasion. Why was he being evasive?

Ecksdorff poured himself another glass of wine and, picking it up, went through to the other room where Katzmann and Winkel were talking together. Schwarzenbach became conscious of Broszat's heavy breathing in the silence of the kitchen. A moment later Broszat went out, leaving Schwarzenbach alone. He stood for a time at the window, twisting his empty glass in his hand. He was perspiring heavily and wondered why Ecksdorff should have disturbed him so much. Enjoyable monstrosities? When Schwarzenbach thought about it, he knew that he hadn't enjoyed killing in the least. But it had been hard to think of it in that way – as murder. Duty was the prime thing; where duty existed, where patterns of behaviour had been allotted to you in advance, you became like a locomotive that can run only on one set of tracks and no other. There wasn't time to stop and think whether there were questions of right and wrong. The duty, the sense of duty, transcended ethical problems. You became a device, an instrument in the hands of the system that survived only because of your enthusiasm for it. There was nothing else. Those who had stopped, who had questioned duty, who had turned round and wondered about ethics – those were the men who had gone insane.

He looked from the window into the darkened street. Two cars had drawn up outside. He stared at them. They were lined up one behind the other, their engines dead, their windows dark. Leaning forward, he felt a sudden premonition, a fear, and yet it was nothing he could locate within his mind. Why had the vehicles stopped there? And why hadn't anyone emerged from them? In one of the windows of the rear car he saw the flash of a match or a cigarette lighter, a brief flare hurriedly extinguished. What were they doing down there? He pressed his face flat against the glass, his skin streaking the pane with perspiration. And then, for a reason he couldn't understand, he experienced panic. Silently he · pushed the window open and the cold night air struck him. He listened. The city around him was dead, noiseless, as though it had been vacated by every living person, and again he felt the touch of fear. Anxiously he leaned over the ledge. Those black windows below, no sign of movement – it seemed as if the cars had driven themselves there and that there was nobody in either of them. He picked a flake of loose cement from the ledge and let it drop and although he listened he heard nothing.

'You're being anti-social.' Broszat was standing in the doorway.

'Look.' Schwarzenbach indicated the cars.

Broszat stared from the window. 'Well?'

'They drew up a moment ago. And nothing's happened.'

Broszat was alarmed. 'What do you think?'

'I don't know what to think.'

As they watched they heard the engines being switched on – first in the front car, next in the rear. And then both vehicles moved slowly away. Broszat closed the window.

'Nothing,' he said. 'It was nothing.'

Schwarzenbach followed him into the other room. Winkel was half-asleep and Katzmann, as usual, was drunk. Ecksdorff was standing at the other side of the room, gazing at the swastika flag.

'A nice touch,' he said. 'It adds to the emotions.'

Broszat said, 'I think it's time for the toast.'

'Which toast?' Ecksdorff asked.

'Loyalty and honour,' Broszat said.

Ecksdorff sighed: 'A dangerous thing to keep alive.'

Broszat was filling glasses. When he had finished they all stood – with the exception of Winkel – in front of the flag. Above the swastika hung the photograph of the Führer, an oddly benign expression on his face, as if he had been snapped unexpectedly at a time when the war was going well.

'Death to our enemies,' Ecksdorff said, and there was mockery in his voice. He clicked his heels and raised his arm in a salute, as if he did not take the matter seriously.

Broszat began to recite the oath. As they spoke together, Schwarzenbach felt an acute sense of fear again, almost as if he had been given in advance an insight into the immediate future. Fear, anxiety, and beyond those feelings a deep encircling blackness that nagged at his mind: why did he feel like that? When they had finished the oath, they raised their glasses. Ecksdorff drank his wine quickly, throwing his head back in an extravagant way, and then he dropped his glass to the floor where he crushed it with the heel of his shoe.

'The custom of the groom at a Jewish wedding,' he said. 'It symbolizes the end of his freedom and the renunciation of his past. Sometimes I feel like a Jewish bridegroom.'

It was Katzmann who spoke first after a prolonged silence.

'Am I imagining things?'

'What things?' Broszat asked.

'I heard something. Outside. On the stairs.'

They were silent again, listening. They heard nothing.

Broszat said, 'You're a nervous bastard.'

'I *heard* something. I'm telling you.'

Broszat moved towards the door. Ecksdorff, as if deliberately wishing to break the spell of sudden silence that had fallen on the room, laughed noisily.

'I don't hear a thing,' Broszat said. He moved away from the door and back towards the flag at the other side of the room. Schwarzenbach waited and knew that he was waiting for *something*; he knew that something was about to happen. He shivered suddenly, wondering why he should feel as he did, and yet knowing the reason. The two cars in the street, empty hearses. The premonition. The fear. He turned his face towards the door and simultaneously so did Katzmann. There was a faint noise from the stairs outside, like a coin falling on stone some distance away, but echoing faintly now.

Someone was standing outside the door. He knew it; he was certain of it. But he hesitated still, lost, not knowing what to do, what course of action to take.

The first loud noise any of them heard was the sound of enormous pressure being placed upon the door and then that of old wood splintering drily. Broszat acted quickly: he went to his bed, which was situated behind the curtain in a recess, and took his old revolver from beneath the mattress. In the confusion, Schwarzenbach heard a single shot, fired from behind the curtain in the direction of the door. It pierced the wood. Outside someone cried out in pain. The door fell inwards, wrenched from its bolts, and the Americans entered the room, guns drawn, their faces surprised, as if they had not expected the door to yield so easily. Broszat fired again. His bullet struck the first American, a Negro, throwing him back against the wall, drawing a fountain of blood from his neck. Schwarzenbach lay on the floor, aware that Ecksdorff – in trying to get past the Americans to the stairs – had been shot in the skull. And Katzmann, his arms raised in surrender, was cowering in the corner of the room. But Broszat was still firing desperately from behind the curtain, his bullets cutting into plaster, shattering glass, ricocheting from the ceiling and walls. Schwarzenbach saw the Americans move towards the curtain and then they opened fire, blindly, their shots tearing into the curtain, shredding it, piercing the wall beyond, and they advanced towards it only when the thin material was soaked with Broszat's blood. The curtain was pulled back. Broszat was lying across his bed, the empty gun still in his fingers. His face had been shot away. The bed sheets were sodden with his blood and the walls of the recess splattered with insane red patterns.

When the gunfire had died Schwarzenbach stood up and raised his arms in the air. One of the Americans searched his pockets while another tore the swastika flag from the wall and smashed the picture of the Führer with the butt of his gun. Schwarzenbach watched the sparks of glass that flew in the air as the photograph slid from the frame to the floor and lay there, upturned, Hitler's face hidden from view. There were seven or eight soldiers in all and they explored the room as if they expected to encounter a concealed army. Winkel was taken out, dragged to the landing where he screamed. Katzmann was forced towards the door, his arms twisted behind his back. Ecksdorff lay near the door, looking frail and strangely insubstantial in death, and Katzmann, as he was moving, stumbled across the corpse. Schwarzenbach was pushed down the stairs. On the last few steps he fell. He was picked up roughly and led out to the street. He was taken round the corner of the building to where the two cars were parked. He was thrown into a back seat. He covered his face with his hands, listening to the sound of the engine, feeling the vibrations of movement as the vehicle slid forward through the city.

The American sergeant asked: 'Do you speak English?'

Schwarzenbach stared at the rifle that lay across the man's knees. 'Yes. I speak English,' he said.

The sergeant was silent, as if content to have discovered one significant fact. Sometimes he whistled through his teeth and occasionally grunted incomprehensibly whenever the driver spoke to him. Schwarzenbach looked through the window. So far as he could tell they were going in the direction of the Berlinerstrasse. Broszat was dead: this fact – as though he had suddenly realized it – caused him a moment of pain. And then he remembered that he had been caught himself. What was he going to say when they started to ask their questions? What lies could he dream up to tell them? His mind was blank. Shrunken into his coat, the collar turned up against the icy night air that came through the open window, he watched the shapeless city flit past. Now the car was turning away from the Berlinerstrasse and moving past the Hippodrome in the direction of Charlottenburg.

The sergeant said: 'I lost one of my men tonight.' He lowered the window still further and spat out. And then he leaned towards Schwarzenbach and struck him hard in the groin with the barrel of his rifle. Schwarzenbach slumped forward, trying to contain the pain, his hands fumbling around the place where he had been hit. He sat back again, gasping. His eyes were watering.

'I shall report this to your senior officer,' he said.

The sergeant rubbed his hands together. 'I could stop this vehicle and put a bullet through your skull. Shot trying to escape.'

Schwarzenbach was silent. The pain had not subsided. Instead it seemed to have given rise to a whole sequence of lesser pains that rippled spasmodically through his body. For some reason he thought of the photograph of Hitler that had been smashed from the wall in Broszat's apartment: and envisaging this again, it was as if he had only just realized that the past was finished, and that everything – everything he had lived through – was finally washed away.

The sergeant looked at him: 'You fucking Nazi. I thought we'd wiped you all out.'

Schwarzenbach watched the black buildings drift past in silence. When the car slowed, and turned into a courtyard, he felt a stab of anxiety.

The office was small and stuffy: before the war it had been the junior clerk's room in a firm of solicitors, now defunct. It was lit only by a single bare bulb that burned weakly, flickering sometimes, throwing exaggerated shadows amongst the shelves of legal documents. Schwarzenbach waited in the room alone for almost an hour before the door opened and Major Spiers entered. He went quickly and silently to the desk, a monstrous wooden rectangle that ran almost the entire width of the office. Seated behind it he looked uncomfortable, as if he had been placed there forcibly and was now aware that the desk imprisoned him. For some time he did not speak, apparently engrossed in a batch of papers that lay in front of him. Smoke from his cigar – which lay burning in an ashtray – masked his face and sometimes he fanned it away with a quick movement of his hand.

Schwarzenbach stared at him: if he resented any single aspect of Spier's power, it was the way in which the man made the mere act of waiting seem obligatory. The silence – almost an extension of the room's lack of fresh air – was intolerable. It lay heavily on Schwarzenbach, exaggerating the sense of shock that he was beginning to feel. The way the Americans had burst into the room, snapping the door back, firing their revolvers – he had dropped to the floor almost immediately – the way they had shot round after round of ammunition into the curtain that covered the recess until poor Broszat's body was broken in pieces: it had seemed to him that his own life was about to be shattered.

Spiers was still silent, shuffling through the papers, dispersing the smoke from the cigar with sharp absent gestures of his hand. And yet it was obvious to Schwarzenbach that he wasn't really concentrating on the papers at all – he was thinking of other things, he was planning how to handle the interview. This realization somehow reassured Schwarzenbach and emphasized something he had suspected before – that Spiers, and Eberhard as well, were basically amateurs, untrained for the game of vengeance and the consequences of the chase. When he compared Spiers and Eberhard with some of the interrogators in the Gestapo the difference was almost laughable. The American was inexperienced and unsubtle and Schwarzenbach felt a little more relaxed now, even if the still unbearable silence beat down on him and the insufferable room choked him.

He leaned forward towards the desk and said, 'How is your back, Major Spiers?'

Spiers continued to sift through the papers. He crushed his cigar in the ashtray, wiped flakes of ash from his fingers, and looked at Schwarzenbach. 'Much improved, Dr Lutzke. Much improved. I was given a very useful liniment that helped in no time.'

Schwarzenbach smiled: 'I'm glad of that.'

Spiers stood up suddenly and leaned against the edge of the desk. A sense of anger appeared to have come over him; his face was red, a nervous pulse moving in his throat. 'I lost one of my men tonight. And another was seriously wounded.'

He thumped the desk and stared hard at Schwarzenbach. And then he was silent for a time, as if trying to control himself, struggling with an anger he felt to be emotional and therefore unprofessional.

'I'm sorry about your men,' Schwarzenbach said. 'At the same time, I would like to protest about the ruthless behaviour of your soldiers.' He watched the Major slump into his chair like a man overcome by a strange fatigue.

'Ruthless?' he asked.

'I was struck by your sergeant and handled badly by one of your soldiers,' Schwarzenbach said.

Spiers was silent again. He lit another cigar and blew smoke upwards at the ceiling, watching the strange shapes that curled around the lightbulb. 'You better have a damn good reason for being in that apartment tonight, Lutzke.'

'Very simple. The occupant of the apartment was a patient of mine. And I was there in a professional capacity. I didn't expect him to have company.'

'Too easy,' Spiers said. 'Too fucking easy. Try me again.'

Schwarzenbach smiled and shrugged. 'The truth is frequently very simple, Major.'

'You're trying to tell me you were Helmut Broszat's physician?'

'That's correct.'

'And you knew nothing about his past?'

'Nothing at all. I knew of his medical past, of course, but nothing else. Needless to say, I was a little surprised to find his apartment so fancifully decorated. When your men arrived on the scene I was about to leave – '

Spiers shook his head. 'Helmut Broszat was wanted by us. And wanted by the Russians. The list of crimes alleged against him is as long as your arm. But am I telling you anything you don't already know?'

'I never asked about his past. He came to me with a minor heart complaint. Thanks to your men, he's been cured of that.'

'Funny man, Lutzke.' Spiers bit on his cigar and yawned. 'We only expected to get Broszat. But it wasn't such a bad haul, was it?'

Schwarzenbach was silent. He felt tired all at once and wanted nothing more than to sleep. He closed his eyes, listening to the sound of Spier's voice as it began to list the men who had either been killed or captured, and the crimes they had committed.

'Well, Lutzke. Where do you fit into that little gang?'

Schwarzenbach opened his eyes. The room seemed blindingly bright. 'I've already told you, Major. I was Broszat's physician.'

'You've got to try harder, Lutzke.'

'I've nothing more to add.'

Spiers got up and began to walk around the room, a stream of broken cigar smoke trailing behind him. 'Swastika. Hitler's snapshot. Come on, Lutzke – convince me of your innocence.'

'You know my war record. I was never SS. I wasn't even in the Party.'

'Sure, Lutzke. You've got all the documents. We've seen your papers. But there's something wrong. Why doesn't it add up? Why?'

'You're professionally suspicious, Major.'

'Not only me, Doctor. Captain Eberhard feels much the same.'

Schwarzenbach spread his hands. The cold night air had filtered into the room and the curtains that hung at the window shook slightly. 'I'm sorry. I'd like to help.'

Spiers smiled for a moment. 'You weren't Broszat's physician. You went to his apartment expecting to participate in a pleasant little gathering of old friends and colleagues. Talk of old times. A few laughs. Just a few of the old SS boys reminiscing. What the hell did you talk about? Auschwitz? Dreams of how you're going to get it all started up again when the occupying armies have gone home? Is that it?'

Schwarzenbach remained calm. It was obvious now that Spiers knew nothing of any substance. He was digging, throwing accusations around, clutching empty air – but he knew nothing.

'I repeat, Major. I was never involved with the SS.'

Spiers went to the window and ran his finger in the condensation that lay on the glass. He traced a series of tiny cubes, as if he were trying to construct a definite pattern.

'Lutzke, it doesn't fit. We pick you up at an SS nostalgia meeting with some pretty murderous characters, and you claim you weren't taking part.'

Schwarzenbach licked his dry lips and watched the Major at the window. What would happen now? Would he be detained during further enquiries? Or would he be set free?

Spiers dropped his hand to his side and stared at his creation on the window. 'What if I told you that Katzmann had talked? What if I said that Katzmann had told us everything about you?'

Schwarzenbach was momentarily confused. 'I wouldn't believe you. For one thing, I don't know Katzmann. For another, he knows nothing about me.'

Spiers drew on his cigar, the end of which was sodden and misshapen. 'Okay. What about this then? In Chelmno concentration camp there was a certain Dr Schwarzenbach who specialized in inflicting pain and invariably causing death. In late 1944, this character left Chelmno and disappeared. Now – what if I told you that Katzmann had informed us that you are Schwarzenbach?'

'I would laugh. Because you think I'm naïve enough to believe you – and because there isn't a bit of truth in that.' Schwarzenbach felt a brief sensation of fear, a burning in the base of his stomach. How far could Spiers go? How much did he know and how much had he simply guessed?

'Reference to this Schwarzenbach was discovered in the papers of Hans Bothmann, commandant of Chelmno, although it appears that Schwarzenbach was something of a mystery. He was never seen around the camp. There are no extant descriptions of him. None of his victims – those that lived anyway – have come forward to tell us anything about him. His job description – according to Bothmann's papers – is more than a little vague. He was a scientist, he was some kind of pain expert, but that's about it. The rest is mystery.' Spiers paused for a minute and turned to look at Schwarzenbach. He returned to his desk and sat down, looking suddenly like a minor bureaucrat in a vast and labyrinthine organization. An expression of puzzlement crossed his face and he stared at the cigar in his fingers as if he were surprised to find it there.

'Katzmann says that you are Schwarzenbach – '

'Katzmann is talking nonsense – '

'That's what he says.'

'And I deny it.'

Spiers shrugged. 'Face facts, Lutzke. You could be Schwarzenbach. Okay, you've got documents that prove you're Lutzke, but there are more damned forged papers in Germany than there are bank-notes.'

'This is a serious accusation, Major – '

'I know it is – '

'And you will have to prove it.'

Spiers opened his desk and took out a revolver which

he laid in front of him. 'I could get you to confess, couldn't I?'

'You underestimate me.' Schwarzenbach stared at the weapon. He realized how simple it would be for Spiers to take it up, aim it, and fire. Who would say that he hadn't killed in self-defence?

'But I don't believe in threats, Lutzke. There are other ways.'

Schwarzenbach couldn't take his eyes from the gun. 'You are doomed to disappointment, Major. You can never prove something that is untrue.'

'It's been done before.' Spiers put out his cigar. 'Someday, sometime, you'll slip up. Or else I'll hear a whisper. Perhaps somebody will come forward and bring me the evidence I need to put you away. You'll never be safe, Lutzke.'

Schwarzenbach listened: but it was nonsense, empty nonsense. He doubted if Katzmann had talked and he knew for certain that if Spiers had anything more substantial than his own suspicions then he would have been arrested there and then. But Spiers was as unsubtle as Eberhard: it was an obvious strategy to say that Katzmann had talked – and then to claim that Katzmann had told them that he was Schwarzenbach. He saw in a flash the nature of the game that they were playing: there was a file on Schwarzenbach, a thin and useless file, and for reasons known only to their tortuous, clerical mentalities, they were desperately keen to close that file. And who fitted the role better than Lutzke – a Berlin doctor with a past that was suspiciously spotless?

'You've got a wonderful imagination, Major.'

'I'll get you in the end, Lutzke. Rest assured of that.'

'You are welcome to your zealous fantasies.' Schwarzenbach stood up: the interview was at an end, and he was free to leave. Spiers had nothing on which to hold him.

Spiers watched him move towards the door. 'Remember this, Lutzke. Somebody knows about you. And sometime he's going to come forward and open his mouth and blow everything he knows about you. I'll wait for that to happen. I'm a patient man.'

Schwarzenbach closed the door and went outside. A desk sergeant was sleeping in the lobby, head propped against his hands. Schwarzenbach passed him quietly. The night air was fresh and clean and as he stepped out of the building into the courtyard he felt suddenly dizzy. He stood for a moment against the wall and when the feeling had left him he continued to walk. The streets around him were silent, bare, unyielding, as if the recent bombardment of bombs and shells had stripped them of their secrets. As he walked he realized that he could not be touched now: there was nothing, there was no evidence that could be brought against him.

But in his sense of jubilation he had forgotten the Jew: and it was only later, when he was climbing into bed, that it dawned on him Grunwald was the man Spiers wanted so desperately to meet. Grunwald was the only man who could send him on the short walk to the gallows.

12

Once – he had forgotten the year – he met Frau Gerstein on the street near the Gabrielen-Platz in Munich. She was trying to cross against the busy traffic, standing on the edge of the pavement, turning her head this way and that. He touched her elbow and she turned, trembling slightly, as if he had disturbed her in the middle of a dream. She looked at him absently, without recognition. She turned away, an expression of contempt on her face, like a spinster accosted by a drunk. She moved forward through the traffic, and reached the opposite side of the street without looking back. Puzzled, offended, he remained where he was, watching as she disappeared in the crowd. Why had Frau Gerstein – whom he had known for some years – why had she ignored him?

Later in his apartment he mentioned the incident to Martha.

Martha said, 'Frau Gerstein's husband has forbidden her to speak to Jews.'

Grunwald looked from the window of their front room down into the street. It amazed him that people could be so narrow-minded. They had known the Gersteins for years. Hans was a salesman who travelled up and down the country with a pigskin suitcase.

'Does it surprise you?' Martha asked.

Grunwald didn't answer: there was a sense of puzzlement, but beyond that nothing. He turned to look at his wife and saw in her expression an appeal to his own awareness of what was happening in Germany.

'It doesn't surprise me,' she said. 'It doesn't surprise me at all.'

Grunwald shrugged: 'Does it matter if Frau Gerstein

and her husband won't speak to us? Who are they anyway?' He realized his voice was rising in cold anger – and yet he knew that he was only trying to justify his own attitudes.

'Who *are* they?' Martha asked, looking at him in surprise. 'They're Germans. They're ordinary, everyday Germans.'

'They're bigots,' he replied. 'Narrow-minded . . .'

His voice trailed off. Martha had gone into the kitchen. He could hear the sound of running water in the sink. He felt furious with himself: he clenched his fists and went into the kitchen. She turned to him and smiled.

'Maybe you're right,' she said. 'Perhaps they aren't really typical.'

He relaxed all at once. He put his arm around her shoulders and saw – but did not recognize – the expression of anguish in her eyes.

He moved blindly towards the Westkreuz station. Of all the things he might have remembered why had he selected so trivial an incident? Frau Gerstein was a meaningless figure from the past. Why remember, with such frightening clarity, an unimportant affair, an incident that – in the light of subsequent events – was insignificant? Did it seem to him now that the meeting on the Gabrielen-Platz contained the infinitesimally small seeds of genocide: the blank silence, the unacknowledged greeting, the face turned silently away? He recalled Frau Gerstein's expression, almost as if she were standing in front of him now and the intervening years had never happened, and he thought he recognized in it the reflected looks of everyone who had ever contributed to the lunacy of the final solution. And if he looked in a mirror now, if he looked in a mirror at his own face, could he justifiably claim that the expression he saw there was entirely different from that of Frau Gerstein? He felt a brief compassion: yes, yes, it was easy to understand, it was simple to conclude that what had driven Frau Gerstein – fear, fear of her husband, fear of being seen associating with Jews – had driven him also, shunted him relentlessly into acts of such monstrosity that he was no better than Frau Gerstein or her husband, or Obersturmführer Mayer, or Hauptsturmführer Schwarzenbach, or the bloody minions who had carted them first to Mauthausen and then to Chelmno in murderous transports, he was no better than any of them and the guilt that lay across the wreckage of the Reich was as much his to share as it was anyone's, because what he had done had been prompted entirely by the worst fear of all – of dying. If he had chosen instead to die, if that had been his way, if he had closed his eyes for the phenol injection in the heart or stepped naked into the gas chamber, now he would be one of the uncounted dead. But he had chosen differently, conscious for the first time in his life of the sheer necessity to exist.

When the door had slammed shut behind him in Schwarzenbach's hut in Chelmno he knew that he did not have whatever extremes of courage it took to sacrifice himself.

There was a great deal of activity around the Westkreuz station. Trucks full of workers were preparing to continue the task of clearing Berlin of its rubble. Men in shabby overalls sat hunched together in open lorries, soldiers milled around supervising the loading, drivers smoked cigarettes and stamped their feet against the cold of the morning. Grunwald stood for a time watching them, conscious of their sense of impending purpose, a tangible thing that seemed to rise from them collectively like the fumes of smoke from their cigarettes. He felt unwell. Sensations of dizziness pierced him and he moved away slowly from the gathering of trucks to sit down amongst a pile of stones that had once formed the wall of a court-yard. For some days now he had been sleeping in different places, moving from one bombsite to another, from one flooded cellar to the next, like someone deliberately trying to obliterate the tracks of his existence. And yet this was futile: no matter how hard he tried he was unable to shift the feeling that life, like a hunted animal, left its own scent behind.

After some minutes the trucks began to move away. They swayed from side to side as they shuttled forward, scraps of tattered canvas billowing like the sails of ships. Grunwald watched them go and then he rose. From Westkreuz he made his way to the Kurfürstendamm, losing himself in the endless drift of people that moved along in listless droves. What were they living for – the grey faces, the eyes tired of war and conquest? They depressed him: he found himself turning his face away from them, as a squeamish person might from the sight of blood. In his imagination they ceased to exist as separate entities, as individuals with regrets and grievances, they merged and fused into one indistinguishable whole. He stopped in a doorway. There was a tight ache in the centre of his chest under the rib-cage: heart? Lungs? He put his hand to the area of pain.

'What are you doing here?'

He turned round quickly when he heard the voice. The woman was in her thirties: she wore a beret on her head and her face was covered with cheap make-up. She looked old and used and unhappy, as if one morning she had woken to find that her youth had dissolved overnight. In the palm of her hand she held a key-ring that rattled faintly.

'Sheltering,' Grunwald said.

'It isn't raining,' she answered.

'There's no law against standing here, is there?' he asked.

'You look filthy,' she said. Her eyes, funereal blue, were cracked with tiny lines of blood.

'I can't help how I look.' He turned away from her.

The last thing he wanted was a conversation with a whore.

'Have you got any money?'

'Not enough for you,' he said.

'Suit yourself.' She stood beside him, staring silently into the street, smiling absently from time to time at men who drifted past. After some minutes she said, 'See what happens because you're standing here? Nobody's interested in *me*. You put them off.'

Grunwald stared at her. She was badly dressed: a cheap fur, looking as if it had never been part of any living animal, was hung around her shoulders; her black skirt was stained with cigarette ash; the lipstick had been drawn carelessly across her mouth and her lower teeth were tinted with a light red stain.

'Got a match?'

'I don't smoke,' he said.

'Shit.' She had taken a pack of American cigarettes from her bag. She held them a moment despairingly and then returned them to the bag. 'You could do with a bath. Really. Haven't you got anywhere to go?'

'I move around,' Grunwald said.

'We *all* move around these days – but don't you have a regular place to sleep?'

He shook his head: did he detect a sound of pity in her voice? He wanted suddenly to laugh. It seemed absurd – being offered comfort by a prostitute whom he couldn't afford to pay.

'Don't you have a job?'

'That's a stupid question,' he said. 'Don't you recognize me?'

'Recognize you?'

'I'm von Ribbentrop.'

She raised her eyebrows: 'I'm Eva Braun.'

'Then perhaps we might have recognized each other,' he said.

She opened her bag and fished inside it. Amongst various objects – hairgrips, a tattered pack of playing cards, cigarettes, items of cosmetics – she produced a scrap of paper with an address on it.

'If you want a bath,' she said, and she smiled for the first time.

He took the paper silently: written on it in broad pencilled letters was an address in the Barbarossa Strasse. He thrust it into his overcoat pocket, not knowing how to react. He felt the need to say something, anything, but he remained silent.

'Sometimes I'm there, sometimes not,' she said.

He looked at her but already she had pushed past him to the street where she was soliciting a passer-by. He saw the man light her cigarette for her and then they became involved in conversation. He watched them move along the pavement, the woman taking the man's arm, the man trying self-consciously to free himself from her grip. Why had she given him the address? Did she imagine that he might one day come into some money and become a regular customer? Or was it something else – some sense of guilt she was perhaps trying to expiate? As he stepped from the doorway into the busy street it did not occur to him that her offer might be genuine and her act one of impulsive generosity, because these were terms that had been erased from his vocabulary.

Schwarzenbach heard the noise a second time: there was someone in the surgery. His first reaction was that Eberhard and Spiers had returned – perhaps with some new scrap of information, perhaps even to take him to their headquarters for intensive questioning. He searched his mind frantically. What had he overlooked? What had he forgotten? Moving into the kitchen and towards the surgery door, he tried to dismiss the Americans from his thoughts: he was becoming obsessed with them. Whoever was in the surgery, it didn't have to be either Eberhard or Spiers – it could be anybody. One of his patients, perhaps, with an emergency case. Anybody. He listened. The sound came again. Someone was moving around the room. He went forward, hesitating at the door that led to the surgery. He wanted to call out but didn't. Catching his breath, he pushed the door open. The surgery – with a window that faced the street – seemed inordinately bright and for a moment, a foolish moment, he thought that the room was empty, that the sounds he had heard had been manufactured – not by some human agent – but by the house itself. And then he saw Franz Seeler standing by the door. He went to his desk and sat down.

'You shouldn't have come here, Seeler,' he said, aware of the way in which his voice was broken and hoarse.

Seeler looked profoundly apologetic: 'I heard what happened last Thursday. I heard about Broszat and the others – '

Schwarzenbach looked up at him. 'You should have been there. Why weren't you?'

'I couldn't make it,' Seeler answered. He sat down. 'Thank God.'

'It's as well for you that you couldn't make it.' Schwarzenbach felt unaccountably nervous all of a sudden, as though Seeler's presence had a deeper and more intense meaning than he could at present fathom.

'And Broszat's dead,' Seeler said.

'They've got Katzmann as well.' Schwarzenbach looked at the other man: Seeler was of a physical type that he couldn't tolerate – a broad, flat forehead that suggested brute idiocy, a nose pushed back against his face like a prizefighter, and thick negroid lips.

'Katzmann?' Seeler asked. 'They took Katzmann but they didn't keep him for long. My information is that when he learned he was to be handed over to the Russians he committed suicide.'

'Katzmann did?'

'So I have heard.'

So Spiers had been bluffing – in all likelihood Katzmann had told the Americans nothing. Schwarzenbach rose

140

from his desk and went to the window. With increasing frequency these days he found himself scanning the street below the window. 'Why did you come here anyway? It's a bloody stupid thing to do.'

'I came to say that I'm leaving Germany.'

'Leaving? When?'

'I go tonight,' Seeler said. 'First to Geneva and from there to Spain.'

'And then?'

'Africa, possibly.' Seeler shrugged, as if it didn't matter where he went so long as he left Germany.

'And you came to offer your farewells?' Schwarzenbach asked.

'Not entirely.'

'What then?'

Seeler was silent for some time, playing with his fingers, cracking the bones in a way Schwarzenbach found highly annoying. He seemed intent on jerking each finger out of its socket.

'I think you should come with me,' he said at last.

Schwarzenbach was surprised. 'How can I?'

'It can be arranged quite easily. You only have to say the word, and I will see that your papers are prepared and tell you how the transport has been arranged – '

'Why should I? Why should I run away?'

Seeler laughed: 'Gerhardt, you persist in fooling yourself that nothing can touch you. You're blind. Do you imagine that you'll be able to live out the rest of your life without the truth being discovered? Do you really think that?'

'I hope so – '

'Just think. Just think about it a moment. All over Germany now people are putting the bits and pieces together. It's like a big jigsaw puzzle. Someday someone will turn up the fact that there's something very odd about Gerhardt Lutzke. I don't know what – but the piece just won't fit the jigsaw. And they'll start to ask questions.

Embarrassing questions for you. Don't you realize that?'

Schwarzenbach felt that he was being patronized: 'It may seem extraordinary to you, Seeler, but I feel much safer here than I would in Spain or anywhere else.'

Seeler made a noise at the back of his throat that might have been either contempt or disbelief. 'Gerhardt, time is running out for every one of us. Why are you so stubborn? Why don't you realize what's going on around you?'

Schwarzenbach moved towards his desk. It was preposterous that Seeler should come here and tell him what to do. Why didn't Seeler simply leave? What did he want? Schwarzenbach felt curiously safe all at once, safe and impregnable, as if nothing could ever touch him, as if he were above and beyond the whole squalid situation. Seeler was the one who wanted to run, to get out: Seeler was the coward.

'I've nothing to say. I'm staying here.' Schwarzenbach touched the various objects that lay on the surface of his desk – paper-weight, pen, blotter – like a man seeking some sort of proof that the external world existed. Why couldn't he make Seeler realize that there was nothing to be gained in fleeing? A life of exile – foreign countries, alien languages, strange food, uncomfortable climates: what sort of existence was that? It was a negation of life: it was unGerman.

Seeler gazed at the upturned palms of his large hands. 'It's your funeral, Gerhardt. Stay in Germany, if that's what you want. But do you *really* think they won't track you down? Do you imagine that they aren't looking for you even now, at this very moment?'

'Looking for *me*?' Schwarzenbach laughed. 'They may be looking for a man called Schwarzenbach, but they aren't looking for me.'

Seeler shook his head incredulously: 'You imagine that you've got it made, don't you? How long do you think your false papers will support you?'

'You won't convince me,' Schwarzenbach said.

Seeler hesitated a moment and then, moving forward, held out his hand. 'Who knows? We may meet again.'

'Perhaps,' Schwarzenbach said. 'And perhaps not.'

'The world isn't such a large place, Gerhardt.'

Seeler shrugged. At the door he stopped and turned, as if he were about to say something else. But he was silent, and when he left he went in silence.

Schwarzenbach went into the kitchen and opened a fresh bottle of cognac. He poured himself a drink and sat at the table clenching the glass tightly. The room was cold. For a moment he wondered if perhaps there was a grain of truth in what Seeler had said; but after a moment's consideration he realized that there wasn't. Poland was a century away and his memories of it now were dismal recollections, like those of some half-glimpsed object brought back to mind. The trail was dead. What did it matter if Bothmann's papers made mention of someone called Schwarzenbach? The Polish landscape hid beneath its surface more crumbling bones and putrefying corpses than there were names to be accounted for: who could say with certainty that Schwarzenbach hadn't died, and was buried there, buried deep in some miserable weed-choked field? There was nothing to prove otherwise.

When he had finished his drink he put on his overcoat and went out.

He kept thinking about the woman. Why had she given him the address in the Barbarossa Strasse? Did she want something out of him? But what? He had nothing to give. There was nothing he could offer her. Walking through crowded streets, considering her, he rejected the possibility that she had been motivated by kindness. It was a concept alien to the post-war world, incongruous in ruined cities where everyone grafted and struggled to survive.

It was turning dark now. A hard wind was blowing through the streets. She was a prostitute and nothing more. She sold her flesh – hadn't he seen her in action? He remembered the painted face and the threadbare clothes, the dead fur that lay around her shoulders. What could he offer a woman like that, even if he wanted to offer anything? And yet it was human contact of a kind, a collision with another being after days of silence and solitude. It broke the barriers he had erected around himself like the last frail fences of sanity, and it had drawn him, however briefly, into a pale memory of what relationships were like. But he was being absurd: she was only a whore – and Berlin was full of whores, every woman would spread her legs for a few ounces of fresh butter – and since she was no more than that it was ludicrous to invest the meeting with a significance it couldn't possibly have.

He took the scrap of paper from his pocket and unfolded it slowly. Peering at the faded letters in the dim light, it occurred to him that possibly he was the butt of a practical joke. What guarantee did he have that the woman *actually* lived there? That it wasn't the address of the local police station, or the headquarters of an organization, or even more likely still a blank bombsite? He tucked the paper back into his pocket. He turned off the Lutherstrasse and into a side street where the wind, travelling full blast, struck him with threats of ice. Frozen, he found his way into a bar and spent the last of his money on a glass of beer.

He stood against the bar and listened to the silence of conversations around him.

Schwarzenbach waited for a break in the passing traffic before he could cross the street. The lamps of vehicles hung in the darkening air like disembodied eyes searching for recognizable objects. Lamps like those had been suspended over rows of barbed wire in the concentration camp: he heard a voice, someone crying out from a point somewhere above, and then he realized that what he had heard had existed only in his imagination. He shook his head. Thinking of Seeler, some part of his mind still wondering if Seeler were right, he found his way to the other side of the street. Muffled in heavy greatcoats, three or four American soldiers passed him, and he heard their excited talk drift away as they receded. Was Seeler right? Was he right to take his chance and run? And exactly how much credence could Schwarzenbach put into Seeler's warning? *How long do you think your false papers will support you?* How long? How long?

The wind blew strongly against him, catching papers and tossing them up in the air as if they were white hands grasping for something solid. Suddenly desperate, a stab of fear running through him, he tried to think of all the precautions he had taken to bury Schwarzenbach: there were the papers of course, genuine government issue, even if the facts on the papers were false; before leaving Poland in the scared chaos of the Soviet advance, he had destroyed the records pertaining to his work in the camp; he hadn't known about the references to himself in Bothmann's documents – how could he? – but these weren't important because without any kind of substantiation they were useless. What had he overlooked? He could think of nothing except that he might have been more cunning; he might have murdered a prisoner in the camp and dressed the corpse in an SS uniform with Schwarzenbach's papers in the tunic – but there hadn't been time. In spite of the fear that the Russians were advancing and would shortly be upon them, he might have considered his own irrefutable destruction more thoroughly. But there simply hadn't been enough time. He had done what he could – but what had he overlooked?

He was allowing Seeler's conversation to worry him inordinately, that was all. He was permitting his imagination to take flight. Nerves, nothing but nerves: that was the effect Berlin could have on a man. The great ragged shadows that seemed to leap alive from nowhere, the streets that deceived you into thinking they led to other streets but ended instead in smashed apartment houses – it was nothing but an attack of nerves.

A drink. He wanted a drink.

There was suddenly some sort of commotion. A bottle went spinning through the air and splintered against the wall. Flakes of broken glass showered across someone's head and someone else, pushing his table back, got to his feet and cursed. Grunwald moved to the other end of the bar away from the action. He saw two men circle one another with ugly slices of glass in their fists. They were breathing wildly and one was already cut: blood ran across his face and into his open mouth. The men were both civilians and whatever had caused the incident, whatever offence, it was obvious that they were thinking of nothing else than how to damage each other. Grunwald watched in fascination as they closed together and the slivers of sharp glass swung like flashing razors through the air, drawing more blood from the men. Both were smeared with incoherent streaks of red and as they clashed together again one yelled out painfully and dropped his weapon to the floor. As he stooped to retrieve it, the other brought his knee sharp and hard upwards into his face, and the man who received the blow went sprawling back across chairs and tables, toppling them, losing his own balance and striking the back of his skull against the wall. For some seconds there was silence and then the barman went towards the unconscious man with a wet towel and began to wipe his face. The other man dropped his piece of glass, picked up his jacket, and began to wipe his bloody hands on his trousers with slow self-conscious movements, as if he were only just aware of the fact that he had inflicted pain and injury and was amazed by the realization. Grunwald lifted his glass and sipped beer. Like people who had frozen into immobility at some

146

prearranged signal, those who had been watching the fight suddenly began to come alive again. Grunwald stared into his beer and wondered why it was that violence – as if it were some kind of magic spell – could silence people.

Schwarzenbach pushed the curtain back from the doorway and before he could reach the bar a fight had broken out. He stepped away for safety since blood and glass seemed to be flying everywhere, and when he felt he was safe he observed the fight closely. In a matter of seconds it was finished. Someone lay in a slashed mess against a wall, motionless, as if all life had been crushed out of him. Schwarzenbach felt as if he had been cheated in some strange way, and the excitement he had experienced during the brief fight remained unfulfilled. Why did it seem that violence had its own peculiar beauty? He watched a barman run to the inert figure on the floor, a towel flapping in one hand.

He pushed the curtain away from his face and moved towards the bar. Halfway across the floor he stood suddenly still: some faint intuition, some vague impulse, made him turn his head to the side. As if frozen he stopped, his arms stiff and numb by his side, his legs – like limbs subjected to a mild electric shock – tingling quietly.

Beyond the bar there was a cracked mirror, faded and brown: in this mirror – in spite of the cracks – he saw reflected an unmistakable face.

For a moment he did not know how to act. It seemed that a paralysis had stricken him. His mind would not function. And then with a great effort of will he turned round, went back through the curtain and climbed the steps to the street. He stood there in the penetrating cold of the night, shaking like a child after a nightmare.

He pushed his hands into the pockets of his coat and moved off some yards from the entrance to the bar. He waited there in the shadows, chaotic thoughts pushing through his brain.

Grunwald put down his empty glass and turned to leave. He examined the scrap of paper and the address yet again. It wasn't far to the Barbarossa Strasse and he wondered if he should go there. What could he lose? At the very worst the woman could turn him away: on the other hand it might mean the chance to sleep under a roof for once – if in fact the whole thing wasn't a practical joke.

He left the bar. He climbed the steps to the street. His breath hung on the biting air. He moved away in the direction of the Barbarossa Strasse.

Schwarzenbach watched the figure go down the street and then, when there was a safe distance between them, he followed.

13

A dark and broken staircase led invisibly upwards. Grunwald waited and then began to climb it, his hand clutching the rail for support. The house was utterly silent: a graveyard building. He wished that he had a match; it was impossible to tell what lay in front of him. He reached a landing and paused to catch his breath. There was a sharp pain in the centre of his chest which touched him like a brief flare of light and then passed.

On the next landing he stopped again. Was that a noise from below? He listened but heard nothing: anyway, there were so many loose fragments of cement around it was likely he had knocked a piece over the side. He continued to climb the stairs, growing more and more certain that he was the victim of a joke. The whole building was apparently deserted. Besides, who could have lived there and not done something about the smell? Excrement, garbage, the stale trapped smells of cooking that might have been years old – these hung in the air with a presence that was almost tangible.

At length he reached the final landing where he stood for a time in the harsh darkness and experienced a sense of desperation. The woman had been taking the piss, there was no doubt about that now. The building was uninhabited. He leaned against the rail and listened. There were muffled noises of distant traffic. But there was something else as well: a very faint ticking noise, as if someone were moving on the stairs below. And yet it wasn't like that at all. Rather it was an after-noise, the tiny whisper you catch after something has taken place and there are only suggestions of echoes. He strained to hear but caught an unresponsive silence. Even so, he was convinced that some*thing* – if not someone – was moving below. He held his breath, waited, aware of his desperation increasing, if only he had a match, a torch, even a candle, some slice of light by which he could see – but he had nothing except the hostile, impenetrable dark around him. Gripping the rail hard, he leaned over and looked down blindly. He called out.

'Who's there?'

His voice was caught in a muffled echo that reverberated briefly and then died. Christ: what was down there? Again, it seemed that he heard a shuffle, a kind of shuffle, as if someone were coming up very slowly. He leaned over to call down again but this time he was dumb. What could he do? The thought of going down the stairs and passing whoever was climbing upwards through the thick darkness was terrifying.

Suddenly from behind there was the sharp flash of an electric light. He wheeled round quickly. A door had been opened some feet away from him. The woman, her features almost invisible, was framed in the doorway.

'Who is it?' she asked.

He moved towards the door and she saw him properly for the first time. She held the door back and allowed him to enter and then she slammed it shut.

He followed her down a corridor that led into a large high-ceilinged room which was in a state of disarray. A mattress lay on the floor and there were a few old books scattered around amongst the dirt, the items of discarded clothing, the tattered newspapers and empty bottles, the bedsheets that seemed to have been ripped from the mattress in a moment of violence, and strewn across the room.

'So von Ribbentrop has come for his bath?' She sat down on the mattress and he looked at her. She was wearing a nightdress loosely covered with a dressing-gown and in her hand she held a burnt-out cigarette. She looked curiously tiny and he realized for the first time just how large the room actually was: it was overwhelming, its ceiling disappeared into shadow some way above the electric light, and yet he felt safe again, as if the mere act of being there behind a closed door had shut him away from whatever terror had existed outside on the darkened stairs.

'You look pale. Is something wrong?'

'Nothing,' he answered. He could not take his eyes from her: she presented a picture of such decadence that it seemed to him she symbolized in a small way the things that had overtaken Germany and ultimately destroyed it. But when he thought about it, he knew he could not pinpoint exactly why she seemed decadent. Was it something to do with her appearance, her broken appearance – especially here in this room which at one time must have been magnificently impressive?

'I'm sorry,' she said. 'The bath will have to be cancelled.'

He looked for a chair and sat down. He glanced along the corridor towards the door, wondering if it were securely closed.

'The plumbing's fucked itself up,' she said. 'I didn't expect you to come here so soon.'

He said nothing. Why had she asked him to come anyway?

'I must have underestimated your dilemma,' she said. 'You really *don't* have anywhere to go, do you?'

'I told you. I move around.'

She got up from the mattress and came towards him. She stared at him curiously for a moment: 'You were in one of those camps.'

'For a time,' he answered.

An expression of pity crossed her face, as if she were genuinely sorry. But how was it possible for him to tell if she really meant it? The face – its features blurred, the

151

make-up smudged and caked and beginning to crack – was like a mask that has been used in too many dramas: equivocal, blunt.

'I'm sorry,' she said. 'You don't know how sorry I am.'

Her hand brushed against his shoulder and then, slumping like someone wilting under intolerable pressures, she returned to the mattress and sat down.

'Are you married?'

'I was once,' he said, retreating from the subject, from the thought of discussing anything that lay in the past.

'What happened?' she asked.

He was silent again. And then he asked: 'I don't know your name.'

'I told you my name. You told me yours. I'll always think of you as von Ribbentrop.' She leaned across the mattress to where an old gramophone lay. She wound it up slowly and put a record on the turntable. A dance band was playing a foxtrot.

'Do you know that piece of music?' she asked. 'An American gave me that record. It's Glenn Miller.' She closed her eyes and clicked her fingers in time to the music. 'It makes me feel very happy whenever I play it.'

Swaying slightly, she closed her eyes. Grunwald watched her. She seemed to have transported herself and she opened her eyes again only some moments after the record had finished and the needle was ticking again and again in the last groove. She looked at him as if she were seeing him for the first time, an expression of surprise in her eyes.

'Why did you give me your address?' he asked.

'I wanted to.'

'But why?'

'Does it matter?'

Grunwald shrugged. Did it matter? Perhaps not; perhaps the only thing that mattered now was – for however brief a time – the end of his solitude. She got up from the mattress and went to the window. She drew the curtain back a few inches and stood there staring absently at the darkness.

'I gave you my address because I felt sorry for you,' she said. 'Does that answer your question?'

Grunwald wondered about pity: there were times when it seemed to him the most deceptive of all human feelings. 'Why did you feel sorry for me?'

She shrugged. 'Who knows? Maybe I felt sorry for myself.' She dropped the curtain and stood in the centre of the room. 'The way you see me now isn't how I have always been. Does that surprise you? I haven't always been a whore.'

'It doesn't surprise me,' Grunwald said. A slight noise made him turn his head towards the corridor: nothing more than a scrap of paper shifting in a draught.

'Do you know why I'm a whore?' she asked.

Grunwald was embarrassed. He felt uneasy with the confessions of other people: they made him feel as if he were simply a deposit-box for vanities and anxieties that weren't his own.

'Hitler made me a whore,' she said. She returned to the mattress and dropped there, very slowly, as if beneath an impossible weight.

'How?'

She picked up a comb and began to run it through her hair but it made little difference to her appearance. 'At the age of eighteen I was selected for duty at the Lebensborn. In accordance with the biological dictates of the Third Reich, I was mated with a young SS officer – of the same racial type as myself – blonde, Aryan, and attractive. Yes, I was attractive then. You may find it hard to believe.'

Grunwald looked away: what impulse had motivated her to tell him her history? They were both casualties – was that it?

She said, 'I became pregnant. I carried the child for nine months. They said we couldn't keep the children.

153

They said we had to resign any claims on them. That was the law of the Lebensborn. The babies became children of the Reich. At first I didn't mind the thought. And as the months went past I knew I wanted to keep the child. It was growing inside me, it was mine, and I wanted to keep it . . .' She lay down on the mattresss, curled in the foetal position. She lit a cigarette and let it burn down between her lips.

'What happened?' Grunwald asked.

'I tried to keep it after it was born. But they took it away from me. What could I do? What could I have done? The child wasn't mine by law. I had signed a document. But that didn't alter the fact that I was the baby's mother, did it?' She turned over on her back and concentrated on the smoke that rose from her cigarette while it drifted and dispersed somewhere above the light.

'What did you do?'

'Nothing. Christ, I didn't do anything. As far as I was concerned the child was dead. But I wanted it. It was a desperate physical need.'

'And the father?'

'A nothing in a black uniform. I can't even remember his name.'

'I'm sorry,' Grunwald said, and the word seemed an empty gesture.

'After I'd lost the child, I just drifted around. I went into one of those places where they kept girls for the SS officers. I suppose I was looking for another father for another child. Do you think that's what I was doing?'

Grunwald got up from his chair and walked about the room. When he closed his eyes it was as if a nightmare were about to set in; a sense of threat, of menace, impinged upon his consciousness. But why? Did it relate to the past? To the way human lives had been taken up and broken beyond repair? Or did it pertain to the future? He shivered suddenly. The future: there was a beautiful, artificial concept. What did the future hold? He opened his eyes. The room hadn't altered, it was still there, it was around him and he could touch it, and the woman hadn't moved from her position on the mattress; and yet he couldn't rid himself of the strange sense of menace.

'I'm sorry to hear about your baby,' he said, and his eyes were drawn again along the corridor to the door as if in the knowledge that only the door prevented the menace from assuming a real shape. What was it? What was out there? What was moving in the darkness on the stairs?

'Then we're sorry for each other.' She rose from the mattress and looked at him. 'You must be hungry. Do you want something to eat? I've got some cheese and bread.'

'I can't remember when I ate last,' Grunwald said.

She went into the kitchen and returned a moment later with the bread and cheese and a half-bottle of wine. She put them on the table and watched while he ate. The food tasted strange to him and the wine made him slightly dizzy.

'Have you any plans?' she asked.

He shook his head.

'Where do you come from?'

'Munich originally. Poland more recently.'

She looked at him sadly: 'Why are you in Berlin?'

'I found myself here when we returned from Poland,' he said.

'Have you any family in Munich?'

'I'm not sure if they're still alive.'

He was silent for a time. He remembered that there had been several uncles and aunts and cousins, some on his own side, others on Martha's. But what had become of them? Had they survived?

'Don't you want to find out?' she asked.

'They're dead. They must be dead.'

'How do you know?'

'I feel it.' He pushed the empty plate away.

'How can you feel something like that? If there's a

155

chance that any of your relatives are alive, even if there's only a slight chance, you must go to Munich and find out.' She had become suddenly animated, as if she had just managed to solve a major problem.

'Why should I go to Munich?' he asked.

'Why should you stay in Berlin?'

Grunwald shrugged. He was tired all at once: fatigue seemed to hang around him, in the folds of his clothes, in his flesh. Munich. It was a city in which the memories of his life were endlessly trapped.

'If you went to Munich you might be able to make a fresh start.'

He said nothing. Martha and the boy, the apartment, the empty apartment, the long road leading to Dachau, Obersturmführer Mayer's room at Gestapo HQ: even if it were true that Munich had been flattened by war, how could he return there with these memories in his mind?

She touched the back of his hand and he was surprised at the smoothness of her skin. 'Could it be worse than this, Ribbentrop?'

He got up from the table restlessly and moved towards his chair. Munich was an impossible distance away. It was a part of his life that he had cut off, like a useless limb.

'I won't go there,' he said.

'You must.'

'It holds nothing for me now –'

'Your relatives –'.

'Dead. All of them.'

She threw her hands up in exasperation as if – having offered him the solution to the dilemma of his life – he were rejecting it entirely.

'I know someone,' she said. 'He sometimes runs a truck down to Munich. You would only have to mention my name to him and he'd take you down there.'

Grunwald refused to listen. She approached him where he was sitting and caught hold of him by the shoulders. 'Don't be so obstinate. I want to help you. Don't you *see*

156

that? You should go back home – '

'I don't have a home! For God's sake!'

'Arnold Neurer,' she said. 'You'll find his garage in the alley that runs off the Rosenheimer Strasse. You only have to mention my name, tell him that I sent you – '

'No!'

'He'll help. He'll take you to Munich.'

'I don't want to go. Can't you understand that?'

Suddenly she was silent. She took her hands from his shoulders and went to the mattress where she sat down. She looked at him for a long time, puzzled by what she saw in his face.

'Why won't you go? All across bloody Germany people want nothing more than to get back to their home towns. Especially those who've been in your kind of situation – '

'You're wasting your time.' Grunwald slumped further into the chair as if to defend himself against her. 'Look, you've been kind to me. You've given me food. You asked me to come here. But I am *not* going back to Munich. Do you understand that?'

'Please yourself then. It's your fucking life, not mine.'

Grunwald watched her as she went first to the window and then to the table, where she stood with her hands on the wooden surface, spreading the fingers as if to catch at something spilled.

'The expression on your face reminds me of the faces we used to see before and during the war. That look of hopeless fear. Not knowing what was going to happen. Always listening for the bad news. Always waiting . . .' She crushed her cigarette on the table, pushing the stub this way and that through a trail of bread crumbs. 'That's what you remind me of: the man who is always waiting for the bad news.'

She shrugged. 'I thought I could help you. I really thought I could help.'

Shutting his eyes, he was suddenly conscious of the heavy sound of her breathing in the silent room. So she wanted to help? She wanted to send him home, turn the clock back, make him feel that nothing had happened, that the events he had lived through were as unreal as the dread of a nightmare? She was holding out a hand towards him, offering him a point of contact, because she saw in him – what? exactly what? – the open wound of the victim. How could it help to go back to Munich where every sight he might see would be a punishment?

'The time when you might have helped is over.' He felt indescribably weary all at once, as if tired of searching for an object he had misplaced, as if having looked everywhere for it he had resigned himself to the fact of the loss.

She played the Glenn Miller record again like someone who finds comfort in constant repetition. The music threw up a barricade that protected her. He listened to the sound with growing annoyance, shifting around in his chair, restlessly. When the music had finished she took the record from the gramophone and held it a moment between her hands. And then, with a deliberate gesture, she snapped the record in two pieces and dropped them to the floor.

'Why did you do that?' he asked.

'Why not?' She stared at the broken pieces as if she were regretting her impulse. She lit a cigarette and, holding it between her lips, smiled at him. 'I can help you in another way,' she said. 'I've been trained to help men. That's what I do best of all.'

Grunwald looked away. 'I don't need it,' he said.

'It's got nothing to do with need.'

'I don't want it,' he said, embarrassed by the sudden change in her behaviour, yet thinking at the same time of her body under the nightdress. There had been no one since Martha and his memories of Martha's flesh were like recollections of events that had never taken place: except that somewhere, buried now under the rubble of his mind, there existed the smallest memory of love. What would it be like to take this woman? To lie beside her on the mattress and feel her body moving against him?

He rose from his chair and crossed the room to the mattress. He sat down beside her and touched the back of her hand. She was crying quietly: tears lay on the thick surface of her make-up.

'Stop it,' he said.

She covered her face with her hands and he put an arm around her shoulder. Why was she crying? It seemed to him so totally irrational that explanation was impossible. Why was she suddenly crying? He was embarrassed: the confession, the offer of help, and now this.

'Please stop,' he said.

She turned her face away. He did not know how to cope with tears: whenever Martha had wept it had seemed to him a statement about his own uselessness. He rose from the mattress and went back to his chair.

'Why are you crying?'

She raised her face from her hands and shook her head: 'I don't know. It sometimes happens. I can't explain it to you.'

There was a whine of self-pity in her voice. Grunwald imagined her rummaging through her mind for past acts that she could regret now, turning over and over again the items of her conscience as if they were pieces of soiled laundry. And suddenly, without reason, he felt a sense of hostility towards her: she had tried to involve him in her life and in turn had tried to become involved in his – and yet there was an element of theatricality in her behaviour, like someone auditioning for a minor role in an obscure play. She wasn't real: the room, the broken record, the pity and the self-pity, the tears, even the joke name she had assumed so readily – these suddenly seemed to him like fragments of a half-written drama. But how could he have expected her to be otherwise? How could he have imagined her to be sincere? And now that he thought about it he realized that nothing was real in the post-war world: there were times when the broken buildings and the armies of the invasion seemed to him like pieces of poor stage scenery, erected for some interminable theatrical event. And this woman, playing her emotional charade, was using him as her audience.

'It's late now. And I'm tired.'

'As you wish.' Grunwald still hesitated: why didn't she ask him to stay? He didn't want to face the darkness of the stairs again. He didn't want to step outside the door and put his foot on the landing and experience the fear he had felt before.

'I'm sorry about the bath. About the plumbing being fucked up, I mean.' She laughed lightly. Several more cracks appeared in her make-up, running from beneath her eyes to the sides of her cheeks. He had the curious sensation that she was coming apart.

'I wish you didn't feel the need to apologize,' he said.

She looked down at the table and shook her head.

Cold, bitingly cold. He had been standing in the dark for what seemed like hours. What was he waiting for? For the Jew, yes, but why? What did he mean to do? He huddled against the wall in the passageway for wamrth. Ice came through the broken front door and sliced his overcoat and he shivered. What was the Jew doing up there? What was he playing at? Schwarzenbach looked towards the door. Faintly he could see a pattern of light falling from somewhere outside against the broken panes of glass. There was a disgusting smell: tramps and deadbeats came here to shit. He pressed himself to the wall and listened. Nothing. No sounds. Why was he waiting for the Jew?

If he closed his eyes it seemed that a black ocean came to beat against the inside of his head and he was trembling, still trembling, ever since he had seen the Jew in the bar off the Lutherstrasse he had been unable to control himself. It disgusted him to think of his own body being out of control. Why didn't it stop? Nerves, as if abandoned, moved inside him, pulsing like the mechanism of some run-down clock. Another shift of stabbing wind blew through the panes of glass and he moved back a few yards down the passageway. The building was so quiet. It was a soundproof shell, a vacuum.

He thought of Chelmno and the time when the Jew had come through the door of the hut. At first he failed to recognize the Jew because he was so emaciated: his flesh seemed to hang on him like flimsy wrappings of loose paper. The SS-Scharführer – a thug, a philistine who enjoyed the infliction of pain – pushed the Jew forward as if he were presenting a human trophy.

'This one has a sense of humour, Hauptsturmführer,' the man said. 'I want to demonstrate to him that to have a sense of humour in a place like Chelmno is something of a disgrace.'

Schwarzenbach recognized the Jew then: at that point he remembered the man's name and face and the ailments that had dogged him during the years of their association. But that wasn't all: the Jew was afraid, it was written all over his face, he was scared to death – and yet beneath the fear, under the surface of the expression, there was something else. A look of intense pity, a look that had said: So you have come to this.

So you have come to this. Schwarzenbach's first impulse was to destroy the man. When the Scharführer had gone and he was alone with the Jew, he had said: 'I am in a position to kill you.'

The Jew said nothing. He had become accustomed to silence: prisoners did not exchange conversation with SS unless they were spoken to first.

'I can kill you,' he said again.

The Jew looked around the hut: he must have absorbed the instruments of surgery because an expression of incomprehension crossed his face. Schwarzenbach had picked up a surgical knife and held it tightly in his hand. He thought of inserting it into the man's flesh, pushing it between the ribs and deep into the heart. But he didn't. He dropped the knife and it clattered across the table that lay between him and the Jew.

'However,' he said. 'I am also in a position to give you your life.'

The Jew's expression changed to one of relief, of hope, and Schwarzenbach thought it strange that they – all the prisoners – should want to retain their grip on their miserable little lives even if they knew that no world would ever exist for them again beyond the barbed wire and the watchtowers. But they were afraid of death, each and every one of them lived in terror of the final moment as if existence were something infinitely precious.

'I can give you your life,' Schwarzenbach said.

'How?' the Jew asked.

'Do you want to die?'

'No. I don't want to die.'

'Then you will do as I say.'

You will do as I say. Schwarzenbach moved towards the stairs, away from the cold. He should have followed his first impulse then and murdered the man: another corpse would have been insignificant anyhow. He should have taken the surgical knife and made the incision there and then and finished the Jew's life cleanly. But he hadn't. He had failed to make the attempt. He had been too clever, acting on the belief that he knew of an even better way of prolonging the Jew's agony.

'I will do as you say,' the Jew answered.

'Entirely,' Schwarzenbach said.

And now it was incredibly cold as if the whole city around him had frozen into a block of solid ice. He moved a little way up the stairs and sat down, his back to the wall.

'What do you want me to do?' the Jew asked.

'First you must know something of the work I do here,' Schwarzenbach said. 'You must not be prejudiced. The work is of a scientific nature.'

'Scientific?' the Jew asked stupidly, as if he were recalling unbelievable rumours he had heard whispered about the scientific aspects of the concentration camps.

'Don't ask questions,' Schwarzenbach said. 'Your life depends upon your ability to accept!'

'Yes,' the Jew said. 'I understand.'

There was a fresh eagerness in the Jew's eyes now, that of the pupil concentrating upon every word of the master, anxious to hear everything and let nothing slip away. He watched Schwarzenbach move around the room, tracking him with his eyes – those bloody eyes filled with hope. Schwarzenbach remembered a sense of growing excitement: the Jew's life depended upon his own whim. It hung on a thread as slender as that.

'The work I do here is connected with the nature of pain and human endurance. It is connected with an understanding of physical, pain. Naturally it would be impossible to study pain in the abstract, as it were. It becomes necessary to inflict it. Do you follow me?'

Schwarzenbach picked up the surgical knife from the table and looked at Grunwald. 'Hold out your wrist.'

Without hesitation, the Jew thrust his arm forward. Schwarzenbach brought the knife down across the Jew's wrist, causing him to flinch, bringing a swell of blood from the broken skin.

'Pain,' Schwarzenbach said. 'Exactly what you felt just then.'

The Jew watched the blood drip from the wound and then raised his eyes to Schwarzenbach. The eyes were expressionless, as if the man had become momentarily detached from his body.

'You want to remain alive, do you?' Schwarzenbach asked.

The Jew moved his head a few times.

'Very well,' Schwarzenbach said. 'I find the pressure of work intolerable sometimes. And I have often thought lately that I need some kind of assistant.'

The Jew blinked. Surprise? Astonishment? It was impossible to tell.

'You will assist me,' Schwarzenbach said. 'Do you accept that as a condition of your survival?'

'Yes.'

Yes. The Jew had accepted. To save his own pathetic life, he had allowed himself to follow wherever Schwarzenbach wanted to lead. He had allowed himself to be taken on one of the roads to hell.

At the door he hesitated, feeling suddenly drained: he did not seem to have the strength to open the door and step out on to the stairs.

'Goodnight,' he said.

There was no reply. He pulled the door open and closed it quietly behind him. The decreasing angle of electric light dwindled finally into darkness, pinpointing fading shapes of things on the stairs below: a couple of old chairs, a table turned upside down, pieces of bedding. And then he could see nothing. He put out his hand until he found the rail and then he started to descend.

Fuck her, he thought: why had she turned him out when it must have been obvious to her that he wanted badly to stay? A few hours more, that was all, at least until daylight. He plunged forward again into the dark. A candle might have helped and yet the thought of light was appalling somehow because of what it might reveal: worse still, a candle would have created moving shadows. If she had really wanted to help him she would have asked him to stay –

A swirling shaft of cold air came up from somewhere below and it penetrated his overcoat like a fragment of ice. Ahead of him the unyielding darkness was a fine skin that had been stretched unbrokenly across space. He moved on until he reached the next landing. Noises. A rat scampering somewhere. Paper rustling. Ordinary sounds – but why did they manage to sound like someone breathing heavily in an enclosed space? If only he had a light. Fuck her again, he thought.

He reached the next landing, the second from the bottom. He paused there a moment, hesitating like a blind man who suspects an obstacle just in front of him. He put out his hand. Again there came a sudden blast of cold air, a shaft sucked somehow into the building from the street outside. He moved on to the steps again, listening all the time for other noises. The rat again. Paper rustling in the draught. Why was he afraid of these meaningless sounds?

He stopped at the last flight of stairs before the passageway. Through the broken glass panes of the front door he could see a faint impression of light that fell upon the glass like indistinct thumbprints. Moving forward, he put his foot on the first step.

Something rose up just in front of him. A figure he could barely make out. A man. A shape that rose up from the darkness of the wall to meet him.

'Herr Grunwald?'

Grunwald stood perfectly still. He opened his mouth to speak.

'It *is* Herr Grunwald, isn't it?'

'Yes – ' The clipped voice was unmistakable.

'Strange to meet you once again,' Schwarzenbach said. 'You'll forgive my rudeness the other day when I failed to recognize you. Sometimes one's memory plays odd tricks. Don't you find that?'

Grunwald said nothing. He moved backwards to the landing behind him. Schwarzenbach struck a match and the flame killed a tiny area of the darkness.

Schwarzenbach dropped the match. 'I was surprised to see you again, Herr Grunwald. I imagined that you were dead. I've been thinking about you quite a bit since then – '

Grunwald moved back against the wall: he touched something soft.

'How did you find me here?' he asked.

'By accident,' Schwarzenbach said. 'You must have imagined you had seen the last of me. Is that what you thought? Did you imagine you wouldn't see me again?'

Grunwald was silent. Schwarzenbach asked: 'Well? Lost your tongue? You weren't so taciturn, Herr Grunwald, when you were begging for your life.'

Grunwald felt the pains in his chest increase. Pain seemed to dominate everything for him, as if the very centre of his life were located in the region of his heart. Why was all this happening to him? What had he done to deserve his life?

'Well, Herr Grunwald? Why don't you talk?'

'There's nothing to say,' Grunwald answered. 'What do you want? Haven't you caused me enough – '

'I haven't caused you anything,' Schwarzenbach said. 'You made your own choice. Don't come running to me, moaning about the past. You did whatever you could to save your precious flesh. And where has it got you? Where are you now?'

Grunwald felt for the handrail and almost lost his balance.

'I should have killed you when I had the chance,' Schwarzenbach said and moved forward on the steps. The Jew wasn't far away: he could hear the quick, urgent sound of his breathing. He reached the landing and struck another match. Frozen in the light, Grunwald was standing with his back to the wall, pressed there as if held in place by some heavy weight.

'I can see you. I know where you are,' Schwarzenbach dropped the match and moved a few paces forward.

'What do you want?' Grunwald asked.

'Do you know what I really want?' Schwarzenbach was silent a moment, waiting for Grunwald's answer. But none came.

Schwarzenbach said, 'All I really want now is some peace. I want to live my life without the bloody past interfering all the time. You must understand that, Herr Grunwald. You must feel the same way yourself sometimes.'

Schwarzenbach again lit a match. Through the curtain of light he could see Grunwald's impassive face. It seemed curiously featureless, as if it had been robbed of its shape. He felt an intense loathing, an excitement that propelled him forward just as simultaneously it held him back: the moment could not be squandered. He would kill the Jew this time. He would kill him with his own hands, without instruments. He would cancel out what remained of the past and he would be safe.

The match burned his fingers and he dropped it to the ground where it flared briefly and then went out. The darkness seemed more complete, more ruthless than ever before.

He reached across the darkness for Grunwald and his hands came in contact with the Jew's overcoat and he caught hold of it, clawing it, dragging Grunwald towards him, pulling the Jew back across the landing, over the debris heaped there, over the upturned chairs and chunks of plaster: it seemed to him that a fire was burning in his mind and that what he would have to do, what it was most important to do, was to destroy Grunwald. His fingers sinking into the moist flesh of the Jew's neck, he swung Grunwald round and thrust him against the wall as though he were no more substantial than a dry stick that he expected would snap at any moment, break in several pieces. The Jew grunted for breath and for life and raised his hands feebly to push Schwarzenbach away. But he held on, clinging, clinging, in spite of Grunwald's scratching fingers that were upraised now towards his face and eyes. He pushed the Jew's head back against the wall and the neck snapped against the flaking concrete, snapping back like a tightly coiled spring. In the years before the war he remembered seeing them standing in sombre queues outside travel agencies waiting and hoping for ships that would carry them to the outside world, waiting in their disgusting queues like servants hanging around tables for crumbs, suitcases under their arms and lines of them marching towards the frontiers and having to run the gauntlet of stormtroopers who mocked them, who rightly mocked them, and he remembered being in Frankfurt on the *Kristallnacht* and seeing the crowds of men clattering along the Friedberger Anlage to the synagogue there with their torches blazing and their feet hammering, hammering, remembered the frozen hollow eyes of the dead and the dying whom he saw sacrifice themselves like cowards on the barbed wire electric fences or be gunned down like rats from the watchtowers. Now the Jew was gasping for his life: he grunted, kicked, scratched, cried out, tried to catch at the remnants of life that were leaving his body. He hadn't a chance: he hadn't a hope in hell.

Grunwald felt his lungs expand and then burst and his ribs catch fire as surely as if lighted instruments were being played along his bones. His fingers, curling as though to clutch at nothing, caught the flesh of Schwarzenbach's face. In a moment he would die. There was nothing to struggle for and no strength remained to fight. His life was rising out of him like a single, dissolving column of smoke. There was nothing left to struggle for.

Schwarzenbach imagined his hands had become weapons made of iron. The thumbs that encircled the Jew's neck were like two bands of metal, digging deeper into the blood of Grunwald's life. In a moment now, in a moment the Jew would stop struggling and then there would be nothing left of him.

Grunwald tried to force his head upwards. He was splitting. At the back of his throat was a constantly growing sensation of tightness and his chest felt empty. He was going to die – He threw his hands in the air, forcing them beyond Schwarzenbach's arms, and thrust the index finger of his right hand deep into Schwarzenbach's left eye. He heard a confused cry and suddenly the pressure on his throat had gone. Stumbling away towards the stairs, he fell down, overcome by weakness. In the dark he heard Schwarzenbach curse blindly and the sound of him fumbling in his coat for matches. A flare of light: it blinded him and he tried to crawl up the stairs out of Schwarzenbach's range of vision.

Schwarzenbach came after him, grabbing him by the collar of his coat and dragging him back down the stairs. Grunwald rolled over on his side, out of Schwarzenbach's reach, and fell halfway down the next flight of stairs. Dazed, coughing, he sat up. More matches were being hastily lit on the landing, flickering in Schwarzenbach's hands like fireflies.

Grunwald crawled into the passageway, listening to the noise of Schwarzenbach on the stairs. If he could make it to the door, and from there to the street, if he could do that then he had a chance of safety. He started to crawl along the passageway, his eyes fixed to the broken panes of glass in the door.

Schwarzenbach called out: 'I'll find you, Grunwald.'

Grunwald reached the door and pushed it open. Barely conscious he stumbled out on to the street. Did he have the strength to run? Outside, he pulled himself to his feet. His neck and throat were numb, no longer a part of him, and his legs would hardly respond. He limped towards the corner and made his way slowly amongst the black buildings. In an alleyway he lay down flat on his face and coughed for a long time. His neck was bleeding and his eyes felt as if they had been injured from within. He turned over on his back, gasping for air, drawing as much into his lungs as he possibly could without pain.

He had almost died. Schwarzenbach had almost killed

169

him. And he had been on the point of accepting the fact, of acquiescing in the event of his own murder.

Schwarzenbach discarded the empty matchbox and made his way towards the front door. Where was Grunwald now? How had the Jew managed to slip away just when it seemed that – Schwarzenbach looked up and down the street and then, turning round, went back into the building.

14

'What is it? What do you want?'

The woman held the door open a little way. Because of the angle of light it was hard for Schwarzenbach to make out her features. He moved forward.

'You want to come in, do you?'

Schwarzenbach said, 'For a little while.'

She held the door open and showed him down a corridor that led into a large room.

'What can I do for you then?' she asked.

She sat on the mattress and looked at him with a bored expression while she began to undo the buttons of her nightdress.

'I didn't come here for sex,' Schwarzenbach said.

'What do you want then?' She left the buttons undone. Her breasts were large and heavy and an attempt had been made to cover the cracked nipples with a scarlet lipstick.

'I want some information,' he said.

'Are you police?'

Schwarzenbach found a chair and sat down. 'There was a man with you not long ago – '

'He's gone, sweetheart.'

'I know he's gone,' Schwarzenbach said and noticed, with some fascination, that his fingers were smeared with Grunwald's blood.

'I can't give you any information,' she said. She lay back across the mattress and fingered her own breasts, as though to excite him. He found the spectacle dreary.

He took some money from his pocket and threw it on the floor.

'Tell me what you know about him.'

'I don't know anything,' she said, and made no move to pick up the banknotes. 'He's a pathetic wretch whose life has been ruined by the concentration camps – '

'I'm not interested in the past,' Schwarzenbach said. 'Did he tell where he was living? Did he tell you anything about his future plans?'

'Nothing.' She shook her head and stared at him. 'Even if I knew anything, I doubt if I'd tell you.'

Schwarzenbach shifted his feet on the bare floorboards. He was in no mood to be buggered around by a whore. If she knew anything, if Grunwald had mentioned anything about his whereabouts, he was determined to find out. He looked again at the blood on his fingers: it was already dry. It was dry and sticky and the sight of it contributed to his frustration. Grunwald had eluded him: the little Jew was free, somewhere in the city, moving somewhere now across the darkness.

'If you know anything, I suggest you tell me,' he said.

'Why should I? If you want him, you'd better find him.'

'I said that you better tell me anything you know.'

'Look, I don't like being imposed upon. I don't like men who get me out of bed in the middle of the night for no reason at all. What do you want him for anyway? He hasn't done any harm – '

'Shut up.'

'I love your manners. You must have gone to all the right schools.'

'Shut up. I'm not interested in your opinions.' Schwarzenbach looked round the room. If the whore knew nothing, he was wasting his time. But Berlin was a large city with a thousand secret places and he could spend too much time looking for the Jew. He got up from his chair and walked around the room.

'Look, I don't like this,' she said. 'Why don't you leave? You know where the door is, don't you?'

Schwarzenbach stood over the mattress, looking down at her. She covered her breasts with the nightdress and

172

tried to sit up. He placed his foot on her body and pinned her down.

'You better tell me,' he said. 'I wouldn't like to think you're keeping something back from me.'

'You're hurting me.' She tried to struggle and he increased the pressure of his foot.

'I can do better than this,' he said. 'I'm not even trying.'

'You're hurting me,' she said again and placed her hands on his foot, attempting to shift it.

He laughed, pushing his foot hard into her belly until her eyes had begun to water. And then he released the pressure and stepped back from the mattress.

'What did he tell you? What did he say?'

'He told me nothing,' she answered. 'What do you expect? It was just a casual encounter, that's all. Do you think he fed me his whole bloody life-story? You're mad.'

Schwarzenbach wasn't satisfied: 'You're lying to me.'

She sat up on the mattress, her arms around her knees, an expression of fear on her face. He looked at her distastefully: in the old days such anti-social elements were sent to corrective camps.

'I'll give you a second to reconsider.'

'There's nothing to reconsider,' she said. 'Christ, I've had enough of this. If you don't leave now, I'll call the police.'

'The police?' Schwarzenbach laughed: 'What makes you think the police will come?'

She was standing now, looking at him desperately: 'Please believe me. I can't tell you anything.'

He went towards her and caught her by the hair. He twisted her neck backwards and then pulled her body towards him. With his free hand he struck her twice across the mouth and then, releasing her, threw her on to the mattress. Her lip was cut: a single line of thin blood ran across her chin.

'You're insane,' she said. 'For Christ's sake, I don't know anything!'

He knelt beside her and placed his hands on her shoulders. He touched the blood with the tips of his fingers: it glistened in the dim reflection of the electric light. He twisted his hand in her hair, coiling strands around his fingers.

'He must have said something to you. He was here for more than two hours. What did you talk about?'

She turned her face away from him. 'We chattered. We didn't really talk of anything important.'

He stared at her a moment. Under the chipped make-up he could see the thin veins that carried life around her body: they were so frail, so simply destroyed. He gazed at his own hands and then, swinging the right arm in a short arc, struck her hard across the mouth with his fist. She cried out, twisting her body away from him.

'You can do much better than you've done so far,' he said. 'You'd better think hard because I don't have much time to waste on you.'

'My front tooth. I think you've broken it.' She held her hands to her mouth to stop the flow of blood.

'You can get another one,' he said.

'Fuck you.'

'Think. Think hard.'

She lay back, defeated, closing her eyes. 'All right. He said something about . . .'

'About what?'

'About Munich.'

'Munich?'

She sat up and looked at him hopefully: 'That's right. He wanted desperately to go back to Munich.'

'You're lying. Why should he want to go to Munich?'

'That's what he said. Munich. To see if any of his relatives were still alive.'

Schwarzenbach clenched his hands together. It sounded wildly improbable. Why should Grunwald want to go back there?

'You're still lying,' he said. 'I don't believe you.'

'Seriously. It's the truth. He asked if I could help him get back to Munich.'

'And what did you say?'

'I gave him the address of a man who sometimes drives a truck down there and told him that he could fix himself up with a lift.'

'Are you telling me the truth?'

She was examining the blood on her hands, wiping her fingers in the folds of her nightdress. 'I swear it.'

'Why didn't you tell me this in the first place? You could have spared yourself some trouble.' Schwarzenbach stood up. He pushed his hands into the pockets of his overcoat and stood in the centre of the room, looking down at her. 'What's the name of this man?'

'Arnold Neurer. He has a small garage in an alley that runs off the Rosenheimer Strasse.'

Schwarzenbach raised one hand to his lips in a gesture of silence. 'We've never met. Do you understand that? If I discover that you tell anyone about our little talk, I'll come back.'

The cellar was flooded: on the surface of the water floated various items of debris that Grunwald peered at through the darkness, as if in the hope that he might find a dry place to lie down in. His neck ached and there was a painfully hard sensation in his throat. He sat down on the steps: water dripped from a place above, running down the damp walls. Closing his eyes, he thought: I almost died. Schwarzenbach almost killed me. To be close to death was like falling into a violent sleep, like dropping endlessly into a place where there was neither light nor warmth nor any kind of sensation. Schwarzenbach almost killed me. Did I want to die?

On the bottom step he reached out and cupped his hand in the water and splashed his face. There was a taste of staleness on his lips and his tongue felt swollen and immense, a foreign object in his mouth. His chest burned, as if heart and lungs had been held and squeezed by a pair of strong hands, and for a moment he imagined that he was bleeding inside. He lay back across the steps and listened to the constant drip of water, trying to recover his strength.

What now? He could go to the authorities and tell them what had happened: piece by piece they would drag his story out of him, stage by stage they would reconstruct the events of his history. He rested his face on the damp concrete. Suddenly he was cold, shivering all over, his body trapped in a cold circuit. He hadn't been so cold since the journey back from Poland: the crowded train that stank of horse dung, the prisoners dead and dying, the icy black Polish sky split by the fire of machine-guns.

The journey back from Poland into the disintegrating remains of the Reich was a trip to nowhere. Nobody would speak to Grunwald: a woman, her hair in rags, an object that looked like a baby clutched against her breasts, spat at him. He felt sad and aloof, wounded by his own pity, betrayed. Did human life mean so much to him? It must have done: it must have meant more to him than anything else. He wiped the warm saliva from his face with his sleeve and looked out of the truck at the dead Polish landscape: fractured here and there by shells and bombs, carrying burned-out farmhouses as if they were the symptoms of some corrosive disease, it had the appearance of another planet. It was hostile – and yet it could not be worse than the train.

How much did these prisoners know about him? How much was just rumour or gossip or suspicion? He looked different from them, he looked cleaner and healthier, his uniform was neater and untorn: but how much did they know about him? At the next siding where the train stopped, he waited until the guards had unbolted the sliding doors of the truck and he took his chance: he slipped out of the truck and down the embankment into a field. Somewhere someone fired a rifle: whether it was aimed at him he could not tell. He ran through fields, field after field, until he came to a wood. He lay down in the cold bracken under a bare tree and realized that for the first time in years he was free: he was free – in a sense.

He listened to the constant drip of water. Raising his head from the steps he looked around the darkened cellar. What now? How could he stay in Berlin now? The very question restricted his choice of movement. He could go anywhere, and yet there was nowhere he could think of: except Munich. The prospect pained him. He was afraid – both of staying in Berlin and of going to Munich. He had heard it said that Munich had suffered damage in the war: the Ostbahnhof had been destroyed, that the Frauen-kirche, the Peterskirche and the Rathaus had been directly hit by bombs, he had heard that most of the city centre had been annihilated. But did these facts mean anything to him? There were two Munichs: the one in which he had lived and worked until the beginning of the chaos and the other – flattened by Allied bombs and occupied now by the Americans. Between the two – between the memories of the Englischer Garten and the Maximilianstrasse, the recollections of Schwabing and afternoons on the Sonnenstrasse, and the thought that all of this had been crippled and killed – there was nothing.

He stared at the dirty water and the floating objects in front of him and it seemed to him that the past was a desperate animal he could not bring himself to unchain.

He knew then that he could not go to the authorities.

A light was burning in the workshop. Schwarzenbach stopped outside the half-open door and looked inside. A truck, partly covered by tarpaulin, stood against the wall and the hood had been lifted off. A man was examining the engine, his body bent over the side. In one hand he held a torch, in the other a spanner.

Schwarzenbach pushed the door open and stepped

inside. The man looked up: he was about fifty, his face smeared with engine grease. He switched off the torch and rubbed his hands on the sides of his trousers.

'I'm looking for Neurer,' Schwarzenbach said.

'Which Neurer?' the man asked.

'Arnold.' Schwarzenbach looked round the workshop. Tools of various descriptions hung neatly from hooks on the wall, and there were cans of paint, a blowtorch, several wooden crates.

'What can I do for you?' the man asked.

'You're Arnold Neurer?'

The man shifted the spanner from one hand to the other. 'What do you want?'

Schwarzenbach said, 'I won't take up too much of your time.'

The man shrugged: 'I've got a run to make in the morning, and if I can't get this bloody engine fixed – '

'I won't keep you.' Schwarzenbach sat down on one of the crates. 'I'm looking for someone.'

The man continued to wipe his hands. 'How can I help?'

'He might have come to see you,' Schwarzenbach said.

'Why should he want to see me?' Neurer looked suspicious now, as if uncertain about Schwarzenbach's purpose.

'He might ask you to take him to Munich.'

Neurer smiled for the first time. 'That's not my line of country. I don't carry human cargo. It's not worth the effort.'

Schwarzenbach frowned. 'The information I have is different.'

'I don't know where you get your information from,' Neurer said. 'But you must have picked it up wrongly. I carry supplies. That's all I ever take.'

'What supplies?'

'That depends.' Neurer leaned against the truck and took a cigarette butt from his overalls. He struck a match

178

on the cab door. 'Sometimes it's medical supplies. Sometimes it's spare parts of machinery. It depends. Take
tomorrow morning, if you like. I pick up some medical
stuff and I run it down to Stuttgart first, then to Munich,
and I come back empty.'

'I'm not from the police,' Schwarzenbach said. 'You
don't have to lie to me.'

'Who's lying?' Neurer weighed the spanner in the palm
of his hand.

'I was reliably informed that you sometimes carried
people.'

'Who told you that?'

'I was told by a woman.' Schwarzenbach paused, and
realized that he had not asked the woman's name.

'What woman?'

'She lives in the Barbarossa Strasse.' Schwarzenbach
watched for Neurer's reaction, but the man's face did not
alter.

'Does she? And she said I sometimes took passengers
along, did she?'

Schwarzenbach felt curiously uneasy: had the woman
lied to him after all?

Neurer stepped on the cigarette, swivelling his foot
round until he had crushed it. 'What's the name of this
person you're looking for?'

'Grunwald.'

'Never heard of him,' Neurer said.

'I think he'll come to see you,' Schwarzenbach said.
'And if he does, I want to know about it.'

'I told you – I don't carry passengers.' Neurer looked
suddenly annoyed. 'It's not worth it. Suppose I took
someone along, and he didn't have the proper papers,
and suppose I got stopped at a checkpoint somewhere –
that would land me in the shit, now wouldn't it?'

Schwarzenbach said nothing: he knew instinctively that
the man was lying to protect himself. Neurer picked up
his torch and switched it on.

179

'Excuse me, I've got this bloody engine to attend to,' he said.

Schwarzenbach rose from the crate. Taking some money from his pocket, he pressed it into the man's hand.

'What's this?' Neurer asked.

'For your trouble,' Schwarzenbach said. 'Have you got a pencil?'

Neurer indicated a shelf where there were several blunt pencils in an old tobacco tin. Schwarzenbach wrote down his telephone number on the nearest piece of paper he could find – an old garage bill – and he handed it to Neurer.

'If Grunwald comes here to ask for your help, I want to know about it. Do you understand that? Have I made myself clear?'

Neurer stuffed the paper into the top pocket of his overalls.

'I know what you want,' he said.

The door at the rear of the workshop was opened, and a boy of about fifteen came in, carrying a mug of what looked like coffee.

'Who's that?' Schwarzenbach asked.

Neurer looked at him in surprise, as if the question were meaningless. 'My son. Why?'

Schwarzenbach shrugged and watched as the boy handed the mug to his father.

'It's time you stopped for a break,' the boy said, and turned to look at Schwarzenbach. Schwarzenbach hesitated a moment, as though he were about to say something else, and then he moved towards the door.

At the door he stopped and looked round. Both Neurer and his son were staring at him blankly.

'Thank you, Herr Neurer,' Schwarzenbach said. 'You know where to find me.'

He went out into the alley, and turned his coat up against the cold. There was something about Neurer that disturbed him but he could not isolate whatever it was:

180

the man behaved suspiciously, he was sullen, indifferent – and yet whatever it was that irked Schwarzenbach, he knew it was none of these things. It was something else altogether: it was as if Neurer were part of some silent conspiracy against him, as if Neurer knew something he would never reveal no matter how much money he was paid. Going down the Rosenheimer Strasse, Schwarzenbach tried to shrug this odd sensation aside but it persisted, nagging him like an ache that he could not quite locate.

Grunwald left the cellar just before daylight and went back up into the street. He had slept irregularly, waking every so often in the intense cold: and yet there was another cold, an inner sense of chill, that seemed to have its origins deep inside him. At least there had been no dreams, and he was thankful for that. The very thought of dreaming acted upon him like a scalpel.

In the street he began to walk, and walked until he discovered his exact whereabouts: the corner of the Ludwigskirche and Fasanenstrasse. At the back of his mind he was conscious of having accepted the necessity of going to Munich. In one sense, he realized that he should never have spent such a long time in Berlin but he had argued against himself that one dreary war-broken city was much the same as another: so why not Berlin rather than anywhere else?

But this was feeble reasoning for the very simple reason that it negated the need to make a decision. It had forced him to believe that nothing he could do would alter anything. And even now he was not sure if he could change, if he had the courage needed to impose order upon his life. When he considered this – the need to make sense of chaos – it occurred to him that whatever he did would not in any way change the nature of his guilt. It might shadow it, it might obscure it, but it would not remove it. Guilt was something he carried around inside him, that constantly broke the fragile surface of his mind and flamed his memories with a sickening fire: it was not possible to purge himself entirely.

He crossed dead streets in the gathering dawn and wondered cynically if perhaps he was being driven – yet again – by fear rather than the desire to shift the basis of his life. He was afraid of encountering Schwarzenbach again, of dying, of being murdered, which seemed to him a more reasonable motive for wanting to leave Berlin than any other, more honourable, compulsion. What would he do in Munich? Pick up some sort of thread and start again? The very idea agonized him: how was it possible to live in Munich and become, say, a bank clerk? The clerical figure, neat in his dark blue suit and respectacle spectacles, whose hands are covered in blood and who lives in fear of at best exposure, at worse assassination – how was that possible? He felt infinitely weary of everything and knew, without having to probe his own motives any further, that he was running again, that he was fleeing from the shapes and sounds of the past and the threats that came like bullets out of yesterday.

Change: how was change possible? He was swapping one landscape for another, when the only real environment was the one he witnessed inside his own mind. And how was it possible to enter into a world of relationships with other people, when all the time – amidst all the superficial contacts – there was a continual process of self-accusation?

Munich was an excuse, a refuge, another place to which he was fleeing.

Schwarzenbach entered the building where he lived and knew instinctively that something had changed in his absence. Something was different. There was an atmosphere. In the hallway he stopped, as if listening for something. Yes, something had changed in the last few hours. But what? He went towards the stairs and then he paused. The electric light overhead blinked and the fringed shade that hung around it shook slightly. He made no move to climb the stairs, aware distantly of some kind of danger. He was reluctant, without understanding why, to put his foot on the first step.

A door in the hallway opened and he turned round quickly. Herr Zollner, the caretaker, a shabby little man who wore a green plastic eyeshade around his forehead, peered out.

'Herr Doktor,' he whispered, beckoning Schwarzenbach forward.

'Herr Doktor, please,' he said again, when Schwarzenbach didn't move at first. He held open his door and Schwarzenbach entered the caretaker's room. It was a large, smelly place: it contained the scents of old age – stale urine, sweat, and a peculiar smell that Schwarzenbach associated with senile flesh.

Zollner stood in the middle of the floor, worrying, rubbing his hands together in agitation. 'Herr Doktor, oh Herr Doktor,' he said, over and over again, as if he were learning a language for the first time.

'What is it? What's the matter?' Schwarzenbach asked. There was a distant sound from somewhere above, like a heavy piece of furniture being toppled over. He felt alarmed.

'Upstairs in your apartment,' Zollner said, clasping at his eye-shade breathlessly.

'What about my apartment?'

'Soldiers,' the caretaker said and looked for a place to sit, and found an armchair where he slumped down in the manner of someone suffering cardiac arrest.

'What soldiers? What bloody soldiers?' Schwarzenbach gripped the old man's arm and shook it.

'Americans. They came here an hour ago. Six or seven of them. Said they wanted to search your room.' Zollner took out a khaki handkerchief and spat into it. 'I couldn't stop them. They went upstairs. They've been banging about a bit. Oh, dear God, I don't know what's going on –'

'Is that all?' Schwarzenbach asked.

'They said if you came back after they had gone, I was to get in touch with them and tell them. But I couldn't do that, could I? How could I spy on you like that?'

Schwarzenbach looked around the room in desperation, trying to gather his thoughts. What did it mean? What were they searching for? Did they now have some definite evidence? Or were they looking for some? Or were they simply trying to harass him? He went across to the window and looked out. Parked on the other side of the street about a hundred yards away were two cars, their sidelights shining.

'Thank you for telling me, Herr Zollner,' he said.

'But what does it mean? What does it mean, Dr Lutzke?'

Schwarzenbach shrugged: 'I'm not sure.'

Still staring from the window, he tried to consider the situation calmly. Had they uncovered some new fact he had overlooked? Again he thought of his talk with Seeler and wondered despairingly if Seeler's prediction had come true. But no – he couldn't think like that. It was defeatist to suppose that they knew his real identity. Quite suddenly he felt secure, for no apparent reason he felt that nothing they could say or do would touch him in any way. It was the feeling he had had while talking to Seeler, it was the extraordinary sensation that he was above and beyond the grubby mundane behaviour of the Americans and that their game of wits could end only with him outsmarting them. He turned to look at the caretaker.

'Thank you again for warning me, Herr Zollner,' he said.

'What are you going to do?'

'I shall do what anyone in my position would do. I shall go upstairs and demand an explanation.'

184

The caretaker clapped his hands together. 'That's the way, Herr Doktor. They come in here, think they can do what they like, I told them, you know, I told them you were a medical man and much respected, Herr Doktor, but they pushed me aside, an old man like me, just shoved me aside as if I was garbage.' The caretaker flapped after Schwarzenbach as he moved towards the door. 'They think they can do whatever they like to Germans, don't they? They think they can push us around – '

Schwarzenbach opened the door and stepped into the hall. He felt curiously elated now, as if his mind were no longer bound to his body. He walked briskly towards the stairs and, glancing back once at the figure of the caretaker, started to climb up.

Grunwald crossed the Pariserstrasse and reached the Kaiser-Allee which he traversed quickly. From there he turned on to the Regensburgerstrasse and walked towards Viktoria-Luise-Platz. At the corner of the Münchenstrasse he stopped, looking this way and that, scouring the empty streets as if for a familiar sign. Not far from here, a few streets away, was the Rosenheimer Strasse. Where was he going? Why was he running again? It seemed to him that the future lay in front of him like a road over which all the electric lamps have failed.

He had reached the intersection of the Münchenstrasse and the Barbarossa. There he paused, as if it were possible to reflect even further on his situation and drag out of himself some vital new factor that would not only explain everything but – like an oracle – would also decide his future action.

Captain Eberhard appeared to be in charge of the search. Cap in hand, briefcase chained as usual to his wrist, he was watching his men move around the apartment. They had already searched the surgery – the place was in chaos – and had now begun on Schwarzenbach's bedroom.

Schwarzenbach stood in the doorway that led to the bedroom.

'I would like an explanation for this outrage, Captain,' he said, noticing that the men did not even bother to replace the objects they searched.

Eberhard smiled and laid a hand on Schwarzenbach's arm. 'An explanation, Doctor?'

'There must be one,' Schwarzenbach said.

The American looked inside his cap and laughed: 'Well, that might be a bit difficult for you to understand, Doctor.'

'I'm prepared to listen.'

Eberhard shrugged: 'We're making a search of your apartment.'

'I can see that.'

'Well? What more do you want?' Eberhard put his cap on his head and moved away from the bedroom door into the kitchen, where he sat down and placed his feet on the table.

Schwarzenbach followed him. 'I want to know why!'

'No reason, Doctor.'

The inane smile was fixed to Eberhard's face as if it were made of cement. 'No reason?' Schwarzenbach slapped the table with the palm of his hand. 'Are you saying that you and your men have come here to search my private possessions *without any reason*?'

Eberhard said, 'That's about it.'

'What's the name of your commanding officer?' Schwarzenbach asked.

'Major Spiers is in charge of our unit, Dr Lutzke.'

There was a crash from the bedroom. Quickly, Schwarzenbach went to see what had happened. The bed had been turned over on its side, the mattress thrown to the floor, and the water-jug, which had been on the bedside table, lay in broken pieces.

'This is outrageous,' Schwarzenbach said.

Eberhard patted his briefcase. 'Well, well.'

186

'Have you nothing to say, Captain?'

'Nothing at all.' Eberhard took out a cigarette and lit it. He stared at Schwarzenbach pleasantly, like someone who has come on a social call but who will soon make excuses to leave.

Schwarzenbach sat on the edge of the table. It was clear now: a policy of harassment. That was the name of the game. Well, Eberhard and his men could search for as long as they liked – they would find nothing. He felt superior: neither Eberhard nor Spiers were really certain of their ground – and so they had stooped to this feeble trick. But he could match them, simply by the act of remaining calm and unconcerned.

One of the soldiers came out of the bedroom. 'Captain, you might like to have a look at this,' he said.

Eberhard turned round: 'What is it?'

The soldier shrugged and handed the Captain a book. Schwarzenbach, animated suddenly, leaned forward. It was a medical book that had been removed from the bookshelf in the bedroom.

He said, 'It's a textbook on tropical diseases. A standard work when I was a medical student.'

'Interesting,' Eberhard said and took the book from the soldier: it lay open at the fly-leaf.

'Are you excited by tropical diseases, Captain?' Schwarzenbach asked.

'Where did you get this book, Doctor?'

'How should I remember? It was a long time ago. I don't know.'

'Think.' Eberhard was staring at him intently.

'What's so important about the book?' Schwarzenbach asked.

'It isn't the book, Doctor. It isn't the book.' Eberhard passed it to him. 'It's the initials in the fly-leaf.'

In faded blue ink: G.W.S.

Schwarzenbach stared at the letters as if they were

187

accusing him of a crime. His own initials inscribed on the flyleaf of an old medical school textbook.

Eberhard said, 'They aren't your initials, Dr Lutzke. Whose initials are they?'

Schwarzenbach said, 'You obviously don't know very much about the economics of being a medical student, do you? Possibly students in your own country are more affluent, but when I was studying it was often necessary to purchase books secondhand. And that must have been one of them.'

He ran a hand across his forehead. Strange, he was sweating. Did Eberhard notice his perspiration?

The American took the book back and slammed it shut. 'Then why didn't you erase these initials – or score them out – and insert your own? I imagine that that would be standard practice, Doctor.'

Schwarzenbach said, 'I was never a great one for material possessions, Captain. I possessed the book. That was enough. Why should it be necessary to inscribe my initials inside it as well?'

'That's what most people do,' Eberhard said.

'You make more generalizations than anyone else I know. Is that an American trait?'

Eberhard looked suddenly angry. He rose from his chair and walked around the room. The chain attached to the briefcase made a soft rattling noise.

'G.W.S.' Eberhard stopped by the window. 'What do those letters stand for?'

'Really, Captain, do you expect me to know? How could I know that? When you purchase a book in a second-hand store, do you ask the name of the previous owner?' Schwarzenbach watched the American's face for a reaction. But there was none: the moment of anger – if anger it had been – seemed to have passed.

'Maybe I'm making a mountain out of the proverbial molehill,' he said, and suddenly smiled, and placed the book on the table where it lay closed. He drew a hand across his face. 'That's the trouble with this job, Doctor. You never get enough sleep. I'm dog-tired.'

'Sleeping pills,' Schwarzenbach said. 'I may have some – '

'I never use them, Dr Lutzke. But thanks all the same.'

The soldiers were beginning to come out of the bedroom, their search over. They lined up casually against the wall.

One of them said, 'We're finished, Captain.'

'Okay, men,' Eberhard said. 'You can go back to the vehicles.'

One by one the soldiers left. Eberhard lingered behind.

'Your men have made a considerable mess,' Schwarzenbach said.

Eberhard said nothing for a moment. And then: 'You had a talk the other day with Major Spiers. He told me about the little discussion you had. I gather you feel that he made certain unfair and unjust accusations against you – '

'More than that,' Schwarzenbach said. 'They were preposterous.'

Eberhard shook his head: 'Sometimes he gets mild fixations, you know. He gets a thing into his head and won't let it lie down. This Schwarzenbach business – '

'Which is absurd – '

'I agree. I think we ought to forget it, don't you?'

Schwarzenbach was surprised. Eberhard held out his hand and they shook hands together.

'Goodbye, Doctor.' He looked round the room. 'Sorry about the mess.'

He saw what it was in a flash. As soon as Eberhard had gone, he knew what was happening. At first he was inclined to think that he was meant to be lulled into a false sense of security, but he dismissed this possibility. It was something else: they were trying now to confuse him.

They were trying to mix him up and then trap him into some fatal error. It was the oldest game of all: the art of confusion. It was all perfectly clear to him. Did Eberhard imagine he would fall for that one? It was so childish Schwarzenbach almost laughed. It was infantile and pathetic – all he had to do was remain firm, reveal nothing, and no matter what strategies they employed nothing would happen to him. All he had to do was stick to his story.

No: there was something else. The Jew. What was the point of sticking to his story if the Jew remained alive as a threat to his safety? He could only be completely safe if every angle were covered and all the approach roads sealed.

Herr Zollner was at the door, rubbing his hands together.

'They've gone, Herr Doktor,' he said.

'I asked them to leave.'

The caretaker tapped his plastic eyeshade. 'Good for you. Good for you.' Herr Zollner did a quaint little dance that seemed to suggest the joy he felt at seeing the Americans leave.

'Funny thing,' he said.

'What's funny?'

'The senior one – a captain, is he? – told me to tell you he was sorry about messing about your apartment.'

'What's funny about that?'

Herr Zollner paused a moment: 'Well, he got your name wrong. He said to me, "Tell Dr Schwarzenbach that we're sorry." That's what he said.'

'There must be some mistake,' Schwarzenbach said. 'He's a little confused.'

'Funny thing,' the caretaker said. 'Dr Schwarzenbach? There's no one here with that name, is there?'

'No one at all.'

Schwarzenbach closed the door.

* * *

190

He picked up the medical textbook from the table where it lay closed. He stared at the initials on the fly-leaf: how many years had passed since he had written them there? Then, with a move of sudden violence, he ripped the sheet from the book and burned it over the sink. As he watched the paper curl in the flame, he knew the Americans would never catch him through their own efforts. They were too clumsy: there was no other word to describe them. They were like ungainly people stumbling around amidst fragile and irreplaceable objects in an antique shop. If they were to trap him they desperately needed help. He washed the charred ashes away and then ran cold water over his hands.

When the last scrap of burnt paper had vanished he went into the surgery to survey the wreckage.

He found the prescription book lying on top of the desk amongst several sheets of paper that had been dragged out of the drawers. Someone had written on it the words: *Chelmno Death Camp, Poland*. He paused for a moment and then seized the pad and ripped off the top sheet. And then he stopped: this kind of erratic behaviour was pointless. He had to remain calm. He had to control himself. If he allowed himself to become harassed he was playing exactly as the Americans wanted him to play. *Chelmno Death Camp, Poland*. He crumpled the sheet of paper in his hand and threw it into the wastebasket. Eberhard was a fool. What had he hoped to prove by writing those words?

Grunwald found the alley off the Rosenheimer Strasse without difficulty. Neurer was in his workshop fiddling with the engine of his truck and turned round as he heard Grunwald approach. Grunwald hesitated: what was he meant to say now? He drew his overcoat around him and said nothing for a time, staring at Neurer who in turn was scrutinizing him closely.

'I'm busy,' Neurer said, and returned to the engine.

'I've got to get this fucking thing moving – '

'You're having difficulty, I see,' Grunwald remarked.

'Noticed, have you?' Neurer spat into a dirty handkerchief he had taken from his overalls.

Grunwald felt like turning round and leaving: why had he come here anyway? He knew nothing about Neurer; he had come only because of the woman's recommendation. He lingered in the open doorway for a time. Neurer was whistling between his teeth while he fidgeted with the entrails of the vehicle. After some moments Neurer turned round again.

'Do you want something? What is it?'

'Are you Arnold Neurer?' Grunwald asked.

'That's right,' Neurer stood upright, his hands on his hips in an aggressive manner. 'Well? Are you going to tell me what you want? Or do we stand looking at each other all bloody day?'

Grunwald opened his mouth: his lips were dry and heavy.

'Well?' Neurer asked.

'I was told to come and see you,' Grunwald said. Why did he find it so painful to come to the point? Was it because he wanted to ask a favour?

'Who told you?' Neurer asked.

'The woman – '

'Which woman?'

'The woman in the Barbarossa Strasse – '

'What's her name?'

'I don't know – '

'Then I don't know who you're talking about, do I?' Neurer bent over the engine again, probing with a screwdriver.

Grunwald felt unaccountably faint. He leaned against the door and discovered that he was breathing with some difficulty. For a moment the workshop shimmered in front of his eyes. He massaged his eyelids with his fingers. Why had he bothered to come? Munich: it was an impossible prospect.

Neurer looked up: 'Describe the woman.'

'Describe her?'

'Go on. What did she look like?'

Grunwald's mind was a blank. He tried to reconstruct the woman from the sudden emptiness of his memories.

'She's a prostitute,' he said. Neurer did not move. He continued to stare at Grunwald coldly. 'I don't know her real name. She called herself – it's ridiculous, I know – but she called herself Eva Braun.'

'Go on. How did she look?'

'Blonde. She looked tired. She enjoyed playing a Glenn Miller record.' Grunwald paused and realized there was nothing left to say. Beyond these bare facts, what else could he offer?

'Anna. You've described Anna.' Neurer said. He put his screwdriver down and wiped his hands on his trousers. Moving forward he held out his hand towards Grunwald and Grunwald accepted it.

'You look tired yourself. I've got some coffee inside.'

Grunwald followed him through a door at the other end of the workshop that led into a tiny square kitchen. The place was immaculately clean. On the gas-stove a pot of coffee was heating slowly.

'Sit down,' Neurer said. He poured the coffee and passed a cup to Grunwald who had taken a chair at the table.

'So Anna sent you,' Neurer said.

'I'm sorry – I didn't know her name.'

'How is she? I haven't seen her in weeks.'

Grunwald sipped the hot coffee. It burned his dry lips. 'Fine,' he said.

'She's never fine,' Neurer said. 'She's more cut up inside than a lump of butchermeat.'

Neurer lit a cigarette and held his cup between his

hands as if he were seeking warmth from it. He gazed at Grunwald a moment.

'Let me guess,' he said. 'Your name is Grunwald.'

'Did she tell you that?'

'No.'

'Then how do you know?'

Neurer reached inside his top pocket and produced a scrap of paper that he placed in front of Grunwald. Grunwald picked it up: it was a garage bill. He turned it over in puzzlement. On the reverse side was written the name of Gerhardt Lutzke. Underneath the name was a telephone number.

'Lutzke?'

Neurer wet the end of his cigarette with his tongue: 'He came here. He was looking for you. He asked me to tell him when you got here. Even paid me for the information. What do you make of that?'

Grunwald pushed his chair back from the table, with the sudden feeling he had walked straight into a trap.

'Relax,' Neurer said. 'Don't worry. I'm not going to tell him.'

'But he paid you – '

'Fuck that. He's got more money than sense.'

'You don't mean to tell him?'

'Why should I?' Neurer paused a moment as though to reflect on something. 'I've seen his sort a hundred times before. If you could get his head off his shoulders and shake it around you'd hear it rattle. Look at his eyes. He'd stab you as soon as piss on you.'

Grunwald stared into his coffee. He could hardly believe that Neurer would not betray him: why was it impossible now for him to accept people at their face value?

'I'm not interested in what there is between you,' Neurer said. 'If Anna sent you here, then that's all right with me.'

Grunwald said nothing. Neurer rose from the table and

rubbed his hands together in anticipation. 'Now, if I can get that bloody motor fixed we'll be out of here in an hour.'

'So soon?'

Neurer clapped him on the shoulder. 'You came at the right time, Grunwald. If you'd left it a bit later, you would have been right out of luck.'

Grunwald looked at him in surprise. 'You haven't even asked where I'm going, have you?'

Neurer laughed. 'I only stop in two places. Stuttgart and Munich. And Munich's the end of the line for me. Which is it to be?'

'Munich,' Grunwald said, and wanted to bite his tongue off for having said it.

'Get some rest on the couch until I'm ready.'

Neurer went back into the workshop. Alone, Grunwald finished his drink and lay down on the sofa. Sleep was impossible. He was going to Munich. *He was going back to Munich.* What would it be like? How much would it have changed? Would he see any faces from the past? Did he want to? He was suddenly scared the way a child might be terrified on its first day at school. He heard noises from the workshop. Neurer was revving the engine. Munich – for God's sake. The place where his life had begun and ended.

A boy was standing in the doorway watching him shyly. Grunwald felt immediately awkward lying on the sofa and made a move to get up.

'Don't get up,' the boy said.

Grunwald stared at the boy. He bore a superficial resemblance to Neurer and was presumably the man's son.

'What's your name?' Grunwald asked.

'Karl.' The boy stood at the end of the sofa, his eyes fixed to Grunwald's shabby coat. 'Are you going on a journey with my father?'

'That's right.'

'Is he taking you all the way to Munich?'

Grunwald nodded his head. The boy was around fifteen, but small for his age. It was years since Grunwald had spoken to anyone as young as this. What did boys of fifteen talk about in the claustrophobic climate of postwar Germany?

'I stay here and look after things while he's away.'

'What things?'

'There are a few mechanical things,' the boy said and brushed hair from his face.

'Are you good at mechanical things?'

The boy's face brightened. 'It's the only kind of thing I'm really interested in,' he said. 'In a few years I should be a fully qualified mechanic. What do you do?'

'I used to be in business,' Grunwald answered.

'What business?'

'Oh, import and export.'

'Import and export what?'

Grunwald had to remember for a moment: 'Jewellery.'

'Real jewels?'

'Imitations mainly.'

'Oh.' The boy seemed vaguely disappointed. 'If you don't mind me saying so, you don't look very well.'

'Perhaps the Bavarian climate will make me better.'

The boy sat on the arm of the sofa. 'My father often takes people with him on his trips. Do you know why he does it?'

Grunwald shook his head. 'Why?'

'He says that we have a duty to help the casualties of war.'

'Does he? And was he a casualty?'

The boy examined his fingers in a bored fashion. 'He didn't fight.'

'What did he do?'

'He was in prison for five years.'

Grunwald felt that he should not pursue the point, but

the boy continued. 'They put him in prison in 1940 because he was distributing anti-Hitler pamphlets. They said he was a communist. He refused to fight Hitler's war. At school, some of the boys boast about what their fathers did during the war. Some of them fought on the Russian front, one or two were in the desert. One boy's father was a high-up in the Waffen-SS.'

'What do you say about your father?'

The boy was silent a moment. 'I keep quiet,' he said.

Grunwald sat up. 'Aren't you proud of him?'

'I don't know,' the boy said.

Neurer came in from the workshop, cleaning his hands on a rag.

'I've got the bugger going at last,' he said. 'Are we ready?'

Grunwald rose from the sofa with some trepidation. He shook hands with Karl and followed Neurer into the workshop. Neurer embraced his son a moment, until the boy withdrew in an embarrassed fashion, and then climbed into the driving seat. Grunwald swung himself into the other seat and watched as Karl opened the workshop doors. Neurer released the handbrake and the truck rolled forward into the alley. Swinging the large wheel round quickly, Neurer turned the vehicle towards the Rosenheimer Strasse. Karl shouted something, his hand raised in the air, but his voice was whipped away by the noise of the engine.

At the end of the alley Neurer said, 'Here we go, Grunwald.'

Go where? Grunwald wondered. And why? And what was likely to happen at the ultimate destination? There were so many questions and he had the answers to none of them. The truck lurched into the Rosenheimer Strasse and turned right. This was the start of the journey.

15

The landscape amazed Grunwald. Drowsy from the stifling heat inside the cabin, his eyes barely open, he watched it stutter past like the images of an incoherent dream. Sometimes when Neurer spoke to him he did not catch the words, partly because of the noise of the engine but mainly because he was so absorbed by the things he saw. People were working in the fields. In small towns and villages there were bulldozers clearing whatever rubble the war had imposed upon them. There was an atmosphere of *purpose* such as he had never encountered in Berlin, there was a sense of having aims and goals to pursue: it was as if the war had intervened only as some minor inconvenience that had left behind a certain amount of superficial damage which now had to be cleared away so that the business of living could go on. Accustomed to the sight of Berlin, Grunwald realized for the first time that while he had spent many months in the capital another sort of life was going on elsewhere. People were picking up the broken pieces and trying to weld them once more into an acceptable whole. There were soldiers everywhere, of course, but even they seemed a natural part of the landscape, as if they had always been there and nothing could shift them.

He fell asleep sometimes, dreamlessly, but would awake puzzled until he realized where he was and where he was going. A new life: was that what he was going to? Sometimes he tried to imagine this idea, he tried to frame the concept of starting anew, but it eluded him tantalizingly. And yet he felt – in spite of himself – the stirrings of hope. But what could he hope for? Forgetfulness? The cancellation of his memory? He looked through the dirty

cab window: wintry morning sunlight flooded the landscape with cold colours. Whenever he opened the window
he was aware of how deceitful the sunlight looked.
Outside it was clawingly cold. Wind swept the fields. Men
and women wore heavy overcoats and scarves. Could he
hope for a new life? He thought of Munich and it was like
thinking of a haunted city: ghosts flitted back and forth
through his brain like people walking endlessly up and
down dusty corridors as if they were seeking the one door
that would lead them out.

Neurer stopped the truck once by the side of the road
and produced a paper bag from his rucksack. He took out
some sandwiches.

'Not very inspiring,' he said, as he passed one to
Grunwald. 'But they'll fill your belly.'

Grunwald accepted gratefully. 'How far have we
come?' he asked.

'We've got a long way to go,' Neurer said. Chewing on
his bread, he stared from the window out across the open
fields. Grunwald felt suddenly secure inside the cab: some
of Neurer's strength and certainty seemed to have affected
him.

Grunwald said, 'I don't have any money. I can't pay
you.'

Neurer looked insulted. 'I didn't ask for payment.'

'Why are you taking me?'

'Do you always think in terms of the profit motive?'
Neurer opened the window and threw the paper bag
outside.

'I'm sorry.'

Neurer was silent a moment: 'I don't blame you,' he said.

'I'd like to thank you,' Grunwald said.

'We aren't there yet.'

'The boy – Karl – mentioned that you spent the war in
jail.'

Neurer lit a cigarette that he had rolled himself from a
tin he kept in his jacket. Everything he did was invested

199

with a sense of purpose and economy: his speech, his movements – nothing about the man suggested excess.

'That's right,' Neurer said. 'Until the end. They took me out of jail and stuck a rifle in my hand and told me I had to defend Berlin.'

'What did you do?'

'I didn't do anything,' Neurer said. 'I wanted to welcome the Russians. I didn't want to shoot them.'

Grunwald finished his sandwich. 'Why didn't you go to war?'

'I didn't make any secret of my contempt for Hitler,' Neurer answered, and then laughed as if at some hidden memory. 'If they'd stuck me in the army I would have been a bloody bad influence.'

Grunwald slumped back in his seat. He could not recall when he had last felt so secure. Neurer affected him like that: he would willingly have placed his life in the man's hands.

'I was an active member of the outlawed communist party until they imprisoned me,' Neurer said. 'I was a member of the anti-Hitler resistance. How could any reasonable man comply with the Hitler regime?'

Compliance. Grunwald opened the window and pushed his face out into the chill morning air. Neurer's simple courage upset him: he was sitting beside a man who had risked life and liberty because of his morality. Jesus Christ: it was more than he could bear to think about. What had he done? *What had he done*?

Neurer said, 'There just wasn't a choice. We weren't blind. We knew what was going on. Not just in Germany but in Poland as well. We were in contact with the communists there. We knew it wasn't just propaganda.'

Neurer threw his cigarette from the window and shivered.

'It's damned cold.' He started the engine and the truck rolled forward. 'But it's all in the past. Why think about it now?'

Grunwald stared at the landscape. The countryside looked icily beautiful, created out of violent extremes of light and shadow and the dead colours of approaching winter. He retreated into himself: Neurer made him feel ludicrously feeble. And guilty. He loathed his own guilt. *How could any reasonable man comply with the Hitler regime?* He pressed the palms of his hands hard and flat together, as if he were trying to crush an object that he held between them. Neurer had risked everything because he was honest and because he had dignity. Grunwald knew he had risked nothing and that he had no dignity left.

Neurer asked, 'Are you married?'

'I lost my wife,' Grunwald replied.

'The same for me.' Neurer turned his eyes back to the road. 'She died of natural causes. At least that's what the medical report said. There's only myself and the boy now.'

'I'm sorry to hear it,' Grunwald said. He watched the road slip away, seeming to judder beneath the constant reverberations of the truck.

The workshop door was closed. Pushing it open quietly, Schwarzenbach went inside. The truck had gone. Where it had stood there were oil-stains on the floor. He paused a moment listening. There was complete silence. He went towards the door at the other end of the workshop and again he stopped.

He opened the door and found himself in a small kitchen. The boy, Neurer's son, was dozing on the couch, a book open on his lap. Schwarzenbach moved silently.

The boy opened his eyes, startled. 'What are you doing here?'

Schwarzenbach sat down on the couch. 'I'm looking for your father.'

'He's gone. He won't be back for a couple of days.'

Schwarzenbach looked at the concrete floor. Long ago

an attempt had been made to cover it with red varnish. He smiled at the boy. 'I came to ask you father something,' he said.

'What did you want to ask him?'

Schwarzenbach sat back, his head against a cushion. 'He was going to do me a favour, you see.'

'What favour?'

'He was going to take a friend of mine down to Munich.'

'A friend of yours?'

'That's right. A man called Grunwald.'

The boy sat down beside Schwarzenbach. 'They've gone. He took a man with him when he went this morning.'

'A Jew?'

The boy shrugged: 'He might have been. How should I know?'

Schwarzenbach felt a sense of despair. Neurer had betrayed him. There was a sickening feeling of loss. The Jew had eluded him. At this very moment he was on his way south in Neurer's truck. Angry, Schwarzenbach rose from the couch. He wanted to break something, he wanted to take some fragile object and break it between his fingers. He stood in the centre of the room. He flexed his fingers. His mind seemed a flurry of violent colours and shapes. 'When did he leave?'

'A few hours ago,' the boy said and picked up his book.

'A few hours – how many hours?'

'Three,' the boy said.

Schwarzenbach moved across the room and stopped in the doorway. 'Goodbye,' he said.

The boy, engrossed once more in his book, didn't answer.

Neurer said, 'There's a checkpoint about a mile ahead. They always examine my dockets, but they never take the trouble to look at the cargo.'

He stopped the truck and opened the door. He jumped

down into the road and looked both ways. The highway was empty.

'You'll have to get in the back, Grunwald. There's a piece of tarpaulin there. Tuck yourself under that.'

Grunwald stepped down from the cab. His limbs were stiff and sore. Neurer unbolted the panel at the back of the truck and Grunwald clambered inside. He found the tarpaulin and pulled it over himself.

'Lie still and quiet,' Neurer said. 'You won't come to any harm.'

Grunwald lay under the tarpaulin. He had a strong sense of unreality, as if none of this were happening to him. He was detached from himself and quite suddenly indifferent: it did not really matter if he were discovered. The worst that could happen was to be sent back to Berlin. He heard the cab door slam shut and then the truck rattled forward, slowly at first, gathering speed as it moved along the highway.

He listened to the sound of the truck slowing down again. In poor broken German he heard a voice ask for Neurer's papers.

Neurer said, 'All in order, I imagine.'

There was a long silence. He heard footsteps along the side of the truck. He lay perfectly still and repeated to himself that it did not matter if he were discovered, it did not matter if he were discovered.

'Medical supplies?' the voice asked.

'That's right,' Neurer said.

Someone struck the side of the truck. 'All right. Pass on.'

There was a soft, whining sound. The truck lurched forward. He heard Neurer say, 'It's bloody cold.'

The voice came back from a brief distance: 'I've met worse than this.'

Grunwald gripped the tarpaulin as the truck picked up speed. Some minutes later he felt it slow down, and then it stopped entirely. Neurer came round to unbolt the panel and Grunwald pushed the tarpaulin aside.

'Easy,' Neurer said. 'I told you it would be.'

Grunwald returned to the cab. He climbed back into the warmth and watched as Neurer let in the clutch.

'They never ask questions,' Neurer said. 'They're bored to tears. It can't be much fun manning a checkpoint, can it?'

'I suppose not,' Grunwald said.

Outside the highway slipped past quickly. Fields stretched to either side. From time to time he saw workers in the fields or someone dragging a horse across pasture or people pushing hand-carts along the side of the road.

Neurer asked, 'What do you intend to do in Munich?'

'Have a look round,' Grunwald said.

'It was hit quite badly. You know that?'

'I had heard.'

Neurer drove with one hand while he lit a cigarette with the other. 'But they're making progress in patching the place up. All I ever seem to see there are lorries going back and forward with rubble.'

Grunwald was silent. Listening to Neurer brought home to him the destruction of the city.

'They're still rooting out all the old Nazis, of course,' Neurer said. 'That's the sport now. You'd be surprised to hear how readily some of the old Party hacks denounce the Hitler regime.'

'I'm not surprised,' Grunwald said.

Neurer undid the window and spat over the side. 'They're a shower of bastards. All they were ever good at was crawling on their bellies. Well, they're still crawling. Only the masters are different now.' He slapped his hands against the steering-wheel. 'Christ, I'd love to see them suffer for what they did.'

Grunwald looked out of the window. The horizon lay in an autumnal haze like a scene from a rustic painting.

'I'd love to make them suffer,' Neurer said again.

* * *

Schwarzenbach slept for less than an hour and when he woke he still felt tired. The room was cold and he rose quickly, dressed as fast as he could and made coffee in the kitchen. He then put on his overcoat and went downstairs. He found Herr Zollner in his room on the ground floor, toasting some pieces of bread by the gas-fire.

'Herr Doktor, I was just having breakfast – '

Schwarzenbach stood by the open door watching the man fuss with his toast. 'I will have to go away for a few days,' he said.

'Oh? Far?' The caretaker searched for his eyeshade, as though it were an essential part of his dress, and snapped it on around his head.

'No. To Hanover.'

'In this weather,' Herr Zollner said sympathetically. 'It's so cold.'

'I will be gone perhaps three or four days. Conceivably a little longer. It's hard to say.'

'What about your patients?'

'You will tell them that I have had to go away, Herr Zollner. Tell them that Dr Scheunes in the Fansaner-strasse will attend to their needs. Perhaps if you pinned a notice to the door of my apartment – '

'Of course, Herr Doktor. As good as done.'

Schwarzenbach went into the hallway. The caretaker followed him to the outside door.

'I hope your journey isn't a sad one. A funeral or anything like that.'

Schwarzenbach said, 'No. No funeral.'

'So much death,' Herr Zollner said. 'So many people have died – '

'Yes,' Schwarzenbach said.

'I haven't been in Hanover for many years. Before the war it was. I well remember the Markt-Platz. And the Herrenhäuser-Allee. Yes, I well remember Hanover – '

'I'm glad to hear it,' Schwarzenbach said. 'By the way, I have locked my apartment. We wouldn't want any more illegal visitors, would we?'

Schwarzenbach went down the steps into the street, and walked quickly away from the building. In the pocket of his overcoat he had folded a bundle of banknotes, all the money he possessed and that he had hoarded inside his mattress, as if he had known all along that the time would come when he would need it hurriedly. His papers were inside his jacket. He had not thought to take any clothes along: those that he needed he would buy wherever possible.

One thought dominated him: one solitary thought circled again and again through his mind.

PART FOUR

Munich, November 1945

16

It was changed: it was different. He had expected the signs of destruction and the absence of familiar landmarks, and he had anticipated the monstrous heaps of rubble. But there was another change: in spite of the damage he detected an atmosphere that he could describe to himself only as one of freedom. People were starving and the city lay in ruins, and yet he sensed that even if these were terrible burdens worse ones had been finally and thankfully removed. The black uniforms of the SS, the outfits of the *Hitlerjugend*, the swastika flags and streamers – they had been obliterated forever, accidents of history, of no more significance than a casual occurrence.

Neurer had parked the truck and they were standing beside it. Grunwald was silent. He felt strange: there was no sense of familiarity, of having returned to a city where he had lived for most of his life, there was no feeling of having come home. But had he expected that?

Neurer said, 'I want you to have this money.'

'Money?'

Neurer had taken some banknotes from his jacket. 'You'll need it.'

'No, really, you've done enough for me,' Grunwald said.

'How are you going to exist?' Neurer pressed the money into Grunwald's hand. 'That's the money Lutzke gave me. You might as well have it.'

Grunwald stared at the crumpled notes and wished that he could express his gratitude. But Neurer had already opened the cab door and was climbing back into his seat.

'Are you leaving?'

'I still have a delivery to make. And it's a long way back.'

'I can't thank you enough.'

Neurer shrugged. 'Who knows? You might do the same for me some day.' And then, laughing, he pulled the door shut. He started the engine and Grunwald watched as the truck edged slowly forward. At the end of the street it swung to the right and passed out of Grunwald's sight.

Alone, Grunwald experienced a sense of dislocation. Munich. Of all places. Why had he come back to a place where he didn't belong? Did he belong anywhere?

He was in the area around the Hauptbannhof: whole streets had been severely bombed and places he might have recognized no longer existed. People wandered around aimlessly, like sleep-walkers, as if the confusion and chaos that surrounded them were too much to accept at a conscious level. He hesitated, not knowing which way to turn. His immediate impulse was to walk in the direction of Neuhausen. But that would have served no purpose. It was enough to have returned to Munich without also seeking out the very place where he had once lived. Neuhausen and the Hirschgarten, the Steuben-Platz and the Rotkreuz-Platz – did they still exist? Or had they been shattered too in the war?

He felt despair. His indecision seemed to have paralysed him. Which way to turn? Was there anyone left alive he could contact? Did he *want* to contact anybody? Lost, like a child abandoned by its parents, he moved away slowly. Around him Munich seemed like a web spun by a crazy, destructive spider. This was the place where he had been born, where he had worked, lived and married, fathered a child: why then was it so hostile?

The bakery shop behind the Gabelsbergerstrasse was still there although it was closed now. Its windows were dusty and dark and the name – Gerber – which had once been written in gold paint over the doorway had been removed.

He paused in front of it, catching his reflection briefly in the filthy window. Moving forward, he held his hand to the glass and tried to look inside. It was empty so far as he could see. The shelves, streaked with dirt, had been removed from the wall and stacked on top of the counter. He shouldn't have come here: what had he hoped to find anyway? That at least one part of the past was intact? He dropped his hand from the window. No, he should never have come here. For a moment or two he leaned against the wall and realized the sheer futility of it all. Beyond doubt, the Gerbers had been taken. Why should *they* have survived anyway? A sixty-year-old Jewish baker and his wife? They hadn't a chance.

He crossed to the other side of the street: it was just possible to make out the name of Gerber where the gold paint had been removed. Where were they now? Buried in some Polish grave? Perhaps they hadn't even got as far as Poland; perhaps they had died here, in Germany. He went back across the street again and tried the door, which was locked. He rattled the handle hopefully but without success.

As he was turning away he heard a voice from inside.

'Hold your horses. I'm coming.'

It was a man's voice, gruff and unfamiliar. Grunwald waited, suddenly tense. He heard footsteps and then the noise of a bolt being slid back. The door opened a couple of inches. He had never seen the man before. He wore an open waistcoat and was in his shirtsleeves: his clothes looked as if they had been slept in. His spectacles nipped the end of his nose.

'What is it?' the man asked.

'I've made a mistake,' Grunwald said.

'Mistake? I was having a nap, just getting my head down for forty winks – '

'I was looking for somebody.'

'Nobody lives here except me,' the man said. 'Who were you looking for?'

211

'Herr Gerber and his wife,' Grunwald said.

'The old baker?'

'Do you know him?'

The man opened the door wider and scratched at his belly. 'I used to know Herr Gerber slightly. A nodding acquaintance, you might say. But it's years since he lived here. Let me see – I've been here since 1941. It's as long ago as that.'

'Do you know where he is?' Grunwald asked.

The man removed his spectacles. There was a white band at the end of the nose where the spectacles had been pinching.

'I don't know,' he said. 'I've heard that he lives in the Schumannstrasse. At least that's the information I've got – '

'Who told you that?' Grunwald asked.

'Who told me?' The man stroked his face and concentrated a moment. 'Wait, it'll come to me. Yes – it was Frau Heinrich, who used to help out in the bakery before the war. She said that she had heard Herr Gerber was living in the Schumannstrasse. But I couldn't swear to it.'

'Where is the Schumannstrasse?'

'It runs off the Holbeinstrasse,' the man said. 'Are you related to Herr Gerber?'

'I'm his nephew,' Grunwald said.

'Well, I hope you find him,' the man said, looking up and down the street absently. 'I hope he's in good health.'

Grunwald turned away. Was Gerber *really* alive? Or was it simply a rumour? He felt suddenly excited, without knowing why: it was as if the possibility of Gerber being alive somehow created a bridge, a frail link, with the better past. He walked to the end of the Gabelsberger-strasse and paused there, trying to remember his way. It was amazing how quickly one could forget directions that not so long ago were effortlessly brought to mind. He began to hurry, like someone rushing to a death-bed before the sick man expires.

In the Schumannstrasse he realized that he did not have the house number. He stopped the first person he saw, a woman carrying a tattered umbrella. She looked at him curiously when he asked if she knew Herr Gerber: shaking her head, she hurried away. He walked to the end of the street and then, crossing, went down the other side. He had a feeling of quiet panic: what if Gerber didn't live here and he was wasting his energy? What if it were simply a piece of false gossip passed on by Frau Heinrich to the man in the bakery shop? He stopped on the corner: it was suddenly important to see Gerber, to talk to him, to remind himself that once upon a time there had been a different world. Two teenage boys came round the corner.

'Excuse me,' Grunwald said. 'Do you happen to know if a certain Herr Gerber lives in this street?'

The boys looked at one another. 'Couldn't say,' one of them remarked. 'What's he look like?'

Grunwald searched his mind for a description, but it was like fumbling for a forgotten word that seems to lie half-formed in the recesses of the mind. How could he describe Willi? Years had passed and Willi must have changed.

'He's old, over sixty,' he said. But it was hopeless.

One boy said, 'That could describe any of hundreds.'

'I'm sorry. I thought you might know the name.'

He watched the boys go and then he stood for a time on the corner and wondered what to do. If Willi lived in this street then he would find him, he had to find him. But where to begin? How to look? He could go into the houses one by one, he supposed, and ask for Willi, and by a process of elimination find him that way. It was a small street and it wouldn't take him long but the prospect overwhelmed him. Talking to strangers in doorways, knocking on doors, asking the same question endlessly: when he considered this he rejected it – somehow such a course of action seemed in a way to be an exposure of himself. He turned and walked back down the street again and when he reached the opposite corner, the junction with the Geibelstrasse, he crossed to the other side.

A man had emerged from a doorway, an elderly man with a brown paper bag clutched under his arm as if it contained his every possession. When he saw Grunwald approach he tightened his hold on the bag like someone who expects to be accosted by bandits on every street corner.

'I'm looking for a certain Herr Gerber – do you know where I might find him?' Grunwald asked.

The man looked suddenly secretive: 'Why do you want to know?'

'I'm his nephew. I haven't seen him for some time. I'd like very much to get in touch with him – '

'Nephew?' The man put his hand into the bag and brought out a piece of bread which he placed in his mouth and began to chew. 'Are you really his nephew?'

'That's right,' Grunwald said.

'I know where you can find him,' the man said.

'Where?' Grunwald put out his hand to touch the man's sleeve, but he recoiled from the contact.

'Herr Gerber doesn't see many people, you understand. He likes to keep himself to himself. You know what I mean?' The man winked then, like someone betraying a confidence light-heartedly. 'I'm not sure if he'd want to see you – '

'I'm his nephew.'

'That doesn't matter, does it? He likes to live his own life.'

'I'm sure he'd like to see me,' Grunwald said, exasperated.

'Maybe. Maybe not.' The man scrutinized Grunwald for a moment. 'Herr Gerber lives in the top flat of this

214

very building,' he said. 'That's where you'll find him.'

Grunwald moved towards the doorway.

The man said, 'I sometimes play card games with him. It whiles away the hours.'

'Thank you. Thank you,' Grunwald said and went through the door.

He felt Willi's rough hands upon his face as he was clasped towards the other man's body and held tightly against him. When Willi finally stepped back, Grunwald saw that his eyes were watering as if he were about to cry but could not find the capacity to weep. He stepped further back, framing Grunwald, like someone taking a snapshot: his expression was incredulous and yet grateful, in the manner of someone receiving a gift of the very thing he had thought irretrievably lost. He did not speak for some time and Grunwald noticed exactly how much he had changed since their last meeting. He was thinner, yes, but that was to be expected: what Grunwald found difficult to absorb was the nature of the thinness – as if his uncle were suffering from some incurable, wasting disease. His flesh had a certain transparency and his eyes protruded prominently, and his hands – with which he had worked all his life – were hardly more than bones at the ends of his emaciated wrists. His hair, always thick in the past, was now sparse and barely covered his skull.

'Leonhard,' he said in a whisper. 'Leonhard . . .'

Grunwald experienced a confusion of emotion. Seeing Willi again was delightful in itself, but there were so many areas of past experience it would be painful to touch. How could he talk to Willi about Poland? The sheer necessity for secrecy was something that Grunwald already felt had come between them, an invisible thing that would always hold him back from Willi. How could he say to Willi: Look, I am guilty . . . ? It was impossible. Why couldn't he accept the fact that they had both survived and that they were having an unexpected reunion? That should have been easy, and yet Grunwald felt an accumulating sense of desperation, as if he were deliberately depriving Willi of the most important thing of all – the true facts of the last few years.

Willi was still standing in the middle of the room. His arms hung by his side and there crossed his face for a flickering moment a suggestion of some internal pain. But he smiled, raised his arms, and held them there in mid-air in an empty embrace.

'Leonhard,' he said. 'This is impossible. How can this be? I feel that if I close my eyes and open them again you'll have vanished.'

Grunwald held his uncle's hand. 'I've been in Berlin,' he said. 'It isn't very easy, travelling conditions the way they are.'

'Leonhard,' Willi said, and flexed his hand feebly around Grunwald's wrist. 'You will not believe me. But only yesterday I was thinking about you. Only last night. I still have some old photographs and I was looking at them, the way an old man does, ransacking his memory the way an old man does, and I looked at the one taken of you and Martha on your wedding day.'

Not that, Grunwald thought. The old man was already plundering the past insensitively. Couldn't it wait?

'Changed days,' Willi said. 'Changed days, Leonhard.'

'Everything changes,' Grunwald said.

Willi sucked in his breath and shook his head. 'Too many ghosts, far too many ghosts.' He went to his chair and sat down and a renewed expression of disbelief crossed his face. 'I can hardly credit it, Leonhard. After all those years. I made enquiries about you. Do you know that? I filled in a form and told the authorities that I wanted to know what had become of you. I heard nothing, of course. One hears nothing these days. And so I thought that you were dead. I thought you must have been killed.'

Willi smiled palely. He sat for a time in silence, shaking

his head, as if he were pondering the terrible absurdities of life.

'And here you are. My God, I can hardly believe it.'

'I went to the bakery first,' Grunwald said.

'The bakery? They took that away from me in 1941 under one of their silly laws. Aryanization of businesses, they said. They stuck a notice in the window and told me I had to get out. I suppose I was lucky to have it as late as 1941. I used to imagine they had overlooked me, that's what I thought, they'd forgotten about me, tucked away behind the Gabelsbergerstrasse. But they hadn't. They forgot nothing.'

Willi paused. He was perspiring. He rubbed his forehead with the palm of his hand. 'But I was too smart for them in the end. I knew they would arrest me eventually, so I cleared out. What they didn't know was the fact that I had quite a bit of money tucked away in the bakery. I moved around from one place to another, keeping just ahead of them, just out of their reach. Who wants to bother with an old man anyway?'

Grunwald looked at the room. There were one or two items of scrappy furniture: another door, to his right, was partly open and he could see a large brass bed.

'In one way it was lucky that they didn't seize the bakery earlier,' Willi said. 'Alice was ill early in 1941 and she died two weeks before they took the business away.'

'I'm sorry,' Grunwald said. 'I didn't know she was dead.'

'How could you?' Willi made a dismissive gesture with his hand. 'She died painlessly. At least I'm thankful for that.'

Grunwald remembered Alice as a thin little woman who never uttered a word unless it had her husband's complete approval. She lived and died painlessly: her existence had always seemed to Grunwald grey and monotonous.

'So you see, I managed to escape the camps,' Willi said. 'In some ways a great blessing, Leonhard. But in others not. For example, sometimes I think of my old friends, all of whom were taken, and I wonder if I would have been better off if they had taken me as well.'

There was a whine of martyrdom in Willi's voice suddenly. He rubbed his hands together vigorously, as if he were trying to spark some mood of cheerfulness into himself. He turned to Grunwald and said, 'I suppose I've been fortunate, especially when you compare me with all the others. Dead, all of them. I'm the only one left, apart from yourself, Leonhard.'

He smiled to himself and rose uncertainly from the chair.

'It's good to see you, to know that you're alive,' he said, and put his hand on Grunwald's shoulder. Suddenly he was weeping, his face pressed flat against Grunwald's arm, his body moving up and down as he cried. Grunwald led him back to the chair and made him sit down: he didn't know how to cope with the old man's tears. His face was moist and the expression one of complete surrender to pain: Grunwald wished he had a handkerchief to offer.

'Don't upset yourself, Willi,' he said. He clapped the back of Willi's hand comfortingly. After a moment the old man raised his head and tried to smile. He sniffed several times, cleared his throat, wiped his face with his hands.

'I'm sorry, Leonhard. Becoming a bit emotional in old age, that's all.' He smiled again and clutched Grunwald's hand tightly.

After a moment he said, 'So tell me what there is to know about yourself.'

Grunwald hesitated: it was the question he knew would come.

'Nothing,' he said. 'I'd rather not talk about it.'

'As you wish,' Willi said. 'I understand your reluctance.'

Do you? Grunwald wondered. He crossed the room to the window, which overlooked a tiny rear yard stuffed with garbage. What does Willi understand? In the yard a couple of children had appeared and they were sifting impatiently through the rubbish.

'The last I heard of you, Leonhard, was that you had been taken. Nobody knew where. Nobody dared to ask questions.' Willi spread his thin hands, like someone looking for warmth from a source of heat. 'Not knowing, you see, that was the worst thing of all. You were dead. I knew that you were dead.'

Dead? Grunwald turned from the window and looked at his uncle. By a peculiar trick of light, Willi seemed no more substantial than a sheet of flimsy paper. He carried the mark of death upon him, as surely as if he had been mortally wounded by a burst of gunfire: he had the appearance of a corpse. What keeps him alive? What drags him from one day to the next? What is he living for? Grunwald stood by the old man's chair.

'I was in Mauthausen,' he said.

'God help you,' Willi said.

'And then I was in Poland.'

'Poland?' Willi half-rose from his chair: 'What have they done to us, Leonhard? What have they done?'

Grunwald looked at the old man. Years ago he had been energetic, strong, filled with an exuberant sense of life. Now, wasting away, it was as if the earlier man had not existed at all.

'After Poland, I made my way back to Berlin,' Grunwald said.

'And you've been in Berlin ever since?' Willi asked.

'Until now,' Grunwald said: a moment of embarrassment arose, conjured up out of seemingly nothing, as he studied the old man's questioning face and realized that Willi wanted to hear more, he wanted as many details as possible.

There was a slow silence. Cries from the yard below penetrated the room. A child was shouting.

'In Poland,' – Willi said, and then faltered. 'In Poland, were you in one of those death camps?'

Grunwald paused: he felt suddenly conspiratorial.

'I was in one of the extermination camps,' he said.

Willi looked puzzled. 'You were lucky then, you were lucky they didn't exterminate you.'

Grunwald said nothing. He was conscious now of the way his blood seemed to race through him, as if it were frantically trying to elude some impending menace. Lucky? For a moment he wanted to open his mouth and make a confession and tell Willi what he had done to survive the camp and the life he had lived, but he could not bring himself to unlock the nightmare, he could not force himself to cross the fragile line that marked the end of the deception.

'Yes,' he said. 'I was lucky. I was fortunate. They could only exterminate a certain number every day. Working at full capacity, they still didn't have time for everybody.'

Willi sighed. 'There's nothing one can say, is there? It baffles the imagination. It bewilders me. How could they have done it? How could they have murdered so many people? It's strange, isn't it? I never used to think of myself as a Jew. I was always a German, a good German citizen, I have medals from the First War, I never thought of myself as being a Jew. And then they forced me to think of myself in that way. But I used to say to myself that it couldn't happen to me, because I was a German.'

'I know what you mean,' Grunwald said.

'I hate them now. I hate all Germans now.' Willi began to cough and wiped mucus from his lips. 'I'm ashamed of them.'

Grunwald was silent. He walked up and down ·the

room, the feeling that he should never have sought Willi out beginning to grow: everything was changed: a volcano had erupted and everything was dressed in ashes and darkness. He looked down at the ragged children in the yard below. They reminded him of the skinny, taciturn children he had seen in the camps. So much human garbage. So much junk. He pitied himself and the world. There was a tight, jagged sensation in his chest and throat. Sickness everywhere. Something healthy – would he ever see something healthy again? He pressed his face to the glass, aware that Willi was rambling on and on about what had happened to Munich. Knappertsbusch, having been banned by the Nazis, had returned to conduct the Philharmonic: a new newspaper, the *Münchener Stadtanzeiger*, had appeared: *Hansel and Gretel* had been performed in the Prince Regent Theatre: the Rathaus bell was ringing again: it was said that the statue of Patrona Bavariae was to be re-erected in the Marienplatz: ten former inmates of Dachau had been elected to the City Council. But Grunwald was barely listening to these snippets: they were insignificant to him, even if for Willi they were the stuff of his daily life.

'I used to love this city,' Willi said. 'But not now.'

Grunwald turned away from the window. The children were gone. The yard was empty.

He shuffled towards the gas-stove and lit the ring under the kettle.

'You can't get real coffee these days except on the black market,' he said. 'So we use this powdered rubbish. But at least it will heat you up.'

Grunwald watched as the kettle began to boil. Willi took two cups from a wooden cabinet and brewed the coffee. He handed one to Grunwald. The liquid was dark and tasteless. They sat for a time in silence, drinking.

And then Willi said, 'I take it you've heard nothing about Martha and the boy – '

'Nothing,' Grunwald answered. 'It's hopeless. They're dead. I know it for a fact.'

Willi shrugged. 'We mustn't give up hope, Leonhard.'

'Hope?' Grunwald failed to recognize the word: could Willi conceivably have some tiny reserve of optimism even now? It was hardly credible.

'They're dead,' he said. 'I know they're dead.'

Willi sipped his drink. 'You have to look forward, Leonhard. Forward, not back.'

Forward, not back. Grunwald stared at his uncle in surprise. What gave the old man his banal philosophical strength? How had he managed to retain his platitudinous shell in the face of everything?

'What's gone is gone,' Willi said.

Grunwald turned his face away. It was more than he could stand to listen to the old man. Willi got up suddenly and went to the wooden cabinet by the stove. He took out an envelope and returned with it to his chair. Opening the envelope, he produced some photographs.

'Have a look at these,' he said. 'They should cheer you up.'

'Please,' Grunwald said. 'I don't like old pictures – '

'Go on,' Willi said. 'It won't do any harm.'

Grunwald stared at the photographs in the old man's hands with a sensation of mounting horror. Photographs. Pictures of the dead. Snapshots of the damned. He closed his eyes, aware of the inconsistency in the old man's approach. If one were to look forward and not back, what good did it do to scrutinize old photographs? He felt the envelope being pushed into his hands. Opening his eyes he stared at the blurred snapshot that lay in front of him.

'Remember that?' Willi asked, suddenly alive and animated. 'Hilda and Josef in the foreground, you and Martha at the back, and Alice and myself to the one side. 1932. Autumn. That time we all went for the weekend to Josef's cabin at Friedrichshafen. Do you remember that?'

Grunwald looked at the photograph. Her eyes screwed

222

up against the sunlight, a straw hat on her dark hair, a white dress hanging on her loosely, Martha had a frozen appearance. He realized he had forgotten how she had been: the eyes crinkled in that characteristic way of hers, the incongruously large straw hat he had purchased for her in Ravensburg that seemed to eclipse her face, the slight forward thrust of the lips as if she were about to launch into an argument. And then the photograph seemed to melt away as he looked at it and he turned it over: Willi had written on the back the words *Friedrichshafen, 1932*.

'Here's another,' Willi said, and thrust a second picture forward. It showed a group of people sitting in a field in front of an outspread tablecloth that lay across the grass. 'The time we drove down towards Rosenheim for a picnic. Funny, I can't remember the year. It must have been 1931.'

Grunwald studied the photograph closely. He had no recollection of a picnic near Rosenheim and so far as he could see he wasn't amongst the group of people on the grass. But Martha was there, seated at the back, half-hidden. Her head thrown slightly back, she seemed to be laughing about something. But a shadow lay across her face and it was difficult to make out the features. Grunwald held the picture a moment longer, his finger moving across Martha's face as if he were trying to impose reality and texture upon the flat surface of the photograph. Willi should never have produced these snapshots: what good did they do? What was the use of stirring up so much dust? Of producing impossible longings? He pushed the photograph back inside the envelope.

'There's plenty more,' Willi said. 'Look – '

'Not now, Willi. Please.'

'You're tired. You've had a long journey.'

'Yes. I'm tired.'

'Then you must get some rest. You must wash and shave. Get some fresh clothes. We'll have plenty of time

to talk about things, Leonhard. We'll have lots of time.'
He suddenly clutched Grunwald, as if he were afraid of
letting him out of his sight. 'Go into the bedroom and lie
down. Rest for as long as you like. You need it.'

Grunwald went into the bedroom, hardly more than a
boxroom that was crowded by the large brass bed, and
lay down. He pulled the covers over his body. Willi sat on
the edge of the bed a moment. And then, leaning forward,
he pressed his lips against Grunwald's forehead.

He got up from the bed, slightly embarrassed by his
own display of affection, and left the room. Grunwald
watched the door shut and then wiped the moisture from
his forehead with the palm of his hand. He should never
have come: it was more than he could possibly tolerate.

Some hours later he woke and heard the sound of voices
from the other room. For a moment he could not remember where he was. The bed was strange to him and the
room, with its tiny barred window, threw him momentarily off balance. He pushed the covers back and stood
up. Brushing his hair from his face, he went towards the
door. The voices had stopped now. He hesitated a
moment and then pulled the door open.

In the other room Willi was sitting by the gas stove, the
envelope of snapshots still in his hands. At his side there
was a woman: she must have been in her late twenties.
As Grunwald entered, she turned round. Willi rose from
his chair, one arm extended in a greeting. Grunwald
stopped: he had not expected to find a woman there.

Willi said, 'Leonhard – let me introduce you to Fräulein
Strauss.' The woman held out her hand and Grunwald
accepted it. It was curiously cold and as he touched it he
shivered imperceptibly.

'My nephew, Leonhard,' Willi said to the woman. 'I've
just been telling her how you've come back from the
dead, Leonhard.'

'Remarkable,' the woman said. 'Herr Gerber has told

me that he had given up all hope for you.'

Grunwald was embarrassed a little: it was as if his uncle had turned him into some kind of hero. He looked down at the floor. There was something about the woman's eyes. He had the odd sensation that she was mocking him. Was it just his imagination? Was it his guilt? Did he assume automatically that he was transparent?

'It takes great courage and endurance to have survived,' she said.

He looked at her again. It was impossible to be certain, but he had the distinct and uncomfortable feeling that she was subtly trying to provoke him – as if his heroism were a blatant lie that she desperately wanted to puncture. But why did he think this? Why did he imagine hostility in her manner? She was half-smiling, her lips fixed, her eyes cutting into him.

There was a moment of silence and Grunwald found that he could no longer meet the woman's eyes: they were clear and sharp, piercing him in a way that he found troublesome. He turned away and went to the window. It was beginning to get dark and he realized he had no idea of time. Was it late afternoon?

'Let's hope that you can re-establish yourself,' she said.

Re-establish? It was a strange word: clinical and formal. Why had she chosen that? What did she mean?

'Let's hope so,' he said. He wanted to shift the conversation and so he asked: 'Are you a neighbour of my uncle's?'

'A neighbour?' Willi interrupted. 'She's far more than that, Leonhard. She's my lifeline. If it weren't for Elisabeth, God knows what I would do. She fetches things for me because I don't get around very much. She gets my rations. She picks up one or two things on the black market for me. Sometimes she even cooks me a meal – '

'Whenever we can get any decent food, that is,' Fräulein Strauss said. She was leaning now against the wall, her hands clasped in front of her. Her eyes had not moved from Grunwald's face since he had entered the room. She seemed to be scrutinizing him, as if she were seeking the solution to an intricate problem. He turned to look at her, fascinated by her expression. He judged that she was about twenty-eight: she was thin, dark-haired, her eyes a peculiar shade of bright blue. Why was she staring at him? What was it that she wanted to understand?

Willi said, 'Elisabeth is a blessing to me.'

Fräulein Strauss smiled. 'We keep each other company,' she said to Grunwald.

Grunwald felt that he was imprisoned by her gaze: it trapped and encircled him, and yet he could not avoid the suspicion that she was examining him as she might have done any stranger who had survived the holocaust, and who was reluctant – for reasons that she could not obviously fathom – to tell his story. Was that it? Did she want to hear how he had coped with the concentration camps? Was he some sort of novelty for her? He tried to clear his mind: he was imagining things. There was nothing extraordinary in the way she looked at him.

Willi said, 'Elisabeth lives in the room along the corridor.'

Grunwald said, 'Does she?'

'Sometimes she comes in and cleans up.'

'When I have the energy,' Fräulein Strauss said. 'But energy, like any other commodity, is at a premium these days.'

Willi sighed: 'It can't get any worse,' he said. 'Things are getting better all the time.'

They were silent again, as if all three knew that this was a lie. The woman began to move around the room, tidying up here and there in a casual fashion. Grunwald watched her a moment and wondered why she helped Willi: charity, pity. When she had finished, and had put the broom away, she said to Willi; 'It's time for your nap.'

Willi groaned. 'I'm not even tired – '

'No complaints,' she said. 'You know that you need it.'

'You're like a nurse,' Willi said. 'She's just like a nurse.
Leonhard.'

She clapped her hands together briskly. 'Come on.'

'You bully me.'

'You wouldn't look after yourself, would you?' She
helped him out of the chair. Willi was laughing, as if the
whole thing were a joke they played out together every
day at the same time. She led him towards the bedroom.
Grunwald watched the door swing slowly shut and listened to the sounds of Willi climbing into the bed. He
looked around the room. It was neat and tidy now. She
had washed the dirty cups and swept the floor and had
tidied the various papers that lay around, stacking them
neatly on top of the cabinet.

She emerged from the room a minute later, wiping a
strand of hair from her forehead.

'He always sleeps for a few hours at this time of day,'
she said. 'He doesn't want to, but it does him good.'

'He's sick,' Grunwald said. 'He's changed so much.'

She looked at Grunwald a moment, her head tilted to
one side.

'He's dying,' she said. 'It's a wonder he's lived as long
as this.' She was busy again, replacing the photographs
inside the brown envelope.

'What's wrong with him?'

'Cancer,' she answered.

'Christ,' Grunwald sat down: the old man was suffering
from cancer.

'Even if medical treatment was possible, it would do no
good,' she said. 'And he knows it better than anyone.'

'I'm sorry,' Grunwald said. 'To come all this way to see
him, and then to find he's dying – '

'I understand. Everything seems so painful these days.'

She had stopped in the middle of the floor. She looked
sad. Her arms hung by her side listlessly. Staring at her,
Grunwald was conscious of the fact that she was attractive: she was by no means beautiful, but her face – which

227

was intelligent, pale, knowing – suggested something far removed from any mundane concepts of beauty. Had she suffered? The question needed no answer: everyone had suffered.

She said, 'I feel so sorry for him. I like to help as much as I can. It makes it a bit easier for him.'

Grunwald felt like an intruder who has stumbled in on some intense personal grief: he felt clumsy and unhappy.

'I couldn't bear the thought of him dying alone,' she said.

She was standing in a peculiar fashion by the door now, as if yielding to some immense weight. Her shoulders sagged and her face had altered: the features seemed to have become blurred. 'Why don't you sit down?' Grunwald offered her a chair and she accepted.

He went to the window and looked down into the yard at the rear. It was empty now and silent: rain, falling softly, swept across the garbage heaps. He turned to the woman: 'How long will he last?'

'I don't know. A month? Three months? He might die tomorrow. You can see how ill he looks.' She paused a moment, closing her eyes, resting her head against the back of the chair. 'He suffers great pain, although he never says anything about it. He hardly complains. This room – doesn't it smell of death to you?'

Grunwald looked round the room. It was impersonal and cold, as if Willi, in preparation for his death, had discarded almost all of his private possessions.

'What do you do?' he said.

'Do?'

'Do you work?'

'No, I don't work.' She was twisting her fingers together in a tormented way. He was on the point of asking about her war years, when he decided against it. In the failing light she appeared improbably pale and bloodless. There were dark circles under her eyes and tiny lines around the corners of her mouth. What was she thinking?

'What's the time?' he asked.

She held up her bare wrist. 'I don't know.'

'I'd like to take a walk,' he said. 'Will you come?'

He didn't know why he had asked or even why he particularly wanted to walk. The room was stifling him.

'It would make a pleasant change,' she said and she smiled. She rose slowly from the chair. 'I'll get my coat.'

When she went out of the room Grunwald washed his face and hands in the sink, and shaved with Willi's razor. For the first time in months he had noticed that there was a distinct smell – from his flesh, from his clothes – of dirt and staleness. It had never bothered him before but suddenly he wanted to scrub himself clean.

Fräulein Strauss reappeared in the doorway, wearing a navy blue raincoat.

'It isn't very glamorous, is it?'

'It'll keep you dry,' Grunwald said, and watched as she turned round: after a moment he followed.

The Americans had entered Munich on 30th April: they had met no resistance. But the city around them had been flattened by damaging air-raids and Grunwald could see the signs of destruction everywhere. It was a sight he had become accustomed to in Berlin except that now, in Munich, it seemed far more personal, more painful, because these were streets and buildings he had known particularly well. Fräulein Strauss told him that between the summer of 1940 and the end of the war, there had been about a hundred air attacks on the city and that thousands of people had lost their homes. She also told him that someone had painted an inscription on the National Socialist shrine, the Feldherrnhalle, that said: 'Concentration camps of Dachau, Velden, Buchenwald, I am ashamed of being German.'

They walked as far as the Maximilianeum and from there they crossed the river to the Widenmàyerstrasse. The Isar looked strangely green and swollen in the gathering darkness and they stood and looked at it together for some minutes in silence. They went on as far as the Luitpold Bridge where they could see the gardens of the Maximilians-Anlagen. Grunwald felt less and less that he had come home and more and more that he was a morbid tourist exploring the scenic grandeur of destruction.

Fräulein Strauss said, 'People don't have much to eat these days. We have ration cards, but sometimes the rations don't seem to be available. It's terrible. You remember what Munich used to be like and it's terrible when you compare it with that.'

Grunwald watched the river and the rain that fell along its surface. She would have been about fifteen years of age when the National Socialists had come to power, no more than a happy young girl, carefree, perhaps experiencing her first love affair: what had she done when the shadows had begun to fall?

Someone was burning something in the gardens across the river. A few sparks rose up in the air, followed by a bright orange flame. He stared at this and then at the woman. In the reflected glow her face seemed to assume a different shape: her eyes, now blank, were directed inwards. Rain had soaked her hair and flat strands were plastered across her forehead. She looked impossibly young all at once, like a schoolgirl savouring the excitement of her first adult dance.

'What did you do?' he asked.

'What do you mean?' She didn't turn to look at him. Her gaze was fixed in the direction of the bonfire around which the shapes of several people had materialized.

Grunwald was silent. He had no right to ask her anything.

'What did I do in the war? Is that what you mean?'

Grunwald nodded his head. Beneath them a motor launch was going down the river and a man was shouting inaudible words through a loudspeaker.

'I did nothing,' she said. 'Like Herr Gerber, I didn't end up in a camp. I stayed in my room.'

He imagined that she was being flippant. 'I don't understand.'

'I thought you wouldn't.'

'What do you mean?'

'Exactly what I say. I stayed in my room.' She was moving away from him and he followed.

'Which room?'

'Oh – it was just a room.' She seemed to want to tease him now: she appeared to enjoy a sense of being enigmatic. He followed her down the Widenmayerstrasse. She was walking quickly, as if she didn't want him to catch up on her.

'Where was this room?' he asked.

'In a house.' She stopped by the side of the street and looked down at the Isar.

'I still don't understand.'

'Between the Kristallnacht and the surrender of Munich, I didn't leave my room. Does that make sense?' She saw his look of puzzlement. 'I was sheltered. Protected. The people with whom I was living protected me. They brought me food. They concealed me. They put themselves in terrible danger for harbouring a Jewess. But they were opponents of the regime and they considered it an act of Christian charity to hide me and support me. Now do you see what I mean?'

'You must have left the room sometimes,' Grunwald said.

'Never. How could I? It was an attic room with a tiny window that was partially boarded up. It contained a bed. It had primitive lavatory requirements. Twice a day these people brought me something to eat and books to read. They gave me cigarettes to smoke and newspapers so that I could keep in touch with what was going on. Except that the newspapers contained nothing but propaganda lies.'

'I'm not sure that I understand you,' Grunwald said.

'Do you mean to tell me that you didn't go out of doors between November 1938 and April 1945?'

'Six and a half years,' she said. 'I stayed in the room all that time. How could I have left it? That would have involved the betrayal of the people who let me live there.'

Grunwald was astonished: 'But what did you do?'

'Don't you believe me?'

'Yes, I believe you. But what did you do all the time?'

'I told you. I read books. I read everything from Kant to German translations of cowboy novels.' She paused a moment. 'That wasn't enough, of course. I had my fantasies as well. I devised games.'

'What games?'

'Paper games. I created amusements for myself. I devised a complex kind of chequers. I planned the assassination of Hitler. I amused myself.'

She was talking flippantly and Grunwald wondered if she were telling the truth. How was it possible to live for six and a half years in an attic room without going out once? He imagined the murderous strain that such an existence would have imposed upon him.

'It's hard to grasp,' he said.

'It was more pleasant than Dachau,' she said. 'I was able to talk to people twice a day, when they brought my food upstairs. I ate reasonably well. I was bored much of the time, naturally, and I longed for the open fields. I used to dream that the war was over and that someone, a lover perhaps, would come and rescue me. I lived in my mind for six and a half years.'

Grunwald caught her by the arm. 'Are you telling me the truth?'

She didn't answer. Instead, she said, 'You can't imagine how much I longed for fresh air and wide spaces. Every day seemed the same as the one before, except for the fact that the room was getting smaller. It was dwindling around me. It was choking me. I couldn't have survived much longer without going insane. Do you know? When the war ended, when Munich had surrendered to the Americans, I was afraid to step outside and put my foot on the ladder. I was afraid to leave the place. Can you *imagine* that? The one thing I *really* wanted to do, and I was scared to death of doing it. It was incredible.'

Grunwald took his hand from her arm.

'Six and a half years,' Grunwald said. 'Who were these people?'

'A Protestant pastor and his wife whom I had known since I was a child. They took me in after the Kristallnacht. My mother, she was a widow, was burned to death that night. I was alone. I had to turn to someone. And they protected me.'

Grunwald looked down at the Isar. The rain had stopped now, but darkness had fallen over everything. He felt a sudden desire to protect the woman, as if she were a child abandoned in a dark place, but the desire was bound up with the sense of pity that he felt. To touch her would be to contaminate her: she had far more courage than he could ever have possessed.

'I would have gone mad,' he said, and the remark lay between them feebly.

'Would you?' She turned round to face him. 'It's surprising how much strength we find when we're afraid. Don't you think that's true? Didn't you find that?'

Grunwald shrugged. They had now come as far as the Steinsdorfstrasse, which led to the Ludwigsbridge. Rain began again, blowing out of the darkness in a squall.

'Anyway,' she said, 'six and a half years isn't much out of a lifetime, is it?'

People moved through the darkness. Grunwald watched their wretched shapes shift through the shadows of buildings: they had the air of predators in a season of famine. They reached the other side of the river and crossed the Mariahilfplatz. He found that he did not want to talk to her, that he had nothing to say to her, nothing to contribute: he had become surprisingly bitter within

233

himself, as if her courage and stoicism were a deliberate affront to him. But how could he be affronted? He had no sense of his own dignity left, and found something curious in the idea that some people did have dignity: Elisabeth Strauss, for instance, could live with herself comfortably. Thrusting his hands into his overcoat, he suddenly wished that she would go away and take her courage with her. He had never been anything other than a coward, afraid of decision, terrified of action and conflict, scared of death.

They returned in silence to the house in the Schumann-strasse. As they climbed the stairs she asked him if he wanted to come into her room. He followed her inside, saying nothing. It was smaller than Willi's room. In one corner there was a bed upon which lay a pile of freshly laundered clothes. She moved them, placing them neatly inside a chest, and then she sat on the bed.

Looking at Grunwald, she asked: 'Why are you so sad?'

'Am I sad?'

'You have a sad expression.'

Grunwald shrugged: 'Your story has upset me perhaps. I don't know.'

'I'll make coffee. Would you like that?' She filled a pot with water and put it on the gas-stove. She said nothing until the water boiled, and then she passed him a cup. 'You're an unhappy man, Leonhard. Why are you unhappy?'

Grunwald sipped his coffee. He looked at her: her damp hair hung down untidily in thick strands, but her face was shining from the rain. He had an urge to touch her, as if by the very act of laying his fingers upon her face he could understand something of her courage.

'Your experiences have made you unhappy, haven't they?'

'They weren't exactly filled with joy,' he answered.

'You know I didn't mean that.' She looked upset and he realized that his reply must have seemed needlessly sarcastic and bitter. 'Why can't you accept the fact that you are alive? That you have a life to lead? You can't go around in such a miserable – '

'Am I miserable?' Grunwald asked.

'Don't ask me. I can only tell you how you look.' She put her empty cup on the floor and lay across the bed propped up on one elbow. She stared at Grunwald for a time and then she said, 'I know terrible things have happened to everybody. You can't meet anyone nowadays without colliding with some tragedy or another. But they aren't important any longer. Don't you see that? It's history. Life has to be a process of going forward, and forward again.'

'You sound like Willi,' he said.

She threw her head back and laughed: 'Do I sound pompous?'

'Not in the least.'

She had stopped laughing and was looking at Grunwald intently, trying to place him in her mind, attempting to categorize him. She sat up on the edge of the bed, crossing her legs, never taking her eyes from his face. He felt again the sensation he had experienced on first meeting her, that somehow she was trying to cut her way into him, as if it were important to her to discover what lay beyond the façade and inhabited the mind. He found it uncomfortable.

'Plans,' she said. 'People have to make plans nowadays.'

'Do you have plans?'

'A few.'

'Such as?'

'As soon as it can be arranged, I'll go to Palestine. Why should I stay in Germany? It isn't the same for me here any more. Even the language sounds harsh because I can remember what it was used for and the kinds of things people said in German. That's bad, isn't it? That the language should have been poisoned for me forever.' She thought for a moment and then added: 'Do you remember when they used to broadcast Goebbels's speeches? We sat huddled round the radio, shaking our heads. That's when it started for me – the feeling that if the language could become so tainted, then it wouldn't be very long before the people followed in the same direction.'

She seemed suddenly to have become imbued with a new energy. She got up from the bed and walked about the room in a restless way.

'And then they started to burn books. Who could ever forget that? Somehow that was the worst thing of all. When I heard about it, I was shattered. It was unbelievable that people could burn books. The twentieth century! It was incredible. Didn't you feel like that when you heard?'

'I considered it the action of a few hooligans,' Grunwald said, and noticed the look of disappointment that spread across her face.

'How wrong you were,' she said. 'Then Kristallnacht. I'll never forget that as long as I live. We were woken up, it must have been around midnight, people were running through the streets and some were being beaten up on the pavements, and there was this awful smell of burning. I woke up and I remember thinking: They've come to murder us. The building was on fire. I got out of my bedroom. The stairs were blazing. I heard my mother scream. And the awful thing is that I could see her through the flames and I couldn't do a thing about it. She was trapped in her own bedroom, she was screaming, I was screaming, she was wandering up and down in a panic, like a trapped animal, and her nightdress was aflame. After that, she just disappeared.'

'What did you do?'

'I rushed through the fire on to the street and started to run. Buildings were burning. People were lying around covered in blood. A stormtrooper caught hold of me and forced me into a side-street. I struggled and eventually I got away. He didn't bother to chase me. I ran until I reached the house of the Pastor and his wife.'

'And then?'

'Then I knew for certain that the position of the Jews in Germany was hopeless.'

Grunwald looked at his hands and imagined that he must have known the same thing as well: why for God's sake hadn't he acted in time to save himself and his family? If there had ever been an answer to that question, it lay buried now.

'Palestine,' she said. 'That's where I shall go. There isn't any other place on earth I want to go to so badly. I want to get away from all those memories. Wherever I turn nowadays I find that everything in Germany is stale and dead and utterly defeated.'

Stale and dead and utterly defeated. For a moment Grunwald wondered if Palestine could offer him a new chance. He imagined sunlight and dust, blind white buildings sizzling in the heat, endless miles of scrubland. But the images were unreal, related to nothing he had ever seen or could hope to see.

'Do you have plans?' she asked.

'Not especially,' he answered.

'You must. How can you live without grand schemes?'

'How could I live with them?'

She stopped walking around and stood just in front of him. She touched the back of his hand with her fingers. Puzzled, he looked at her, but she was staring at his hands. Folding her fingers, she caught his wrist gently and held it a moment: and then, stooping slightly, she pressed her mouth to the tips of his fingers. He drew his hand away abruptly as if something unbearably hot had been dropped there.

'What's the matter?' she asked.

'It's nothing,' he said. 'Why did you do that?'

'Because I wanted to think you might be happy.'

'You don't know me.'

'I still don't like it if you're miserable.'

'Why did you want to touch me?'

'You seem lonely.'

'For God's sake.'

'It wasn't pity, if that's what you're thinking. You must have a very low opinion of yourself if you suspect people of pitying you.'

He got up from his chair: he had to get out of her room. He went in the direction of the door.

'Are you going?'

'I'm tired.'

'Are you staying with Herr Gerber?'

'For the time being.'

She smiled at him: 'Then we'll meet again tomorrow.'

Closing the door behind him quietly, he left. He stood for some time on the landing, thinking of the woman. He drew his hand from his pocket and stared at it: what had she been trying to tell him? What had her gesture meant? He imagined that he detected in it an expression of humility: she had put her lips to his fingers as a person with incalculable wealth might wash the feet of a beggar.

Willi was still sleeping. The sound of his snoring filled the tiny apartment. Grunwald went into the bedroom and looked at his uncle for a time. Mouth open, arms thrown back behind his head, the old man was breathing with some difficulty. He would be dead before long: and after he was dead, who else would be left?

Grunwald went into the other room and pushed two chairs together and lay uncomfortably between them. Fatigue settled on him like a heavy stone and he fell sharply into an undisturbed sleep.

17

He was fortunate to find a hotel room since – as the manager so hastily pointed out – the world was full of homeless people and soldiers of the Allied victory, and somebody had to provide shelter for them. It was only when he was in the room that Schwarzenbach realized how dangerous it was for him to have come to Munich. People had long memories: a chance acquaintance on the street, a face glimpsed across a room – he might be recognized by almost anyone. And yet he felt that this would not happen. He had changed: he was not the same person who had left this city to journey to Poland. There were his papers, for one thing. And if anybody looked at him curiously, with flickers of recognition, he would say that they were mistaken. His name was Lutzke. He had surrendered to this fact long ago.

The room was miserable and depressing. The chairs were made of gold wicker, dragged out of the hotel ballroom because they were no longer needed. In the corridors of the hotel he saw American soldiers – captains and majors mostly – who occupied an entire wing. He felt contempt for them. When they walked past him, he imagined that they were scrutinizing him closely and coldly. When he saw them in the hotel dining-room where they invariably managed to eat well – certainly better than the few Germans in residence – he was acutely aware of how much he hated them. They laughed, they stuffed themselves, they were insensitive to the state of chaos around them. He wished sometimes that they would leave, go home, vanish forever. The only people who knew how to repair Germany were the Germans themselves: the

Americans and their friends were ignorant of the nature of German life and feelings.

The bed in his room was narrow and had a padded headboard, a luxury from the past. Beside the bed was a telephone that didn't work and above it a lamp that had no bulb. When he turned on the taps of the wash-basin the hot-water faucet gave out a strange rust-coloured liquid that was lukewarm and the cold water one emitted a gushing liquid that he was loath to drink because it carried particles of dirt. The wall by the window was black and charred because there had been a fire in the room at one time. He despised the place and yet he felt secure there. From his window he could look down into the street and see the ruins of buildings across the way: military jeeps – a whole line of them – were parked in the shadows of the ruins.

On his second day in the hotel the chambermaid tried clumsily to seduce him. He found her making the bed as he came in from the lavatory in the corridor, a thin, scraggy girl with tiny breasts. She caught him by the elbow as he walked past, and like someone offering a free sample undid the top button of her blouse. He gazed at her a moment and then turned away.

She asked: 'Why not?'

'You don't interest me.'

'Are you a German?'

'Yes.'

She shook her head: 'I should have known. The Americans are more sociable.'

He watched her a moment longer.

'You don't have to look at me like that,' she said. 'I've got to live somehow.'

She finished making the bed and then she went to the door.

'Wait,' he said. 'Do you want to make some money?'

She paused by the door. 'I'm interested.'

He took some notes from his pocket and passed one to her.

'Can you give me some information?'

'It depends.'

'I want to know a little about the black market in Munich.'

She clenched her hand around the money. 'What do you need?'

He sat down on the bed. 'I have an old revolver from before the war. I want to get rid of it. Do you know of anyone who deals in such commodities?'

'You want to sell it?' She thought for a time. 'I wouldn't have much use for a black market in weapons, would I?'

'Not personally, no.'

'But there is a dealer in the Marienallee, near the Isar. He has a shop there. I don't know the name. But I believe he has a reputation for dealing in almost anything.'

Schwarzenbach gave her some more money. 'Weapons too?'

The girl smiled: 'Perhaps. But I wouldn't know, would I?'

She went out, closing the door quietly behind her.

At the end of his second day – during which he had left his room only once to procure a copy of a scandalous newspaper called the *Süddeutsche Zeitung* (financed, no doubt, by American money) – he felt curiously lethargic, as if he were in a state of suspension and time had ceased to exist. In two days he had accomplished nothing: time had drifted away, he had allowed it to slip through his fingers like worthless grains of dirt. The thought of going out in the broken streets appalled him. He felt that his mind had become a sieve through which important things were allowed to filter and that his purpose in coming to Munich was receding with every second into the past. He stared at the charred wall or at the useless electric lamp for hours on end and sometimes he gazed down into the street in the manner of a man expecting a sensational occurrence. His thoughts drifted out towards the Jew:

how easy would it be to find the Jew? The question tantalized him for a time until he realized, with a detached awareness, that he felt more rational than he had done for many weeks.

The American – a journalist called Peters – said to him in the hotel bar, 'I suppose you feel resentment against us for being here, don't you?'

'Why should I?' Schwarzenbach said. The bar was crowded and Peters had a loud voice that he found slightly embarrassing. He was a big man with a brown moustache that drooped over the corners of his mouth. Incongruously, Schwarzenbach thought, he was wearing a spotted bow-tie that hung from a band of elastic under his collar.

'Well, I guess I would have resented it if your people had invaded the United States. I guess I wouldn't have liked that very much.' Peters was drinking scotch in liberal measures. When Schwarzenbach had asked for beer the barman had told him that there wasn't any: most of the barley these days was being used for bread.

Peters said, 'Would you resent it if you knew we had come here to stay?'

Schwarzenbach looked round the bar. Why did Peters have to talk so noisily? 'I'm not sure if I would,' he said. 'Perhaps it might be better if you did what you have to do, and then clear out.'

'You think so, eh?' Peters prodded Schwarzenbach with the index finger of his right hand. 'You mean you want us to clear out?'

'I didn't say that, did I?'

'It was your tone of voice.'

'Look, that's not what I meant. Perhaps the German nation could protect its own destiny a little better than your people could – '

'That's a laugh. You made a great job of it the last time.'

Peters sipped his drink and indicated to the barman that he wanted another. Schwarzenbach could not help noticing how quickly Peters was served.

'There were mistakes,' Schwarzenbach said.

'That's a joyous understatement.'

'There were errors of judgement – '

'Hey, you're really on the ball.'

Schwarzenbach was silent. Peter's aggressiveness disturbed him. He looked into his scotch and Peters, as if noticing that he had offended Schwarzenbach, clapped him on the shoulders in a friendly manner.

'Don't get sore. This is just a little discussion, that's all. A little democratic discussion.'

'If you say so.'

Peters lit a cigarette with a gold-plated lighter. 'The thing I *really* hate is the way you people have just bowed down. You all seem to have died. You let us walk all over you. You don't have any get-up-and-go qualities about you, do you?'

'What do you expect? A defeated nation – should we have carnivals every night?'

'I'm talking about spirit. There's no spirit left in this whole damn country.'

Schwarzenbach shrugged. He felt uneasy: other faces in the bar were turned in their direction and Peters appeared to enjoy the attention he received.

'Know what I would do in your position?' Peters said. 'I'd get a bit of good old-fashioned resistance going. I'd hand out a few pamphlets: Americans go home. Fuck the Americans! What right have they got to be here? Fuck the war! Let the Germans get on with their own lives.' Peters drew on his cigarette and laughed: 'Instead, you let them take your women, your cars, your hotels, your houses. They've only got to snap their fingers and you people come bowing and scraping. No, it's too easy. You've surrendered everything.'

Schwarzenbach finished his drink. The talk wearied

him. His head was spinning from the effects of the alcohol and from the constant rattle of Peters's voice.

'No offence,' Peters said. He appeared drunk now: his eyes were cracked and bloodshot. 'No offence intended.'

Schwarzenbach was jammed into a corner by Peters and another scotch was thrust into his hand.

Peters said, 'I'm writing an article on the survival of the Jews.'

'Yes?' Schwarzenbach asked, and looked up from his drink. Now there was music somewhere, a recording of someone playing Bach on an organ.

'Maybe you can help.'

'Help? How?'

'You were here during the Hitler period?'

'I was in Germany,' Schwarzenbach said.

'Our readers are interested in what happened to the Jews. Do you know how many Jews there are in New York alone?' Peters smoked another cigarette and frowned slightly: 'Did you see any persecution personally? How did you feel?'

Persecution: it was the most fashionable word of the moment. Everywhere people were screaming about persecution. Schwarzenbach shook his head.

'I saw nothing,' he said.

'Like one of the brass monkeys, eh?' Peters's face vanished a moment behind a cloud of smoke, but the earlier aggression of his manner was present still. 'I don't understand. I talk to people, and I ask them the same questions. But I don't get it: Dachau is about eighteen kilometres outside this city. There's even a street going up that way called the Dachauerstrasse. And yet every damn person I talk to saw nothing, heard nothing, and didn't raise a single fucking whisper – '

'I saw nothing,' Schwarzenbach said again.

'All right. All right. So you saw nothing? Didn't you know what was going on?' Peters stabbed his cigarette forward, as if he meant to burn Schwarzenbach's hand.

'There was a newspaper called the *Völkischer Beobachter*. There was a rag called the *Stürmer* – didn't you ever read those? You can't expect me to believe you didn't read in one of your newspapers of the measures that were being taken?'

'I tended not to read the papers you've mentioned,' Schwarzenbach said, profoundly irritated now.

'So you deliberately took the easy way out, did you?'

'If you mean to ask whether I ignored things, the answer is yes. They weren't interesting me, don't you understand that? So far as I was concerned, the acts perpetrated by the National Socialist regime were undertaken in the name of German strength. I neither agreed nor disagreed. I went about my business. Does that answer your question?'

'I makes me puke,' Peters said. He was leaning for support against the bar, the cigarette stuck between his lips, his eyes half-closed against the smoke that rose upwards from his mouth.

'Then we have nothing more to discuss,' Schwarzenbach said. 'You are prejudiced – '

'I'm disgusted.'

'You are prejudiced because you know nothing of the conditions under which we lived – '

'I'm disgusted. You make me sick. What have you got inside you for a heart? What do you feel? You're a cold bastard, you feel sweet fuck all – '

'I'm sorry,' Schwarzenbach said. 'But I don't think you have a right to express opinions on something you don't have first-hand personal experience of.'

'I visited bloody Dachau!' Peters shouted. 'When I first arrived in this miserable, shitting country I got off the boat at Hamburg and I went to Neuengamme. From there I went to Bergen-Belsen and then to Ravensbruck. No personal experience? No fucking personal experience? You cold-hearted bastard – the things I saw would give you nightmares for the rest of your life. You – and all the others like you – just went about your private business, ignoring everything. Concentration camps? Never heard of them. Jews going to gas chambers? Impossible. Furnaces burning corpses? Uncivilized.'

Peters caught Schwarzenbach by the lapel of his jacket and drew his head down level to his own. He whispered, 'They were using bulldozers to sweep the bodies into mass graves. Did you know that?'

Schwarzenbach shook his head: 'I knew nothing,' he said.

'And you feel nothing?'

Schwarzenbach turned round and walked across the bar.

Peters shouted after him: 'And you *still* feel nothing?'

Schwarzenbach went to the stairs, climbed them slowly, and when he was back in his own room he locked the door and lay across the bed. He was sweating and there was an ache in his head. Peters was a bore, one of the new liberal bores, one of the chroniclers of victory authorized to probe around the ashes for the titillation of his readers. It made him feel sick. He took two pills from his jacket and drew a small amount of the dirty water from the sink. He swallowed both pills quickly.

He stood for a while at the window, looking blankly out at the few lights flickering in the street. Below, he saw Peters stagger out of the hotel and into a waiting car. And then the vehicle had gone. He despised Peters: it was very fine and very noble of the man to preach and criticize and condemn – but his sentiments were hollow. They were soft-centred and somehow indecent. How could the man know? How could he know *anything*?

He woke, fully dressed, in the early hours of the morning. He washed his face in the rust-coloured water and then dried it thoroughly. He felt somehow impatient now, as if conscious of the fact he had wasted too much time staying in the hotel, doing nothing, making no efforts, subjugating the real reason for coming to Munich to his own lethargy. The sense of impatience grew in him and reached proportions of panic. The room was shrinking around him: its bleak walls depressed him and the ancient black and white print of Hindenburg that hung askew over his bed unnerved him. There was no more time to waste. He had to go outside into the streets. Every second that passed had sudden significance: every minute was another point to Eberhard and Spiers in their search for the truth. He imagined that they might have discovered something in his absence: after all, if he had overlooked the medical textbook with his own initials in it, what else might he have forgotten? He searched frantically and hopelessly through his mind. He could think of nothing, yet somehow there were phantoms and shadows that rose in his mental images to disturb him. But he could not identify them: they lay like gaunt clouds shapelessly crossing a landscape.

Behind the Von-der-Tann-Strasse he found the tiny office of the Jewish Agency in a building that looked as if it hadn't been swept or cleaned since the outbreak of war. Dust lay heavily everywhere and the windows were grimy: on the outside wall an attempt had been made to scrub off a swastika painted in white, but the mark was still visible against the grey stone.

In an inner office there were two desks, both occupied by Jewesses. Schwarzenbach took a chair by the desk near the window. The woman who sat behind it was about thirty years of age. She looked at him sympathetically, half smiling. Her attitude reminded him of a doctor's receptionist and he almost expected her to enquire after his health. She picked up a pen from the desk and rolled it between her fingers.

'What can I do for you?' she asked.

'It's very important that I find someone. I imagined you might be able to help.'

'We might,' she said, taking a piece of paper from a scrap-pad.

Schwarzenbach said, 'He's an old friend of mine, you see. A really old friend. And I'm very anxious to know if anything's happened to him.'

'I quite understand,' the woman said. 'Are you Jewish?'

'No, does that matter?'

'But your friend is Jewish,' she said.

'That's right. We were at school together. We were always very close, you understand. Nothing could keep us apart.'

The woman was silent for a time. 'When did you last hear about him?'

Schwarzenbach closed his eyes, as if recalling a painful memory. 'He was taken away. To Poland, I think. I had heard that he was taken in one of those transports to Poland.'

She looked suddenly very efficient. She placed the tip of the pen against the sheet of paper. 'What is his name?'

'Grunwald. Leonhard Grunwald. From Munich.'

She was thoughtful for a moment. 'Will you please stay here until I check our files?' She got up and went behind her and, turning round, Schwarzenbach could see her flick through a filing-cabinet. A moment later she returned.

'I'm afraid we have no record of the whereabouts of the man in question,' she said. 'You must appreciate how difficult it is to keep track.'

'Yes. Yes, I do,' Schwarzenbach said.

'But the name rang some kind of bell,' she said after a pause. 'According to our records, we have another enquiry for a Leonhard Grunwald who used to live in the Wendl-Dietrich-strasse of the Neuhausen district of Munich. Would that be the same Grunwald?'

Schwarzenbach sat forward in his chair. 'That's the one.'

'It may be that the earlier enquirer has some new

information. Sometimes such things happen without us knowing anything about them. People turn up, arrive back in the city, and frequently it happens that we are not informed.'

'This other person – '

She interrupted him: 'I was about to suggest that you contact the other person and see if he has any new information.'

'Yes. Yes. That's a possible idea.' Schwarzenbach put his hands into his pockets: they were perspiring heavily.

'It's worth a try anyway,' she said. 'I'll write the name and address on this piece of paper for you. It's a Herr Willi Gerber who lives in the Schumannstrasse. Grunwald's uncle, according to this form. He was concerned about the fate of his nephew.'

Schwarzenbach accepted the piece of paper, aware that his hands were now not only moist but also shaking noticeably.

The woman said, 'You mustn't build your hopes up too high. It's a long chance. But worth following up.'

He folded the piece of paper into his pocket and stood up.

'How can I thank you?'

She smiled at him: 'There's a donation box as you go out. The organization badly needs capital, both for overheads and for the purpose of raising funds to send displaced Jews to Palestine. If you don't have any money, don't worry about it. If you have any to spare . . .'

'Thank you again,' he said, and turned, walking towards the door.

'Good luck,' she said.

He stepped outside. He could not express the jubilation that he felt. Taking some coins from his pocket, he placed them inside the box and started to go down the stairs. It did not follow that he would find Grunwald at the address in the Schumannstrasse, but at least he had some information. At least, he had a point of departure.

18

Fräulein Strauss had lived in the room in the Schumann-strasse since the end of May. Isolated at the end of a corridor, but still sufficiently near to Willi Gerber's rooms for her to feel confident of reaching him quickly in an emergency, it suited her and she felt fortunate that at a time when there were so many homeless people and thousands of refugees living in bombed-out cellars she had a place of her own. By any pre-war standards it was inadequate: dampness, a faulty gas supply that lived an irregular existence of its own, a lack of carpeting and loose floorboards by the window – these had ceased to irritate her. She was thankful instead, accepting the room's faults as one might the flaws in the emotional structure of a much-loved person. It sometimes surprised her she was not claustrophobic, remembering her life in Pastor Neumann's house and the endless days she spent in the attic.

There were a couple of prints on the wall that she had found by accident amongst a pile of rubbish being cleared from a derelict house. One depicted the Old Rathaus on the east side of the Marienplatz; the other the Café Helbig in the Hofgarten. Both reminded her of more pleasant times and there were occasions when she would stare at the prints and be unconscious of time passing. Yet at other times she was acutely aware of how her life seemed to be slipping away while she chased it, finding it as elusive as her own shadow, pursuing it foolishly as one might chase the wind. With this disturbing awareness came another scrap of self-knowledge: that in Germany her own life was an impossible concept, something she could neither envisage nor imagine, like some creature out of mythology. Leaving Germany was the only important thing now. Obtaining information on Palestine, enquiring about the possibility of making the voyage and the chances of establishing herself there, these were her preoccupations. But it wasn't easy: the more she pursued Palestine the further it appeared to recede, like a piece of seaweed being sucked back by the tide.

Much of her time was given to caring for Willi Gerber. He was pathetic, sick, dying, and yet she did not help him for those reasons. Rather she helped him in the manner of someone labouring under a debt of great gratitude. She owed him nothing, certainly, in the sense that she had never received gifts from him that she felt bound to repay: instead, in some oblique way, she felt that she was somehow clearing off certain moral arrears – the six and a half years, perhaps, when she had been protected by Pastor Neumann and his wife. She was giving as much back as she possibly could. If Willi Gerber were to survive for as long as six and a half years – even longer – she knew that she would still be there to look after him. Because of this responsibility her dreams were continually being shoved back and away from her and there were days when she felt that she might never see Palestine. But it remained, it persisted, a mirage that sustained her.

She never thought of the war years nor of the years of terror and persecution before that. They lay firmly embedded in the past, sometimes dancing across her memories as an image might flit across a mirror: but for the most part these were disjointed recollections and were therefore irrelevant. What did it matter to her now if she might recall her own tears and awareness of isolation when she discovered that she could no longer sit in the same classroom as her friends? Or when she observed stormtroopers marching under their anti-semitic banners? Or when she was accused of putting Christ to death and had therefore to expect punishment? None of these mattered. If they surfaced in her mind at all, they did so at a level where they entailed no painfulness. Part of her had always been conscious of anti-semitism anyway and she had accepted it as a fact of nature: some people, for irrational reasons, hated the Jews. When she saw it grow, when she saw what it had led to and the dark corridors of misery down which it prowled, she had given up hope but she had never accepted despair – which she could not allow was a part of the human condition. Bonfires of books, her mother's death, everything engulfed by flame – all of this seemed unreal now, acts perpetrated in some mythical past. Her six and a half years in Pastor Neumann's attic were also a blur: the days were sucked one into the other and every day was the same as the one before. The world was static and dreary. But out of all this she had constructed – if not a sense of joy – then at least a realization that nothing could ever be as bad again. The thought made her happy. When the war ended, and she had taken her first tentative step on the ladder down from the attic, helped by the pastor and his wife, it was as if a happy silence had suddenly descended on the world. No guns. No noise of bombs and anti-aircraft fire. No more destruction. And when she had looked round Munich for the first time since the Kristallnacht, she knew that there could never be any more destruction. Peace: the battling nations had stopped, and like infinitely tired men, had closed their eyes to sleep. She had looked at the battered houses and the homeless, gaunt faces and she wondered at the fact that she had managed to survive it all. Like a child discovering the seasons for the first time, she had wanted to run and leap and clap her hands and say: I know, I understand now. But to have done so would have been tantamount to laughing at somebody's funeral. *She* had survived, but beneath the ruins and buried crudely in the rubble there were thousands of dead.

Forgetting the past, or suppressing it because it was no longer significant, tending to Willi Gerber's small demands in the knowledge that one day soon the demands would cease, she had created a kind of life for herself. The room was an anchor. She had things to do. She had plans to make. There were dreams she had to mould into the substance of reality. And with all this had come a certain contentment and peace of mind.

Why then had the sight of Leonhard Grunwald shattered all this?

The sick, the maimed, the homeless, the hungry, the returned survivors of the death camps – she had seen them all at one time or another. They were the intrinsic personae of the new world, mutants, the grotesques spewed up by the war. But Grunwald was different in a way she could not entirely fathom. He was thin and weary and lost, all of which were predictable. He was afraid and his life revolved around his fear – how could she expect otherwise? None of these things about Grunwald surprised her and yet the sight of him, the awareness of him, had suddenly upset the delicate balance of her life.

At first, as if she had had a sudden attack of dizziness, she had attributed his difference to the workings of her own imagination and allowed the matter to settle there. But the feeling of strangeness persisted. She could not get close to him, she could not understand him, she could not see in his expression any betrayal of what he was really feeling. She felt like a nurse trying to take a fevered patient's temperature with a broken thermometer: he frustrated her because he remained constantly detached, as if he were outside himself, circling and wheeling around the real nature of his own existence like a bird of prey surveying a small, dying animal.

To get near him she had kissed his fingers, a futile gesture that seemed to express her own failings. Why had she done that? He accused her of pitying him and although she denied it, she knew it was partly true. But it was a pity of a kind she had never felt before. Pressing her mouth to his hand had been like some numb conversation, a language of signs, a way of breaking down barriers. Yet he remained aloof, afraid of speech, perhaps even afraid of her affection. And this strangeness had disturbed her: it had become a kind of light that suddenly threw into relief the inadequacies of her own life. All because of Grunwald and the impossibility of getting near to him. All because of the expression she had glimpsed in his face – a concentration of pain – when they had been looking at the bonfire in the Maximilians-Anlagen. For a second the expression had terrified her. And then she felt that she wanted to understand it, she wanted – if such a thing were possible – to get inside it and see it from a different point of view. What had been going through his mind? What was going through it now?'

That morning, after his first night in Munich, he had come to her room dressed in some of Willi's clothes. For a long time he stood in the doorway, as if afraid of entering her room properly, and said nothing. Staring at him, she resolved not to speak until he did.

After some moments he said, 'I want to apologize to you.'

'Oh? Why?' She held her breath, for some reason very tense.

'I was abrupt last night.' He turned his hands over and looked at them.

'Don't apologize,' she said. 'There's no need.'

'Please let me say I'm sorry.'

'Well, you've said it. Are you happier now?'

He didn't answer. Wanting for some reason to justify herself, she said, 'It was impetuous. I should apologize to you. I don't normally behave that way.'

'Don't you?'

She shook her head: 'I just felt – and still feel – that something is troubling you. I wanted you to smile. I did what I did because I imagined it might make you feel happier.'

He gazed at the window, recalling something. 'You find me cold, don't you?'

'A little.'

He put his hands into his jacket, as if they were the offensive objects under discussion. 'It's a long time since I've been in the world of living people,' he said.

'I understand,' she said.

'That's all I want to say.'

She found his sudden relapse into silence unnerving. To break it, she laughed. 'Look don't you think we're making something out of nothing? It was an innocent gesture. It wasn't a prelude to my seducing you. I didn't intend that – '

'No, of course not.' He turned away from her. 'I didn't imagine that for a moment.'

When he had gone she sat on the bed for a time staring at the vacant space in the doorway. Her mind had become blank. She didn't know why she had acted as she had done. She didn't know why her inability to pin him down or communicate with him should leave her so puzzled. There were many people with whom she couldn't communicate and yet they never troubled her. But Grunwald did. Grunwald troubled her. She shrugged the thought aside and a little later she went out. The room had become suddenly narrow and restricting.

On the morning of his third day in Willi's small apartment, Willi said to Grunwald, 'You must think of making a new life for yourself. You have been given a chance.'

Grunwald looked at his uncle curiously: a chance of what?

Willi said, 'I've never been a religious man, Leonhard. You know that. I haven't been a *bad* man, at least I don't think so, but I was never one for the claptrap of worship or prayer. But it strikes me that if you have survived death, God must want you to go on living. He must want you to make something of your life.'

Grunwald was standing facing his uncle. It was odd to hear the old man talk as if he were a child again: the implicit acceptance of God's will, the blind acknowledgement of inscrutable cosmic purpose. Momentarily Grunwald was embarrassed and then he realized that the prospect of death had caused in his uncle a mental regression of some kind, a clawing backwards at old and forgotten values.

'God has spared you. You must accept that gift,' Willi said. Because a cloud had crossed the watery morning sun the room became suddenly dark. Grunwald walked back and forth. His own religious faith in the past had been a matter of convenience: a social club that he visited frequently. Gradually what little belief there was had dwindled to the point of non-existence. Rejection of faith took place at an emotional level. Religion had perished somewhere between the ghetto and the crematorium: it had died piece by piece with every crystal of Zyklon B and with every new corpse shovelled out of the gas chambers; it had been demolished in anger and sorrow, fear and disbelief.

'You have been spared, Leonhard. Grasp it with both hands.' Willi, fingers clenched together, looked at Grunwald with his head to the one side, awaiting a reaction.

'What are you suggesting, Willi?'

'I'm not suggesting anything,' Willi said. 'But you are not an old man. And the ruins won't last forever. Someday you'll want to make a new life for yourself.'

'Possibly,' Grunwald said.

'Possibly? Possibly? Is that all you can say?'

Grunwald was silent. Truth was like a fragile article in a shuttered and darkened room: if you brought it out into the light it perished. He wanted to tell Willi about Chelmno but there weren't the words to describe what he had seen and done.

Willi said, 'Fräulein Strauss, for instance – '

'What about her?'

256

'All right, I'm an old man, it's no business of mine. I know that. But she's a nice girl. You could do far worse for yourself. She's been like a saint to me.'

Grunwald stopped by the window and turned round to look at Willi. The old man was sitting hunched in his chair, silent now, seemingly engrossed in his own thoughts.

'Are you matchmaking, Willi?'

'Matchmaking? Me? Don't be foolish.'

'It sounds that way to me.'

Willi shook his head. 'Look, you're lonely. She's lonely. What could be more natural?'

'More natural than what?' Grunwald asked.

'You and her getting to know one another better. That's all.'

Grunwald thought for a moment of the absurdity of his uncle's suggestion. It *was* absurd. A relationship with a woman was far from his mind and besides if such a thing were to happen in connection with Elisabeth Strauss, how could he live with the knowledge that she was stronger than he was? He felt inexplicably feeble for a moment, drained of his energy.

Willi said, 'Forget it. Forget what I've said. Put it out of your mind. It's none of my business whether you start afresh or not. It's got nothing to do with me.'

Grunwald answered: 'I appreciate your concern.'

In the early evening, just as it was beginning to get dark, he went walking with her in the direction of Schwabing. It had been her idea and he had complied reluctantly. For a long time they walked in silence along the Widenmayerstrasse, turning down the Prinzregentenstrasse and past the Englischer Garten. It had turned cold and the darkness was falling imperceptibly, and as it fell it seemed to accentuate the forlorn appearance of the streets and buildings around them. She had said nothing so far and he wondered what was going through her mind. Her silence seemed potentially explosive, as if she were gathering herself together to say something of profound importance. As they walked, time and again they passed squads of American soldiers and trucks parked along the sides of the streets. It was all vaguely unreal: it was as if – having inflicted such damage on the city themselves – they had come as interested spectators intent on assessing the extent of the wreckage.

There were crowds of people on the Ludwigstrasse, which led up to Schwabing. She seemed suddenly alarmed to see so many people and she held his arm tightly, looking for comfort and safety. They passed beneath the Siegestor and into the Leopoldstrasse, and from there they walked down darkened side-streets. In the Giselastrasse she said, 'There used to be a restaurant here. My mother and I used to come up this way about once a month and eat here. Do you remember Schwabing then?'

'I remember,' he answered.

She was silent again. Schwabing had had enormous gaiety for her. Here, more than anywhere else in Munich, she had felt alive. She remembered music in the restaurants and beerhalls, tables on the streets, lights and sound, dancing everywhere. Interesting and intense people argued over their beers and thumped the tables and made passionate speeches in front of any audience that would listen.

A solitary street lamp burned at the corner. They stood beneath it and for some reason Grunwald said, 'Willi thinks we should get to know each other better.'

She turned her face away. 'Does he?'

'That's what he said.'

'And what do you think?'

Grunwald shrugged. He was being distant again. She felt him drift away from her.

'Don't you think anything?' she asked.

What did she expect him to think? He looked up at the

258

pale light from the street lamp. He was conscious of noises around him, as if through the darkness people were scurrying silently away to secret conventions. She was staring at him and he felt nervous. Why did she have this effect upon him?

'You don't have to say anything,' she said. 'You don't have to be forced into talking.'

From the expression on his face, she tried to enter his thoughts. But it was hopeless. He was surrounded by barbed wire. For a moment she held his hand between her own and was surprised at the icy feel of his flesh. Why was he so cold?

'You're freezing,' she said.

He took his hand away. What was the point? He had to protect himself: to drift into a relationship with her would ultimately entail having to tell her the truth, and he couldn't face the prospect. He stared at her face. Her expression was expectant, but more than that she looked as though she were prepared to wait, with infinite patience, for as long as it was necessary.

'You're strange,' she said.

'Am I?'

'If you were a house, you would be haunted.'

'Willi's a fool. His mind is going.'

She didn't want to talk about Willi. She felt that time had become concentrated on a single pinpoint, that the time they had between them was already dying: why waste it talking about Willi? But she didn't understand the sensations she experienced. Why should there be a sense of urgency? And why in any case should she allow Grunwald to affect her?

He said, 'Elisabeth, what's the point?'

'The point in what?'

'You're always asking for definitions.'

'The point in what?' she asked again.

He didn't answer her question and she felt that she was

on the edge of losing something: but it was a peculiar sense of loss – as if she had never possessed the missing object in the first place.

'For God's sake,' she said. 'What's wrong with you?'

He shook his head. They moved away together from the circle of lamplight.

'I don't know what it is,' she said. 'I don't understand you. Ever since I saw you I've *wanted* to understand you. I've wanted to get inside your head. Oh, Christ, does that make sense?'

'Not really,' he said. He wondered why he couldn't find it in himself to say something warm, something that would make her smile.

'I can't *talk* to you. I don't get *through* to you.' She felt conscious of her own desperation. The world had become focused on this single thing: getting through to him.

'Why do you want to? Why do you want to?'

She looked at him vacantly. Why couldn't she find an answer to that? 'I don't know,' she said. 'I wish I did.'

He felt unaccountably sad all at once. He sensed her despair and knew that he couldn't help her. They began to walk again, a fresh silence constructed around them. They reached an area that had been heavily bombed, where the houses had been crushed into the ground. Even though it was dark the job of clearing the rubble was still going on. Arclights had been erected and they burned against the shadows of the men who were piling the shattered concrete into trucks. Around the lamps were other people, idly watching what was taking place because they had nowhere else to go and nothing to do. More victims, Elisabeth thought: everywhere she turned she experienced the brutal wounds of the age.

'I don't like looking at this,' she said to Grunwald.

Grunwald hesitated. One of the clearance workers had cried out and several of his colleagues moved across slowly to the place where he stood. They grouped together and looked down at something in the rubble.

After some moments they pulled out the body of a man and dragged him towards the trucks. Elisabeth noticed his face as he came into the direct glare of the lights. It was expressionless and grey: congealed blood covered his skull and ears and she thought that one of his hands was missing. The corpse was dumped beside one of the trucks and a blanket thrown across it.

'Let's go,' she said.

She started to walk away and Grunwald followed her. He thought of the dead baby he had discovered in the ruins of Berlin months ago. He thought of the cold blue lips and the shut eyes. Catching the woman by the arm, he said, 'I'm sorry that you saw it.'

'It doesn't matter,' she said.

She was shivering. Again a feeling of sadness overwhelmed him. He was still holding her arm and he tightened his grip. Her softness surprised him. He had forgotten how soft it could be to touch another person.

She turned to him: 'Don't ask me for an explanation, please. But all I want to do is to get near to you.'

'Why? Tell me why.'

'No explanations.'

'What do you mean by near?'

'Don't you know?'

She was staring at him. He said, 'I used to know.'

'Then you must try to remember.'

They had reached the Luitpold Bridge where for a moment they stopped. Looking at his face, she was surprised by its thinness, by the way the cheekbones were high and seemed to protrude and the eyes were sunken and distant. She put her hand to his face and left it there a second, as if she were trying to transmit a message to him that could not be conveyed in words. He thought of the corpse that had been disinterred from the rubble and of the arclights burning mercilessly in its face: he imagined that death was nothing more than the absence of expression – was that what he had been afraid of?

Conscious of the woman's hand against his cheek, he experienced a sense of sorrow: it was as if he knew that he was destined forever to be trapped inside himself with no possibility of release, no chance of freedom.

'You're cold. Your skin's like ice,' she said, aware that he was slipping away from her again. She wanted to hold him, to hold his face tightly against her body and to possess him, as if the mere act of possession would entail the knowledge that she was seeking. Yet she could not overcome the feeling that he was a stranger, growing outwards with every minute that passed in a direction she could not possibly follow.

They crossed the Isar. She said, 'Willi told me you were married once.'

He said nothing: the bare fact – stated like that – might have been an entry in an encyclopaedia.

'Let me ask you something,' she said, and then paused for a time. 'Do you still love your wife?'

'Do I love her memory?'

'Yes. Perhaps that's what I mean.' She waited for his answer. It was suddenly important to know if all his emotions had been buried in the past.

'I can't honestly remember,' he said. 'I had forgotten her face until Willi showed me an old photograph. I remember now what she looked like. But I don't recall anything else.'

'Don't you remember how you felt?'

'No.'

'Do you have any feeling left?' Why did it always seem that she was interrogating him? Questions and questions: she wished that she could stop asking them and accept Grunwald on his own terms. Each question he answered seemed to cause him pain, seemed to expose yet another area of agonizing sensitivity. She thought of herself: an impoverished Jewess in the shabby wreckage of what had once been Munich. Well, unlike Grunwald, she at least had feelings left even if they baffled and perplexed her.

She was alive, she was aware of each new mood and sensation that passed through her mind, conscious of her own body and the nerves and pulses that operated every time she performed a simple physical act. This was what war had done: it had created for her a penetrating new awareness of herself as an entity in the world. Suddenly she wished that she could get some of this feeling across to Grunwald. If she could shake him, change him, erase from his mind whatever memories remained there and reconstruct him afresh. And then she realized this was impossible. Whatever it was that haunted him could only be exorcized by him. She was powerless to act, she was weak and useless: she felt like a sea-wall that can no longer contain the force of a tide.

'You don't need to answer my question,' she said. 'It doesn't matter. It's none of my business.'

'I don't know how to answer your question,' he said. 'So even if I wanted to, I wouldn't be able.'

'I shouldn't have asked,' she said.

'You can ask whatever you want,' he answered.

'Are there such things as unanswerable questions?'

They had reached the Schumannstrasse and they paused on the corner. She reached out and took his hand and held it a moment: momentarily she wondered if the only thing she could offer him was a fragment of hope. The little she knew of his past had created an overwhelming impression of darkness in her mind. Against that, could she give him something to hope for? A transfusion of optimism?

They entered the building and climbed the stairs. She found that she was breathing heavily and perspiring as if in anticipation of some momentous event. What could she do? If she wanted to offer him hope, if she wanted to reach the foundations of his despair, what could she do?

He followed Elisabeth into her room. She looked nervous and uneasy. Her eyes had dark circles beneath them and her flesh was pale. She sat down on the edge of the bed and clasped her hands together. The feeling of ridiculousness had not left her. Why did she think she could offer this man some salvation? Why did she even *want* to? Could this be the extent of her pity?

She had never had a lover in her life. The fact of her virginity sometimes startled her. It surprised her now. She wanted Grunwald to have her body and yet she felt curiously detached from the possibility. She imagined him lying across her, his breath against her face, his eyes open. Her own lack of experience frightened her suddenly. But nothing was going to happen anyway. Nothing was going to take place. He wasn't interested, she could tell that he wasn't interested in her body. He was standing by the sink, gazing at the print of the Café Helbig that hung beside the mirror.

'Do you want some coffee?' she asked.

'I'm not thirsty,' he said.

'Come over here. Sit beside me.'

He moved towards the bed and sat down beside her. She reached for his hand and took it, pressing it tightly in her own.

'What do you want from me?' he asked.

'I could ask the same question of you.' His face: how could she erase the sufering that seemed to have been inscribed upon his face?

She waited a moment. She felt stiff and tense. 'Do you want to sleep with me?'

'Why do you ask?' When he saw that she wasn't going to answer, he said, 'Do you want me to?'

'I think so,' she said. 'I think I do.'

He shook his head. 'It's hopeless. Can't you see that?'

'What's hopeless? What is it, Leonhard?'

'Involvement. Why should we become involved with one another?'

'Leonhard, what is it? Why can't you tell me what's troubling you?'

He got up from the bed. Looking round the tiny room,

he realized that she had created a life for herself. All the incongruous trappings of normality were evident: the clothes that lay on top of the wooden cabinet, the framed photograph of a woman who was possibly her mother, the prints on the walls, the toilet items neatly arranged on a ledge beside the sink, two pots hanging from nails, the kettle on the gas-stove. This was her life: how could he contaminate it?

'Shall I tell you something?' she asked. 'I've never had a man. A lover, I mean. I don't know why I feel slightly ashamed of the fact, but I do. I had boy-friends in the past, but never a lover. Some of them were kind, and nice, but there was none of them I ever particularly desired. Do you suppose I was saving myself for you?'

He turned to look at her: 'You're imagining things. You're playing games, Elisabeth. It's understandable. You're lonely. You want to construct love out of nothing but the pity you feel for me.'

'That isn't true. It just isn't true.'

'It has to be true,' he said.

'Christ – it's not true. Not in any way.' She rose from the bed, suddenly feeling that she had humiliated herself. Her mind was turning over and over in a bewildered way. 'Leonhard, please listen to me. I can't explain what I feel about you, or even why I feel it. All I know is that I don't want you to reject me like this. I'm not playing games, I'm not imagining things. I swear to you that I'm not.'

She had followed him to the window. She felt that somehow she was begging now, imploring him to give at least something of himself. And the more she begged, the more exposed she felt and the further away she seemed to drive him.

'I don't want anything from you,' he said.

She placed her hands on his shoulders and made him turn round to face her. 'Please, Leonhard, why won't you accept what I've offered?'

'Because I don't want anything from you.'

In despair, she turned away from him. He saw her expression in the mirror and wanted to go towards her and somehow explain why he behaved as he did. But he didn't move.

She said, 'Will you leave me alone now?'

She sat down on the bed and stared at her hands. How could he be so hurtful? How could he cause so much pain to her? And then she considered herself and thought it stupid that she had offered her body as if it were a meaningless thing.

He put his hand out and touched her hair lightly. 'You're a good person.'

'What has that got to do with anything?' she asked.

'You're a better person than I could ever hope to be.'

'Does that matter? Does goodness matter?'

He lowered his hand from her head: 'It matters to me.'

'I don't understand you,' she said. What was he trying to tell her? What was he trying to say?

'Don't you?'

'For God's sake, of course I don't understand you. You talk in riddles. Why am I any better than you? What does that *mean*?'

'It's a question of courage,' he said. There was a silence: he wanted to say nothing more. He wanted the puzzle to remain. She got up from the bed and stood for a time, head bowed, in the middle of the floor. Then, as if she wanted to occupy herself, she started to rearrange the clothes that lay on top of the cabinet. She became tired of this and threw them aside.

'A question of courage,' she said. 'What does that mean? I can't think what it might mean. You must have more courage than me, Leonhard. You survived the camps. All I ever did was to hide away like a coward. How can you possibly have any less courage than me?'

He shrugged. Everything seemed to melt backwards into the past, dissolving like hot wax only to assume more monstrous shapes later. He hated himself. He thought with disgust of his life and the contrast between himself and Fräulein Strauss. He imagined that to touch her would cause her skin to burn, as if he carried in the tips of his fingers some fatal germ.

'Aren't you going to answer me?' she asked.

'There's nothing left to say.'

'I can't say that I love you,' she said. 'I don't know what love is, and I don't know how to recognize it.'

'I don't want you to say that,' he answered, awkwardly aware of her nearness.

She stepped back from him. It was true: love was unrecognizable. It was as if her emotions had lain dormant for so many years that she could no longer be sure of what she felt. She pushed her hair away from her face, conscious of the way he was staring at her. What was he thinking now?

She dropped her hands to her side. 'I don't know what I feel.' She smiled at him: 'I think we've all been robbed of our emotional vocabulary.'

She sat down on the bed and watched him. He was like a nervous adolescent, standing there in the centre of the room as if uncertain about what to say or do next. He pushed his hands into the pockets of his overcoat and she noticed a gash in the material that ran for about six inches from the hem of the pocket down.

'Your coat's torn,' she said.

'Is it?'

'Let me stitch it for you.'

'It doesn't matter.'

'Why not?'

'My appearance doesn't matter.'

'For God's sake.' He wouldn't allow her to do anything: he wanted to remain private, locked up in himself.

'It's an old coat,' he said: he had taken it from the corpse of a Polish peasant he had stumbled over in a muddy field.

'Just the same, I could repair it for you.'

267

Why was she fussing so much about the coat? He felt irritated.

'It doesn't matter.'

'I'm sorry. I'd forgotten. Nothing matters to you, does it? It doesn't matter if you live or die, does it?'

A feeling of frustration rose inside her, as if she had just realized that he was hollow and empty and that the enigma she was trying to explore was merely a thing of her own making. Seated on the bed, he looked forlorn and abandoned, adrift from the objects around him. In spite of herself she wanted to reach for him and protect him against whatever it was that threatened him.

'Leonhard,' she said whispering.

He raised his face to look at her. She approached the bed.

She repeated his name a second time. Then, moving slowly, she sat on the bed beside him: she was conscious of the space that existed between them. She wondered about his life: what had his marriage been like? Willi had told her that there had been a child, Hugo, and that both mother and son had been taken away one day to an unknown destination. What had Grunwald's wife been like? She fumbled for some understanding. Was it because of some desperate loyalty to his wife's memory that he remained so detached? Was it because he did not want to betray her, even in death? These questions seemed to emphasize not only how little she knew about Grunwald, but how small her own understanding of herself was: and she had been blind enough to think that survival had brought a sharp, new self-awareness! There were elements of her own nature hidden away from her, parts of her that defied analysis. She was groping in a darkened room, stumbling against things, breaking things apart: a blind, blind person. She moved nearer to him, noticing that he was now motionless as if any sign of movement would consistute encouragement to her. She put out her hand to touch him and then she froze. She did not think she could stand to be rejected again. She tried to imagine that she was someone else, another person, the sort of person endowed with enough emotional equipment to absorb rejection. The kind of woman who was not afraid of making approaches to a man. She saw nothing in his eyes, a blankness, as if he had vacated himself and the man in front of her were an illusion. She did not know what she wanted from him, or what he was prepared to offer, but her mind wheeled again and again around the prospect of shattering his privacy, breaking the walls down, entering him and knowing him and understanding his existence.

Love – could love flourish in the space of forty-eight hours? She was ignorant of passion and what she knew she had simply reconstructed from love stories of her teenage years when men and women whispered undying devotion and unending faithfulness, and held hands and clasped bodies in firelit rooms, or expressed their feelings with glances and secret signs in fashionable restaurants. It had all been so correct, stiff and clinical. There was nothing of sweat or fear. Heroines trembled, but only in anticipation of the perfect orgasm induced by the perfect lover. There was nothing of undressing, or undoing laces or clips or buttons, because clothes disappeared miraculously as if they had never existed. She remembered all this and wondered if it could be like that, and then realized that such a thing was impossible. She was dealing with a substance that had never materialized in books – reality. The man beside her on the bed was real, she could smell him, touch him, fall against him, and because he was real she was trembling. She moved her hand against him and waited, conscious, incongruously conscious, of the rent in his coat. Her mind was racing ahead of itself, shifting this way and that: what did she want from him? what did she really feel? how could she isolate and categorize her feelings? Six and a half years in one room had ossified her and when she recalled the time and the days crawling one after the other like snails in some grotesque race she was amazed, staggered that she could have survived so long. I want him, she thought. I want to know him. I want him to know me. The only important thing is to seize the chance. To create the opportunity. I want him to feel me. I want to feel him touching me.

He turned to look at her, shifting his head only slightly. Her eyes magnetized him. He found himself thinking of Martha. He had made love to Martha for the first time some months before their marriage. In a holiday chalet at Tutzing. He could no longer recall the details, except for the heat which sizzled inside the tiny, shuttered room and the noise of a solitary fly buzzing against the wall. Later, they had gone to the Café Dreher and drank beer in the garden and he remembered being acutely conscious of the fact that it was summer, as if for the first time, as if for all of his life until that moment he had been unaware of the sun or the heat or the fact that seasons changed. But that had been years ago and Martha was dead: remembering Tutzing now was like perversely savouring the image of making love to a corpse.

He felt Elisabeth's hand cover his own and his resistance seemed suddenly to weaken, as if it had been undermined by the memory of Martha. Confused a moment, he imagined that the hand that lay across his fingers was Martha's and that somehow Martha had been resurrected, returned to him intact. He experienced a strange sensation of joy and relief that lingered just as long as he kept the image of Martha in his mind. Turning around, he pulled the woman towards him and for a long time they lay together without moving, like people afraid that any sudden movement would change everything inexorably. He thought of the long grass on the Rosen-Insel and of how he had held Martha against him for what appeared to be hours, while they listened to the sounds of insects and the motion of water against the shore. They had constructed a web around themselves: even the noise of the steamer that ploughed down the lake towards Tutzing did not penetrate it.

Her hand rose to his face and then dropped against his shoulder, but her eyes remained constant and fixed. It was the expression he observed in the eyes that unnerved him: her stare was a tangible thing, a fine thread that linked him to her. He tried to remember the long grass on the Rosen-Insel; he tried to conjure out of the backwaters of his memory the sight of the mountains that could be seen from the edge of the Starnberger See – the Wendelstein, the Benediktenwand, the Brecherspitze, and all the others – but although he could recall the names as clearly as if he had seen them on a map, he could not recreate the image.

She said something to him, but he did not catch the words. She pressed her face against his neck and her fingers moved between the buttons of this coat. He felt that he was slipping down the greasy side of a slope, frantically trying to get a foothold. Lying in the long grass, Martha had spoken only once and her words had been whipped away by a sudden breeze. What had she said then? He would never know.

Elisabeth sat upright and began to undo the buttons of her blouse. She did this slowly, as if ashamed. Turning his eyes away, he gazed at the ceiling for a time. He heard her remove her clothes: faint sounds, like people whispering in silent rooms. He felt no urge to move: there was neither the impulse to escape from her, nor the compulsion to remain. He was outside himself, floating, unable to control or to predict the course of events. He was waiting. It was as though he were suspended. Acts, decisions, urges, feelings – these had fallen into a state of abeyance.

She leaned over him and took his face between her hands. He was extremely thin and for a moment she imagined that without his clothes he would cease to exist. She felt nervous again, yet she knew that she would not suddenly stop and take a backward step. Closing her eyes, she lowered herself against him. She heard him undo the buttons of his coat and draw his arms from the sleeves. Underneath he was wearing a clean grey shirt that she recognized as one of Willi's. She had washed and pressed it herself.

She shivered because now the room was cold. Her perspiration froze upon her body. She drew the sheets back from the bed and lay beneath them, her limbs stiff. She watched him undress, half-turned away from her. It occurred to her that he was as nervous as she and that all his reluctance boiled down to the fact that he was frightened. He was frightened of climbing into the bed beside her. She stared at the objects in the room and wondered if she would bleed when he entered her. She despised her own ignorance: how could she have remained a virgin so long?

She stared at the print of the Café Helbig and noticed that Grunwald's shadow, thrown by the electric light, fell across it. He was stripped to his trousers. His ribs were visible and his skin was blotchy in places. She felt suddenly very sorry for him and for whatever it was that he had experienced in the past and she wondered if, after all, she could offer him hope.

She held out her hand towards him and he hesitated a moment before moving slowly forward.

'The light,' she said. 'Put the light out.'

He touched the switch and stood for a time in the darkness. From the other side of the room he could hear the sound of her breathing. She called out to him softly but he did not move until his eyes had become accustomed to the dark. She lay like a shadow on the bed, both arms visible over the top of the sheets. Looking at her, he felt strangely calm and collected. His mind was devoid of thought, empty for once of the sounds of accusation. It was as if he had been listening to a clamorous noise for many long months that had suddenly been shut off, leaving behind it the kind of silence that could only exist on an empty planet.

She said, 'It's cold.'

He drew the sheets back. In the blackened room her body was pale and immobile and her hair lay across the pillow like an intricate pattern of dust. When he touched her she trembled. She threw her arms around his neck and he felt her eyelashes close against the side of his face.

19

Half of the buildings in the street had been blown away.
Those that remained were scarred and tattered like old
men malingering in a place where they had no right to
be. At open windows curtains flapped in the rain and
sometimes a face could be seen beyond the panes of
broken glass. Here and there official notices and procla-
mations were pinned to walls and lamp-posts – strictures
against black market activities, curfew warnings, items of
information. Everything had been touched by a dead
hand.

He walked through the wreckage, looking around without really seeing: the things that passed in front of his
eyes seemed somehow distant from him. He crossed the
Königs-Platz, pock-marked now with the signs of the
conquerors. In the Briennerstrasse an American land-
rover swept past. He felt that he could transcend these
things and yet he was weary of them. This was no longer
Munich: it might have been any city in any defeated
country.

He went down a network of narrow streets that were
vaguely familiar to him: but landmarks had been
destroyed and street-names had disappeared. He stared
at the broken faces of houses and realized that he might
have attended the sick in such places. It all seemed so
long ago and the memories – rising in the dead of night to
deliver a baby, hurrying up stairways to scenes of death –
were thin and bare. The weariness of the past struck him.
He wanted to forget.

He found the shop in an alley near the Isar. It was the
only building intact in the street. A ragged sunblind hung
across the window which had been taped to prevent

breakage. In the apartment over the shop a window was open and he could faintly hear the sound of a radio announcer. He stepped into the doorway and paused a moment in the shadows. Then – surprised a little by the noise of a bell – he pushed the door open and went inside.

There was a smell of damp. On rows of shelves there was a large variety of objects – old cameras, toys, garments, mirrors. Beyond the counter a curtained door led into another room. He listened to the radio announcer: 'Volunteers are required to assist in clearing rubble from the centre of the city. Assembly will be held at the Frauenkirche at ten hundred hours tomorrow morning.'

Impatiently he moved towards the door behind the counter. He drew the curtain back and stepped into the tiny room beyond. A man was seated behind a table in the corner, examining some papers beneath the pale glow of a lamp. Seeing Schwarzenbach, he looked up in surprise.

'I heard the bell,' he said impatiently. 'I was coming, I was coming.'

Schwarzenbach looked round the room. 'I can't wait forever,' he said.

The man rose from the table, adjusting his spectacles. 'Everybody is in such a hurry these days. For God's sake, what is there to hurry for?'

The man paused in the middle of the floor and stared at Schwarzenbach a moment. He was a Jew: the features were unmistakable. The irony of this amused Schwarzenbach.

'What can I do for you?' the man asked.

'I want a certain object.'

'Otherwise you would not be here.' The man sighed impatiently and half-turned away. 'What sort of object?'

Schwarzenbach wondered how he had managed to escape death. He thought of the two Jewesses in the office behind the Von-der-Tann-Strasse and wondered: how many others?

'What sort of object?' the man asked again, returning to the table and his papers.

'A revolver.'

The man took off his spectacles and looked at Schwarzenbach incredulously. Then he laughed: 'What sort of joke is this?'

'It's no joke.'

'A revolver! You're mad.'

Schwarzenbach followed him to the table. 'Are you telling me that you don't have such a thing?'

The man shuffled through his papers. 'That's exactly what I'm telling you.'

'You have a certain reputation. They say that you can supply anything.'

'You might as well ask for a Messerschmitt.'

Schwarzenbach laid his hands on the surface of the table.

'I don't have much time to waste. It would be better if you told the truth from the start.'

The man looked at Schwarzenbach and, as if sensing menace for the first time, spoke seriously: 'Where would I get a revolver from? Answer me that.'

'The source is your problem. It hardly concerns me.'

Rising from the table, the man fidgeted nervously with his papers. 'Take my word for it, I do not have the merchandise you require. Now – '

Schwarzenbach laid his hand on the man's shoulder: 'Think again.'

The man shrugged. 'It wouldn't be impossible, of course, to obtain such a thing. But it would take time. And money.'

'I don't have time,' Schwarzenbach said. 'I want it now.'

'You're being ridiculous. Please – '

Schwarzenbach tightened his hold on the man's shoulder and forced him to sit down. 'I'm never ridiculous. Let's begin our conversation again, shall we?'

The man slipped off his spectacles and polished them fussily on his sleeve. 'All right, all right, sometimes such things pass through my hands. Anything is possible these days. But at the moment – '

Schwarzenbach swept the glasses from the man's fingers. They slithered across the desk and fell to the floor.

'You have your reputation to think of,' he said. 'You can supply anything. Can't you? Can't you supply anything?'

The man attempted to reach his spectacles but Schwarzenbach prevented him.

'What sort of revolver?'

'The question is academic. I want a gun with cartridges. And I want them *now*.'

'My glasses. Please.'

Stepping aside, Schwarzenbach allowed the man to retrieve the spectacles. The man was breathing heavily and perspiring and his fingers shook as he placed the glasses on his face. He turned to Schwarzenbach.

'Can you pay in dollars?'

'I will pay in German notes.'

The man shook his head slowly: 'No transaction. I'm sorry. American dollars or nothing.'

'Nothing?'

Schwarzenbach caught the man by the wrist and, swinging him round, forced him to bend across the table. He pressed the full weight of his arm against the man's neck and held him there for a moment.

'You're choking me. Please – '

'German notes,' Schwarzenbach said. 'Or nothing.'

He stood back and the man straightened up slowly. 'Very well. Very well. As you wish.'

The man went towards the stairway that led to the apartment above. Schwarzenbach followed him. In an upstairs room the man opened a small wall-safe and took out a package wrapped in oilskin. He handed it to Schwarzenbach who immediately undid the wrapping.

The revolver was almost new. Heavy, immaculate, it gleamed against the oilskin.

'An American service revolver,' the man said. 'There are cartridges in the chamber and another box in the wrapping.'

Schwarzenbach fingered the weapon lightly. He wanted suddenly to try it out, to select a target and take aim.

Nervously the man said, 'All right. You have your gun. We must discuss money.'

'There is no basis for bargaining,' Schwarzenbach said. 'So that you won't insult me by asking for more than I can possibly afford, I shall name my own price.'

The man was uneasily silent. He watched as Schwarzenbach took some notes from his pocket. He accepted the notes and counted them quickly.

'Absurd. This is barely a tenth of what I paid for the weapon.'

'No bargaining,' Schwarzenbach said. He began to cover the gun with the oilskin.

'But – '

'No bargaining.'

The man followed Schwarzenbach to the stairs.

'It's robbery! Daylight robbery! Do you think you can get away with it?'

Schwarzenbach paused at the foot of the stairs and looked up. 'Why don't you report me to the military authorities if you feel like that?'

A door slammed. Schwarzenbach went on to the street, the package inside his pocket.

Last night he had seen Grunwald: he had seen the Jew in the company of a woman leaving a house on the Schumannstrasse. He had followed them across the Isar and along the Ludwigstrasse into Schwabing. He had tracked them down side-streets and then back again to the Schumannstrasse. The woman puzzled him. Was she Grunwald's girl-friend? A relative? Her presence was a complication certainly, but there was no particular problem involved. If it was necessary he would kill her as well.

He was conscious of the revolver in his pocket as he walked back to his hotel. But he thought of it less as an instrument of murder – more, much more, as an instrument of peace.

Willi said, 'According to this newspaper, they are asking for volunteers to help with the clearance of rubble. Interested persons are required to present themselves tomorrow morning at the Frauenkirche before ten o'clock.'

Grunwald looked at his uncle, who was sitting in the chair with the newspaper folded across his knees.

'Well?'

'Why don't you go along, Leonhard? Physical exercise will do you good. Besides, it will help to keep you occupied.'

'I don't have the strength,' Grunwald said.

'I'm not surprised,' Willi said, opening out the newspaper.

'What does that mean?'

'It doesn't mean anything.'

Grunwald was silent for a while. He had returned to Willi's apartment just before dawn while Elisabeth was asleep. His first impulse had been to leave, to clear out before Willi and Fräulein Strauss were awake. He had crawled between the armchairs silently, drawing a woollen blanket around himself. Had Willi heard him return? Had he deduced for himself what had taken place? He looked at the old man and wondered what was running through his mind.

'You'd be doing something useful, instead of slouching around here all day long.'

'Are you tired of having me here? Do you want me to leave?'

Willi folded the paper and let it drop to the floor:

'Don't get so cross, Leonhard. You know that you're welcome here for as long as you like. I'm thinking only of you. Don't you get bored sitting around doing nothing?'

Grunwald shrugged: he did not know why he was being so aggressive. Willi was simply being considerate and constructive. But he was thinking less of his uncle's suggestion than he was of his memory of the woman. Before dawn, just as he had awakened, she had placed her arms tightly around his body and confessed – if confession were the word – that she was in love with him. He wanted to laugh, but didn't: instead, he was silent, wondering if she would still want to love him when she discovered the true facts of his miraculous survival. He attributed it all to her loneliness: she was making a desperate attempt to fill the gaps of her life. And there was pity, of course. As he was dressing to leave her room she had suggested that they go to Palestine together: a new life lay out there, just waiting to be embraced. He said nothing. What was there to say? If she had asked him what he felt, whether he loved her or didn't, he couldn't have answered. He might have mouthed a few select sentiments – but to go as far as saying that he loved her would have been a lie. Love – if it was to be recognized – required the kind of scrutiny of himself that he wasn't prepared to make. What was love? Was it any more than the act of sex that had taken place? It was easy to be confused, as indeed he felt that she was confused, falsely labelling her feelings with the nearest descriptions that came to mind. Love: it was the kind of word that contained meaning only in the creeping hour before dawn, dragged out of some sleepy exhaustion, a moment of gratitude for the fact that he had been her first man.

'Why don't you go along to the Frauenkirche in the morning, Leonhard?' Willi asked.

'Because I don't feel like it.'

'That's as good a reason as any, I suppose.' Willi got up from his chair and crossed the room, surveying his nephew's face. 'How is Elisabeth? I haven't seen her this morning – '

'How should I know?'

'You went out with her last night, didn't you?

'We went walking.'

'I think she's attracted to you. That's what I think.'

'She isn't attracted to me at all.'

'God, you're so bloody cynical.' Willi flapped his hands in an angry way. 'You make me sick sometimes.'

'Sick?'

'Practically throwing herself at you, that's what she's doing. A blind man could see that.'

'You're talking nonsense.'

'Am I? Look, she's practically going down on her knees before you. And what do you do? You fart around this room with a face like thunder. I know you've had a bad time, Leonhard, but the misery can't go on forever.'

Grunwald turned angrily to his uncle. 'Mind your own business. Why don't you?'

Willi's face clouded with despair. 'All right. I'm an old man. I'm wandering in the head. Forget it.'

He returned to his chair where he sat down. He picked up the thin newspaper – which he had already read several times – and turned the pages. Grunwald watched his anaemic hands shake against the paper.

He said, 'I'm sorry, Willi. Forgive me – '

'Forgive you what?'

Grunwald went into the bedroom and sat down on the bed. The best thing to do would be to leave. Willi would die, and Elisabeth had enough strength to live out a useful life. As for himself, it barely mattered. He did not want to see Elisabeth again. It was better that way.

A moment later he heard her voice from the other room. And then the bedroom door opened and she was standing there. She looked different somehow.

'I found a piece of ribbon and tied my hair back – do you like it?'

He said that he did. She closed the door and sat down on the bed beside him. She took his hand and pressed it against the side of her face.

'Do you think I'm silly?' she asked.

'In what way?'

'Because I said what I did say.' She paused for a second: 'When I woke up this morning at first I thought it had all been a dream. But it happened, didn't it? It actually took place.'

'Yes, it happened.'

'What's the matter?'

Her hair smelled of soap: the ribbon was scarlet and tied in a bow like a little girl's. It was an incongruous splash of colour.

'Is something wrong?' she asked. 'You seem so gloomy.'

'Do I?'

She sat up, her face blank: 'You don't regret what happened, do you?'

'Of course not.'

'Well, what's wrong?'

'Nothing.'

'There must be something.'

He stood up and went to the small, square window. There were children playing below: every day at the same time they played amongst the garbage. He watched them chase each other around the yard and wondered what he felt: what did he feel about her? Did he resent himself so much that he felt nothing? Or was he afraid of emotion? These questions struck him as being banal and irrelevant to his real dilemma: wherever he went, whatever he did, he carried the past upon his back like a sack of lead.

'Elisabeth,' he said.

'What is it? Tell me what's the matter.' She was standing beside him at the window. Light set fire to the red ribbon.

'I don't think that you genuinely feel love for me.'

282

'I think I do,' she said. 'I don't know why I do, but I do.'

'You must appreciate that I don't want you to,' he said, as if he were dictating a letter cancelling a magazine subscription.

'I know what makes you say that.'

He faced her quickly: 'Do you?'

'I think I've worked it out, Leonhard,' she said. 'Because of the way things are, I mean because of the bloody misery and depression everywhere, you can't see any hope for anything – including our relationship. Isn't that it?'

He looked at her and thought it remarkable how easily she could rationalize obstructions out of existence, even if her deductions were the wrong ones.

She said, 'But that doesn't worry me. It doesn't worry me at all. You must know that I have enough hope for both of us.'

He felt her fingers close around his hand and for a second he wished that what she was saying were true. It would be simple to resign his responsibility, to discard it entirely, and let her carry all the loads. If she had hope then perhaps after a time it would infect him as well. Was it possible? Could he still hope for something? He shut his eyes, pressed his face flat against the glass, heard the shouts of the children rising from below, and in that single moment was seized with a paralysis of despair.

'I can't accept your hope,' he said.

'Leonhard, you must. It's more important than I can say. You must let me help. I'm strong, you said so yourself, I'm strong enough for both of us. It won't always be like this.'

She stopped. Willi had come into the bedroom.

'Private conversation?' he asked.

'No, not really,' Grunwald said.

Willi looked at the woman: 'Make him come to his senses. Make him get a grip on himself.'

'For Christ's sake,' Grunwald said.

Elisabeth smiled at the old man. 'I'm trying, Willi. I'm trying.'

Willi sat down on the bed. 'If I were a young man again, you wouldn't have to try so hard with me, Elisabeth.'

Grunwald looked out of the window. He had the impression that he was travelling on a huge ship through a dangerous minefield. One false move would blow everything apart. He tried to imagine Elisabeth's reaction if he told her about Chełmno. Hatred? Revulsion? Would she damn him?

She said, 'I'll make some coffee. Would you like that?'

'I'm as dry as dust,' Willi said.

She went out of the room.

Willi turned to Grunwald and said, 'She could do a lot for you. If you'd let her.'

In his room Schwarzenbach took the revolver from his coat and put it down on the bed. Retreating to the other side of the room, he stared at it for a time. After a moment it seemed to lose its shape and purpose: its ugliness was appalling. But when he returned to pick it up, it became meaningful again. He polished it on the edge of the blanket and then put it back into his coat. He hung the coat upon a peg fixed to the door and noticed that the weight of the gun distended the garment slightly. He rearranged the coat to disguise the bulk of the gun and he was satisfied after some minutes that nobody entering the room could possibly tell, just by looking at the coat, that a revolver lay in the left pocket.

Later, he went down to the restaurant. The food, consisting of a watery soup and scraps of meat surrounded by potato substitute, was abysmal. But he ate hungrily, absorbed in what he was doing, completely unconscious of the waiter who served him. When he had finished the meal the waiter lingered by his table, as if he had been assigned solely to serve Schwarzenbach and no one else. After a time, Schwarzenbach realized that the waiter was staring at him.

'It's all right,' he said. 'I don't think I need anything else.'

The waiter approached the table. 'Excuse me, sir.'

'I said that I don't want anything else,' Schwarzenbach remarked.

'I'm sorry if I seem to have been staring, sir,' the waiter said.

'Were you? I hadn't noticed.' Schwarzenbach shifted uncomfortably. Across the room, upon a raised dais, two violinists were playing a selection of tunes from Strauss. There was something of the pre-war atmosphere in their music, but their evening suits were drab and threadbare.

The waiter, smiling, said, 'I was trying to place you, sir.'

'Place me?' The music had become louder. He was aware now of the number of uniforms in the dining-room.

'It's just that I seem to recall your face, sir.' The waiter, smiling in a watery way, lowered his head. 'It seems familiar. I'm trying to remember where we've met before.'

Schwarzenbach wiped his lips and threw his napkin upon the table. 'You're mistaken. I haven't been in this hotel before.'

'No, not the hotel. Somewhere else.' The waiter reached for Schwarzenbach's empty plate and the discarded napkin. 'I hope you don't think me rude. Somehow I think we've met before.'

'Impossible,' Schwarzenbach said, and yet he knew that the waiter's face contained the germ of recognition. An old patient? Someone from the past?

'I'm certain that I've seen you before. Years ago.'

'Hardly likely. I didn't visit Munich often.'

'Didn't you?' The waiter piled the plate and cutlery upon his tray. The cuffs of his shirt were yellow and

285

scruffy and his fingernails unclean. 'My mistake, sir. You reminded me of someone.'

Schwarzenbach rose from the table and walked towards the foyer. He heard the waiter behind him. Damn him: was he going to remember something?

Suddenly the waiter called out: 'Dr Schwarzenbach!'

Schwarzenbach did not turn round. He walked across the foyer and towards the stairs. A sense of dizziness touched him. He reached the first step and grabbed the handrail. The waiter was immediately behind him.

'Isn't it Dr Schwarzenbach?' he asked.

Schwarzenbach turned round: 'Sorry. You must have made a mistake. My name's Lutzke.'

'Oh.' The waiter seemed disappointed. 'The resemblance is quite remarkable. You're thinner than Dr Schwarzenbach and you don't have as much hair as he had, but otherwise you could pass as his twin brother.'

'These resemblances happen,' Schwarzenbach said and moved up the stairs.

'It's just that I visited him when I was a schoolboy. An emergency case, it was. I cut my wrists on some rusty metal. He was a good doctor.'

'Was he?' Schwarzenbach looked down at the waiter: for the life of him, he couldn't recall the man's face.

'Very good indeed, sir. Knew what he was doing.'

'Glad to hear it.'

Schwarzenbach continued to the first landing. The waiter had gone. He climbed up to his room and lay on the bed, gazing at the coat against the door. What a bloody nuisance, to be recognized by a waiter. But had he convinced the waiter of the mistake? Had he persuaded him? What if the waiter was still unconvinced? No: he had to relax. He had to close his eyes and forget about the waiter. Soon he would no longer have any use for the hotel and the incident would be forgotten. He got up from the bed: it was impossible to relax. He took the revolver from his coat and fingered it gently for a moment. He walked up and down the room, the gun hanging in his hand.

At the window he looked into the street. In the reflected light of the hotel he saw a group of Americans in their greatcoats huddled together below. They seemed to be talking in an animated fashion. He drew the curtain across the window. Outside it was perfectly dark.

She felt that she had laid herself bare in front of him: it was more, far more, than the uncomplicated nakedness of her body. She had torn large pieces out of herself and held them raw in her hands and offered them to him. And what had he done? What had he done? He had turned his eyes away, shifted his head, refused. Now what more could she do?

She looked at Willi, half-asleep over his crumpled newspaper. He was dying slowly, as if death could ever be a slow process: his head bent forward, the palms of his hands upturned, a trickle of white saliva at the corner of his lips. She felt frustrated, as if she had become a prisoner of her own sensations. Why wouldn't Grunwald speak? Why wouldn't he accept?

He was standing at the window where he always seemed to be, like a man scouring the sky and hoping for some crack to appear in the fabric of the universe. Was that what he wanted? Did he want to destroy himself? These questions beat like waves against her brain and she knew she was tired, she knew she should never have become involved with him. She felt miserable and depressed: she felt like an obsolete object that has been used only once and then discarded.

She said, 'I'm going to my own room. Are you coming?'

Grunwald turned round and looked at Willi, who was snoring now. Saying nothing, he followed her along the passage. He entered her room behind her, noticing that her face was flushed and that she had removed the scarlet ribbon from her hair. She had worn it like the flag of some triumph: now it lay across the dresser, abandoned. He wanted to run. He wanted to get out. But the world wasn't large enough to offer him refuge. He listened to Elisabeth's silence: it was hard and cold, containing as it did the seeds of her despair.

He held out his hands: he imagined that bloodstains lay in the hollows of his palms. Schwarzenbach used to make him mop up the blood that had dripped from the table to the floor. He used to ask him to pass various instruments, the names of which he had learned willingly and quickly. Grunwald watched the experiments in pain like some macabre spectator. The hollow shells of people that were brought into the room by the guard were stretched across the stained table and Schwarzenbach, immaculate in his white coat, would come forward as if he were about to perform a life-saving operation. All the time, all the painful time, Grunwald wondered what was happening inside him: why did he feel nothing? What was it costing him? What was disintegrating within him?

Elisabeth yawned. She sat on the bed and gazed at the floor.

'Well?' she asked. 'What's going to become of us?'

'I wish I knew the answer,' Grunwald said.

'You could give me a clue. Some sign. Anything.'

He detected the desperation in her voice: it shocked him that she should be asking so much from him.

'What can I say?' he asked.

'Do you feel anything for me?'

'How should I know?'

'If you don't know, who else could?'

'It isn't easy, Elisabeth.' He paused and sat beside her on the bed.

'But don't you realize that I could bring such a great deal to you? I could change your life, I really could.' She looked at him in a determined fashion: she might have

288

been talking about a slab of clay she was about to mould into a determinate shape.

'Look,' she said. 'I understand. I know the difficulties. You don't want to become involved – '

'Please, Elisabeth, I don't want to talk about it.'

She sighed and shrugged her shoulders in an exaggerated way. She had imagined that everything would be so much simpler, now that she had managed to reach him: but everything was exactly as it had been. Rising from the bed, she walked across the room and stared at her face in the mirror above the sink.

'Am I ugly? Is that it? Do you want someone more attractive than me?'

'You're attractive enough,' he said.

'Then for Christ's sake what is it?'

He felt that he was composed of dead tissue: that he had been standing for too long in a storm and emotion had congealed in his brain. He was numb. He could not rid himself of the sudden thought that but for a stroke of luck, an accident, she might have ended up in Chelmno herself. What then? Could he have watched Schwarzenbach assault her? He knew the answer to that question.

She had covered her face with her hands, as if she did not want him to see her. 'Do you intend to leave? What do you propose to do?'

'I'm not sure.'

'Why are you so indecisive?'

'Decisions seem so irrelevant,' he said.

She turned back to face the mirror, looking at it as if she might smash it, shatter the image that came back to her like someone sick not only of her face but also of her life. Their whole relationship seemed a protracted interrogation, as if at its very foundation there was a terrible mystery to solve. She was weakened by it, it plagued her and harried her. She felt that she was running towards a distant object that never came any closer. What had begun as pity – as the kind of pity a nurse might feel for a dying patient – had deepened into something else: a need.

'I'm not playing games. Not now,' she said.

He spread his hands hopelessly and was silent.

'Last night, when we slept together – how do I begin to explain to you the significance of that. Did it mean anything to you? Was it just nothing to you?'

She was aware of her own voice in the quiet room, rising into a whine: why did he make her so weary of herself? Four days before she had been totally unaware of his existence. Why couldn't she simply go back to that state of affairs and forget the interlude entirely? She had had a life of her own, something she had created herself: it was a tunnel into which she had retreated, burying her face in her hands so that she might see and hear nothing of the external world. She wasn't interested in the struggle for Europe, the squabblings of politicians over tracts of territory, the petty differences between the Allies. She had her own small world, bounded by the room, the need to eat, and caring for Herr Gerber.

But how *could* she simply allow him to disappear from her life? She could be patient, strong, she could encourage him to exist again no matter what she had to do or how long the process would take. She could protect him and help him – if only he would extend his hand and accept her.

'Anything you want from me,' she said. 'You only have to ask. You only have to ask. What could be more simple?'

Schwarzenbach rose from the bed and seized his coat from the back of the door. He struggled into it and then left his room. In the foyer he met Peters, who was drunk and aggressive.

'Sneaking out to visit some little fräulein, Lutzke?' the American asked. 'Plenty of them about, plenty of them.'

'Taking a stroll before bed,' Schwarzenbach said.

Peters stroked his moustache: 'Got a bottle of something nice in your pocket anyway – cognac? scotch?'

'Cognac,' Schwarzenbach said, dropping his hand over the bulge made by the revolver.

'Aren't you going to offer me one little shot from it?' Peters moved closer.

'I don't want to open it just yet,' Schwarzenbach answered.

'Well, that's just fine,' Peters said and slapped him across the shoulder. 'You want to save it for your little fräulein, eh? I've got you taped, Lutzke. I know what your game is.'

Peters laughed suddenly and Schwarzenbach felt obliged to smile.

Peters said, 'You prowl around the damn streets at night, screwing all the women you can lay your fat kraut hands on – that's your game. You're a sex maniac.'

Schwarzenbach tried to pass the American, but Peters had a hold of his arm.

'You look like a sex maniac, come to think of it,' Peters said. 'My God, you must send the shivers up their spines when you give them a dose of that old cold eye of yours.'

'I have an important appointment. Will you let me pass?'

Bowing in a mocking way, Peters said, 'Of course, sir. Pass on into the night. Happy hunting.'

Schwarzenbach went through the front door and stood for a time on the hotel steps. When he turned round he observed, through the glass panel, that Peters was making a telephone call from the reception desk. The man was a bore, a nuisance. He put his hand into the pocket that contained the revolver and he walked away.

Silence was a sort of cone: Grunwald sat within it, waiting for Elisabeth to speak.

'I think I'll take a walk. Some fresh air,' he said.

'Do you want me to come with you?' she asked.

'If you feel like walking.'

'That wasn't what I asked,' she said.

'Yes. All right. I'd like you to come.'

'Can't you put some more enthusiasm into it?'

'I'd like you to come,' he said again, in the same flat way.

She found her raincoat and draped it across her shoulders. She followed him down the stairs, noticing how the lamps on the landings flattened his shadow against the walls. She was being stupid: why didn't she recognize the fact and come to her senses? He wanted nothing from her no matter how hard she tried. Perhaps it would be easy just to shed him, forget the encounter had ever taken place, and slip back into her own life and her own preoccupations. In the Schumannstrasse he was walking a yard or so ahead of her. Quickening her pace, she caught up with him.

'Are you trying to win a race?'

'Was I hurrying?'

'Perhaps you were trying to get away from me,' she said.

She was like a child, with her eagerness to please and her fear of rejection: he wondered if six and a half years had somehow retarded her mental development. She took his arm and laid her face against his shoulder.

They walked towards the Zeppelinstrasse, crossing the Isar by the Reichenbach Bridge. A flotilla of small craft lay unsteadily on the surface of the water. He watched the boats, many of them covered in tarpaulins, and wondered why it was that he couldn't tell her the truth: the answer to that was simple – he could not bring himself face to face with his guilt. Or perhaps he could not share it. What would become of her feelings if he told her? What would she say then?

They crossed the Gärtner-Platz and in a tiny side street, miraculously untouched by the bombs, they found a small café that was open. Outside, gathered around the lighted windows as if to savour an illusion of heat, there were six or seven ragged people huddled together. They did not look at Grunwald and the woman as they went through the front door into the café.

Schwarzenbach found himself walking across the darkened gardens that lay beneath the Maximilianeum. The shrubbery cast weird shapes, black outlines frozen against the lighter darkness beyond. Suddenly he remembered the fact that Peters had made a telephone call immediately after he had left the hotel. Who had he been calling? Why had he made a call just after his encounter with Schwarzenbach? Was there a connection? He remembered the waiter who had recognized him and it seemed to him that there were links, vague but threatening links, between these two events. Did Peters suspect something? Was he a journalist as he claimed? If not, what was he? Had the waiter spoken to him? If these two suspected some thing, how many others in the hotel did?

He was in the Maria-Theresa-Strasse now where the presence of a few street lamps seemed to dispel his fears. After tonight, he would not need to return to the hotel anyway.

They drank tasteless lukewarm coffee that Elisabeth paid for and sat at a table away from the door. The café was barren and cold: its cheerlessness made her feel that she would have to make a real effort to appear happy. She held his fingers in her hand. Most of the other tables were empty but here and there sat American servicemen with their German girl-friends: sometimes someone would laugh but the sound always seemed forced and artificial.

From a distant back-room there came the blurred noise of a radio drearily playing tuneless dance-music. She could not have wished for a more accurate external representation of what she felt inside herself. Grunwald was miles away, but just the same she had been talking for what seemed like ages, listening to the empty noise of her own voice and the meaninglessness of her words. Palestine – why didn't he make the decision to go to Palestine? As if desperate to convince, she lumped one argument upon another, creating illogical spirals of reasons. Germany was dead, a corpse; he had no family left, other than Willi; there was nothing in Germany to keep him there; how could he live in any case in a land of ghosts; she would look after him when they got to Palestine; they could build a place to live and work the land and what they didn't know they could easily learn. Yet the more she sought convincing reasons, the more it seemed that Palestine was slipping and slipping away from her.

Grunwald did not appear to be listening. Yet he heard her words although he could barely make sense of them: the one name, Palestine, recurred again and again. He sipped his coffee: at the back of his mind was the urge to tell her about Chelmno, as if he somehow thought that she had a right to know. The urge increased and the words lay upon his tongue. She had a right to know why he was so cold towards her: she had a right to know, after what had happened, why he could not respond in the way she wanted. But he said nothing, listening to the sound of her voice as it washed over him.

'Are you listening to me?' she asked.

'Of course I am.'

'I wasn't certain,' she said.

'You were talking about Palestine.'

She lifted her cup: 'How much did you actually hear?'

'Everything you said,' he answered.

'And how do you respond?'

He finished his drink, turning his face towards the misted window: outside, thrown in silhouette against the glass, were the figures of several people. At the other side of the room, behind a counter, a waitress in a black frock counted coins in the palm of her hands.

'If I went with you to Palestine, what would happen to Willi?'

'He's going to die.' She felt callous suddenly and wanted to explain herself: 'We don't have to go until he's dead –'

'So we wait around like vultures – ?'

'You know I didn't mean that.'

He played with the empty coffee cup between his fingers. Visions of Chelmno crowded his mind: how could he ever bring himself to tell her? He saw in her face an expression of such hopefulness that to destroy it would have caused him agony. She was waiting, waiting for his reply as if her entire life revolved around the moments of patience. She was offering him a kind of salvation: what did he have to do to accept?

'Leonhard,' she said, and she covered his hand with her fingers.

He remembered sleeping with her: once, in the middle of the night it had seemed to him that he had woken himself up calling out Martha's name – now, remembering, he could not decide if it had been part of a dream. Why did the past cling so tenaciously to him?

She said, 'You don't have to hurry your decision. We've got lots of time.'

But somehow she didn't believe herself: it appeared to her that time, like an object caught in the wind, was drifting and dwindling away.

Schwarzenbach stopped in the Schumannstrasse. An American patrol car had gone past. On the corner it braked and stood there a moment, its engine ticking over. He pressed himself inside a doorway and waited. He watched the driver light a cigarette and then the vehicle moved forward and out of sight. Crossing the Schumannstrasse, Schwarzenbach entered one of the buildings. In the hallway he took the revolver from his pocket and looked at it beneath the light of the lamp: it gleamed upon the flat of his hand and he was impressed by its perfection. Why, when they created objects of destruction, did men design such beautiful, economical things? He put it back into his overcoat and moved towards the stairs. He imagined he heard the sound of someone moaning, but it was only the wind rattling through the broken glass of the landing windows.

'How do you propose to travel to Palestine?'

She caught his hand tightly, as if his question had excited her.

'There are organizations who arrange such things,' she said. 'Usually refugees go by boat. It isn't easy, but it can be done. I have the address of one organization – '

'And what does one do in Palestine?' Grunwald asked.

'We wouldn't be alone,' she answered. 'I know several people who went there before the war.'

'How does one eat?'

'From the land,' she said.

He wondered at her idealism: *from the land* – it was so vague it was almost absurd. When he thought of Palestine he thought of miles of scrubland and desert. Yet he admired her for her incredible optimism, for her ability to perceive another world beyond the depressing horizons of Germany. And she wanted him to see and understand the same vision. She stared at him, wondering why she was breathing so quickly: was it possible that he was going to commit himself? Palestine was an excuse, she recognized that fact: a commitment on his part to Palestine was really a commitment to her.

Waiting for him to speak, she was aware of the empty noises around her: a kettle boiling, money being counted, the distant wireless uttering some trivial announcements. Please, she thought: please say that you will come. Please, please decide in my favour.

He looked at her, feeling a revitalization of his shame.

* * *

Schwarzenbach saw that the name had been written on the wall beside the door in faded chalk letters: *W. Gerber.* Outside the door he hesitated, drawing the revolver from his coat. The building was silent. The revolver seemed suddenly weightless, as if it were not an object that he held in his hand, as if all at once his fingers were unaccountably empty. He flexed his hand around the weapon for reassurance and observed his shadow dropping across the door, distorted by the warped wood. Now: now, he thought, and caught the doorknob with his free hand, surprised that the door wasn't locked and opened just as soon as he touched it, fell open into a dark, shapeless room.

No. He could not bring himself to tell her. The words became congealed lumps in his mouth. He could not force himself to be honest with her even when her face, her expression, her whole being demanded honesty. He watched the coffee cup slip from between his fingers and shatter on the floor. Two clean pieces. He bent down and picked them up, placing them on the table in front of him. She was watching him all the time. He wondered why he could not look at her eyes now but even without turning his head he knew that they were burning into him, he felt them just as surely as if she had touched him.

She asked, 'What's wrong? Why are you so nervous?'

He laughed slightly: 'I don't feel nervous,' he said.

'Leonhard, you're trembling. Look at you – you're shaking like a leaf. What's the matter?'

She lifted his hand to her mouth and brushed her lips against it, as if she were trying to smooth away a wound. How *could* he tell her?

There was the noise of someone snoring. When his eyes had become accustomed to the dark, Schwarzenbach realized that another room led off from the one in which he was now standing. He moved towards the door and pushed it open. Faintly, in the dimness, he could make out the shape of someone sleeping on the bed. He raised the revolver at the figure, moving forward towards the bed. And then he realized that the man wasn't Grunwald.

He switched on the light. The man on the bed sat up, staring wildly around the room.

'Leonhard?'

Schwarzenbach motioned him to be silent.

'Who are you? Where's my nephew?'

Schwarzenbach asked, 'Herr Gerber?'

'Where's my nephew?' Willi pushed the blankets back and shakily rose to his feet. He shivered in the cold room. It was then that he saw the weapon.

'What's that for?'

Schwarzenbach stared at the weapon: 'Where's Grunwald?'

'Out.'

'When will he be back?'

Herr Gerber shrugged: 'I don't know. How should I know?' He stared at the revolver and Schwarzenbach noticed that his lower lip was trembling, as if he were about to burst into tears. He raised the weapon in a direct line with the old man's skull. One blast would shatter it like an eggshell.

Herr Gerber clasped his hands together, muttering below his breath like someone praying. It was a sound Schwarzenbach had heard before: sometimes they used to pray in whispers, facing death they used to pray to God with their useless words. He lowered the revolver to his side.

'What do you want with Grunwald?' the old man asked.

Schwarzenbach was silent. The bedroom smelled. He noticed it for the first time, a peculiar odour that seemed a mixture of sweat and incense. He loathed it: it seemed to catch at the back of his throat and choke him. He pushed the window open and stared out into the darkness. The old man did not move from the bed: as if paralysed, he could not take his eyes from the gun.

Grunwald said, 'There's something I ought to tell you.,'

She smiled: 'You mustn't feel under any obligation to tell me anything,' she said.

'I ought to tell you,' he said: and then he paused. How could he find the words? How could he tell her about Chelmno and the sight he saw every morning from the barred window of his tiny room, the naked figures crossing the muddy yard just before dawn, walking to the gas installations just as if they were about to be deloused prior to a medical inspection? How could he tell her he had seen this happen from the safety of his tiny room without doing anything to prevent it? Without feeling the temptation to join the shuffling queues himself? The women, the children, the men, all curiously desexed and alike, crossing through the mud and the rain to reach the installations: and he could see his own face, framed against the window, as if he were watching it from the viewpoint of the victims, and he knew that he despised his own blank expression that stared down as the queues shifted forward and kept shifting until the chambers were packed to capacity. Where were they all going? What was the purpose? How could he tell her about the hut, and the medical instruments scattered around the place like the elaborate toys of doom, and the bodies that came into the hut because they had been selected to further the cause of National Socialist science? How could he tell her that he had complied with the insanity, he had grown mad himself, crazy for life as if it were a prize that could only be won by debasement and defilement?

'Well? Aren't you going to tell me, Leonhard?'

He looked at her. Her mouth was partly open, her hands clasped on top of his.

He shook his head: 'On second thoughts, it isn't important.'

'Are you going to use it?'

The question surprised Schwarzenbach because he had quite forgotten about the old man. Looking from the open window he had been thinking of his own peace of mind and how close to him the prospect seemed. He would be alive again, regain something of contentment: with Grunwald dead, the past would at last be over.

'Do you intend to use that thing?' Herr Gerber asked.

'It's getting late,' Schwarzenbach said. He felt impatient: he wanted to finish the deed and then forget.

'Are you going to use that on my nephew?' Herr Gerber asked.

'Shut up. Sit down on the bed and shut up.'

It was cowardly: he had run away again. Faced with the prospect of a confession, he had rejected it. Was he destined forever to lack real courage? He used to help Schwarzenbach dispose of the corpses: they were taken outside the hut into a small rear yard and thrown on to a truck, where they were covered over with old scraps of cloth. Once a week one of the guards would drive the truck to the crematorium: at least Grunwald had always imagined that the bodies were taken to be burned. It seemed fitting somehow that they should be set on fire: whatever function they had once served, they were meaningless now. Why hadn't Schwarzenbach simply killed him?

Elisabeth said, 'It's getting late.'

They got up from the table. He followed her into the street. Along the pavements people were sleeping, huddled together to keep warm. A strong stench of staleness rose from their bodies and the sight of them made him feel despondent. Everything had become so grey. He tried to imagine sunlight and constant brightness and he thought of Palestine: did the sun burn all the time there? Was it always bright and hot? He longed for warmth: he longed to take his clothes off and lie in the sunlight.

She took him by the arm. The gesture, so simple, moved him. She was prepared to change her life just to accommodate him: why did she care like this?

'Let's go back to the house,' she said.

He thought of lying beside her in her narrow bed and sleeping with his arms around her body, safe, certain, protected. For a moment the prospect relieved him of his guilt and he imagined he could live the rest of his life blindly, keeping secrets from himself.

'Palestine has a warm climate, hasn't it?' he asked.

'It has a beautiful climate,' she answered.

'What was that?' Schwarzenbach asked. He had heard a noise on the stairs: a sound of thin laughter.

The old man stood up in alarm. Schwarzenbach caught his arm, and twisted it, and forced him to sit down again.

They stopped at the top of the first flight of stairs. She could not explain to herself why she felt so happy. She wanted to laugh: it was irrational, because he hadn't *actually* committed himself, but she felt within herself that he had at last decided. She put her arms around his thin body and tried to imagine him strong again, his flesh filled out, she tried to envisage him as he would be with a sense of purpose.

She held him against her a moment longer. They said nothing to one another and yet she felt that she had accomplished something: she experienced a sensation of triumph, as if she had conquered some terrible adversity. Holding him against her, she realized that she did not want to let him go. She had discovered him. Now he seemed more relaxed than ever before, as if she had achieved some miracle of chemistry and had managed to dissolve the taste of the past for him.

301

'The climate is beautiful,' she said: and she didn't want to stop talking about Palestine. 'I've read all the guide-books and travel-guides, and according to them all the climate is almost unbelievable – '

He silenced her by putting a finger to her lips. From somewhere, somehow, he would find the courage to tell her about Chelmno.

'Keep quiet.'

Schwarzenbach raised the revolver at the old man and, crossing the floor, went into the other room. As if dazed, Herr Gerber followed him.

'One word. That's all.'

Schwarzenbach stood behind the door. His entire life had become intensified upon this single, waiting moment. The gun. The Jew coming up the stairs. Behind him, Herr Gerber stood in the middle of the room, a blanket drawn tightly around his body.

Schwarzenbach lifted the revolver. And he waited.

'Shall we go into my room?' she asked.

'Yes.'

'Do you want to?'

He hesitated a moment, wondering even now why he was holding himself back. 'Yes, I want to.'

She took her key from her coat and dropped it. As she bent down to pick it up, she said, 'Perhaps I ought to look in and see if Willi is comfortable first.'

'He's all right. Don't worry about him.'

'No, I really should.'

Grunwald shrugged: 'If you feel you must.'

She started to move along the corridor towards Herr Gerber's room.

Herr Gerber moved as quickly as he could towards the door. Wheeling round, Schwarzenbach struck him across the throat with the revolver. The old man tried to speak but couldn't, yet he still persisted in trying to get past. Schwarzenbach pushed him back, conscious of the footsteps coming along the corridor. The old man lost his balance but he did not fall. He caught the arm of the chair, raised himself upright, and reached the door just as Schwarzenbach had started to open it.

'You old fool!'

She did not understand at first: she saw Herr Gerber, wrapped in a blanket, and she imagined that he had had a seizure of some kind. His arms were raised in the air and it appeared to her that he was trying to say something, but the only sound that issued from him was a low, tearful cry. Because of her concern for the old man, she was barely conscious of the other figure that stood just behind him, a darker, taller figure that she saw only from the corner of her eye. The blanket slipped from his body and he moved slowly forward towards her and, quickening her step, she rushed to catch him because it seemed that he was about to fall. Yet he did not fall although he appeared to have lost his balance, and it was only when she was about eight feet away from him that she wondered who the other person was. Suddenly, as if he had been conjured out of existence, Herr Gerber was no longer there. Willi! Willi! Had she called out his name? Or had the voice been that of Leonhard, who was standing several yards behind her? Dizzy, sickened, she looked around for Willi, and thought she saw him sprawling across the floor, his hands upraised, when she became conscious of a loud noise and a single second of flame that seemed to her an echo of an earlier noise that she had hardly registered in her concern for Herr Gerber. Pain was spreading through her, starting in her chest and rising with the force of lightning to her neck and brain: stiff with panic, she suddenly discovered that she could no longer stand up. She went down on her knees, aware of someone rushing past her, aware of the third and fourth noises that

303

shattered the fading echoes of the previous sounds. She put her hands to her throat. Leonhard! Leonhard! Where was he? Why hadn't he come to help her? It was silly, she was imagining things, he would be at her side in only a moment with an explanation for all this –

'Leonhard,' she said, 'Leonhard, please.'

The old fool had got in the way. And then the girl, the stupid girl. Ahead of him, rushing down the stairs, he could hear the frightened sounds that Grunwald left behind him like the scent of a dying animal.

For Christ's sake why didn't her body respond to her demands? Move. Move. *Move!* And why was she alone now? Alone with this awful silence. Frozen, her back flat against the wall, she was conscious of blood falling from her body and yet when she looked at it in her hands it wasn't her own blood, it wasn't even real blood, it was some substitute matter that might have been used in an amateur theatrical. Not her blood. Christ, the pain had anaesthetized her scalp, there was a numbing, tingling sensation. Like the kind you experienced at a dentist's when you were falling asleep and couldn't stop yourself. Was she falling asleep? It felt that way because it had become more difficult to make out shapes around her, they were distorted, dream-shapes, they wouldn't keep still and the dream seemed to be erecting a fog of blindness around her. Leonhard. Leonhard. He would come in a moment. He was bound to come. She whispered his name. Leonhard, I love you, I pity you.

20

He paused in a dark semicircle of trees. Before him lay an open stretch of lawn. He raised the revolver upwards and suppressed the sudden urge to fire it blindly through the branches of the trees. There was a half-moon, partly enclosed by cloud, and the bare branches were imposed upon it like a complex of scars.

The Jew. The Jew was around here somewhere. Hiding. But there was always an end to hiding, a moment when the barricades of concealment were finally broken down. He would find the Jew. It was a matter of time.

He thought of how the first bullet had gone through the old man's neck; and the second had struck the woman in the chest. He remembered the expression of surprise on her face and the sight of Grunwald lurking somewhere behind her, a dark shape thrown by the lamp against the wall.

Clutching the revolver against his side, he crossed the lawn until he reached the lamps that burned along the side of the Isar. He took the box of cartridges from his coat and replaced the two he had already used. He snapped the chamber shut.

Turning, he walked back across the gardens to the trees.

The Jew was here. Somewhere in these gardens.

Breathless, Grunwald lay with his face flat against the mud, his hands sinking into a puddle of water beside him. After some minutes he became conscious of his predicament. He sat up, his body still heaving, and peered through the darkness. A light wind rustled in the trees and shifted the shrubbery, drawing out tiny, echoing sounds. Along the empty streets he had heard Schwarzenbach's footsteps: he heard them even now, the clatter of feet running over the concrete. When he had reached the gardens he had the advantage of complete darkness, and the terrible disadvantage of no longer being able to hear whether Schwarzenbach was still behind him.

He lay down, his hands in his pockets, and felt that he wanted to sleep. He wanted simply to close his eyes and drift out into the forced unreality of a dream. How else could he cope? He tried to think of Elisabeth, and imagine that she was well and that she had fallen down because she had suffered a superficial flesh wound. Yet he could not obliterate from his mind the stark realization that the bullet had entered her body somewhere and that by now she was probably dead: or close to death. Why was it that everything he seemed to touch surrendered itself eventually to death? Why did he drag so much suffering and loss behind him? He tried to imagine that he was kneeling beside her, holding her head in his hands, consoling her, and yet the image would not assume a definite shape: instead he saw her lying across the floor, her arms thrown back, her blouse discoloured with blood. She was dead. And he had run away.

He had run away.

Running, running, running: I know about myself. I know exactly what I am. I see how transparent I am: a thin, filmy thing held up to the light, penetrated as if by an X-ray machine. As transparent as that.

Turning over on his side, aware of a violent pain that racked his chest, he seemed like a spider creating and spinning around itself a poisonous web that inflicted fatality at a single touch. Elisabeth. Elisabeth. The hand he had held in the café and in the street, the eyes that had reflected the bonfire across the Isar, the body that had been offered to him like a sacrifice: these things had become hideous because he had touched them.

Straining, he rose to his feet and stumbled through the

darkened gardens. Some yards away he saw a lamp that he moved towards: below he saw the black surface of the Isar. Why had he run? Why had the first impulse been that of self-protection? Cowardice was more than a frame of mind, or an attitude: it was a disease that had spread and permeated through the entire self. He felt like going over the wall and into the water. He imagined the experience of drowning, going down time and again to the very bottom of the river until the lungs burst and the heart collapsed.

He turned away from the river and was conscious suddenly of how the lamp exposed him. He moved back towards the edge of the darkness and stood for a time beneath a tree, his face flat against the cold bark. Involuntarily he envisaged Elisabeth and the picture tortured him, not because he saw her this time as she would look now if she were dead, but because he imagined her as she had been in the café: alive, intense, hanging on to him and waiting for him to make the decision that would change his life. He couldn't remember whether he had decided; all he could recall was the feeling of warmth he had experienced, as if he had realized for the very first time that she contained all the future possibilities of his existence. Palestine! It sounded like a fabled word, a talismanic piece of apparatus that would open, like some magic key, the hundred doors that were closed to him, and that were suddenly closed to him again. It all seemed like an improbable dream that, left to itself, would dissolve and fade like salt in water.

He moved amongst the trees silently. The world around him seemed empty, a great crazy sphere suspended – to no apparent purpose – in an irrational universe.

He heard a faint crackling sound behind him and he caught his breath. Somewhere in the darkness he was being tracked by Schwarzenbach: the name, the man's name, seemed branded in the memories of his mind.

* * *

He gripped the revolver. To get to Grunwald he had shot the old man, Herr Gerber, and the woman as well. They were nothing – distant, impersonal events. They were surgical. Cold operations. It all seemed to fall into place as he thought about it: in the scheme of things, some people had to die so that others could live. Those who had to die expired in shabby rooms, wrapped up in their solitude and insignificance: and yet, given the pattern he had imposed upon reality, their deaths were not exactly meaningless – because they had died simply that others, like himself, could go on living. It was a system of hierarchies, within which certain people had an elected right to existence while others perished dutifully. And he recognized this now as an immutable law of nature. Some had their grasp on a kind of immortality. It was an overpowering concept and as he framed it it seemed to him that the death of the Jew was just another trivial fact within the design of life.

He moved through the trees slowly, the revolver levelled in his hand. The Jew was around somewhere: like an habitual hunter, he knew instinctively – as if he could read signs into every infinitesimal movement created by the night – that the object of his search was nearby. The Jew was close at hand, about to die his necessary death.

Grunwald froze against the tree. He heard the sound a second time. Someone was moving towards him. He had been holding his breath so long that he felt as if the cage of his ribs was about to crack. He put out his hand like someone trying to map the geography of a darkened room. He thought of his own death, which he felt was very near, drawing nearer with every sound that he heard. The thought scared him, and yet he wondered why it should: you feared only the unknown and death, by now, wore the mask of a habitual visitor.

Turning round, he moved silently away from the tree. Slipping, he fell forward into the grass. It seemed to him that he had created a noise that could have been heard a mile off. He lay quietly with his face pressed to the ground.

'Grunwald!'

Schwarzenbach heard his own voice vanish among the trees. He paused a moment and listened.

'Grunwald!' He called the name a second time.

Grunwald crept up the slope. He clutched the icy grass as if it were a rope supporting him on his climb up a treacherous mountain. He heard his own name echo around him in the darkness like the blank and fading after-sound of gunfire. He reached the top of the slope and wanted suddenly to be sick. The muscles of his throat tightened. Why didn't he stop running? Why wasn't it simple just to get to his feet, stand up, and offer himself as a target? But he couldn't do that. He couldn't do it. The urge became stronger. It became more difficult to resist. He *wanted* to stand up. He *wanted* to get to his feet. It was as if he were standing at a great height and looking down, contemplating the dizzy possibility of throwing himself over.

'Grunwald!'

Schwarzenbach's voice came through the trees like the sound of a night bird beating its wings in panic. He lay perfectly still while wave after wave of nausea surged through him.

The revolver. The revolver. He imagined pressing it against Grunwald's brain and pulling the trigger. He imagined the mechanism of the weapon functioning cleanly in a split second and the fraction of time it would take for the bullet to be forced out of the chamber, along the barrel, and into Grunwald's skull. He pushed forward through the shrubbery.

Again. The feeling Grunwald was near. Something

moved to his left. Clearly defined against a tree. He raised the weapon and fired twice.

Grunwald ran across a stretch of lawn. It was a minefield: at any second he expected to be blown up. He reached a clump of bushes and stopped. Behind him he heard Schwarzenbach crossing the lawn. There was another gunshot and a faint flash of light and he heard the bullet whip into the shrubbery. Disturbed birds rose out of the trees and filled the darkness with a desperate, hawking noise.

Branches slicing his flesh, thorns tearing at his overcoat, he pushed his way forward and ran until he had reached the other fringe of the gardens. Beyond he could see a street of derelict buildings and the thought crossed his mind that perhaps he could hide amongst the ruins. Perhaps he could find safety there. He moved through the outer fringe of bushes and reached the shattered, upturned concrete that had once been the street.

Schwarzenbach followed him across the wrecked street and saw him make his way across the piles of rubble. He put the gun into his pocket and started to run. Ahead of him, Grunwald was stumbling across the charred remains. He could see the Jew's shape as it dodged between broken columns and fallen beams. He followed, running into the rubble blindly, aware of the dragging weight that the revolver made in his pocket. He saw Grunwald pass through an opening in a wall: seconds later he went through it himself.

A place. A safe place. Somewhere there would have to be a hole in which he could hide. He kept running, drawing his strength from unknown reserves of energy. The ruins around him were endless: the whole area must have been completely devastated. Charred walls, shaped illogically, were still covered with faded patterns of wallpaper. Chimneys led up to nowhere. Window-frames were empty, wood twisted. It was a landscape of utter desolation. It was a landscape that might have been conceived in a flash of lunacy: it was somehow as if it had never been built but had been left this way, half-created, abandoned, its plans forgotten in the office of the municpal architect.

He scampered over the rubble, unaware of the fact that his ankles were bleeding from where he had collided with the sharp edges of stones. He was beyond panic and fear now. He was running – not for his life, his survival – he was running because he had become involved in some insane competition that made it necessary for him to spring across these ruins without once stumbling or falling. In blind moments he seemed to forget that he was being pursued by Schwarzenbach. In fragments of seconds he seemed to realize that survival had nothing to do with this endless race, that he was running because he was suddenly insane, deluded into thinking that if he finished this obstacle course he would be decorated with medals.

He paused a moment to catch his breath. His lungs were burning and his heart hammering insanely. There had to be some way out, some way to win the race, the race, there had to be a finishing-tape he would break through before Schwarzenbach. He looked anxiously through the dark and then upwards at the splintered remains of a chimney.

Clutching the harsh brick face he started to climb, forcing his fingers into crevices for holds, shuffling his feet against the flaking edges of bricks. His breath was coming in short snatches, mist frozen on the air. A way to win. A point where he could stop and claim victory. The darkness was filled now with sound. Voices? he wondered. Voices of acclaim? Was he in front?

He stopped, hanging to the chimney like a drowning man grabbing chunks of vacant air in sheer desperation. He clung to the fragile brick, eyes shut, the light in his mind suddenly black, snuffed out like a candle in a draught. He could hang on forever. He knew he could. A matter of strength. I have great strength, reserves that the war could not touch, that the concentration camps could not violate. I can wait here, suspended above the world, forever. Dizzy, he forced his eyes open. Somewhere below he could hear Schwarzenbach.

Schwarzenbach stopped. The Jew had disappeared. Somewhere between the last opening and the wall that lay ahead. Where was he now? Where? Seized with the impossible realization that the Jew had slipped away somewhere, he took the revolver from his coat and began to pick around the rubble as if the object of his search were something small enough to hide beneath stones. The darkness was difficult. He wished he had a torch, Meticulously he continued to probe around and then, with a feeling of desperation, he sat down. Where was Grunwald?

He listened. He concentrated all his strength on listening, straining hard. Silence surrounded him. He felt the weight of the revolver in his hand and realized that – without the target – it was a remarkably futile instrument.

He called Grunwald's name, the first time quietly, almost in a whisper, the second time so noisily that the sound reverberated mockingly around him. He wished that he could see Grunwald – not to kill him immediately, not simply to thrust the weapon against the Jew's skull and pull the trigger – but to talk to him. To converse with him. To hold a brief conversation before the event, the inevitable event, took place.

What might they say to one another? What could they talk about now? Conditions in post-war Germany? Politics? The past? The dark of the past?

Schwarzenbach shook his head. The silence was getting through to him, causing his mind to wander and his concentration to dissolve. Conversation! The absurdity of the prospect struck him. There was nothing to say, he realized: there was nothing.

I can wait here until daylight, until dawn, in spite of my fingers bleeding. I can wait until the darkness vanishes and my sight returns. Until then I will not move. I will not shift an inch. I'll hold my breath, freeze myself. Nothing can make me move now.

Grunwald. Grunwald!

From a point below, from the bottom of the world. Can Elisabeth be dead? Can it be? But how? The gunshots on the darkened stairs. Willi fell first. If I remember rightly, Willi fell first.

Grunwald!

He looked down. How far was it through the dark? Thirty feet? Forty? His fingers were stiff and sore, his legs ached. But he could wait for as long as it was necessary.

Schwarzenbach walked through the broken slabs of concrete. For some reason he remembered the expression on the Jew's face on that day in 1935 in his surgery. How could that look be best described? Dumb? Numb? Unbelieving? He clenched his fist around the revolver and realized that even then, so many years ago, he had been struggling with the powerful urge to destroy the Jew. To destroy and obliterate. Had he experienced a premonition on that day? A foretaste of the future?

He leaned against a wall, suddenly weary. When all this was over he would sleep. He would crawl into bed and close his eyes and then there would be nothing.

He stiffened. There was a sound, a scraping sound, followed by a sharp cry.

The fall surprised him. One minute he had been there, gripping the side of the chimney. The next he had been dropping in a shower of bricks. Why had it given way like that? Why had the cement split and the brick crumbled? It seemed almost a perversion of nature, an abortion. He fell swiftly through the dark, conscious not of the fact that he would strike the ground with some force but of the realization that his strength had finally deserted him.

He struck the rubble and cried out in pain. Somewhere in his leg there was a sharp sensation, a razor drawn across his muscles. Yet the pain was an abstract thing, experienced by a ghost, something outside of himself. He lay for a moment flat on his face and then crawled forward towards an opening in the wall.

Schwarzenbach groped along the wall to the source of the noise. A sense of excitement rose inside him. The revolver was smeared with perspiration from the palm of his hand and had become slippery, difficult to hold.

'Grunwald.' He called the name like someone calling in his pet cat at nightfall. He followed the wall as far as it went and then he stopped.

'Grunwald.'

There was a slight, blurred echo.

An opening in the wall. He lowered his head and, hearing a faint noise from below, went inside. A flight of stairs led downwards.

A cellar. The smell was terrible. It was as if something had lain trapped inside for months and was now in a state of putrefaction. He couldn't breathe. The air that he managed to take into his lungs was stale and poisonous. The place was flooded with several inches of water on the surface of which floated a thin scum that adhered to his hands as he crawled forward. He reached the far wall and lay there, unconscious of the discomfort of his sodden clothes. Exhausted, he closed his eyes. Was he safe here? Safe from what? he wondered – as if he could no longer recall why he had been running so fast and so hard. His mind was blank and empty and all his energy had been sucked from his body. He felt that he had never existed – or that he was just about to exist for the first time. He wondered what it would feel like to be born again: would he be trapped again, destined to travel the same route that he had already come along? He opened his eyes suddenly, realizing that he had almost fallen asleep. He couldn't sleep. He felt the water against his legs and arms and the smell seemed to crush him. When his strength returned he would get up and leave the cellar. And then?

He thought of the house in the Schumannstrasse and it seemed very important to him that he discover what had happened to Elisabeth. She wasn't dead: he had imagined that because he had been afraid. She had fallen because she wanted to get out of the way of Schwarzenbach's gun. That was it. His fears were utterly irrational. Elisabeth was alive. Together they would go to Palestine after Willi was dead – Willi? What had happened to Willi? Had Willi been shot? But he couldn't cope with both Willi and Elisabeth: his brain couldn't emcompass them both simultaneously. She wasn't dead. It had been foolish of him to think that. Why was he so damned tired? Why couldn't he keep his eyes open? It was very important not to fall asleep and yet sleep was just out there, circling him in its own deep shadows.

He splashed some of the filthy water on his face to keep himself awake. As he did so, he heard the sound on the steps.

'Grunwald?'

Schwarzenbach was up to his ankles in water. He waded forward into the cellar.

'Grunwald?'

He heard his own voice, a muffled echo.

He raised the revolver. There was a faint splashing sound from the other side of the cellar.

* * *

Grunwald rose slowly to his feet. The water that had seeped through his coat and shirt was cold against his skin. The fact that Schwarzenbach was in the cellar somehow didn't scare him now: he was more frightened by the prospect of not seeing Elisabeth again. Had he come all this way to be shot in a bloody cellar by Schwarzenbach? It seemed almost pitiful. His back to the wall, he tried to move towards the steps. He stumbled against a heavy, wooden object. In surprise he cried out.

There! Just there!

He wheeled the gun round between his fingers and fired quickly. After the echo he heard a low moan and he moved towards it, splashing through the water.

Grunwald felt the pain somewhere in his side. He put his fingers to the wound and when he raised his hand it was covered with blood. He undid the buttons of his coat, aware of the need to make some kind of bandage and put it over the wound. It was the most natural thing to do. Somehow he had to stop the flow of blood. And yet, as he considered this, he felt that such an action would be ridiculous. His body was broken and punctured, and therefore no longer important. He became detached from it. He was thinking of something else, a strange thought that eluded him although he pursued it through the shadows of his mind until eventually he found it: if Hugo was alive, how old would he be today? How old would the child be? He imagined that Hugo was in a refugee camp somewhere, waiting for his parents to collect him and take him home. Every night, he had kissed the child's eyelids: it became a habit – the boy wouldn't sleep until his father had kissed him.

He clutched his side. Millions of miles away something was splashing through the water in his direction.

* * *

Schwarzenbach fired the revolver again: from a distance of roughly five feet. He heard Grunwald cry out and saw him – a dim shape – slip down into the water.

There was an ache above his heart. He felt the water circle his mouth and nostrils and the texture of the liquid so disgusted him that he pushed himself up into a sitting position. Why wasn't he dead? He had been shot twice, perhaps more than twice, and he wasn't even dead.

'Why don't you kill me, Doctor?'

His own voice sounded hoarse and incomprehensible. His blood had mixed with the water: it swirled into the film of dark scum.

Schwarzenbach cursed the gun: the mechanism had jammed. He fumbled with the chamber and rejected the last cartridge into the water. Shaking, he took the box of cartridges from his pocket and forced four of them into the empty chamber.

'Why don't you kill me, Doctor?'

Schwarzenbach could barely make out the words. The Jew was sitting up against the wall, staring at him. For Christ's sake, he should be dead. He should be dead by now.

Grunwald felt the water around his fingertips and it seemed that his fingers themselves had turned to liquid: how absurd it was to be talking to the man, like two people greeting each other in a restaurant or a beerhall. After all, I have nothing to say to him. He is destroying me and I have nothing to say to him.

Schwarzenbach slammed the chamber shut and raised the gun. Do it! Do it! His index finger circled the trigger and he hesitated. He loathed himself for the fact that he was suddenly trembling.

* * *

317

It was like taking a walk through the grounds of a hospital after a long convalescence. A fresh awareness. Sunlight flaming on everything, Burning, burning. Palestine was like that. He had visited the place. He had been to Jerusalem and stood at the Wailing Wall. He remembered how deeply the sun had burned him. Beside him a woman was walking and the landscape was yellow with wheat and the season was summer, it was summer, and the woman held an umbrella that shadowed her face darkly. Who was she? Her name was unimportant. He touched her arm and saw her mouth move into the shape of a smile and inside the smile were several shared secrets. Everything was so clean. He saw the future as clearly as if it were a detailed map laid out in front of him. They were purchasing boats. Refugee ships. Shifting all the casualties of Europe off to the Holy Land.

He had been standing on the deck for hours now and the boat was anchored in unbelievably blue water and the deck was crammed with refugees staring at the shores of the promised land. He saw Hugo coming towards him and he clasped him in his arms. He kissed the child and then turned his face back to the shore. Suddenly a cloud went over the sunlight like a hand drawn across a candle. He felt a sense of panic. What was he doing here? Why was he lying in a cellar? Why was he surrounded by water? He had to get to his feet, away from this place, he had to shed his flesh to rid himself of this awful pain. But he couldn't move and then realized that there wasn't any real pain and that the flooded cellar existed somewhere else, miles away, far away from him. He was drifting through a series of old pictures, like ragged snapshots taken from the past, torn from some dilapidated family album. Holding a hand. Holding a hand. A woman's hand. Looking into somebody's eyes. Face shielded. Faces shimmered and changed. Little Hugo was wandering along the deck. He mustn't get lost. Must he, Martha? Coffee and cakes in the Café Fürstenhof on the Neuhauserstrasse.

A glass of *Zitronenwasser* in the Wintergarten. Cold beer in the Spatenbräu of the Bamberger Hof. He mustn't get lost. Why were they smashing all that glass? Glass being shattered and fires being lit. Somewhere, somewhere at the back of everything, an awful sense of pain. And then the snapshots again. Holding somebody's hand. Suddenly important. Holding somebody's hand. *Gänsebraten* in the Schwarz, the Jewish restaurant on the Schlösserstrasse, a treat, *Gänsebraten* served with *Spargel* and followed by *Erdbeeren*. A treat. Someone's hand. Suddenly very important. Martha and Hugo smiling at him across the table. The empty plates. The empty apartment. Martha's hand reaching out towards him.

Schwarzenbach waited for what seemed to him like several minutes with the gun pressed to Grunwald's head. Why wasn't the little Jew scared? Why was he dying with such nobility? Why wasn't he begging?

Schwarzenbach clenched the trigger. Suddenly, with a sense of horror, he saw Grunwald's hand rise in the air and grip his own. He shrugged it aside desperately and stepped back. The Jew said something, words that he couldn't catch.

But they were unimportant now.

He pulled the trigger and the revolver exploded.

Grunwald jerked with the impact of the bullet. Slowly his body slipped down the wall and he fell over sideways, as if he were broken, and his face sank beneath the surface of the water. All that was visible of him now was the back of his head: and his hands were stretched out on the surface of the water, but sinking gradually, like those of someone too cold and too numb to swim any further.

Schwarzenbach wiped the gun against his coat and then dropped it. It vanished under the water. Turning, he walked out of the cellar and up into the freezing night air.

PART FIVE

Berlin, November/
December 1945

21

The journey from Munich was slow and tedious. The train was cold and he slept fitfully, waking sometimes in the middle of the night and staring out at the unresponsive landscape. Small towns, barely lit, hostile, drifted past like lights on a river. The deserted platforms of railway stations stretched endlessly backwards and it seemed that every time he opened his eyes the train had halted in some minor town or village, neither discharging old passengers nor accepting new ones. When dawn came he went into the corridor and threw open the window, letting the sharp morning air sting his face.

There had been a sparse fall of snow in Berlin. It lay like the skeletal remains of white feathers on the ledges and rafters of bombed buildings – as if it were intended to mask the grotesque scenes of destruction. Yet it emphasized it. The thin white lines exaggerated the waste and the barrenness. He walked briskly through the streets. Underfoot the snow was already crisp.

When he reached his apartment he tore down Herr Zollner's notice from his door. He sat down in the kitchen, conscious of the heavy silence that seemed to lie between the rooms. He poured some cognac and carried it into the bedroom. He lay across the bed and shut his eyes. Relief flooded him. It was over now: it was finished. He had come to the end of his anxiety.

From the bedroom window he saw a handful of winter birds pecking pointlessly at the frozen surface of the snow. He found some stale bread in the kitchen and threw it from the window. Suspiciously the birds circled the scraps for a time and then they swooped down to eat. He watched for a moment. The birds devoured the bread joyously and when the last crumb had been eaten they lingered, as if expecting more.

He went into his surgery and sat behind the desk. Somehow he expected the place to have altered in his absence and although he looked round – and sifted through the papers in his drawer – everything was as it had been. It was unchanged – yet why did he feel a sense of difference? The room was a static entity: it could not alter by itself. He drew the blinds back from the window. He realized that *he* was the only thing that had changed. He was the single difference in the room. Liberated, free, suddenly aware of a future that was untrammelled by the demands of the past, he realized that he was simply *seeing* the room differently. It was as if Schwarzenbach had finally been killed and cremated, and only Lutzke remained alive.

Herr Zöllner gripped his hand: 'It's good to have you back, Herr Doktor. How was Hanover?'

'Changed,' Schwarzenbach said.

Zollner sighed: 'Ah, well, show me something that hasn't.' Zollner was making a pot of tea by the stove, his arm engulfed by the steam that rose from the kettle. 'Did you walk along the Herrenhäuser?'

'I didn't get the chance,' Schwarzenbach said. He paused a moment. Zollner had set out two cups. 'Tell me – are there any messages for me?'

Herr Zollner plucked at his green eyeshade. 'Several. Look, I wrote them down.' He wandered around the room, searching for them. At last he produced several scraps of paper from beneath a tea-caddy.

Schwarzenbach took the papers and sifted through them. They were mainly routine: Herr Lachenbauer had finally passed away; Frau Kolakawski had a recurrence of her shingles; Fräulein Grassmüller was certain that this time she was pregnant; Herr Niedereder wanted some sleeping-pills. The final message was that Major Spiers had telephoned, and would call again.

'Major Spiers? What did he want?' Schwarzenbach asked.

'He didn't say,' Herr Zollner answered. He poured tea and passed a cup to Schwarzenbach. The caretaker then sat down and removed his eyeshade. There was a white line, like a scar, across his forehead from the impression of the elastic band.

'But he said he would call again?' Schwarzenbach asked.

'Precisely.' Zollner sipped his tea fussily. 'How is your tea?'

'Enjoyable,' Schwarzenbach said. What did Spiers want this time? For a split second he wondered if somehow he had been followed to Munich; if his every action there had been observed. An unlikely fantasy. No one had followed him to Munich.

Herr Zollner said, 'I wish we could walk through the streets without seeing great empty spaces and piles of rubble. And soldiers, come to that. I'm sick of seeing soldiers.'

Schwarzenbach stared into his cup. A few leaves floated on the surface of the pale tea. The man called Peters. The waiter who had recognized him. Was there a connection between the two? Had they been placed there deliberately? Meaningless questions. They did not deserve consideration. He was free.

He thought of the sight of Grunwald slipping beneath the surface of the water in the cellar; his blood spreading across the scum. He thought of the echoing gunshots in the dark emptiness. Again there was relief – but beneath that another and more nebulous feeling: a triumphant sense of having worked out his own salvation.

Looking secretive, Herr Zollner began to rummage amongst the junk in his apartment. He produced a gramophone record and held it in the air. 'Look what I found the other day. Let me play it for you. Do you mind?'

Sweeping several soiled items of clothing from the top of his gramophone, Zollner began to wind the handle. He placed the record on the turntable and sat back, eyes closed. The music was the band of the Liebstandarte playing 'Unter dem Doppeladler'. Schwarzenbach listened a moment and then got quickly to his feet. He removed the needle from the disc.

Zollner opened his eyes: 'Is something wrong?'

'Although I enjoy the music personally, Herr Zollner, it would be foolish to give any eavesdroppers the impression that you make a habit of harking back to the past.'

'Eavesdroppers?' Zollner seemed stunned by the suggestion. Sighing, he removed the record and held it against his chest. 'Nothing is sacred any more,' he said.

'Nothing at all,' Schwarzenbach said. He finished his tea.

But the echoes of the music remained faintly in his head even when he had returned to his own apartment. They invoked images that he knew he could no longer think about – the old things, the old scenes, all the fragments of the past. It had become a locked room, the key to which lay lost forever beneath the filthy water of a flooded Munich cellar.

He would start afresh. Devotion to duty, caring for the sick, comforting the mourners – he would begin again in a new way.

At the beginning of December Spiers and Eberhard came to his apartment. They exchanged remarks about the coldness of the weather. They spoke about the approach of the first Christmas since the end of the war and Spiers mentioned something about goodwill – and the word lay in the silent room like a stone dropped from a great

326

height. Schwarzenbach could not take them seriously any longer. For the first time in their confrontations he felt in complete control of the situation. He was calm, relaxed, untouched by anxiety or suspense. He found some spare glasses and offered them cognac and they drank together, toasting the future at Spiers's suggestion.

Eberhard stood at the window, where his shadow fell across the room. Schwarzenbach waited as the silence dragged on and he wondered – even if he did not care – about the purpose of their visit. The Major coughed, a rattling sound deep in his chest.

'You should take something for that,' Schwarzenbach said.

'I get the same damn thing every winter,' the Major said.

Spiers coughed again into his gloved hand. He wandered around the room while Eberhard picked up his briefcase and snapped it open. For a second Schwarzenbach was uneasy. The briefcase again. Always the bloody briefcase. Eberhard took out some papers and spread them across the desk. He shuffled them, rearranged them.

'An army marches on its bureaucrats these days,' he said as he fidgeted with his papers.

Schwarzenbach, smiling politely at the feeble joke, wondered about the papers. However inexpert they might be in other ways, Spiers and Eberhard were gifted in the art of circling around the margins of whatever they wanted to say.

Schwarzenbach leaned forward: 'What can I do for you this time?'

'It isn't so much a question of that,' Eberhard said. 'It's more what we can do for you.'

'I don't understand.'

'This Schwarzenbach business,' Spiers said.

'Schwarzenbach?'

'Well, as you know, Dr Lutzke, for some time I've

thought that you were the notorious doctor Schwarzenbach. I don't have to go into the reasons for my suspicion – '

'It's preposterous anyway,' Schwarzenbach said.

Eberhard rattled his papers and suddenly produced one, holding it up in his fist. 'The plain fact, Dr Lutzke, the plain fact is that we've received some fresh evidence that clears you.'

'What evidence?' Schwarzenbach felt a moment of tension. What evidence could there be?

Eberhard said, 'Several of the former SS guards at Chelmno were captured by the Soviets. Some escaped, but others weren't so quick off the mark.'

Eberhard paused. Schwarzenbach said, 'And?'

'According to the testimony of one of these guards, a man called Hörselberg, he witnessed the death of Schwarzenbach. Hörselberg claims that Schwarzenbach was murdered by an unknown prisoner during the final evacuation of the camp.'

Schwarzenbach felt blank. 'And this man's evidence clears me entirely?'

'That's right,' Major Spiers said. 'It clears you completely. Without a blemish.'

Eberhard stared at the sheet of paper a moment longer. 'The prisoner apparently stole a pistol and gunned Schwarzenbach down in the camp compound.'

He gathered his papers together and swept them back into the briefcase. Spiers said, 'We've caused you a lot of trouble for nothing, Dr Lutzke.'

Shrugging, Schwarzenbach got to his feet. 'These things happen.'

'What can we say?' Eberhard asked, but the question was rhetorical. He looked across the room at Major Spiers. It seemed to Schwarzenbach suddenly that this glance was meaningful, even if he could not grasp the meaning. It was as if they were sharing a lie between them.

Major Spiers beat his hands together. 'I guess that just about wraps it up.'

He lay on the bed and closed his eyes. The name Hörselberg meant nothing to him. Even if there had been a guard of that name there was no reason why he would have known the man. The more he reflected upon it, the more he felt that Eberhard and Spiers were playing new tricks. They had invented a false testimony because they wanted to induce a mood of false security. Hörselberg! It was exactly the kind of fatuous thing the Americans would do. The whole thing was an elaborate charade, designed – like all their other fabrications – to make Schwarzenbach feel dangerously secure. Hörselberg!

The joke, finally, was made at the expense of Eberhard and Spiers. They did not know that Schwarzenbach felt completely secure now. They were like amateur conjurers totally unaware of the fact that Schwarzenbach was a master magician who knew all the tricks. The entire thing amused him. He was safe. They would not catch him now. Not now.

A few days later he started to make tentative plans. He had become tired of Berlin. The time had come to move on, to get away from the brutality of the city to a place where war had been little more than a shadow on the horizon. He studied maps and considered places like Augsburg, Bad Tölz, Weingarten, Landsberg. He envisaged himself in a small country practice, walking the hills during his leisure time, growing old in peace, dying, being buried in the local churchyard.

As he constructed these plans a new sense of peace overcame him, a new awareness of the future stretching out in front of him. Nothing could touch him now. He had finally transcended the fear of discovery and recrimination. Slowly he began to believe that Schwarzenbach had never existed, that he had been Lutzke all his life. He began to forget the past and sometimes wondered if his past actions had really occurred. There was no blood on his hands. He had no responsibility for events within the Third Reich. When he spoke to Herr Zollner or one of his patients he found himself denouncing the acts of National Socialism and the SS with enthusiasm. It had been a blind, bad time in the history of Germany, an age of pain. Now the suffering was over.

He threw himself into his work. He slaved long hours on hopeless cases. He felt clean and pure. He experienced a strong desire to return to the Bavarian countryside. And so he made plans and began to believe that Schwarzenbach was truly dead.

He had started all over again. He was beyond reproach.

On Christmas Eve he decided to go to the late service in the church. It was many years since he had last done this: as a boy, holding his father's hand, trailing after his father through the sharp iciness of the night. There had been a sense of wonder then, a feeling of being drawn into the elements of some supernatural experience. Would it be possible to recover some of this sensation? It was important for him to know the answer to the question. The process of purification was unlimited.

Crossing the Kurfürstendamm, the wind whipping at his coat, he reflected on the last few weeks. He had become so involved in his work, so exhaustively sucked into the lives and illnesses of his patients that it sometimes seemed he had ceased to exist. This feeling of nothingness, of abstraction, acted upon him like a tonic. It made the rejection of the past complete. It made anticipation of the future sharply acute. He was Dr Lutzke, respected by his patients. He was considering an exploratory visit to Landsberg where – if things went according to plan – he would acquire a country practice. He was Dr Gerhardt Lutzke, walking to church on Christmas Eve.

He cut off the Kurfürstendamm and into the narrow streets that led away from the thoroughfares. The church wasn't far away now. It would be filled with people who were his patients. They would worship together: they would pray and sing and the organ would play and perhaps he would afford himself the luxury of remembering the Christmas Eves of his childhood. Perhaps he would.

Ahead he saw the church. Its front door was open, a square of yellow light. People were filtering towards it, thronging through the doorway. The spire, picked out by a solitary spotlight, rose upwards into shadow. He walked towards it slowly, his hands in the pockets of his coat. It was intensely cold. The yellow square of light suggested warmth.

He paused to allow traffic to pass along the street.

Something made him turn his head round. A dark car, moving slowly, had come around the corner and was approaching him. He tugged the collar of his coat against his face and stepped back. The car crept towards him and he stared at it as it went past.

The face in the front was Eberhard's. Frozen, immobile, indifferent. But that wasn't what had interested Schwarzenbach. He crossed the street and reached the doorway of the church. There he paused. Inside an organ was playing.

He watched the car disappear around a corner. It wasn't Eberhard's face that had interested him. In the rear of the car, half-hidden by shadow, momentarily illuminated by a streetlamp, there had been someone else. Another familiar face. Another face he had seen before, long before Eberhard had come into his life. It was the face of the Sturmmann who had regularly, painfully, and with increasing pleasure, escorted the victims into the hut at Chelmno.

Schwarzenbach went into the church and sat down in a pew at the back. The air was cold around him and he stared blindly at the faces of the worshippers.

The Sturmmann. Could he have been mistaken? Could he have been confused by the mixture of light and shadow? There was a chance, a slight chance. But if he hadn't made a mistake, if he had been correct, then what was the Sturmmann doing in Eberhard's car? If he were being taken for questioning, how much was he likely to say?

Someone nudged Schwarzenbach. It took a few seconds to realize that the congregation had risen to its feet. Stumbling upwards, paralysed by the dramatic chords of the organ, he opened his mouth and began to sing.